ASCENDANT

Also by Diana Peterfreund

Rampant

ASCENDANT

Diana Peterfreund

HARPER TEEN
An Imprint of HarperCollinsPublishers

HarperTeen is an imprint of HarperCollins Publishers.

Ascendant
Copyright © 2010 by Diana Peterfreund
All rights reserved. Printed in the United States of America.
No part of this book may be used or reproduced in any
manner whatsoever without written permission except in
the case of brief quotations embodied in critical articles
and reviews. For information address HarperCollins
Children's Books, a division of HarperCollins Publishers,
10 East 53rd Street, New York, NY 10022.
www.harperteen.com

Library of Congress Cataloging-in-Publication Data
Peterfreund, Diana.
    Ascendant / Diana Peterfreund. — 1st ed.
        p.   cm.
    Summary: When sixteen-year-old Astrid Llewellyn,
now a fully trained unicorn hunter, joins the quest
to discover the Remedy at a laboratory in the French
countryside, she begins to question her love for Giovanni,
her loyalty to the Cloisters, and even her duty as a hunter.
    ISBN 978-0-06-149002-6   *453 8 0 762 3/11*
    [1. Unicorns—Fiction.   2. Hunting—Fiction.
3. Supernatural—Fiction.   4. Dating (Social customs)—
Fiction.   5. France—Fiction.]   I. Title.
PZ7.P441545Asc   2010   2010003097
[Fic]—dc22   CIP
                                                   AC

Typography by Larissa Lawrynenko
10   11   12   13   14   CG/RRDB   10 9 8 7 6 5 4 3 2 1

❖

First Edition

*For my father, who taught me
about science and strong women*

THE HUNT FOR THE UNICORN

In ancient times, royalty hunted unicorns for sport. They'd sally forth from their castle, gaily dressed, armed with spears, bows, knives, dogs, and their secret weapon: a virginal maiden. Without this girl, the unicorn could never be captured. Noble of birth and pure of body and heart, the virgin would enter the depths of the forest and allow the men to tie her to a tree. There she would wait, chaste and silent and still, until the elusive unicorn, attracted to her as if by magic, would come forward and lay his head in her lap.

Once the unicorn was subdued, the virgin would grasp its horn and trap the beast with her. The men would spring forth from their hiding place and stab the dangerous unicorn as it lay in the gentle virgin's arms. And so it was that brave and glorious men would be able to kill a unicorn.

Never mind that it was the virgin who had its blood on her hands.

1

Wherein Astrid Follows Her Duty

The unicorn drew its last breath. Within its chest, its heart shuddered and stopped. Twenty yards away, I felt it die, and the world settled into normality. Fire and flood ebbed, the tunnel widened, and my thoughts became my own. I lowered my bow and ran to the corpse—a human run, at a human pace, sluggish compared to the recent rush of hunter-granted speed. I bent over the body and withdrew my arrow. It had pierced both lung and heart, and the alicorn arrowhead was soaked in the almost black arterial blood of the kirin. Steam escaped from the corpse at my feet, twisting around my legs and mingling with the early-morning mist in the field. I wiped the arrow off on the grass and returned it to my quiver. These arrows were not so common that we could afford to lose any. I withdrew my knife and knelt by the unicorn's head. Its yellow eyes were flat now, snuffed of the bloodthirst that had so recently filled us both.

I was carefully carving into its skull by the time Cory arrived. "Didn't need backup after all, then?" she puffed.

"For a single kirin?" I replied without looking up. Over the past month, carving out an alicorn had become a perfunctory postmortem operation. In through the eyesocket to the orbital, a quick jab up to break the nasal cavity, and then use the alicorn itself as leverage to shatter the top part of the skull and peel back the ligaments and skin protecting the base of the horn. In the early days, we'd simply sawed off as much horn as we could grab, but now we were trying to dig as deeply into their heads as possible to retain the venom reserves.

Cory watched me work. "How many kills does this make for you?"

"On this hunt?" I asked, and cracked the alicorn free. "Four?"

Cory said nothing. I swung my braid back over my shoulder with my less-bloody hand and looked up at her. "You?"

"Zero."

I stood. "Really?"

She gave me a tight smile. "Someone always marks them before I get a chance."

If the statement was intended to sting, I could hardly feel it over the burn of alicorn venom. Beneath my sweater, droplets of sweat prickled the tender skin of the scar at the base of my shoulder blades. "It's not a competition," I said.

Her smile grew even more strained. "All evidence to the contrary."

Together we doused the ground around the unicorn with flame-retardant, then took out our vials of gasoline and lit the corpse on fire. It was the only way to deal with the bodies, we'd learned. No vultures, no bugs, would touch unicorn carrion. The bravest among us had even tried the meat, wondering if—as with so many other aspects of the animals—hunters possessed a higher tolerance to unicorns. But apparently the flesh was vile. Even Grace, who ate Roman-style tripe with glee, spat it out. So cremation was our only option.

Cory and I returned to the rendezvous point without further conversation. In all honesty, I couldn't see the source of her pique. When I took a unicorn, it was more out of reflex than anything else. The magic took over. It was just me, my prey, and my weapon. There was no discussion with the other hunters about whose "turn" it was. Hesitation might result in one of us ending up dead. A unicorn moved too fast for us to stop and think about how many kills we'd each gotten. If I had a shot, I'd take it. The alternative was a horn in the gut.

I knew that all too well.

Two of the other hunters who met us in the clearing were splattered with dark kirin blood, though only one of them clutched a horn. Grace was twirling hers like a gory baton, and Ilesha looked baffled. "Its horn was broken off," she explained, wrapping a bandage around her leg. "Teeth still worked." The rest of the hunters stood in readiness, their bodies drawn as tight as any bowstring, their chins lifted, their eyes shrewd and darting.

"Give it a rest," Cory grumbled. Alone among the unsuccessful, she slumped, the tip of her bow dragging in the dirt. "There aren't any more."

She was right, of course. The sun was already rising over the distant hills, burning off the morning mist and sending any unicorns back into hiding until twilight. They were crepuscular creatures, active at dawn and dusk, when shadows and mist would be most likely to shield them from human eyes and memory. It was a rare kirin who would stay out in the full light

3

of day. I stretched my senses to the limit but caught no lingering trace beneath the scent of burning fuel and wet earth.

I looked at the other six girls in the clearing. Only a few short months ago, they would have been an unthinkable sight in their blood-spattered clothes, clutching pieces of the monsters they'd slain. A couple of months ago, few people believed there had ever been unicorns. And even if there were, they hadn't been venomous, man-eating beasts—but gentle, sparkly, magical creatures. That was the story, anyway. And it was about as accurate as the one that held that medieval noblemen kept virginal maidens around simply as unicorn bait. Why complicate the issue? We virginal maidens could do more than simply attract and capture the animals. We could shoot them ourselves. The women of my family had been unicorn hunters since time immemorial—except for those hundred and fifty–odd years in which we'd erroneously thought that unicorns were extinct.

Unicorn hunters may know more about the monsters than the average person, but even we make mistakes.

Actually, if I started cataloguing the things we didn't know about unicorns and our own unicorn magic I'd be here all day. And my morning had already been long enough.

I finished my perusal of the circle. Had I really killed more than my fair share? Ilesha had three, Grace five, Melissende and Ursula two apiece, and Zelda one. I frowned and flicked a sliver of skull off the back of my hand. Perhaps I was on the high end of the scale, but it certainly wasn't outlandish. And, as I'd told Cory, it wasn't a competition, either. We hunted as a group, and helped one another with kills if the initial shot didn't bring the animal down.

Of course, as often as not, my "marking" a unicorn meant

4

ending its life. Gone were the days I'd risk anything but a killing shot. Two weeks ago, I'd hit a unicorn in the leg, and before I could string a new arrow, it had reared up and kicked Valerija in the face. She was still drinking her meals through a straw.

Seventeen was large for a kirin pack, though, and I was about to say so when Grace spoke up.

"We cleared out two packs, I wager." She'd stored the alicorn she'd obtained and was inspecting her sword for chips. "Or the remnants of two. I bet Ilesha's broken one was a losing alpha."

"It was a female," Ilesha said. "And I don't think they have alphas like wolf packs."

"We don't know what they have, do we, *Cory*?" Grace pointed out. Cory slumped farther.

"I don't see *you* doing any research!" I snapped at Grace.

"And I don't see *her* killing any unicorns," Grace snapped back. "And perhaps if you stayed home from a few of these trips, we'd be doing more with that laboratory of yours than just buying beakers."

"Since when do I have a doctorate in pharmacology?" My hands were on my hips now, or more accurately, resting on the hilt of the alicorn knife in my waist scabbard. "Yes, we're rebuilding the scriptorium, but there's no way we're going to wake up one day and the Cloisters will be the Gordian labs—"

"Thank heaven for that," Ilesha murmured.

"We don't have the equipment or the know-how to . . ." I trailed off because I knew I sounded like a broken record. Grace was as accurate with her verbal barbs as she was with a bow and arrow. She knew exactly where to hit me to make it really sting.

Rebuilding the ruined library-cum-lab in our crumbling monastery had been the joint brainchild of Cory and Phil—not me. They'd decided I needed a project to help me get my mind off what had happened in Cerveteri last month. How they figured putting together the equivalent of a high school chemistry lab would make up for the destruction of a state-of-the-art research facility was beyond me. And a high school dropout with aspirations to a career in medicine could never duplicate the skills of the man she'd allowed to be killed right in front of her.

I shut my eyes for a moment, allowing the memory to fill my mind, drowning any remnants of hunter bloodlust in bitterness and regret. Marten Jaeger, his face twisted in pain as karkadann venom rocketed through his system. Perhaps I could have stopped it, could have saved him.

By the time I tuned back in to the conversation, Cory had achieved full-on rant mode.

"Furthermore," she was practically yelling at Grace, "until you take a more active role in the administrative responsibilities of the Cloisters, you don't have a right to complain about the choices we do make."

Something pricked my awareness and my hand tightened on the hilt of my knife.

Cory shouted on, though I could hardly hear her over the rush of blood in my ears. "Value to this order is not determined by quantity, and I resent—"

Grace drew her sword, whirled, and plunged it into the heart of the kirin colt bearing down upon us. The monster slumped over the blade, dead.

Cory froze, but the rest of us were not surprised. The other four girls and I had all drawn our weapons; all stood crouched in readiness. Cory's hands remained empty, her mouth open in shock.

Hadn't she felt it? To judge by their expressions, the other hunters were just as curious.

Grace tugged her blade free. "That makes six for this hunt," she said coolly. "Now, what were you saying about how useful you are?"

"I just don't understand it," Cory said for what must have been the fiftieth time.

We were replacing the alicorn weapons on the wall inside the Cloisters's chapter house. No one was sure if it was advantageous to keep them stored down here, but we figured it couldn't hurt. The ancient hunters had displayed them on the wall, so we would as well. There was very little argument that the chapter house was the most magical chamber in the building. So if it could make the hunter magic stronger in us, maybe it could spare a little for the weapons?

"I'm a hunter. I know I am. I can feel it," Cory said. "Bonegrinder still bows before me. So the powers aren't gone. They're just . . . *depressed*. Is that possible? I don't understand it."

Rosamund paused over her beloved piano keys and blew a strand of red hair out of her face. "Is it possible for you to not understand it someplace else? Some of us are trying to practice in here."

Cory snarled. "What, am I throwing off your tune? A sour note inside your perfect hunterly echo chamber?" She hooked another bow onto the weapons wall with a lot more force than it deserved and flounced down the steps, brown curls bouncing indignantly.

Rosamund looked stricken. "You know that's not what I meant, Cory. Perhaps it is something far simpler. Perhaps you are like a piano and need to be tuned."

"Don't pianos need to be tuned only if they aren't in use?" I asked, then immediately regretted it. Cory had been *trying* to hunt, after all. It wasn't her fault she was sucking at it. And if anyone should be suffering from lack of practice, it ought to be Rosamund. She'd managed to weasel her way out of participating in the last three hunts, preferring instead to remain in the chapter house and play her precious music.

Lucky. I wished I knew her trick. I wasn't keen on killing animals at dawn, either, but I had not yet found the strength to stay home.

I wasn't sure what that said about me.

Not that I wanted to spend time in the bone-strewn chapter house. Though the room rarely gave me headaches anymore, it still had the power to drive me bonkers. I didn't like being surrounded by so much death. Most of the other hunters were just as happy spending their off time in the dorm or the courtyard, and only Rosamund and Valerija seemed to like it down here.

"No, I like this idea," Cory was saying. "Maybe we just need regular checks, like a car." Her face brightened for the first time in what seemed like ages. "And we know precisely how to do it, too."

Rosamund shuddered. Despite her avowed love for the Cloisters's chapter house, there was one unicorn artifact she went out of her way to avoid: the enormous alicorn throne, composed of dozens of unicorn horns intersecting and weaving around one another in a series of terrible patterns. The throne was a gift from the people of Denmark in honor of a corps of hunters who had once saved a city from unicorn-induced decimation. Each horn in the throne was taken from a unicorn that had killed a hunter. Last month, we'd discovered the throne's purpose. Like every other unicorn artifact in the Cloisters, its presence attuned us to the monsters' thoughts and movements, made us better hunters.

Our inborn hunter abilities lay dormant unless we were in the presence of an actual unicorn. Having the artifacts around, being close to our pet zhi, Bonegrinder—it all functioned like antibodies in the bloodstream, boosting the body's ability to fight. The Cloisters was a giant tuning instrument. However, if the building was like an immune system, the throne was like a shot in the arm.

Of course, the quickest way to improve your hunting abilities was to let a unicorn tear a hole through your body. I was living proof of how well that worked. A mildly less agonizing, though no less violent, manner was to sit on the throne and let the magic of the murdering alicorns seep into your body.

It felt like fire, and your mind would be filled with visions of the bloody battle in which the ancient hunters died, visions that would forge pathways in your brain to make way for the alien communion with the hunters' quarry. I still didn't understand how it worked. All I knew was that it did.

For a hunter, anything made of unicorn was imbued with magic. For everyone else, it was nothing more than horn and bone.

Cory approached the throne and cautiously sat down, bracing her body for the expected onslaught of pain and horror. She squeezed her eyes shut.

Rosamund grimaced. "What's happening?"

"I see the field of battle," Cory replied. I shuddered, remembering the blood-soaked earth, the wormy gray sky, and the moans of the dying beneath the battle cries of those who still fought. Cory went on, her voice toneless. "But I feel nothing."

Last month, fresh from a unicorn stabbing, I'd touched the throne and did not feel the usual flash of fire. It had occurred to me how similar the pain of the throne felt to the agony of alicorn venom, which is when I'd gotten the idea that you could use the throne to force a quick hunter attunement. The experiment worked, and that first time, we'd realized that a subsidence of pain had been a signal that the process was complete.

If Cory felt no pain now, it should mean that she was ready to hunt. But she still wasn't sensing the unicorns as the rest of us did, and I couldn't understand why.

Cory turned to me. "Well, Dr. Llewelyn? What's your diagnosis?"

I said nothing.

"Forget it." Cory slammed her hands down on the arms of the throne, pushed herself out of her seat, and bounded out of the room.

Rosamund and I stared after her. "Should I go apologize?" she asked.

I shook my head. "Just let her cool off for a while." After three months of sleeping in the same room, I knew that Cory's moods were best handled by avoidance, not comfort.

"I am sorry I made her feel worse," Rosamund said. "She knows she doesn't make the music go bad."

"Does it ever go bad?" I asked, half joking. Before coming to the Cloisters, Rosamund had been headed toward a career as a concert pianist.

The Austrian colored. "When Phil is here. Yes, a little."

I shut my eyes.

"Please don't tell Phil," Rosamund added, clearly sorry that she had even told Phil's cousin.

I took a deep breath and opened my eyes. "Of course not," I lied, and Rosamund, because she would never lie, believed me. But of course I was going to tell Phil, if only because my cousin would hate the idea of her presence being a burden on anyone here. I left Rosamund to her instrument and took the stairs to the first floor, feeling the tension ease somewhat as soon as I was away from the pull of those bones.

But the pressure never really dissipated within the walls of the Cloisters. Unicorn remnants were laid into the very masonry. The light fixtures were composed of hocks and hooves, and the empty eye sockets of skulls leered from every archway. I passed into the rotunda and found Cory, hands behind her back, contemplating the giant tableau of my ancestor Clothilde Llewelyn attacking the karkadann that history told us was Bucephalus.

"I'm sorry for snapping down there," she said without preamble, and also without looking away from the mannequin's placid face.

"No problem." I shrugged and took a place by her side, studying the tableau. The real Clothilde had looked nothing like this lush, golden-haired doll in her spotless white gown.

"I know it doesn't seem this way," Cory said, "but I really am getting better with that whole temper issue of mine."

I put my hand on her shoulder.

"I've been trying so hard," she blurted, and I no longer knew if she was talking about her temper or about hunting.

"I know you have," I said, because it was true on both counts. Cory had been the one to bring back the Order of the Lioness, to reopen the Cloisters, to find us all.

Cory took a deep shuddering breath and gestured helplessly toward the mannequin. "I just wish . . ."

What? That Clothilde could step off the dais like a goddess come to life and solve all our problems? Explain to us the true nature of our powers, wreak vengeance upon the unicorns for killing Cory's mother, do it all without wrinkling her silk dress?

The tableau was a lie, every bit of it. The real Clothilde Llewelyn had been scarred and dirty, with blood-soaked hands and arms that looked like ragged ropes of muscle. The real Clothilde Llewelyn's hair had been shaved short so you could see the scar that ran the entire length of her scalp. The sword the mannequin wielded wasn't even real—I owned Clothilde's claymore. The real Clothilde had not died in battle with the karkadann Bucephalus; she'd cut a deal with the monster that allowed her to leave her life of hunting, a deal that sent unicorns into hiding for more than a hundred and fifty years.

I brushed my fingers against Cory's bouncy brown curls. This life wasn't pretty. If we kept it up, would we end up like Clothilde? Bitter, broken, desperate to find a way out?

"I just wish they were gone," Cory finished. "I wish I could wipe every last one of them out. If there were no more unicorns, we wouldn't be in danger. Our families wouldn't be in danger—no one would ever have to live like me." She bowed her head. "I was a beacon that called death to my mother's door."

"Been working on that chorus a while, huh?" I asked.

But Cory had stopped listening again. "All I want, all I've ever wanted, is to get rid of them. I would kill every last unicorn on earth if I could." She squeezed her hands open and closed reflexively, a tic I hadn't seen since we first attuned ourselves as hunters. "And I can't even do that. I just have to stand by and watch you do it."

I stiffened. Kill every last unicorn on earth? I stared up at the giant stuffed karkadann that might not even be a karkadann but was certainly not the karkadann Bucephalus, the unicorn warhorse that had marched with Alexander the Great, that had known my great-to-the-fifth grandmother Clothilde . . . who had, last month, saved my life.

Kill all the unicorns? Drive the entire species to a true extinction? Was that what I had really come here to do?

2

WHEREIN ASTRID LOSES
AN UNEXPECTED BATTLE

🗡

I found Phil in the don's office, stacks of paper piled high on her desk, phone glued to her ear.

"Well, can you take a message, then? Yes, Philippa. One L, two Ps, and then Llewelyn is two Ls and then one L— well, no, the first P is in there, too—look, it doesn't really matter to me how you spell it, just get him the message. Order of the Lioness. Unicorn hunters, that's right. Yes, I'm completely serious."

She hung up the phone, blew out a breath, then smiled at me. "Hey there, Asteroid. Ever have one of those days where you feel like you walked out of *Ghostbusters*?"

I plopped down on the chair across from her. "In *Ghostbusters*, didn't they just capture the ghosts and keep them in a containment unit that ended up exploding all over the city?"

"Okay, can that metaphor." Phil shifted some of the folders. "How are you doing?"

I shrugged. "Killed four unicorns this weekend."

Phil grimaced. "I wasn't looking for a score count, Cuz."

Of course she wasn't. Phil had been worried from the

beginning about what exactly it meant to protect humanity from the threat of killer unicorns. Where did it end? Meanwhile, I'd been content to rationalize the benefits of killing particular unicorns that were actively endangering people in populated areas. The hunters had taken out a kirin that was terrorizing a farm, a pack of zhi that had been hunting in a suburban schoolyard playground, a re'em that had prowled the streets of Rome. Unicorn hunting had never been meant as a long-term-planning kind of thing, because the people who'd first invented the Order of the Lioness, centuries ago, had no concept of preserving other species—especially not dangerous ones.

And now I realized that the person who'd revived it—Cory Bartoli—didn't either.

Killing unicorns might be what we did, but we had to plan for the endgame as well. Nowadays, people didn't *get* to hunt species to extinction. Or they shouldn't, anyway. And that's what Phil wanted to make sure of.

"Who was on the phone?" I asked.

Phil rolled her eyes. "The intern to the assistant to the assistant secretary to the Deputy Secretary of the Department of the Interior."

"So you're really getting somewhere with this little crusade of yours?"

"It's better than it sounds, honestly."

I just shook my head. "Has it occurred to you that this isn't really on their radar? Right now, they're concerned with keeping the parks safe. They're still trying to figure out why they can't just go out with a rifle and shoot a unicorn that comes into populated areas. They're not going to put a conservation plan in place until they've done studies on the animal they're hoping to conserve. These things take time."

Phil smiled, but it wasn't her usual wide, gorgeous grin. "Well, I've got one semester before my volleyball coach replaces me on the varsity team and cancels my scholarship, so it's pretty much now or never." Her hands flittered around the desk, rearranging files and shifting papers from one pile to another. The don's ring glinted on her thumb, its cabochon stone shining like a droplet of fresh blood. "I've got four months to save the unicorns."

I nodded, mouth shut. Perhaps it would be a good idea for Cory and Phil to coordinate. My roommate would probably be a bit unhappy to learn her extermination plans were being undercut by my cousin's quest for conservation. A quest with long-distance phone bills coming straight out of Cory's pocket.

"A tall order," she went on, not quite meeting my eyes. "Even if I were still magic."

I heard a jingle, then Bonegrinder trotted out from the don's private wing, gait still stiff from disuse, eyes still half-closed with sleep. The little unicorn yawned, showing her long pink tongue and her sharp white fangs.

"C'mere, Sweetheart!" Phil called to the zhi.

Bonegrinder looked at her, unimpressed, then pranced to my side of the desk and bowed at my feet. I patted her head behind her screw-shaped horn, and she bleated happily. The don's ring was supposed to keep Bonegrinder docile in the presence of nonhunters like Phil and Neil. But lately, Bonegrinder had been acting more bored with it—and them—than subdued by its allegedly awesome magical unicorn-controlling abilities.

Phil became very busy with her files. "I heard from Neil earlier," she said. "He's bringing in two new hunters in the next month."

"That's great!" I said as Bonegrinder shoved her face into my lap so I'd scratch underneath her little billy-goatlike chin scruff. Perhaps more useful than training hunters to overcome the unicorn threat would be figuring out what made the ring work and getting it into mass production. Chalk it up as another piece of the magic that nobody understood.

"Yeah, we've got to build our numbers back up, right?" Phil shoved a lock of her dirty blond hair behind her ear. "We're dropping like flies, you know."

"Phil," I began.

She caught my eye. "I was *joking*, Asterisk. Please don't treat me like a china doll. Believe me, I do not miss murdering innocent wild animals who are only responding to their own survival instincts."

No, she wouldn't miss that. Bonegrinder put her front hooves up on my thighs, the rough edges digging into my flesh. I pushed her off and she growled, pouted, then lay down beside my chair. I picked fluffy white hairs off my jeans.

Phil pretended not to notice. There'd been some talk about getting my animal-loving cousin a kitten or something, but then we realized that Bonegrinder would probably eat it.

"How do you do both at once?" I asked. "Fight to make unicorn hunting illegal while running an organization that hunts unicorns?"

She laughed. "The irony has struck me, too. But it's all part of the same goal, right? We want to keep people safe from unicorns. The Order does it in the old-fashioned way: killing them. But we don't have to go by the old rules anymore. I still think people are more important, and I'm willing to do what it takes to make sure they are safe . . . for now. But I also think we can find a way to protect people that lets the unicorns survive. Like your pal Clothilde." She shrugged. "But with the force of law so it sticks this time."

I regarded her skeptically. Phil was way more optimistic than I was.

"Have you talked to Aunt Lilith recently?" Phil asked.

"Last week," I said. "She's been busy." Since leaving the Cloisters and heading back to the U.S., my mother had launched a new career as a unicorn consultant. Phil might not be able to get the government's attention, but local television stations were more than thrilled to showcase my pretty, blond, arguably expert mother on their programs. The fact that she tended toward the crazy didn't faze them, especially since she'd been vindicated about the fact that there actually *were* killer unicorns out there all along.

From the safety of air-conditioned television studios and radio stations, my mom expounded on the history and mythology she'd spent half a lifetime reciting only to me. She sounded tough and well-informed and, if "former head instructor of a unicorn hunter training camp" was a bit misleading, well, at least it wasn't hurting our cause. My most recent phone conversations with my mother were mostly about whether she needed a booking agent to land a national program, and Grace and Melissende liked to get together and snicker—loudly and within earshot—at the online video clips where my mother rhapsodized over her supposed glory days as a hard-core unicorn hunter.

"How about Uncle John?" I added.

"Still leaving messages. Mom says he 'needs time to process all this' or something." Phil shrugged. "I can't decide if he's maddest that I lied to him all summer, that I'm training unicorn hunters, or that he wasn't there to protect me."

I reached across the desk and laid my hand out, palm up, for her to hold. "I'm guessing it's the last one."

She glanced down at my hand, at the bowstring calluses along my fingers, at the blister forming near the base of my thumb, at the curlicue marks of alicorn scarring on my palm, and didn't let go of her files. "China doll, Astroturf."

I withdrew. "Right."

She stood and stretched. "Okay, how about some target practice? Winner buys the loser a gelato." She glanced down at Bonegrinder, who was still settled at my feet. "And you can't bring her. That's cheating."

Bonegrinder bared her teeth at my cousin.

"Astrid!" Dorcas called up the stairs. "Giovanni's here!"

I closed the book I'd been reading, grabbed my bag, and headed down to meet my boyfriend. Giovanni had planned the date today, but he hadn't told me where we were going— just to wear something comfortable. Luckily, I owned sturdy shoes in abundance.

If I knew him, we were probably headed to a museum. He'd already taken me to the Borghese Gallery, the Vatican, and more churches with Michelangelo statues in them than I could count. One of the hazards of dating an art student: there was always more art to be seen, especially in a place like Rome.

Of course, the hazards of dating a unicorn hunter were far more obvious and deadly, so perhaps I shouldn't complain.

I found Giovanni in the front courtyard watching Ursula as

she sat in the shade, sketching. The twelve-year-old had only very recently taken up drawing. Melissende, Ursula's sister, had asked her parents to send pastels and a notebook. Phil thought it was great for her to have an outlet that had nothing to do with hunting.

I wondered what Phil would think of Ursula's subject. She'd leaned her bow and a quiver of arrows up against the side of the fountain. *Still Life with Weaponry.*

"The water is the hardest part," Ursula said, shoving her dark hair out of her face and squinting at the fountain. "How do you do the water?"

Giovanni pointed to a spot on the sketchbook. "Think about the reflection. Water is going to reflect everything, especially from this angle. The fletching on the arrows, the edge of the bow, the top of the fountain, the sky . . ."

"But all squiggly," Ursula said.

"Yeah," Giovanni replied. "And if you don't think it's squiggly enough, throw a pebble in and draw quick."

Ursula laughed, then promptly stopped as she saw me standing by the door. Giovanni looked up, and his eyes softened the way they always did when he saw me. I smiled.

Ursula scooted. "Thanks for the advice," she said stiffly.

Word around the Cloisters was that she'd developed a little bit of a crush on Giovanni after he'd carried her out of Cerveteri last month. She'd been injured during the battle with the kirin, and he'd been the only one with enough energy to pick her up after she'd hurt her leg.

Obviously, I couldn't blame her for her preference, but I didn't begrudge her it, either. If Giovanni noticed the way Ursula blushed in his presence, or how she'd mysteriously taken up drawing because she knew he liked art—he didn't say anything about it. Like Ursula's sketchbook, her crush on Giovanni was probably good for her.

I know he was good for me.

"Where are you taking me?" I asked, coming to meet him.

"A picnic," he announced proudly. Ursula bent her head over her drawing.

"Wow, so no art?" I asked.

"Did I say that? I don't think I said that."

I put my hands on my hips.

"Astrid," he began. "Where was the last place you took me?"

"A battle with a pack of killer unicorns."

"And what time of day was it when you took me there?"

I sighed. "Dawn."

"And what happened?"

"The kirin tried to kill you and succeeded in destroying the van you'd borrowed from your school."

"Without their permission or knowledge," he added.

"Right."

"So by comparison . . . ?" he prompted.

I laughed. "Art is an amusing and relaxing alternative."

He slipped his arm around my waist. "And safe. No one was ever killed by art."

"I'm sure there is some record of a statue falling over on someone sometime," I argued.

He pretended to consider this. "Was it a poisonous statue hell-bent on devouring my flesh?"

"No," I admitted.

"Then I still win. Now let's go or we'll be late for the train."

* * *

"So Cory's determined to exterminate them and Phil's every bit as determined to set up some sort of endangered species protection, and neither of them really knows what the other is up to!"

"Hmmm," said Giovanni, beside me. He tore a silvery leaf off an olive tree as we passed and began dissecting it. "So are you going to sit them both down and make them hash it out as peacefully as possible?"

"Peacefully?" I scoffed. "You've met them, right?"

Giovanni chuckled. "Okay, well, hide your weapons first. Maybe get them outside the Cloisters altogether."

I tilted my face into the sun. "You're right. Something like this would be a far more peaceful venue for the coming Armageddon."

Giovanni dropped the leaf and grabbed my hand. "Next time. Now it's just us."

We were wandering around the Villa Hadrian, a green oasis of ruins and olive groves beyond the city. In ancient times, it had been the summer palace of a Roman emperor. Now it was far less posh, but the qualities of quiet, warm, sunny, and secluded remained intact. We'd packed a picnic lunch, and I split my time between keeping my mind open for the presence of unicorns and enjoying the feel of Giovanni's hand in my own as we wandered the walkways between the crumbling marble courtyards and algae-covered pools.

"How about here?" he asked as we crested a hill and looked down over the villa. High above us, an Italian pine spread its branches and protected us from the late summer sun.

I sniffed the air. No scent of fire or flood. No unicorns at all. "It's safe."

"I meant, 'Do you like the view; do you want the shade?'"

"Oh." I blushed. "That, too." We spread out the blanket and sat down. Giovanni unpacked cheese, bread, fruit, and mineral water.

"I miss Manhattan water," he said as the bubbles fizzed in the plastic glasses he'd brought. He handed me one and went back to rummaging in his bag for silverware. "Huh. I can't find my knife." He looked at me. "You didn't happen to . . ."

My eyes went wide. "You want to cut *cheese* with my alicorn knife?"

"Well, it's clean, isn't it? We're not going to poison ourselves with unicorn blood or anything like that, right?"

"The blood's not poisonous. At least, I don't think it is." I sighed, reached into my purse, and handed it over. "Be careful, it's an antique."

Carved from a single piece of alicorn, the knife had been the relic of my ancestor Clothilde Llewelyn's first kill. Though the hunters tended to share our small store of ancient weapons, I'd laid an early claim to the knife, and no one—not even Melissende—had challenged me for it. I kept it on me at all times. I'd brought down my first unicorn with it.

Giovanni began sawing into the bread and I looked away, a little sick to my stomach. The knife was a killing tool, not an eating utensil. He handed it back to me, and I ran my hand along the flat, brushing bread crumbs from the creamy exterior.

"Astrid," Giovanni said, and I tore my eyes off my weapon. He gazed at me, his expression a mix of care and concern, and held out a piece of bread with cheese smeared on top. "Stay with me."

I pursed my lips. "I'm sorry. I just find the whole concept of

23

using this for food a little morbid, that's all."

"Any port in a storm," Giovanni replied, and stuffed a piece of bread in his mouth. "So, let's spend five minutes not talking about Cloisters politics, or unicorns, or how this knife we're using on the cheese is usually covered in blood and guts. It's a gorgeous day and there are no monsters in sight."

"Fine." But I sat, silent and dumb, and munched my bread. What was there to talk about? I hadn't seen any movies. I hadn't read any books. I didn't even know what was going on in the news right now outside of my mom's television appearances and the semiregular reports of unicorn attacks, or worse, the failed attempts by nonhunters to stop the unicorns themselves.

I will give credit to my mother for this—and only this— she was doing her best to spread the word that the only people capable of handling unicorns were trained unicorn hunters. If we could just convince people to keep out of areas infested with unicorns, and above all to not try to hunt them themselves, we'd probably be halfway to reaching Phil's goal of noninterference.

Only, who decided which places were going to be reserved for monsters?

Giovanni stared out over the rest of the villa and volunteered no topics of conversation, either. Great, now I was the boring girlfriend. What did I have to offer other than ruminations about bloodthirsty, magical beasts? I leaned over and kissed his neck.

"Thank you for doing this," I whispered against his skin, filling my senses with Giovanni until even the memories of unicorns were obliterated. "It's so beautiful here."

We forgot about bread and cheese and knives for a bit.

When Giovanni lifted his head at last, we were both a little breathless and warm, even in the shade of the tree. My lips felt swollen and flushed from his kisses, and I could see beads of sweat had formed on his temples.

Since Giovanni had learned the truth about the unicorn hunters, he'd become rather militant about keeping strict parameters when it came to getting physical. We kissed—*a lot*. But nothing more. I wasn't sure how much longer he'd be satisfied with that arrangement. I wasn't sure how much longer *I* would.

He lay above me, breathing hard, and traced his finger over my lips.

"Do you ever wish—" I asked.

"No." He fixed me with a look. "Never. I'll take you on whatever terms I can have you, Astrid. You're a hunter, which means you've made a commitment. A meaningful one. An important one." He sat up and resumed staring out over the greenery and brick ruins. "Summer's ending."

"Yeah," I agreed. I sat up and smoothed my hair back down.

"Have you thought at all about what you're going to do for school?"

Phil had brought up enrolling me in an international program once or twice, even petitioning Neil and Cory for the funds, but we'd never followed up on it. Now, after losing the money Gordian was providing us, I worried that the Bartolis had enough trouble keeping the Cloisters open on their own dime. I knew Cory was wealthy in her own right, but I had no idea what she could afford. The ancient monastery was in constant need of repair. Neil was in talks with representatives of the Catholic Church to see if they would contribute anything to its upkeep, but he and Phil worried that church involvement in the Order of the Lioness would bring with it restrictions that we weren't ready to accept.

Things like forbidding make-out sessions in Roman ruins with my boyfriend.

"It's still a little up in the air," I said at last. "There's so much work at the Cloisters." How would I fit in classes and homework with my grueling training schedule and my hunting trips? Could I squeeze in calculus problems between life-and-death moments on the battlefield?

"You need to finish high school," Giovanni said. "If you were in college or something, I could understand taking a year off, or even a few—people in the military do it. Phil is doing it. But you need to think about your future as well."

"For all I know, this is the only future I have."

"Don't say that!" he said, turning back to me. "Astrid, someday this is going to be—over. Somehow. And you're going to go to med school, just like you wanted."

I folded my hands in my lap and studied them. They were strong hands now. Killing hands.

"That's still what you want, right?" Giovanni asked.

I shrugged. "Yeah, but I could also die on a hunt tomorrow."

He said nothing for a long time.

"Tell me again what you saw that day?" I asked him. "In the tombs? What could you see?" Giovanni was one of the few non-hunters who'd witnessed us in action. I wondered what it would be like to stand outside of us, outside of the magic. What was a unicorn to one who couldn't read its mind or see its speed?

"Blurs, mostly," he said. "You move so fast. Like streaks of color, like streaks of light. And behind you, corpses. And screams. And these creatures—animals I've never seen, could never imagine."

26

"Some art student you are."

He snorted. "Okay. It looks like a nightmare. Like Hieronymus Bosch at his very scariest." He lifted his eyebrows as if to tease me. "Better?"

"Much."

"And the smell—" He made a face. "But then you stop, Astrid, you snap out of it, and you stand there, covered in wounds and weapons, and you look like a goddess. Like a hero in a comic book. Like a statue in a temple. Athena."

"Diana."

"Whoever." When he turned to me, his expression was somber, but his eyes practically shone. "You look breathtaking. Beautiful and terrible all at once."

I gave him a skeptical glare. "And you're attracted to that?"

"I'm terrified not to be." He thought for a moment. "I never really saw the little black ones until they were dead."

I laughed at the idea of a zebra-sized kirin being called "little."

"But the big one, I could see it. I saw it try to trample Ursula. It was— Where can something that big hide?"

Bucephalus. I often wondered that myself. I hadn't seen the karkadann since he killed Marten Jaeger and escaped before anyone could kill him in return. If I did see him again, would I be obligated to hunt him? A unicorn? A man-eating killer? No matter that he was the one who had explained my power to me, who had saved my life many times over? No matter that he was thousands of years old, that he'd struck bargains with Alexander the Great and Clothilde Llewelyn and me?

"I'm losing you again," Giovanni said.

"I'm sorry. I'm right here, I just—"

"I know." He sighed. "When I first met you, I knew there was something different about you. And the more I saw of Astrid the Warrior, the more amazing I found it all. But don't get lost in her. You were someone else before you were a hunter, and you'll be someone else after."

I blushed again and looked away. Before was a world away, and after seemed like a fantasy. Even here, on this sunny hillside, with the sound of summer insects in my ear, and Giovanni warm and wonderful beside me, and no trace of unicorns as far as I could sense—the old Astrid was beyond my reach. And the strangest thing of all was that I hadn't even noticed her slipping away. For a few moments we were quiet, our arms brushing against each other as we watched the tourists scrambling over the ruins.

He turned back to me. "I have something to tell you."

I froze. Like "no offense," that phrase was rarely followed by anything good. "Okay."

"I got into an art program back home."

That wasn't what I'd been expecting. "But I thought you needed to pass your summer course before your college would let you back in." And he hadn't passed. He'd been expelled for destroying the van. Or letting unicorns destroy it. For me.

Expelled again. First from college for fighting and then from his second-chance summer school—because of me. Good to hear you still got third chances.

"This is a different school. I'm not going back to SUNY. This one—Pratt—it's in New York City—"

Each word was a jolt of alicorn venom. "You're leaving."

"Yes."

I nodded, and felt my throat closing up. I wasn't immune to this.

"I have to," he said. "I have to finish college. I can't just keep bumming around. It's not like Phil, who is running the Cloisters. This is *my* job. Being a student."

"I understand," I said. "What . . . about us?"

Another pause, but he followed it with, "I want to be with you. I don't care if there's an ocean between us."

I laughed then, a horrible, bitter sound. "Why, Giovanni? Why? It makes no difference to me."

He flinched. "Don't say that."

"I'm a celibate unicorn hunter living in a nunnery. I'm that whether you're here or a million miles away. But you don't have to have that. Back in New York, there are thousands of girls. Girls who aren't like me." Models, actresses, artists, coeds. I couldn't breathe, thinking about all the girls he could have.

"I don't want girls who aren't like you," he snapped back. "I like unicorn hunters."

"Ew, don't say *that*." I shuddered.

"I like *you*, Astrid. There are other girls in Rome and I like you. It'll be the same in New York."

I rolled to my feet, filled with the need to run, to leap, to shoot something. "You say that now, but in a month or two, you'll forget about me. You'll find someone . . ." The words choked me. I felt trapped by my body, imprisoned until the moment a unicorn came and set the magic free.

And then I felt Giovanni's hand slip into mine and the storm calmed.

"Are you saying you don't want to try?" he asked softly. "You want to break up?"

"I don't *want* to," I whispered, folding myself into his arms, hoping he'd hold me tight enough to keep me there. Every

29

second I could get of Giovanni would be worth it when he was gone. "But what choice do we have?"

What choice did I ever have? Dating Giovanni was my only taste of normalcy, the only part of me that remained tethered to my old life, the old Astrid. Giovanni reminded me that hands could be used for holding people, not swords, and that my heart could pound when I wasn't in pursuit of prey. He took me outside the Cloisters for art, not battle, and used my hunting knife to cut cheese. Giovanni had helped to make me a warrior, but he knew that I was also a girl. If he left, what would be left of me?

3

Wherein Astrid Receives a Message

The night before Giovanni left, an unseasonable storm blew in from the sea. I stood on the parapet overlooking the Cloisters courtyard and watched the clouds moving over the terra-cotta rooftops of Rome.

Maybe his flight would be canceled.

Wasn't it just the way of things? There was one guy in the world who didn't care about me being a hunter, and he had to move to New York City. Last I heard, the island of Manhattan was still, blissfully, unicorn-free. What possible reason would I ever have to go there?

I watched the hunters in the courtyard scatter as the rain began, and Cory joined me at the parapet, shaking droplets of water out of her curls.

"All right?"

"Not really."

Cory braced her hands on the stone balcony and rocked back on her heels. "Maybe this is for the best?" She turned to me. "You know I like Giovanni, but your relationship had to end sometime. You can't be with someone and be a unicorn hunter."

"Um, I have been. All summer."

Cory sighed. "This is hard for all of us, you know. You aren't the only one who has had to give things up."

"Have you left a boyfriend back home?" It'd be the first I'd heard of it. I only knew she missed her pet dog.

"No." Cory watched the storm. "I've never had a boyfriend."

"Then don't try to imagine what it feels like," I said, my tone clipped.

"You think I don't know loss?" Her clipped tone tore mine to shreds.

I swallowed. "I'm sorry. I didn't mean to imply—"

Cory's anger dissipated. "And I didn't mean to be insensitive. Of course you're upset about Giovanni. I don't see it your way, but it's obvious he's quite important to you."

My lip quirked. Is this what passed for comfort from Cory? I supposed it would have to do. "Thanks. You know, outside Giovanni, meeting you is one of the only good things about coming to Rome."

"What's another?"

I considered. "Gelato."

She snorted. "I'm happy to rank higher than ice cream, then."

"I didn't say *higher*," I corrected, and she laughed. For a few seconds, we stood there looking out over the storm. Then she spoke.

"I care about you a lot, Astrid. I hope you realize that."

"I do." Of course I did. We'd saved each other's lives, over and over. Sisters at war.

She took a deep breath. "And if Giovanni is who you love, then I'm sorry you're being parted from him. I'm sorry when anything happens to make you sad."

I wasn't sure how to respond to that except to say, "Thank you."

Cory stood silent beside me, staring down at her hands against the stone. Presently, she lifted her head. "Want to raid the refectory for some of that gelato you like so much more than me?"

I smiled. "Sure."

In the dream, Bucephalus called to me in the voice of Marten Jaeger. The karkadann could speak to me only through the telepathic link unicorns shared with all hunters. When it came to the lesser unicorns, the link allowed us to feel their emotions, intentions, movements—allowed us to predict better where they were and how to kill them. But the ancient karkadann had somehow developed the ability to *put* thoughts inside my head—to dredge from my memory images and voices that, with time and very painful practice, I'd learned to translate into a rough form of communication.

Somehow, with the sort of logic that made sense only in a dream, I knew it was Bucephalus who spoke, though it sounded like poor dead Marten. I was searching for him, stumbling through a tangled wood, my feet catching on roots and vines determined to stand in my way.

I hadn't seen the unicorn since the battle at Cerveteri. He'd vanished, clearly fearing our partnership would dissolve once we'd dealt with the threat of the rogue kirin. Though I'd scoured reports of unicorn attacks and sightings for any description of an elephant-sized monster, I'd found none. Bucephalus remained in hiding.

The wood in the dream suddenly gave way to a clearing bathed in moonlight, and I stopped short in recognition. It was the garden outside the Borghese museum, the spot where I'd first kissed Giovanni. The place where I'd first met the karkadann.

Bucephalus was there, as massive and deadly as always. In the voice of Marten Jaeger, he spoke.

The price has been paid.

What price? my dream self asked. Bucephalus was in no debt to me, if a creature such as him could think in terms of debt and repayments. If he could ever imagine himself owing anything to us. Even hunters, we were powerless before him. He'd almost killed Ursula. He'd killed Marten, though I'd begged him not to. I couldn't stop it, or him. Giant, three-thousand-year-old monsters could do as they pleased.

The karkadann stepped aside, and there, on the ground near his hooves, lay the body of a young man, his face bathed in blood.

It was Giovanni.

"Astrid!"

I sat up in bed at the sound of my name. It wasn't quite dawn; the rooftops beyond the window were dark and indistinct beneath purple clouds and lingering rain. In the bed across the room, Cory remained unconscious.

"Astrid!" The voice was a distant cry, and for a moment, I wasn't sure if it was inside my head or beyond it. The karkadann? At the edge of my mind, I sensed Bonegrinder wake, her instinctive fascination with hunters rousing as I did. My new cell phone lay dead on my desk—it never kept a charge within the Cloisters walls.

"Astrid!" At the third cry, my brain clicked into recognition. Giovanni, shouting to me from the street. I shot out of bed, even as I felt Bonegrinder slamming against the walls of her cage down in the don's office.

Great. She'd wake the whole nunnery if her growing interest in our visitor turned to out-and-out bloodlust. I bolted down the stairs in bare feet and pajamas, sprinted across the mosaic tiles of the entrance hall, and opened the bronze doors as silently as I could.

Giovanni stood in the street just beyond the courtyard. A car sat idling behind him, a very amused Italian in the driver's seat.

"There you are!" he cried.

"Shush!" I reached the gate. "What are you doing here? You're going to wake everyone up. You're lucky we finally got a cage Bonegrinder can't chew through." Yet.

"I tried to call." His shirt was wet. He wore no jacket and carried no umbrella to protect him from the rain. It looked very sexy on him. I shuddered to think what it looked like on me. Water was already soaking through my tank top and cotton pajama pants.

I crossed my arms over my chest. "You're supposed to be on a plane."

"I couldn't leave it like this," he said as I opened the gate. "Astrid, we're not breaking up."

I almost slammed the gate shut again. "Says who?" He could not hit me with that before dawn. A killer unicorn I could handle. But not Giovanni on my doorstep, wet through and begging for . . . for what, exactly? I remained on the threshold of the Cloisters, my hand on the gate. "Are you staying here?"

That stopped him short. "No, I—"

"Then we can't. We talked about this." We'd laid out several very well-reasoned and dispassionate arguments as to why long-distance relationships never worked and were far more hurtful in the long run to the people who tried to have them. The fact that Giovanni could go off free and clear and I was staying in my *nunnery* didn't help.

"We can talk until our lungs give out," he said, "and it doesn't make a difference." He laid his fist against his chest. The water had rendered his white shirt translucent and sticky, and the darkness of his skin shone through. "I can't talk myself out of the way I feel. Don't you know that by now? Don't you know how hard I tried, all summer long?"

I hugged my arms tight around myself and buried my chin in my chest. "Stop."

"I couldn't give you up when there were rules and family and deadly mythical monsters standing between us, Astrid. What kind of person would I be if I let something as stupid as an ocean succeed?"

I squeezed my eyes shut.

"And not even a big ocean, like the Pacific," he added. "The Atlantic? It's a puddle."

I flatly refused to smile. The rain pattered down all around us. The cracks in the cobblestones filled with water, washing away the dust of two thousand years. How many people had died on this street? How many lovers had stood here, just like us, and said their final farewells? Giovanni was a fool to think it couldn't happen to us, too.

"Astrid," he said. "Please."

I couldn't. Losing him now was hard enough. Later, I'd only care more; it would only hurt more. I was already teetering at the edge. How could I risk it? "I'm afraid," I whispered in a breath softer than the rain.

But he heard it, nonetheless. "You?" he said, and I heard the smile in his voice, and when I lifted my face into the rain, I could see the smile in his eyes. "But you're the bravest person I know. I'm not giving you up, Astrid the Warrior. I can't."

And I knew at that moment that I couldn't, either. Even if it would be easier. Even if it would be the rational, practical, non-magical thing to do. The old Astrid could have been so dispassionate. But if I wanted to hang on to any shred of her, I had to believe in this—even if it made no sense.

"We'll make it work," Giovanni promised. "We'll e-mail, we'll call, we'll write. I'll see you at Christmas. I'll come here for spring break."

"And what will I do?" I asked. The rain poured down around us, but his skin was hot against mine as we flowed into each other's arms.

"You," he said softly into my damp hair, "will make me a promise. Survive."

A week after Giovanni's departure, we were repairing our weaponry in the shade of the Cloisters courtyard and trying to avoid the worst heat of the day. Bonegrinder, chained to the wall, lay panting on her side with her little pink tongue thrust between her fangs and watched us with sleepy blue eyes.

After discovering last month that arrowheads and knives

made with unicorn horn worked better against the creatures than alloy blades, we'd turned away from our more modern equipment to the weapons from the walls of the chapter house. But, unicorn magic or no, they were still a century and a half old.

In our last big battle with the kirin, we'd broken four standard bows, a sword, two crossbows, and countless arrows. We'd lost even more in the month since, and Grace, who possessed a natural affinity for weaponry, had taken it upon herself to learn to make new weapons and repair the slim store that remained. Though Cory had offered to lend her the records we had of the ancient hunters' weapon-making techniques, Grace had brushed her off and turned to the Internet. Though so far she'd had little success at creating new arrowheads, the repaired ancient tips on new fiberglass shafts were both sturdier and more accurate than our old warped arrows.

I was polishing the claymore that had once belonged to Clothilde Llewelyn. Like the alicorn knife I believed was made from her first kill trophy, I preferred to use this weapon at close range. As I ran a soft cloth over the blade, I wondered why we had Clothilde's knife and sword but not her bow. Had it, perhaps, been broken or lost in the fight that had supposedly claimed her life?

Rosamund sat a few feet away, repairing an arrow tip and singing snatches of what she called "weaving songs": short, repetitive songs designed to help groups work in unison. Ursula and Ilesha leaned against a double alicorn-spiral column, their heads bent close together as they giggled. Zelda and Dorcas had long since abandoned their weapons to pore over fashion magazines, and Valerija sat in a corner, earbuds in place, and concentrated on sharpening one of her many knives. Melissende and Grace were working on a new method of knapping arrowheads off a smooth kirin horn, and Cory was making her way across the bright courtyard, her arms filled with ancient books.

Bonegrinder lifted her head and growled. All the hunters, including Cory, stopped and stared at the little zhi, who was baring her teeth in Cory's direction.

"Hey!" I swatted Bonegrinder on the nose. "No growl. Bad girl."

Cory shook her head and continued over to our side. "What's going on?" She knelt and set down the books, and Bonegrinder sniffed at her and thwapped her tail against the paving stones. "What is happening to me?"

"Do you have something to tell us?" Melissende asked, wagging her eyebrows at Cory. "Hiding a little boyfriend somewhere?"

Cory blushed as most of the other girls tittered.

"Of course not!" she snapped. "I know the rules—" She cast me a guilty glance. "I am not dating anyone, no."

This only made them laugh harder. Valerija looked up from her knives, shook her head in disdain, and returned to her work.

"The rules?" I asked Cory wryly.

"You know I don't approve of you dating Giovanni," she said. "We're hunters. We're supposed to be celibate."

"I am celibate." My hands tightened on the hilt of my sword. "You can date someone without having sex with him."

"Yes." Melissende smirked. "It's especially easy when he lives on a different continent."

More giggling. I ignored them and returned to my work. The day after Giovanni's revelation, I'd visited Marymount International School to see about registering for classes and was told succinctly, but not rudely, that they'd begun accepting applications for this term last January—before anyone knew anything about unicorns at all—and that it was far too late to consider me now. But if I brought my parents in, maybe they would work something out for the spring semester.

I got a similar response at three other schools, then gave up. Perhaps Cory and Neil could find room in the budget for a tutor. Maybe Phil would suggest we both go back to the U.S. to start a North American Cloisters.

And maybe Bonegrinder would decide to give up ham hocks for broccolini.

Finished with the blade, I took out a leather cleaner and started working on the wrapping over the hilt. It had aged poorly, cracking in several places, and there was only so much leather oil could do to improve its condition. I wondered when we'd get a real weapons expert into the Cloisters to—if not repair our entire stockpile—at least give us some tips on how to keep things in good shape.

As careful as I was with cleaning, the leather was unraveling. I tugged on a frayed end and bits came off in my fingers, revealing tarnished metal underneath.

"Oops," I said, and held up the leather pieces.

Grace shrugged. "Probably time to replace, anyway. I'll look for some swordmaking hints about leather hilt wrapping." She tossed me a rag and a pot of polish. "Good opportunity to clean underneath, though."

I unraveled the rest of the hilt and began working the crud

out of the nooks and crannies of the metal. As the silver began to brighten beneath my fingers, I saw a pattern emerging on the hilt, one of curves and right angles. Roman block letter script. I scrubbed harder.

Bonegrinder began to growl again, and this time, when we looked up, we saw that Neil and Phil had entered the courtyard with a black-robed priest.

Neil cleared his throat. "Ladies, this is Father Guillermo, and he's here from the Vatican."

I tried to catch Phil's eye, but she was smiling cheerfully at all the girls and wouldn't focus on me.

Which, in my experience, was a bad sign. It meant she was in "donna mode" and would be pretending, for a little while at least, that being her cousin afforded me no special privileges. It was an attitude she adopted under two circumstances: when one of the other girls had complained about the cliques and whenever what was about to happen would upset me very much.

Now I looked to Cory, whose gaze was boring similar holes in Neil's direction. Like Phil, his face stayed placid, his attention directed toward the group as a whole. In her corner, Bonegrinder tested the security of the chain binding her to the wall until Zelda issued a sharp command and she slumped down. The zhi knew she was no match for a courtyard full of hunters.

"Buon giorno," said Father Guillermo, and bad as my own Italian remained, I detected something awkward in his syllables as well. "It makes me so happy to be welcomed into this beautiful convent, to see so many young women devoted to doing the work of God."

Cory put down her book.

"As you all probably know, the Order of the Lioness in these

41

Cloisters has long been a vital and treasured part of the Church. We were so sorry to see it die out in the nineteenth century and are thrilled to witness this revival now."

Ilesha folded her knees up to her chest and rested her chin on them, watching Father Guillermo curiously.

"And of course," he went on, "we have been watching this rebirth with much interest. The renovation of the Cloisters has given us much joy. The recruitment of Sister Lucia from her own convent to be your cook, the tacit approval of the monks who live next door . . ." He folded his hands in front of his robe and smiled at us. "We feel that until now, we have been supportive and yet unnecessarily distant."

Cory grumbled under her breath, "Fantastic. They wait until the heavy lifting is done then choose to stick in their oar."

"We wish to offer you whatever help we can," Father Guillermo continued, "though we are aware that this incarnation of the Order of the Lioness—well, it's not a religious order at all."

I looked at the other girls. He could say that again! In searching for eligible hunters, Neil already had enough of an uphill climb without requiring that they be Catholic as well. In fact, I was pretty sure only Rosamund, Melissende, Ursula, and Dorcas had any claim to Catholicism, and of those, only Rosamund was devout enough to attend mass.

"Had we been consulted," the priest said, his smile somewhat faded, "we would have encouraged you not to utilize the trappings and name of a Church organization. But," he said with a sigh, "we were not."

Cory's hands balled into fists.

"However, we are very happy to offer our assistance, even in these unusual circumstances. I suppose"—and here he placed his hand on his large stomach and gave a little chuckle—"that you could call it the opposite of a faith-based initiative. For you are a secular organization receiving Church funds."

Phil's composed smile was now frayed at the edges.

"I will be the liaison between your group and the Church, and I look forward to assisting you and seeing you work these miracles firsthand."

"That sounds like a pretty dangerous idea," said Grace, cleaning under her fingernails with an alicorn arrowhead. She shot him a crafty smile, then pricked her fingertip with the point. A single drop of cherry red blood welled and plopped to the cobblestones before the wound knit together.

Bonegrinder, who'd been lying on the floor pouting that she wasn't allowed to eat the priest, raised her head and sniffed at the scent of blood in the air. Father Guillermo took a few steps back.

"Besides," said Melissende, "we aren't miracle workers."

"Nonsense," said Father Guillermo. "Your skills in battle, your gift of healing—what are they but miracles from God?"

"Sorcery?" Melissende suggested with a shrug. Rosamund scowled at her. "What is your word for pagan magic?"

Phil's smile had completely withered and thunderheads were brewing in Neil's expression. Ursula tossed a polishing rag in her sister's direction to shut her up, but Melissende was on a roll.

"Our hunter gifts were bestowed on the line of Alexander the Great by the ancient goddess Diana," she said. "Certainly you know that."

Father Guillermo didn't miss a beat. "Certainly I know what the old pagan myths say. They are very pretty stories, to be sure,

43

and they were all the ancients had, since Christ had not yet been born. No, my dear, trust me: your gifts are miracles of God. The powers you wield, the Order of the Lioness, are like the Pantheon—an ancient pagan artifact that has long since been refocused to give glory to the one true God. I will pray that you glorify Him and that He keeps you safe on your next mission." He made a sign in Melissende's direction.

The real miracle, if you ask me, is that Father Guillermo shut her up.

He nodded as if the matter was settled. "Now I want to take a few moments to discuss a few policy adjustments we'll be instituting in the coming days." He took in our shocked faces. "Don't worry, my dears. This is nothing drastic. We're not requiring you to take holy orders. There are simply a few things we at the Church think will better reflect our core values."

I shook a few fold wrinkles out of the material and turned around to face Phil. "Well? How do I look?"

My cousin bit her lip to keep her grin contained. "I think it's . . . cute."

"Cute?" I snapped, and my headscarf slipped down over my forehead. "I'm wearing a camouflage *habit*."

"But a cute one," Phil pointed out.

All up and down the dorm hallway, I could hear the other hunters groaning as they tried on our new hunting uniforms. The outfit consisted of thick, polyester, camouflage-patterned split skirts that fell all the way to our ankles, a long camo headscarf, and matching long-sleeved, high-necked jackets.

Cory stomped into the room, the hem of her skirts dragging several inches in her wake. "I'm melting," she whined. "Literally and figuratively." She gathered up some of the extra material. "Who did they make these things for, Amazons?"

Valerija followed her, wearing the split skirt and a grubby, V-neck white undershirt.

"Amazons are pagan," I reminded Cory, and scratched at my neck, where the stiff material of my jacket irritated my skin.

Phil folded her feet up beneath her on my bed. "Certain religious sisterhoods are required to wear particular clothes at all times—even during day-to-day activities. These uniforms have been adapted from those nuns' hunting outfits."

"But I thought we didn't have to become nuns," I said.

"And you aren't," Phil replied. "But the Church would prefer that we aren't gallivanting around Rome in tank tops and shorts, that's all. Think of it like going to Catholic school: you don't have to be Catholic but you still have to wear the uniform."

Cory groaned and fell back on her bed, dislodging her headscarf.

"I like it," said Valerija, doing a few practice squat-thrusts on the shag carpet between Cory's bed and mine. She stroked her recently healed jaw and hiked up the waistband of her skirts. "It is roomy."

Zelda appeared in the doorway. "They aren't so bad. Not high fashion, but sturdy. I've torn holes in the knees of most of my trousers. These will hold up better."

"You should see what I have to wear," Phil said. "I don't even get a split skirt."

"Is yours camo, too?" I tried running in place. The split skirts were much heavier than the microfiber cargo pants my mom had packed with me to come to Rome. Still, in the thrall of hunter magic, sprinting after my prey, would I even notice them flapping against my thighs?

Phil brushed her bangs off her face. "Why would I need camo? I'm not a hunter."

"Why would *we* need camo?" I asked her. "We're not hiding from unicorns when we hunt them. We can't." The monsters had the same magnetic sense of our position as we did of theirs. This was why untrained unicorn hunters were a danger to themselves and others. For some reason, unicorns were attracted to hunters—we drew them in like sirens drew hapless sailors.

Oops, there I went with the pagan references again.

Cory sat up abruptly, her headscarf askew and her corkscrew curls sticking out from her head like wacky antennae. "I'm going to talk to Neil. There has to be another option."

But the conversation proved fruitless. "I'm sorry, Cory," Neil said to her later, when it was just the four of us. "But the Vatican has been quite explicit about their expectations for our behavior if we want their financial support. The habits are just the beginning."

"What?" I said. "What else is coming?"

Phil sucked air in through her teeth. "Let's just say it's a good thing that Giovanni went back to New York."

"No boys?" I asked. "So we're back to that, then." And I'd be back to sneaking Giovanni around when he came to visit over Christmas.

Neil cleared his throat. "You have to understand their position. We moved into their sacred space and turned it into a summer camp."

"They were using it for storage!" Cory smacked her hand

against the upholstered arm of her chair. "It was a ruin. Some sacred space. The art was crumbling, the catacombs were filled with rubbish, the scriptorium was burned to a crisp. We paid them their going rental rates, and we restored some of its former glory—"

"And they appreciate it," said Neil. "Which is why they're looking the other way at some of the more unorthodox policies we adopted. They accept that in this day and age we cannot limit the Order to Catholics or to young women willing to take lifelong vows. But you must expect that they would like to have a say in what happens with their money. Are some skirts and kerchiefs really worth all this fuss?"

Cory folded her arms across her chest.

I couldn't blame her. When she'd first sought to reclaim the Cloisters and gather together a new Order of the Lioness, Cory had put all her trust in Gordian Pharmaceuticals, and for the most part, they'd let her have free rein. But then everything had gone south, and Cory had defended Gordian's actions longer than anyone. When they took away our archery trainer and left us without weapons, she'd found a way to justify it. When we couldn't reach Marten and Giovanni told us that the Gordian CEO had been trying to sabotage Phil and me all summer, she hadn't believed it. I still wasn't sure how much of Cory's attitude was due to actual denial and how much was her fear of losing the control their patronage had afforded us.

After all, today it was "some skirts and kerchiefs." But what was next?

As the argument dragged on, I slipped out of the office and out into the courtyard. Father Guillermo was still there, admiring the mosaics and watching as a few of the girls practiced target shooting. Our weapons still lay in a heap all over the walkway, and Bonegrinder panted near an empty water bowl. I shook my head, refilled her bowl, and went back to cleaning my sword. After a few more swipes with the polishing rag, I could actually read the inscription.

DOMITARE UNICORNE INDOMITUM

Where was Giovanni when you needed him? He'd spent half the summer reading Latin transcriptions on ruins and artwork. He'd be able to translate this for me with no problem. Well, the "unicorn" part was pretty obvious, at least.

"Are you Astrid Llewelyn?" said a voice above my head. I looked up at Father Guillermo.

"Yes." I wiped polish from my palms on my new camouflage skirt, then stuck out my hand. He grimaced. Oops.

"I have heard that you are particularly blessed," he went on.

"You heard wrong." I inclined my head toward Grace, who was currently kicking butt at target practice. "She's above and beyond the best here. And the most dedicated as well."

"Modesty is a very noble trait, Señorita."

"You're not Italian, are you?" I asked.

"No. At the Vatican, priests come from all over Christendom. I am from Peru. We have no unicorns there."

I decided instantly that Peru was where I wanted to live when I grew up. "I'm serious, though. It's a false rumor, about the Llewelyns. At least it is with me. I'm certainly not the best hunter here. Grace has killed way more than me."

"I see." Father Guillermo said, smiling slightly. "My family does not believe that I have lived up to the potential of our

48

name, either. They are all businessmen. I became a priest. And not a parish priest but a policy maker. I am in business for my God."

Okay, then. I nodded and returned to my sword, and the priest spoke to the back of my head.

"You see, Señorita Llewelyn, sometimes what our family thinks we should be good at is correct. But not in the way they think."

I turned to look up at him, but he was still giving me that same impenetrable smile. Did he somehow know about my tête-à-têtes with the karkadann? But how could he? I doubted Phil or Neil would have told him something like that. It made us sound nuts.

Then again, Father Guillermo wasn't one of the wildlife or biology experts Phil was contacting for help. He was a Church official. He believed we had magic powers—that our gifts were from God. Saint Joan of Arc had been a warrior who experienced divine visions—why should a member of the Order of the Lioness be any different?

"Do you know what it says?" he asked me, pointing at the sword.

"No," I replied. "This is my ancestor's sword. A Llewelyn sword."

He lifted it from me and turned the blade over in his hands. "It is an incantation. Like the Paternoster, what you call 'Our Father.' It is a prayer, carved into the sword to sanctify the weapon to the glory of God. *Domitare unicorne indomitum.* It means, 'To Vanquish the Savage Unicorn.'"

4

Wherein Astrid Falters

Dear Giovanni,

I'd send you an e-mail, but wouldn't you know, they don't have Internet in this tree stand. So instead I scribble on this paper, back to the trunk and feet dangling out over the forest floor . . . and hope that nothing happens to make what I say irrelevant by the time I get home and have time to type this in.

You know, like me dying during the hunt. Or breaking my neck.

I've been out here since three A.M. and there's no sign of unicorns. The sun will be coming up soon, though, and that's usually our best hunting time. Have I ever told you that?

Of course. You saw it for yourself in Cerveteri when they tried to turn your van into a coffin. That morning seems like so long ago now. Back then, I felt like all this was almost over—like all we had to do was show one herd of kirin that we meant business and they'd go back where they came from, that we'd never have to deal with unicorns again.

Now, I can never imagine this being over.

*Sometimes it's hard for me to remember that they're ani-
mals, that when they kill, they do it for the same reasons as a
shark or a grizzly bear. They're hungry or they're protecting
themselves. It's so much worse for me to do what I do when I
think of that. It's easier to believe they're evil, that they really
have it in for these cows sleeping in their paddock in the farm
below.*

*And if it's hard for me to remember that, it's got to be
nearly impossible for Cory.*

I looked up from the paper, peering through the leaves at Cory,
stationed a half-dozen trees to the north. Her eyes roved the
ground, her body taut and clearly straining for the slightest
sense of unicorn. There wasn't any.

*Who am I kidding? I will never send this to you. I'll get
home, wash the blood off, and realize that these ~~foxhole~~ tree-
stand ramblings of mine are only going to bore you, or scare
you, or turn you off. And that's before I describe to you, in
detail, the seventeen yards of ultra-flattering camouflage
polyester they've wrapped me up in. Sexy, right?*

*I hope you're doing well. I wish you called more often. Phil
says they make international phone cards that are only like
seven cents a minute from New York to Italy. Can you look
into getting one of those?*

*I worry that I disappointed you with the school thing. I
promise I tried, but all the schools here wanted me to apply
like six months ago. Father Guillermo is seeing about getting
us tutors, though. Apparently there are lots of nuns that are*

teachers, so that's cool. I can be a Catholic schoolgirl and a unicorn hunter.

And take the PSATs and start thinking about college applications and hope that the next unicorn I meet doesn't put its horn through my heart.

I stopped writing and looked down the page. My handwriting wandered helter-skelter over the paper, but what could one expect from writing in the dark? I tore the page into bits and let them flitter to the forest floor. Later, I'd gather them up and burn them along with the corpses of any unicorns I managed to kill.

Violet fingers of light began to creep through the trees, signaling the arrival of dawn. According to the farmers' reports, we weren't dealing with kirin this morning, but information beyond that had been pretty scarce. There were monsters. They were eating the livestock. They had horns.

Looked like a job for the Order of the Lioness.

I touched the blade of the alicorn knife strapped to my hip, lifted my bow, and readied an arrow. The air smelled damp, with a tinge of forest and beyond that, the scent of farm animals, straw, and manure. No unicorns yet. Across the boughs, Cory scanned the area for any sign of the beasts. I narrowed my eyes. Couldn't she tell? How much was she attempting to compensate for her decreased hunterly attunement? Perhaps we should have taken this into account before letting her go on this trip.

The acrid scent of fire wafted past my nose, and with it, a touch of cloyingly sweet rot. The unicorns had arrived.

I closed my eyes and nocked an arrow on the string. Magic rushed through my system, and with it, the consciousness of the unicorns below. There were five of them in the pack: three adults and two juveniles. They were picking their way east through the forest, drawn in equal parts to their livestock food source and a strange new sense they couldn't understand but were attracted to anyway. *Us.* They pushed forward, unafraid, unconcerned that their deaths awaited them in the trees above their heads.

I trained my sights on the spot where they'd break through the clearing, opened my eyes, and waited. Ten seconds. Now five. They were moving faster, getting ready to break out of the woods and run for the paddock. I drew back the string. Now I could hear them, though their passage through the under-growth was almost soundless. The world slowed.

Five zhis rushed out of the woods, each as white and woolly as Bonegrinder. I froze.

I'd never killed a zhi. Some of the others had—in fact, I think Zelda had once demolished a pack this big all by herself. But I'd never faced down something that looked just like Bonegrinder and put an arrow through its heart. My drawing hand shook, and I softened the tension on the string.

The pack passed into Cory's line of sight, and she fired. The arrow thunked into a tree trunk and the zhis scattered, their silent thoughts broken in a cacophony of panicked, growling cries.

"Astrid!" Cory shouted as she swung herself down from her stand. "Hurry!"

I drew back again and blinked to clear my head of the image of Bonegrinder frolicking in the courtyard, a pink bandanna tied around her neck. Below me, an adolescent female zhi herded the two youngest away from danger. The babies were weaving in and out of her legs, and her panic radiated out to me as all three crowded and cowered in a small hollow beneath my tree's roots. Were they drawn to this tree because a hunter was inside it? If I dropped down before them, would they flee, attack . . . or bow? After all, they were zhis. The wild zhi I'd met in the woods back home had submitted to me only moments before tearing a hole in my ex-boyfriend Brandt's leg. Zhis never attacked hunters.

"Astrid!" Cory cried. "What are you doing? Shoot them!"

I pointed my arrow down at the hole. Three zhis blinked up at me with wide blue eyes. *Three little Bonegrinders all in a row; I move fast and they move slow.*

Out of the corner of my eye I saw Cory slashing with her knife. One of the adult unicorns screamed and went down, hooves flailing. My string hand began to ache with the tension of keeping the bow drawn. Inside the heads of the unicorns below me, I felt panic, terror, and underneath that, awe.

A hunter, a hunter . . .

They'd follow me anywhere. Back to the Cloisters, to be chained and confined like Bonegrinder, or over to Cory, where they'd bow in turn and offer her their necks for slaughter.

"Astrid!" Cory yelled for the third time. "What are you waiting—" And then she cut off as the second zhi tackled her from behind.

All five zhis were shrieking inside my head—the three little ones in horror, the older male in the midst of its death throes, and the female—the female in fury. And over it all, in my actual ears, I heard Cory's screams. I leaped to the ground and sprinted toward her. The zhi was stomping and biting as Cory covered her face with her arms and tried to shove it away.

"Stop it!" she screamed as the zhi clamped its fangs into her side. "Stop!"

I closed my hand around the zhi's horn, yanked backward, and slit its throat. The unicorn bucked once, then twitched and gurgled as I threw it aside and knelt by Cory's knees.

"You okay?"

Cory's eyes were wide and she panted, clutching her torso with two bloody hands. I saw the scratches of the zhi's alicorn close and vanish on her forearms, but the wound in her side had been inflicted by teeth, not horn. It was a problem.

"Let me see," I said as the unicorn behind us died. The male was fading fast, and at the edge of my consciousness, I could sense the young ones making a break for it. Smart move. I pried Cory's hands away from her tummy and blood spurted forth.

I unzipped my waist pack and pulled out a length of gauze bandage. "Here, hold this against your wound."

"The others . . ." She gasped.

"The others are gone," I told her, distracted. The others had never felt the slightest compunction to attack. Would the female zhi have done so if Cory hadn't stabbed her mate? Aggressive zhis were unheard of. "I'm going to run and get the farmers. You need medical attention."

"You have to kill the others," Cory persisted as the male near us breathed his last. My head cleared a fraction more.

"You're not thinking straight," I said, wrapping another length of bandage around her waist to hold the bunched gauze in place. The unicorns were almost out of the range of my thoughts now, and they were still running. "They're juveniles. They're terrified."

"They'll come for me."

I blew out an exasperated breath. "And what?" I asked. "Bow? They're zhi. You'll be fine." I stood. "Stay here and try not to move. I'll be back with a truck as soon as—"

She leaned forward and grabbed my leg with a bloodstained hand. "Astrid! They'll kill me! I don't . . . I can't . . ." She grimaced, her eyes squeezed shut. "I'm . . . broken."

"You're wounded is what you are," I said. And how wily of the zhi to have used her teeth and not her horn. I hadn't seen that before from a unicorn, not even the devious kirin. "And badly. I have to get you help *now*."

Her eyes bored into mine, wide and filled with panic. *"Do not leave me here alone to die."*

At once I understood. Sybil Bartoli had died just like this, as an untrained Cory had tried valiantly to hold off a family of zhis with nothing but her hands. I handed her Clothilde's knife.

"You'll die for sure if I don't get you some help." And then I ran.

They rushed Cory into the surgery room of the tiny country clinic, leaving me standing in the drab, prefab waiting room, blood still staining the knees of my pants and drying in strange patterns on my arms and hands. It would take almost four hours for Phil and Neil to get up here. Four hours of me standing outside the door to the clinic, wringing my hands and wondering if I should be back out there in the woods, chasing down those juveniles and breaking their necks. After all, they were unicorns, and they needed to eat *something*. Any human in the woods was still in danger. All those animals on the farm were still at risk.

Or maybe I could just convince the farmers to leave the occasional ham hock out in the woods as tribute. Bonegrinder loved pork.

Bonegrinder looked so much like that unicorn I'd just killed.

I drew my legs up to my chest in the hard clinic chair, pressed my eyeballs against my kneecaps, and rocked.

"Asteroid," came Phil's soft voice. I felt her hand on my shoulder and flew out of my seat, blinking in the afternoon sun that streamed through the windows.

"I didn't mean to fall asleep."

"Don't worry about it," said Phil. She was dressed in her regulation Cloisters uniform: loafers, a simple, dark blue skirt that fell halfway past her knees, and a starched, white, high-necked blouse. Her hair was in a low ponytail, though she wore no scarf. "You were up half the night in a tree stand. I know how this works."

"How's Cory?"

"Physically?" Phil shrugged. "She'll be fine. No organs were affected, and the doctors stitched her up. Luckily zhi teeth aren't quite as long as their horns."

"How did it know? How did it know it could do more damage with its mouth?"

Phil shook her head. "I don't know. And maybe it didn't. It could have been an accident that it bit instead of gored. Maybe the angle at which it attacked made using its horn impossible, or maybe Cory was able to fend it off. I don't know. She's got some pretty nasty bruises all over her chest and legs from its hooves, too, not to mention a sprained ankle. She's going to have to take it easy for a few weeks, but it's nothing we haven't seen before."

I took a deep breath. There *was* something new about this attack, though, and it wasn't anything a doctor could stitch up. Cory's hunter abilities had somehow been compromised and were deteriorating fast. A few weeks ago, she hadn't sensed the kirin approaching our group in the forest, and today, she'd had a clean shot at the male zhi and missed. Afterward, she'd admitted what I'd already suspected: Cory was hunting blind.

"Can I see her?"

"Better wait until Neil's done talking to her." Phil cast a concerned glance at the door to the ward. "She's not taking this too well."

"Since when has she ever taken things well?" I blurted, then followed up immediately with, "I'm sorry."

"Don't apologize to me," said Phil. "We both know what she's like, but we also know why. This means more to her than it does to any other hunter in the Cloisters."

Phil was about to say more when the conversation inside the ward suddenly got very loud. The door flew open, revealing Neil in the threshold, still looking back at the bandaged figure on the bed. "I *shall* tell you what to do, Cornelia Bartoli. Like it or not, I am your guardian, and I'll be hanged before I let you die like your mother."

He came out and slammed the door shut behind him, breathing heavily. He ran his fingers through his dark, wavy hair then noticed us. "All right, Astrid?"

"Hi," I said. I looked from Neil to Phil. "Should I . . . ?"

"I can't deal with her defiance," Neil said to Phil. "She refuses to see me as an adult." He sighed. "In her eyes, I'm not her uncle and guardian telling her these things; I'm her bossy older brother."

"You're her only family," Phil replied, coming close. "She'll come around. She always does."

Neil didn't look convinced. "I need a coffee." He spun and headed off down the corridor to the break room, and Phil followed, leaving me alone. I watched them move down the hall, saw Phil place her hand on the small of his back in comfort.

I entered the ward. Cory was making a valiant attempt to get out of the hospital bed, flailing around with crutches and wincing every time she had to bend.

"Careful," I said. "You're not going to heal so quick this time." Her shirt was folded up, and thick bandages wrapped all the way around her waist. There were other bandages on her arms and legs, and several bruises sprouted on the fair skin of her face. Her mop of brown curls lay flat and listless against her head.

She glared at me, her eyes overflowing with tears. "Did you hear what he said to me?"

"I think the entire village heard."

"How dare he!" she said. "How dare he—" She cut off then turned away, burying her chin into her chest. "I've been hunting unicorns for months. I've killed kirin, I've killed re'em—it would be rather foolish if I were killed by a zhi. *Just like my mother.*"

I nodded, and kept my voice soft. "It was wrong of Neil to say that. He didn't mean it. He was just so frightened to see you like this. We're all scared about what this might mean—"

"Oh, I know what it means!" she said. "It means I have to leave. It's too dangerous for me to stay at the Cloisters if I can't be a proper hunter, if Bonegrinder will leap on me as soon as look at me. And Neil says he'll go with me, since we're already a ring short. I'm too young to be a proper don, so I'm the one who has to go. Not Phil. Me." She sniffled.

My mouth opened. "But you can't leave!"

"I know. I practically rebuilt the Cloisters, stone by bloody stone. And this is how it ends! I didn't *do* anything wrong! I don't know why this is happening to me. I don't know why I can't . . ." She seemed to collapse over her crutches, defeated. "This isn't fair. There's no reason I should be losing the magic."

I couldn't think of anything to say. It wasn't fair. Not in the least. "I don't know."

"You're quite the doctor, Astrid," she snapped.

"Well, maybe you should go see a real doctor!" I cried. "Maybe you're sick—something completely normal and non-magical, but your hunter powers are suppressed the same way that, I don't know, your immune system might be depressed from some other illness."

"Like what?" she asked. "Like a cold? I don't have a cold."

I remained quiet because "like cancer or something" wasn't going to go far in calming her down.

"And look at this!" she cried, and thrust out her arm. A brand-new, glistening red alicorn scar peeked out from beneath the edge of her sleeve. "I'm still immune to the poison. It's just the hunting that I can't muster—why?"

"That's what I mean," I said. "It's too dangerous for you to go. We don't know what powers are still working for you. I mean, look at it this way: if you were in a coma, you'd be unable to hunt, but you'd still be a *hunter*. You're still going to draw unicorns to you. That's why we need to train all the girls with hunter abilities. Even if they don't stay here, don't work for the Order, they at least need to know how to protect themselves."

Cory straightened. "You're right. Astrid, that's brilliant."

Phil probably wouldn't thank me for that particular stroke of brilliance.

"They can't let me go or then I really might die. The woods on our land are simply infested with zhis." She narrowed her

60

eyes. "Zhis just like the one today. Zhis just like the ones that killed my mum."

"Zhis just like the one living in our nunnery?" I replied.

But Cory was not to be gainsaid. "Grab my boots, will you?" she said, swinging her crutches toward the door. I followed half-heartedly, boots in hand. This couldn't end well.

One screaming match in a small country clinic and half an exceedingly awkward and unbearably silent car ride back to Rome later, I remembered that I'd never gone back to burn the scraps of paper that were all that was left of my letter to Giovanni.

No matter. I stared out the window at the rolling Italian countryside and began to compose another e-mail in my head.

Dear Giovanni,

Today we found out that Cory's hunting abilities are mysteriously diminished, and Neil and Phil have concluded that it is too dangerous for her to remain active in the Order of the Lioness. Cory is furious, but all I can think is "I wish it were me. . . ."

5

WHEREIN ASTRID REACHES OUT

The sun beat down on the cobblestones in the Cloisters courtyard, shimmering off Phil's blond ponytail as she stood before us on her yoga mat.

"Now," she said, "exhale and bend your left leg until the left knee is perpendicular over the left ankle. You want a straight, ninety-degree angle between your shin and the ground."

We all moved on our mats.

"Keep breathing," Phil said. "Lengthen your torso. Put power into your right leg. Feel the energy in your right leg all the way through your toes and into the earth."

And under the ground to the chapter house of the Cloisters, where the bones hummed in tune to the beating of our hearts. What Phil didn't know is that the rhythm of our inhalations was not dependent on her instructions. All hunters breathed together in the Cloisters—the entire nunnery respired like a massive iron lung.

"Now, on the next breath in, sweep your hands up and out at the level of your shoulders. Think of your arms as arrows pointing straight and true."

I loved warrior pose. I increased power to my core and looked left over the tips of my fingers, imagining them as arrowheads aimed directly at the heart of a kirin.

But in my sights I saw instead Cory, bandaged foot elevated against a column, reading a magazine and drinking lemonade. Her side of our room was packed, and she was headed back home to England this week. No amount of arguing with Neil had resulted in a change of heart. As far as he was concerned, the Cloisters was a gravity well of hunter attraction. Neil's flat in London, however, would be safer.

"Warrior Two," Phil was saying as we deepened into the pose with every breath, "is a position of power but also of focus. A Zen archer aims his bow for years before ever releasing an arrow."

"Doesn't kill many unicorns that way, huh?" Melissende said with a snicker. Some of the younger girls laughed.

Phil lifted her chin and went on. "You are arrows, straight and true. You are spears, strong and focused. You are warriors."

Grace ignored her friend, for once, and closed her eyes.

I, too, turned inward.

The bones in the masonry sang around me. In the shade of the Cloisters, Bonegrinder sat in watchful stillness, her chain anchoring her to the wall. I felt her presence like a livid pinprick in my mind within the net of buzzing artifacts.

And beneath that, I felt my fellow hunters. Grace, solid as a rock, her energy radiating outward from her arms like the points on a compass. The other girls, bright or dim depending on the strength of their concentration. Beyond my fingertips, I felt Cory sizzling like a frayed power cord. Farther out were the others: Valerija resting in her room; Dorcas on the computer; Rosamund coming up the stairs from the chapter house into the rotunda.

I breathed and sank deeper into this new awareness. Inside my head a chord began to ring. I'd heard it before, the music of the Wall of First Kills. I'd only heard it from the other hunters once, just before our battle against the kirin in the necropolis of Cerveteri last month.

I'm an arrow, I thought to myself.

You are an arrow, said Phil's voice inside my head. But no, it wasn't Phil. It was Clothilde Llewelyn. The Clothilde who lived inside the memory of the karkadann Bucephalus.

You are the arrow of God, said Clothilde, *on a mission to vanquish the savage unicorn.*

I lost my balance and went careening into Ursula, who knocked into Ilesha, who elbowed Melissende hard in the stomach. We all collapsed to the floor.

This time, Grace did laugh as she swept up from her pose and smiled smugly at the tangle of hunters at her feet. "Too challenging?"

"Get off me!" Melissende shoved her younger sister, Ursula, out of the way and blew her black hair out of her eyes. "Yoga is dumb."

I put my hands over my eyes trying to clear the dizziness.

"Asteroid?" Phil said, narrowing her eyes in the glare of the afternoon light. "You okay?"

"One too many sun salutations today, I think," I said. I pushed myself to my feet and dusted off my knees. "I'm going to get some water."

The last time I'd heard Clothilde's voice in my head, it was

64

because Bucephalus had put it there. The last time I could feel hunters the way I could feel unicorns—the way I imagined that unicorns could feel us—Bucephalus had been there.

Inside my head, I called out to the karkadann. But there was no reply.

Figured. I had no idea what Bucephalus would be doing in Rome, anyway. Despite the city's network of parks, abandoned, stray-dog-infested ruins, and endless underground catacombs, it was hard for a unicorn the size of a rhinoceros to find a good hiding spot. I hadn't seen him for months, hadn't even dreamed about him for weeks. He'd told me he was going away, and yet I still searched.

Because he was the only one I knew who had any answers.

As I passed through the door into the rotunda, I saw Rosamund standing with Father Guillermo, their heads both bowed in whispered prayer. I stopped, afraid of interrupting them, and after a moment, he made the sign of the cross over the girl's auburn head, then smiled at her.

"*Vaya con Dios, Hermanita,*" said Father Guillermo.

"*Vielen Dank,*" Rosamund said. "I am feeling much better now." She turned and caught sight of me. "Astrid!"

I shied behind the edge of the stuffed Bucephalus. "I didn't mean to interrupt—"

"No," Rosamund said, and beckoned to me. She gathered up her music, which was arranged in a pile at her feet. "Ever since I heard of Cory's . . . problem, I have not been able to sleep. I am so afraid it will happen to us all. I asked *Herr Pfarrer* to bless me. For protection from . . . whatever this may be."

"I will be happy to bless you as well," said Father Guillermo.

I looked down. "No, thank you."

"Or any of the other hunters." He took in my clingy yoga clothes. "I take it you have been exercising?"

I swallowed. "Yes. Yoga. In the privacy of the Cloisters courtyard. We are all alone here." Couldn't embarrass him or the Church or the Order.

He shook his head and smiled. "*Señorita*, please do not be alarmed. This is not a police state, and I am not your enemy."

I brushed past them both and took the stairs to the dorm floor. Yeah, well, the last time some strange man holding the purse strings told us that, he was Marten Jaeger.

And when he'd tried to destroy us, I'd turned the tables and let him be killed.

In the shower, I washed off the sweat of the Italian afternoon and tried to rinse the memory of Clothilde's voice from my brain. As a nun—even a lapsed one—Clothilde would have been Catholic. She would have been raised in the original Order of the Lioness, the kind that carved prayers into their swords and truly believed that they were vessels of God, charged to kill unicorns and dispense doses of the Remedy as the Church saw fit.

That was the Order that Clothilde had rebelled against. That had been the life she'd faked her own death to escape.

I wish I'd known more about her, this mysterious, revered, misunderstood ancestor of mine. It was well documented in Cloisters's records that most hunters who sought to escape their duties turned to the services of what the Order had long called "actaeons," after the mythological man who'd spied on the hunter goddess, Diana, in her bath. An actaeon was a fancy name for a lover—a guy specifically employed to divest a unicorn hunter of her virginity and thus her magic. The mythological Actaeon had been punished for his boldness when Diana had turned him into a stag to be torn to pieces by his own dogs. When the ancient Order of the Lioness caught an actaeon in the act, they fed him to their house zhi.

Yes, I was part of a long line of extremely hard-core nuns.

But Clothilde had not gone the actaeon route. She was still a hunter—had to have been to be able to communicate—when she made the deal with Bucephalus that had sent every unicorn in the world into hiding and had convinced the world they'd become extinct.

Naturally, all records of Clothilde had disappeared from the history. I did know, however, that she'd married and had children. I was a direct descendant, on my father's side. A father that my unicorn-obsessed mother had long ago tracked down and seduced. Possibly—I had recently realized with disgust—for the sheer purpose of getting a hunter daughter with a more prestigious lineage.

Lucky Lilith, not to have borne a son.

The Order of the Lioness may not know what happened to Clothilde, but my mother somehow did. She'd found my father once, though she'd told me he knew nothing of our lineage. And yet, the only thing she'd kept from their tryst (aside from me) was a single golden, blown-glass vial of the Remedy—the only one in existence. A vial she'd kept my whole life, until the day my boyfriend Brandt got gored by a unicorn in the woods and she'd cured him with it.

Naturally, my father, whoever he was, would have no knowledge of its value. To him, it may have been nothing more than a family antique. Maybe he didn't even know my mother had it.

I wondered where my father was. I wondered if he had a family—daughters who may not know what kind of danger they were in. Untrained hunters were in the same position as Cory—unable to help themselves or their loved ones when the unicorns would inevitably be drawn to them.

I left the bathroom, got dressed, and tied my hair into a damp braid whose hard elastic end slapped against the alicorn scars on my back as I took the stairs to the don's office.

The desk was covered with the usual piles of paperwork: reports of unicorn attacks, family trees and other genealogical records to trace the location of possible unicorn hunters, and the newest, disturbing addition—letters from people across the globe begging for help from the Cloisters. *Please, come get the unicorn in our town. These monsters have already killed three people. We can't figure out how to stop it. They've had to close the park/the school/the logging operation . . .*

Well, maybe I didn't so much mind that last one.

The letters came from all over the world, especially remote locations that would be nearly impossible (and cost-prohibitive) for us to visit. Tiny villages in the Canadian tundra, mountaintop monasteries in Tibet, cattle ranches in South America. There weren't many, but it was clear that as people began to learn who we were, the requests would increase. We needed more resources, even than the Church could provide. And we needed more hunters.

My mother answered the phone on the second ring. "Astrid?"

"Hi, Mom." Probably best not to lead with a request. Our relationship had been strained enough since Phil and I had kicked her out of the Cloisters. "How are things?"

"Great," she said. "My agent is in talks with the networks for a major exposé."

Not that she appeared to have suffered too greatly.

"We might come back to Rome and tour the Cloisters if this goes through."

"Have you spoken to Phil and Neil about it?" Not to mention Father Guillermo.

Lilith was quiet for a moment. "Well, Sweetie, there's quite a bit of money involved. Given how tight things have been around there recently, I figured they'd welcome an influx of cash."

Translation: she hadn't planned on asking for permission.

"Actually," I said, "we've been getting some support from the Vatican."

Lilith snorted. "Right. The habits. Well, they'll look better on TV, at any rate. Do they hinder your hunting at all?"

Typical. First my mother worries about the aesthetics and only then concerns herself with little practicalities like whether or not her daughter's life is in danger. "They were designed as hunting costumes."

"Really?" I picture Lilith, her eyes glowing with interest. "Now that's an angle."

"Mom, would you like me to actually *take* some religious vows? You know, to help with the ratings?"

"Ooh, would you? We'd make prime time!"

I almost swallowed the receiver.

"That was a joke, Astrid." Lilith clucked her tongue at me.

Funny how lightly she could take this all now. She'd barged into the Cloisters, determined to whip us into shape, judgmental and dismissive of the Bartolis' policies and their more inclusive, democratic attitudes. She'd run the place like a boot camp reminiscent of the ancient Order, and dreamed of hunters victorious in every battle.

The truth, unfortunately, was not quite as glamorous, and when I'd been severely injured the first time she'd sent us out against a group of kirin, she'd flipped out and tried to close the place down. Phil and I had risen up against her and sent her packing back to the States.

From a few thousand miles away, though, I guess the gory reality of unicorn hunting seemed a tad more rosy. I guess she forgot what it was like when I almost died. Maybe her concern was related to proximity, and now that she lived across an ocean, she'd gone back to buying the hype she spewed on television about our "glorious destiny."

Maybe things with Giovanni would go the same way: out of sight, out of mind.

Time to change the subject before I got too angry to speak. "I need to ask you a few questions about my father."

"This again?"

"You found him once, Mom. Don't you think we owe it to whatever family he has to try to find him again?"

"For someone who dislikes hunting so much, you are terribly eager to consign your potential half sisters to the lifestyle."

I clenched my jaw. My potential half sisters would be sitting ducks unless they were informed of their power to attract killer unicorns.

"You have to make up your mind," I growled into the phone. "Either you want me to come home and be safe or you want me to be your unicorn-hunting rock star of a daughter."

For that was the real reason my mother refused to hand over information about the other half of my gene pool. If there were other descendants of Clothilde out there, then they might be the ones to possess the super cool, descendant-of-Clothilde-

Llewelyn unicorn-hunting skills that had, so far, failed to manifest themselves in me.

It was so ironic. The people at the Cloisters thought I was supposed to be the best hunter because I was a Llewelyn. My mother thought I was supposed to be the best hunter because I was descended from Clothilde Llewelyn, in particular. The Llewelyn who had killed the karkadann. Even the karkadann had come to me instead of to one of the other hunters, because he held a similarly misguided belief about Clothilde's legacy that if he could talk to her as easily as he'd once talked to Alexander the Great, he could talk to me as well. And he *could* talk to me—but I think he could talk to the other hunters, too, if they tried.

What did I believe? That it was all a lie. The facts were incontrovertible: I was *not* the best hunter in the Order. Why was it that the only people who seemed to recognize this besides me were Melissende and Grace? Grace was the best hunter here. Ilesha was a close second. I liked my place farther down the list.

My mother sighed into the phone. "Sweetie, you made your position quite clear before I left Rome. It's *you* who wants this now, not me. And *you* who reserves the right to whine about it, too. I gave you the chance to come home. You gave me a long-suffering speech about duty. You've caught a fine case of holier-than-thou from these priest friends of yours."

How was it that she could do this to me? How did she always manage to turn everything around like that? Her dismissal of Father Guillermo and his support of the Cloisters almost had me on the priest's side, camouflage habits and all.

"Oh yeah?" I said. "And what would you say if I told you I wanted to come home now?"

"Whatever you want, dear," my mother lied, her tone both blithe and bored. She knew I was bluffing. I wouldn't come home because of my duty, and if I did, she wouldn't like it because of the supposed glory involved.

"Fine," I said. "Book me a ticket. Or I'll book it. Give me your credit card number."

My mother hesitated. She wasn't the only one who knew how to call a bluff. "Certainly. Of course, you know you can't come here as a hunter. The danger aspect would cause far too many complications. You'd need to give up your . . . eligibility."

I swallowed. "Fine. I'll . . . do that, too. I'll stop by . . . New York on my way home."

"How very unsentimental of you," my mother responded.

"You're one to talk," I snapped back.

"I hope you won't regret it when you see people in danger of dying from unicorn attacks. Knowing you could have saved them but would rather just come home and live a small and useless life."

I gritted my teeth. We had all the steps to this dance down pat. Sometimes I wondered if I was to blame for my mother's disregard. If Phil and I hadn't kicked her out last summer, would she still worry for my safety? Had I killed that off in her? And if I had, how strong could her love have been?

Sometimes I wondered. Other times, I was too busy fighting for my life and the lives of those I'd pledged to keep safe. "Mom," I said. "You have to tell me where my father is. His family is in danger. You just admitted it!"

"Oh, darling," she said. "It was so long ago. I hardly remember."

That was utterly untrue. Once upon a time, my mother had

been a historian, a Ph.D. candidate whose research had uncovered our hunting legacy and awoken in her this monomaniacal obsession with Clothilde Llewelyn and our magical legacy. She had notes—somewhere—about my father's family.

"Can't the Bartolis do something? They've been so good about finding all the other hunters. Too bad they're so bad at everything else. By the way, how is the search going for that horrible boy who raped Phil?"

I slammed the phone down. My fingers itched for a bow to shoot. My arms ached for a sword to swing. My hands reached for the knife usually strapped to my side, and found only the leg of my pants. I twisted the material in my fist, breathing hard, choking on rage so strong I could almost scream. I leaned over the desk, pressing my palms hard into the wood. In the corner of my eyes, I could see my arm muscles flexing beneath my skin. Though I'd never been as athletic as Phil, since coming to the Cloisters, my body had changed. It wasn't just the scars that twisted along my back and my arms, wasn't just the magic that coursed through my blood and my bones. Back home, I'd been soft, with slim, round arms that never did more than carry books or push wheelchairs during my candy-striping volunteer hours at the hospital. Now, my arms were muscled, defined like the curves and kinks of an alicorn.

I looked like a bodybuilder. It wasn't feminine. It wasn't beautiful.

The anger condensed into tears that boiled from my eyes, and I sank to the floor behind the desk and crawled into the darkness underneath. Screw duty. Maybe my mom was right that it wasn't worth all this.

With shaking hands, I grabbed the phone and stretched the

cord into my little cave. I took a deep breath and dialed his number.

"Hello," said a stranger in New York.

My mouth refused to open until I could speak without shuddering.

"Hello?" the guy repeated.

"Hi," I said, and it came out like a squeak. "Can I speak to Giovanni, please?"

"Uh, he's in class," the guy said. "Can I take a message?"

Tell him I miss him. Tell him I love him. Tell him I can't take this anymore and he needs to come back to Italy and get me out of this hunting gig once and for all.

"Can you, um, tell him that Astrid called?"

"Who?"

I caught the sob in my throat before it could escape. "Astrid," I somehow managed to get out. This was going to go poorly, I could tell.

"Ass trig?" The guy sounded utterly skeptical.

I heard someone else in the background. *"That's the girl-friend, man. The nun?"*

And, under the desk in the convent in Rome, my face turned the color of spaghetti sauce.

"Right. Astrid!" the guy said, his tone turning merry. "How are things with the unicorns?"

"Fine," I blurted, more out of surprise than anything else.

"You keep up the good work," he said. "I'll tell G you called. I'm Steve, by the way."

"Hi, Steve," I said.

"You know, he's practically living at the studio these days. You'd probably have a better chance of getting in touch with him on his cell phone."

"Oh," I said. Giovanni had a cell phone?

"You take care! Bye now." Steve hung up before I could ask for the cell phone number. Which I didn't want to do, because that would mean admitting that my boyfriend had a phone I didn't know about.

Why wouldn't Giovanni have told me about his cell phone? Would it mess with his calling plan? Maybe I couldn't make international calls to his cell without racking up some sort of ridiculous charge.

Or maybe he didn't want me crying to him all day and night about how much my life sucked. Maybe he was living it up back in New York City, and thoughts of me were a downer.

No, that wasn't fair. After all, his roommates seemed to know who I was. They'd called me his girlfriend.

Though they'd also called me a nun, which wasn't entirely accurate.

I reached up to replace the phone on the desk, then buried my face against my knees. Back in America, my mother was turning into a TV star and my boyfriend was fulfilling his artistic dreams. Here in Italy, I was a high school dropout, a fake nun who weekly risked her life in battles against poisonous monsters.

What if, last spring, I'd done what all my friends at school thought I should? What if I'd done what my ex-boyfriend Brandt had wanted me to do? What if I'd slept with him? I'd never have been a unicorn hunter. I'd still be in school, still candy-striping at the hospital, still the youngest girl in AP chemistry, still applying for college science scholarships, still imagining becoming a doctor.

It wouldn't have been just me, either. If I hadn't been a hunter that night in the woods, Brandt and I would never have been attacked by that zhi. Brandt would never have taken my mom's only dose of the Remedy. Maybe he wouldn't have run away from home as the publicity of being the only known survivor of a unicorn attack started to weigh on him. Brandt wasn't my favorite person in the world—what with publicly dumping and humiliating me in the lunchroom after I'd saved him from a "rabid goat"—but he'd been a nice enough guy while we were dating. He'd been a champion swimmer, likely to get a college scholarship. And who knew what he was doing now?

Then there was Phil. If I hadn't come to the Cloisters, there'd be no way she'd have followed me here. If I hadn't come, she'd be back in college, kicking butt on the volleyball court. She'd have never met Seth. She'd never have been raped.

I'd have never met Cory or the other hunters; I'd never have met Giovanni. But then, I'd never be here. I'd never have understood magic or know what it felt like to kill. I'd never be scarred. I'd never be alone in a convent, hiding under a desk, terrified of what the next hunt would bring.

6

WHEREIN ASTRID DISCOVERS A SECRET

"This is a rather bad time for a trip." Neil's voice drifted into my brain.

"Any time is a bad time for a unicorn attack," Phil replied. "But the fact that there was a survivor? That it was a teenage girl? That says 'hunter' to me, and so do some of the other details in the report. One of us needs to investigate this, and bring her here if we can."

I blinked my eyes and lifted my head, neck muscles protesting. Somehow, I'd managed to cry myself to sleep beneath Neil's desk.

"I already have a responsibility to Cory," Neil said. "I *must* get her away from here."

I began to crawl out, intending to alert them to my presence, but Phil's next words stopped me cold.

"Oh, sure. Run away again, just like last time. Whenever things start to get hard—is that your MO?"

I froze and retreated.

"Not *hard*," Neil said softly. "Confusing."

Phil was silent. I imagined them staring at each other. "Admit it," she said at last, her voice harsh. "Cory is an excuse."

"She needs my protection."

"Protection?" Phil repeated. "You're not a hunter. They're the only ones that can protect her. Or *this*—"

"Put that back on!" Neil ordered.

"*You* put it on!" Phil ordered back. "Stop acting like a martyr for me!"

There was a thunk, and the don's ring fell on the floor, rolled a few inches, and stopped. I could see it, shining red and gold, in the gap between the bottom of the desk and the floor.

"I'm not playing games with you, Pippa," said Neil. "You put that ring on this second or . . ."

"Or what?" I could almost see Phil staring him down. "We keep Bonegrinder chained. We have to, with two dons around and only one ring."

"Bonegrinder isn't the only unicorn on Earth. And with the number of hunters we have here, we're in the epicenter of a storm. You're in danger."

"*You're* in danger every single day we're both here. Don't you think I know that? Don't you think it weighs on me whenever I see that ring on my hand?"

"Which is why it would be better for me to leave."

"But not the only reason, huh?"

I clapped my hands over my mouth.

Above me, everything was silent for several long moments, but the blood in my ears roared. Had they heard me?

"No," said Neil at last. "Not the only reason. Are you happy now?"

"Of course not."

"Then what was the point of forcing a confession?"

"So that we can talk about it!" There was a thump on the desk above my head. I curled into an even tighter ball, unsure whether to announce my presence now or try to will myself into deafness. I should *not* be hearing this. "So we can maybe *do* something about it." Another thump.

Come out? Stay hidden? Rip my ears off with my bare hands?

"There is nothing to be done," said Neil. "I'm going back to London. It will all be forgotten."

"Why?" Phil asked, and for the first time, I heard the hurt in her tone.

"You know why." And the hurt in his.

Heck, even I knew why. There was, for starters, the age difference.

"I'm not a child," said Phil. "I'm in college. You're barely out of it."

There was the fact that when she'd first come here, she'd been under his guardianship.

"I'm not a hunter anymore," said Phil. "I'm a don, just like you."

And, worst of all, there was Phil's all-too-recent experiences.

"What's *really* bothering you?" More of an accusation than a question.

I squeezed my eyes shut. Some things I should never, ever hear.

"I'm sorry!" I shouted from beneath the desk. I scurried out and stood, taking in their astonishment and humiliation.

"Astrid!" Phil gasped.

"I'm sorry," I repeated. "I'm sorry! I—"

"Good Lord." Neil's expression was stricken. He turned and beelined for the door.

Phil didn't even watch him go. She stared at me, eyes wide, chest heaving. "Astrid. *What* were you *doing* under the *desk!*"

I hung my head. "Sleeping?"

"What were you doing *sleeping* under the desk!" she cried again, her tone even more exasperated. "Why were you sneaking around? Why were you—" She dug her fists into her eyes. "Why were you in our office?"

"I *am* sorry," I parroted. "I had no idea. I would never try to spy on you—"

"It doesn't matter," she said, hands still covering her face. "It doesn't matter."

"What's going on with you two?"

I instantly regretted asking. She fixed me with a glare that would make a kirin quake in fear—hunter powers or no. "I'm sure you eavesdropped enough to hear the answer to that. *Absolutely nothing.*"

"I can't apologize any more than I already have, Phil," I said, coming close to her. I reached for her hand. "I wish I'd just stayed down there."

"What, to hear more?"

"No! So I wouldn't have embarrassed you. Or interrupted you," I added. Because it sounded as if they were about to hit some sort of breakthrough.

"How thoughtful of you," Phil drawled, and pulled away. "Just . . . don't tell anyone about this, okay? Especially not Cory."

No worries there. Half the Order suspected it, anyway. I'd always thought their relationship was inappropriately flirtatious, but I never figured there was anything more to it—especially on

Neil's behalf—until the night Phil was attacked by Seth.

Then, of course, we'd all had far more important things to deal with than who had a crush on whom. And now, well, I suppose we still did, but that didn't mean it didn't matter.

"But Phil," I said. "If you care about each other—"

Phil slammed her hand down on the desk and snorted. "My God, Astrid, you're such a child." She shook her head, tendrils of her blond hair falling into her face. "Please leave."

So I did.

I didn't go down to dinner. I was way too embarrassed. I hid in my room, cuddled up tight with Bonegrinder, my face buried in fur that smelled of flood and fire. And a bit like pepperoni.

My stomach growled.

"There you are," said Cory. I took in her form, crutches and all, highlighted in the hall, and curled even more tightly toward Bonegrinder and the wall. "We missed you at dinner."

I doubted that.

She came into the room then stopped dead. "I didn't realize she was here."

Bonegrinder and I both sat up. "Seriously?" I asked.

Cory tossed a package wrapped in napkins at me then plopped down on her bed. "Rub it in, why don't you?"

Bonegrinder nosed at the napkins, but I yanked them away from her and pulled out a sandwich.

"Sorry," I said between bites. "I just don't get it." Bonegrinder blinked at Cory. Inside her head, her thoughts were mild, adoring, and certainly of the I-heart-unicorn-hunters variety. There was none of the latent bloodlust I usually sensed whenever she was around Phil or Neil or even Father Guillermo. And yet, unlike all the other hunters, Cory couldn't feel Bonegrinder's presence, or sense her thoughts.

"Well, that makes all of us." She looked around our shared room. "Will you miss me?"

Since her injuries, Cory had mostly chosen to sleep in the don's quarters rather than brave the treacherous spiral staircase up into the dorm. We'd already packed most of her things in preparation for her trip back to England.

"Are you kidding?" I replied. "All I ever wanted was a single."

Cory chuckled. "Don't get too used to it. We'll be getting more hunters soon."

I wasn't so sure about that. Neil had returned from his last few recruitment trips empty-handed. It was difficult to convince teenage girls or their parents that their best course of action to protect themselves from the threat of killer unicorns in their neighborhoods was to send the girls off to a convent with a gorgeous twenty-something British man and stick a bow and arrows in their hands.

The fact that my mom had been all over the plan might, in fact, be proof of her mental state.

Besides, Neil was crying off the newest recruitment trip to babysit Cory.

As reports of unicorn attacks spread, even fewer eligible hunters were willing to risk putting themselves in the line of fire. Even those hunters who hadn't yet experienced the phenomenon of attracting unicorns had heard of incidents on the news. Unicorns left few survivors, and it didn't surprise me that many eligible hunters would choose to isolate themselves rather than risk joining the Order and confronting the animals head—or horn—on. My mother wasn't the only one who preferred that the concept of unicorn hunting remained in the abstract . . . and far in the distance.

Some eligible hunters had informed us they were moving away to isolated islands or into the depths of cities too developed or crowded to support unicorns. One family had even split up its daughters and sent them to separate cities, lest their combined attractive powers made unicorns risk traveling into urban areas, the way the Cloisters, with its concentrated population of hunters, had drawn unicorns from far and wide into Rome.

Bonegrinder's thoughts turned menacing, and she'd started to growl even before I heard the light tapping on the door. I slipped my hand through her collar and looked up.

Neil stood on the threshold. "Good evening, Astrid," he said, flashing the don's ring at Bonegrinder until she settled. "Have a moment?"

I stared into my lap. "I guess."

Cory flipped on the light as Neil came inside and shut the door behind him.

"I need to ask a favor of you," he said, commandeering Cory's desk chair. I still couldn't look him in the face. "I had planned to accompany Cory back to England, but now it seems that I have other . . . commitments."

And now I raised my eyes to meet his. "What?"

He swallowed. "I'm going to the United States to investigate the survivor of a recent unicorn attack. We have reason to believe she might be a hunter, though her family history is unknown."

It was nothing new. Ilesha was also a hunter of unknown provenance. We'd found her when it had been discovered she was keeping a zhi as a pet.

"What about Cory's *protection*?" I asked.

Now it was Neil's turn to look away. "It has been pointed out to me that I'm hardly in a position to protect her from a unicorn. Not like you."

"What about your going back to school?"

"That, too, can wait until things at the Cloisters are a little more settled. Phil is putting it off for a few months. I should be able to at least as much as . . ." He looked away. "I was hoping that you would step into my place."

"England?" I asked. "But isn't the point of sending Cory away that she won't be around any other hunters?"

"Please come, Astrid," Cory said, beaming. "It won't be quite so miserable to be stuck in England—"

"If I'm stuck there, too?" I finished, and shrugged. "Being a hunter in Italy or a hunter in the UK—doesn't make much of a difference, does it?"

"I'm sorry if my company is so distasteful to you," Cory snapped.

I buried my hands in Bonegrinder's fur. "It's not that, Cory."

"I understand," said Neil, "if you want to stay near Phil. I can ask another hunter. I simply assumed since you two are so close—"

Cory shot me a look and I interrupted him. "No, I think it's a good idea. Don't mind my crankiness." Nothing that involved hunting, be it in Rome or London or Timbuktu, was going to make me happy right about now. My mother was nuts, my cousin hated me, my boyfriend couldn't even be bothered to call me back.

"Eventually," said Neil, "the idea is to let all the hunters go

84

back to their homes. With training, they will be safe from any unicorn that might be drawn to them, and trained hunters can simply respond to urgent calls closest to them. It's the best situation for everyone involved if we don't return to the old paradigm of an actual, permanent convent here in Rome."

"But we're not there yet," said Cory. "Not hardly, if we can't even figure out what's wrong with me."

"Astrid, you're one of the hunters who has progressed the most in her training," said Neil, and I was relieved that for once he didn't pursue the myth that I was, in fact, the best. "And unlike, say, Grace, you have a bit more autonomy when it comes to being moved. I don't have to ask your mother for permission to send you to England."

If he could arrange not to let her know at all, I'd probably be grateful.

"I also thought"—Neil squirmed a bit in his seat—"that you might welcome a switch-up. Phil mentioned you've been having a rough time adjusting to some of the new restrictions."

I shrugged again. So was Melissende, and I didn't see her getting to go on vacation with Cory.

"And that maybe a change of pace might be in order."

"So even Phil wants to get rid of me?" I said before I could stop myself. "Sorry," I added. "Like I said, I'm cranky. Do you really think me playing bodyguard to Cory is the best use of our limited hunter resources, though? With all the requests we've been getting?"

Neil shrugged. "Hunter resources notwithstanding, we don't have the physical or monetary resources to send hunters to Tibet or any of the other really remote places that have been requesting assistance. Helicopters to get you up the mountains, mobile medical units in case something happens to you while you're up there—until Phil can get official support from some large government or organization, we're limited in terms of what area we can reasonably service, even with the few hunters we have. Perhaps I am biased, but there's an argument to be made that a good use of our resources right now is to protect our own."

I frowned. "This sucks. I hate the idea that I could help, but I can't get there." What was the point of having magic if it was so incredibly limited? On top of speed and aim and telepathy, couldn't Diana have arranged for worldwide instant teleportation as well? Add it to the list of things the goddess got wrong with this "gift" of ours.

"That's always the case, though, isn't it?" Neil said. "It's the same frustration felt by any relief organization. We have the grain, but we can't get it to them. We have the ability to cure the disease, but it requires machines or facilities that the people in question don't possess."

Beside me, Cory sniffled. "What is the point?" she asked softly. "Why are we trying so hard if we still can't save people?"

Neil's jaw was set. "I can save *you*," he stated. "I'm getting you out of here. And we're going to figure out what's wrong with you. I promise." He looked at me. "Well?"

I glanced at poor Cory and her leg. I thought about Phil's face this afternoon, pictured another month of traipsing around Rome in a habit remembering what it had been like when Giovanni was here. At least in London I'd be away from the weapons and the throne and the constant reminder that my world was nothing like it used to be.

Bonegrinder began pulling on her collar, her thoughts radiating her hunger and her curiosity regarding how delectable a

86

nice raw haunch of Cornelius Bartoli would taste.

At least in London I wouldn't have to worry about a house zhi.

"How long would it be for?" I asked. "And what about school?"

"I don't know," said Neil. "A few weeks at least—whatever it takes to make sure Cory is well again. And as for tutors, we could engage Cory's old instructors. They can teach you both."

"Ah, the penalty of returning home," said Cory. "More calculus."

Yay, more calculus!

"Oh," said Neil, and exchanged glances with Cory. "There is one other thing."

Cory wriggled in her seat and clapped her hands together.

"What?" I asked.

Cory squeaked.

Neil shook his head at his niece. "Would you like to tell her?"

Cory nodded vigorously. "We think we've found Seth."

Bonegrinder must have sensed my adrenaline spike, because she began to grow restless and growled.

"What do you mean 'we'?" I asked.

"Remember the private investigator we hired to help us track hunter lines?" Neil asked. "We've also had him investigating the whereabouts of the bas—young man."

"Bastard," I agreed.

"Yes," Cory seconded.

"We know Marten Jaeger helped Seth elude authorities, and now we have a lead. There's a young man who matches his description staying in a hotel in Limoges, France, and using a credit card that bills to Gordian Pharmaceuticals."

"You're kidding," I said. "Still? But when the police called them after Marten's death, didn't they say they had no idea where Seth was?"

"Are you surprised they'd lie?" Neil asked. "They were experts in lying to us. At any rate, I had been planning to fly to Limoges myself, under the pretense of leaving with Cory—"

"Wait, pretense?" I looked from one Bartoli to the other. "Why have you been keeping this from us? From Phil?"

"You may have noticed," Neil said, "that Phil is utterly disinterested in discussing what happened to her."

I nodded. So what? I'd want to put it past me as well.

"When I first broached the topic of hiring an investigator to search she was a good bit more than merely disinterested. It's not that she doesn't want him caught, but she balked at diverting any of our resources to the mission."

Of course she did. Things were stretched thin enough already, and Phil would probably deem hiring a PI just to track down her rapist as falling under the heading of "china doll treatment."

"Unfortunately," Neil continued, "I can't conform to her wishes on this matter."

"So you're going behind her back," I said. "How happy do you think she'll be when she discovers this?"

"Hopefully, she'll never need to know. Seth will be arrested by the police, and the case will resume as before. However, Phil has already purchased my flight to the United States for this recruitment trip, so I cannot go to France." He met my eyes again. "But you, Astrid, you can."

"Why do we need to go at all?" I asked. "I thought there was a European arrest warrant out—"

Cory shrugged. "It's not exactly top priority, is it? And maybe he's even got a fake passport with a false identity to go with his fancy credit card. But if you were there and went to the police as an eyewitness to a fugitive, the warrant would pop right up. All you have to do is take one look at him then call the authorities."

Neil handed me a sheet of paper: a credit card file that listed the address of a hotel in Limoges.

"Come on, Astrid," Cory said. "Don't you want to be there when they nab him?"

Oh, I did. And I wouldn't mind giving him a good scratch with an alicorn as well. "But what about you?"

She tapped one crutch against the other. "Hardly in any shape to go chasing some criminal around the south of France."

"Exactly," I said. "Or even to go to London by yourself. Who will protect you?"

"It shouldn't take long," Neil said. "Cory had arranged to stay in the airport hotel until I arrived in London. We don't think she's under much danger of a unicorn attack inside the airport. You can do this, then board the next flight to London."

I had to admit, it sounded marvelous. I would love to look Seth in the eye right as he was tackled to the ground by the French police. I would love to come back to the Cloisters, dragging Seth by the collar, and throw him at Phil's feet. Avoidance or not, she'd have to forgive me then.

And maybe that had been Neil's inspiration as well. "Why are you doing this?" I asked him. "Why do you care so much?"

"He hurt a hunter under my care," Neil replied coldly. "What kind of don would I be if I allowed that to stand without

89

response? We don't use unicorns to carry out our retaliations any longer, Astrid, but I will see him pay the price for his misdeeds."

I caught my breath. From time to time, I could actually see that Neil was descended from warriors.

"In this case, the price is a stay in an Italian jail cell." Neil stood. "Please let me know when you've made your decision."

"I have," I said. "It's yes."

"Good. I'll go make the travel arrangements." He stood and headed back to the door, then paused.

Bonegrinder prepared to strike, and I swatted her on the nose to settle her down.

"Astrid," Neil said into the door. His shoulders hunched, and for a moment, he looked much younger. Almost as young as us. Certainly as young as Phil. "I hope . . . I hope you're not under the impression that I think any less of your cousin after her ordeal."

I focused as hard as I could on Bonegrinder.

"What *are* you talking about?" Cory looked back and forth at the two of us.

"On one level, you are right. I am doing this for Phil, as much as I am a don doing this for a hunter," Neil went on, and every word seemed a struggle.

"You're *joking*," Cory cried. "Neil, you wanker."

He took a deep, shuddering breath. "I don't know what she feels. I can't know. But one concern is . . . I'm not sure if any interest on her part can be genuine for her right now. I worry that she might want . . . a new relationship to cleanse her last one out of her mind."

And what about the fact that she'd liked Neil even when she

was dating Seth? But I didn't point that out. After all, it was only one of the many barriers for them. Plus, that secret wasn't mine to tell, and I'd already betrayed Phil enough for one day.

"Neil," Cory said, dumbfounded. "Have you gone mad?"

He continued to ignore her. "I can't be part of that, no matter how much I care for her. Perhaps because I care for her so much."

"Neil!" Cory shouted.

He grabbed the doorknob like a lifeline and vanished.

Things happened very quickly after that. In the morning, Neil came up to tell us that he'd booked tickets for us back to London. Leaving tomorrow. We broke the news to Phil, who continued to avoid my eyes whenever we were in the same room. It was too weird. A large part of me wanted to believe that she was staying at the Cloisters because I was there. But clearly, my presence in Rome wasn't as big an influence on her as I'd thought. She quickly changed the subject from our departure to her most recent attempts to confer endangered status on the unicorns.

Of course. What did it matter that she'd be down two hunters when she wasn't overly crazy about killing unicorns in the first place?

As I watched Phil bustle about the Cloisters—going over plans to update the wiring in the chapter house, making sure that Zelda had mended the hole in Ilesha's cargo pants, typing up reminder e-mails to each of the congressional assistants she'd contacted through her Save the Unicorns campaign—I realized how smoothly she'd transitioned into her role as donna. She wasn't the girl who'd shown up here last May looking for a free Roman vacation. She'd traded in her cutoffs for a knee-length skirt, her volleyball for a pile of file folders. And yet, she seemed happy. Maybe the only reason I thought she wanted to leave and go back to her old life was because *I* wanted to.

I bid farewell to the other hunters, taking in Melissende's and Grace's barely concealed glee, Zelda's and Dorcas's envy, Rosamund's fear, and the young ones' curiosity. Valerija was as hard to read as ever. She didn't even come down to our going-away dinner, though Lucia had pulled out all the stops and bought us gelato in six different flavors.

I'd miss Lucia, an elderly nun who, luck would have it, was descended from a unicorn-hunting family. Word was that food in England wasn't quite as good as in Rome.

Bonegrinder grew more and more agitated as she watched the commotion around her and had to be dragged bodily from our door to be locked in her cage for the night. All night long, I felt her gnawing at the locks that held her in, terrified for some unknown reason of being let free, only to find us gone. Stupid unicorn. Of all the hunters in the Cloisters, Cory liked the pet zhi the least.

I reminded myself to keep my thoughts as calm as possible when I said good-bye.

The next morning, Neil picked up his car to drive us to the airport, and Cory and I waited for him in the Cloisters rotunda. I ran my hands over the bone-encrusted walls, feeling them shiver beneath my fingers, getting flashes of the unicorns they once belonged to. I studied the tableau of Clothilde and Bucephalus that dominated the center of the room. Perhaps in England, with Sybil Bartoli's genealogy research, I could finally track the location of my father and his family.

Clothilde stood in frozen, well-dressed splendor, forever

holding her fake sword up to the karkadann's fake horn. Her real claymore would remain here in the Cloisters's armory, since it wasn't feasible to take it with me. However, Cory and I had packed alicorn arrowheads to fit onto shafts in England, and the alicorn knife was nestled into my checked luggage. I probably shouldn't be taking that, either, but I couldn't bear to part with both it and the claymore at once, and only one was small enough to sneak into my bags.

Cory waved at me from the door. "He's here. Ready?"

I loitered in the courtyard. Was Phil so mad she really wouldn't say good-bye?

After another thirty seconds, I decided she must be. I was climbing into the car when I heard "Asteroid," and felt her hand covering the alicorn scar on my back. I launched myself at her, and we wrapped around each other so tight I thought for a moment our skin would melt together.

I love you! I shouted at her inside my head. *I love you so much it'll be a miracle if I don't kill Seth the second I set eyes on him.*

"I'll miss you," I said aloud.

"You take care of yourself," she whispered into my braid. "Don't you dare die on me. You do and I'll kill you, I swear."

"You, too," I said. "You keep that ring on at all times, you hear? I don't care about Neil."

She pulled back and met my eyes. "Well, I do."

Sometimes you don't get to have what you want, whether it's medical school or a life without violence or a person who means more to you than they should. I knew that now. What I failed to understand is how we could know our duty took precedence and still ache so hard for the things we sacrificed?

Phil took a deep breath and bit her lip as if she were about to say more, then averted her gaze and pushed away. "Go on."

I felt my way to the car, blinded by tears, and we drove away in silence.

The flight was extraordinary. Safe within the little tub of recycled air, thousands of feet away from the nearest unicorn, I found myself feeling almost drunk with freedom. I would have started laughing maniacally, but my seatmate was already looking nervous about my bloodstained cargo pants.

I wondered what would happen if I explained to her that I was a unicorn hunter. Would she give me a bye, or get angry that our organization hadn't quelled the unicorn menace in her particular hometown? I'd seen the hate mail directed at the Cloisters, though Phil and Neil had done their best to hide it from the other hunters.

One benefit of hunter magic I'd never realized is how easily I could feel the alicorn knife and arrowheads tucked away in my luggage, now that I was beyond the net of unicorn artifacts in the Cloisters. I knew without a shadow of a doubt that my luggage had made the flight along with me.

When we landed in Limoges two hours later, I retrieved my knife from my suitcase and stored the luggage with the airline, then headed off to the hotel the private investigator had listed. Apparently, there was a blond American teenage boy with a Gordian Pharmaceuticals credit card checked into that hotel under the name Brad Jaeger.

I held tight to the handle of my alicorn knife through the canvas fabric of my purse as the cab zipped through the streets on the way to the Hotel Lion d'Or: the Golden Lion. How appropriate.

Do not kill the bastard, do not kill the bastard, do not kill the bastard. . . .

All I had to do was find him then phone the police. I was shocked to feel excitement rushing through me, as strong as any magic. Hunting unicorns was fine, I supposed, but tracking down the boy who'd hurt my cousin was infinitely more gratifying.

Unfortunately, when I got to the hotel and asked if they could connect me to his room, it turned out that "Brad Jaeger" had checked out.

I didn't realize what a mess I was until I burst into tears at the counter. The concierge looked embarrassed, and the bellhop standing by the luggage carts seemed even more concerned. And though their English was way better than my French, I doubt I managed to convey the exact reason for my dismay, since when I was waiting out by the taxi stand to head back to the airport, I felt a tap on my shoulder.

"*Mademoiselle?*" It was one of the girls from the counter. "Your boyfriend, he goes to the shop?" She cast about for the word. "*Il a besoin de faire réparer sa moto.*" She mimed handlebars and climbing on a bike, then pointed down the street.

I started running.

The man at the motorcycle shop nodded when I asked in halting French if he'd seen an "*Américain avec cheveux jaunes,*" and pointed me toward the café around the corner. I had to force myself to leave my knife in my purse. I approached the café, heart practically beating through my shirt. My alicorn scars tingled, and for a moment, I felt as if unicorn magic was going to break loose on this quiet French street. It had been too long since I felt adrenaline over anything other than a

95

hunt. The world seemed incredibly fast, blurring in real time as I approached prey that didn't make me feel like a superhero. That had made one of my own feel very small and powerless indeed.

The alicorn knife sang to me from the confines of my purse, and I crushed my fingers into fists to keep myself from grabbing it. There was the café, with a smattering of metal and plastic tables outside on the sidewalk. And there was a blond boy sitting, sipping a Coke from a slender glass bottle.

My breath hitched in my throat. It wasn't Seth. Not even close.

His blue eyes widened as he saw me, and he started to stand. I remembered the forest floor, the screams, the blood. I remembered the way he'd humiliated me in front of everyone I knew in the lunchroom the day after. I remembered exactly the way his hands felt on my body.

"Astrid!" said Brandt Ellison. "How did you find me?"

7

Wherein Astrid Saves a Life

It was over six months since I'd considered sleeping with my boyfriend, Brandt, to secure my social standing in our high school pecking order. It was over six months since we'd been making out in the woods when a zhi attacked us and speared him in the leg. It was over six months since my mother had saved his life by giving him the last known dose of the Remedy.

I stood on the Limousin street and stared at my ex-boyfriend, struck dumb.

"I can't believe it's you!" he added, smiling. Brandt had a fantastic smile—the most devastating smile in our high school class, if I remembered correctly. It beamed upon me, making it even harder to talk. "You look . . . amazing."

That helped break the spell a little. Amazing? In my blood-stained hunter pants and a faded T-shirt that probably still had some of Bonegrinder's fur clinging to it?

"It's the hunting," he said. "Must keep you in excellent shape."

I hugged myself, suddenly self-conscious of my bare, muscled arms. The last time I'd spoken to Brandt, he'd thought unicorns were crazy talk. I tried to keep that in mind.

"Say *something*." He shook his head, still staring at me. "You're starting to scare me."

"What are you doing here?" I managed.

"Waiting for them to patch up my tire." He nodded toward the motorcycle shop. "Such a pain."

"I mean—in France."

His smile broadened. "Ah, that's a bit more complicated." He pulled out the chair next to his. "Probably won't believe me if I said working on my French."

I stepped forward and sank into the offered chair. "You'd need something drastic." Brandt had failed intermediate French in high school.

He laughed. "There's the Astrid I remember." He waved at the shopkeeper inside the café and signaled for two more Cokes. "I suppose I deserve it, too. But I *am* working on my French, among other things." As the man brought out our sodas, I reached for my purse, but Brandt put his hand on my arm. "Nah, I got it."

He'd paid for everything back when we were dating, too. I'd tallied up every soda, every latte, every slice of pizza on some giant internal scoreboard. *If he spends this much money, you have to let him get to first base. If he spends this much, second. If he takes you to prom, you really should go all the way.*

That person, that Astrid—I didn't even recognize her thought processes anymore. I wasn't sure if that made me more rational or less.

"First of all," he said, handing me my drink, "I owe you and your mother a huge apology. You saved my life and I treated you horribly."

I took a gulp of soda. This was true.

"Can you forgive me? I was such a jerk to you, Astrid. Even before that thing with the 'mad goat.'" Brandt leaned over the table and his blue eyes stared me down.

Brandt. Brad. The Bartolis' private investigator had never been following Seth. They had the wrong blond American guy, the wrong ex-boyfriend, all along.

Sometime after Phil and I had come to Rome, Lilith had heard that Brandt Ellison had run away from home. No one knew where he'd gone or why. But now I remembered I'd told Marten Jaeger of Gordian Pharmaceuticals the name of my wicked ex-boyfriend, the one who'd so cruelly dumped me even after my mother saved his life with the Remedy.

"You didn't run away from home," I whispered.

"Well, in a manner of speaking." He sat back in his seat.

The puzzle pieces began to fall into place. "You're . . . working for Gordian?"

"Also, in a manner of speaking." He took a swig from his soda. "I'm the only person alive who's actually gotten a dose of this stuff they're trying to reinvent. So they tested me, trying to see if they could, I don't know, get antibodies or whatever out of me."

"Could they?" I asked, recalling Marten Jaeger's last words. *I know the secret.*

"Nope." Brandt set down his bottle. "But they paid me anyway. And it was better than sitting around our little school and waiting for a swimming scholarship to State that was never going to come. When they offered me a more permanent position at Gordian, I booked out. I'm underage, so I guess, technically, I *did* run away from home. They could take me back if they knew where to find me, so I use a fake name." He eyed me and his lips quirked a little—a shadow of their full potential. "You didn't answer my question."

"What question?"

"Can you ever forgive me?"

I was saved from answering by a whistle. We turned to look up the alley and saw the man from the motorcycle shop waving.

"Great." Brandt threw back the last of his soda and pointed at mine. "Finished with that?"

I'd barely touched it but took it with me as we walked up the hill. "Couldn't Gordian get in trouble for, I don't know, hiring you without your parents' permission?" Among other things, like ordering Phil's rape, blackmailing Valerija, and hiding a herd of murderous kirin.

You know, for starters.

"Gonna tell on me?" Brandt asked as we entered the shop.

Brandt and the shopkeeper conversed a bit in French and kicked the tires of a gleaming silver motorcycle. Brandt's language skills had, I could tell, improved enormously. He handed the repairman a credit card and leaned against the counter.

"So on to more questions you haven't answered," he said.

"I haven't answered any of them," I replied, joining him and placing my soda bottle near his elbow.

"True." He reached for the end of my braid and flicked it, the way he used to back home. "I've been way more forthcoming. Here's one back—what are *you* doing here?"

"I'm looking for someone," I said. "Maybe you know him. Seth Gavriel?"

His expression turned serious. "Yeah, or at least I know of

100

him. I know what he did, and I'm really sorry. Phil was always nice to me. She deserved way better than that. How is she?"

I stiffened. "Wait, you know? Do you know where Seth's been hiding?"

Brandt looked away. "That's also pretty complicated."

"Now who isn't answering questions!" I hissed. The shopkeeper returned with Brandt's receipt. "If you know where Seth—"

"I shouldn't be the one to tell you this stuff, Astrid. Look, maybe you can come with me, talk to my boss. I don't know everything, anyway."

"Come with you?" I said. "Where?"

"Gordian's got a facility about a half hour ride from here. Come with me and you can get all the answers you need."

"No way!" Walk into Gordian Pharmaceuticals after everything they put me and the other hunters through? After they abandoned us? After they set the kirin on us?

After I let the head of their company be killed by a unicorn?

I stepped back. "If you know so much, then you'll understand why there's no way I'm going to any Gordian facility. That company doesn't mix well with unicorn hunters."

"That company," said Brandt, "is chock-full of them."

I stared at him.

He shook his head, smiling at me indulgently. "I really think you're owed an explanation, Astrid. Come on. We've known each other forever. I know I was awful to you last year—but other than that . . . you can trust me, right?" He held out his hand.

I backed up farther. "Not as far as I can throw you."

"*With* a unicorn around or without one?" He winked. "Yeah,

I know all about your special powers now, too. Blows my mind. I'd love to see them in action."

I hugged my arms again, wishing I'd remembered to bring a cardigan or something. I felt naked under Brandt's blue gaze. "I can't. I have to go to London. I'm on assignment. This was just supposed to be a little detour. . . ."

"And this will be another one. What did you come here for if not answers?"

What, indeed?

Brandt insisted on buying me a helmet. He looked at the selection on the shop wall. "What color do you want?"

"Anything that's not camouflage."

He laughed and pulled down a ridiculous purple and black, tiger-striped one. "Kinda like a kirin, huh?"

I shot him a look. "You've seen kirin?"

"Dead ones." He plopped the helmet on my head and toyed with the straps. "It's totally you. Like wearing the skin of the beast you've slain."

"This is tiger-striped," I said. "Nothing like a kirin. And I think you're talking constantly about unicorns to make up for the fact that you scoffed at me last spring."

He closed the clear visor over my face. "You're a smart girl, Astrid. Way too smart for me. That's precisely what I'm doing." He gave a thumbs-up to the shopkeeper, who went to print out another receipt.

I reached for my purse again.

He waved me off. "Stop it. Seriously. Gordian is rolling in it. The least they can do after everything they've put you through is buy you some safety gear."

"It's not my money, either," I said. "It belongs to my friend Cory."

"All the more reason." Brandt snatched up the new receipt and wheeled his bike out of the shop. "Ready?" He picked up his own helmet, which was just as silver as the motorcycle, and strapped it on.

"You promise this will only take a few hours?"

"Absolutely." He examined the sky, which had turned slate gray. "Uh-oh." He slipped off his jacket and handed it to me. "Put this on or you'll get cold."

"What about you?" I slipped my arms into the sleeves. The leather creaked at my elbows and I smelled Brandt. Back home, he'd sometimes let me wear his letter jacket. It smelled like this, too. His deodorant, his skin, his sweat. No fire, not even a hint of flood.

"If one of us is going to get cold, I'd prefer it be me." He swung his leg over the bike. "Okay, hop on."

He hadn't had a motorcycle back home, either. I climbed on behind him and put my arms around his waist. My seat was higher than his, forcing me to lean forward and rest the chin of my helmet against his shoulder.

"We won't be able to hear each other well once we're going," he said, and I suddenly wondered how he knew this. "So if you need anything, just give me a squeeze."

The first bump in the road threw me hard against his back. Our thighs pressed together. I squeezed, mainly from nerves, and even over the wind and through our helmets, I could hear him laugh.

I closed my eyes. This morning, I was a nun chaperoning another girl back to London. Now, I was riding through the

French countryside in purple tiger stripes, clinging to the back of a motorcycle, pressed up against a boy I'd once almost slept with.

If Phil knew, would she kill me, or cheer?

The Gordian "facility" looked more like a mansion, with high walls made of yellow stone and dozens of windows. Beyond the building, I could see the top of a huge greenhouse in the rear and the front lines of what appeared to be woods.

"This doesn't look like a lab," I said after we'd motored up the endless driveway and stopped in front. I slid from the back of Brandt's bike, arms and legs still vibrating to the speed of the engine. I pulled off my helmet and tried to smooth my hair; I stretched my calves and flexed my thigh muscles until they stopped shaking. Forget about Phil. Father Guillermo would probably have a heart attack.

"Looks can be deceiving," he said. "It's also a home. Actually, it was once some sort of sanitarium."

"Like an insane asylum?" I stared up at the windows and around at the manicured lawn.

He set his helmet down on the seat of his bike. "More like a spa for rich, sick people to test out miracle cures." He shook his hair out, and it looked even better than it had back in the city. "Hasn't really changed all that much, now that I think about it. Let's go."

Brandt led me into a well-lit marble entrance hall, furnished with antique end tables and vases that overflowed with flowers in autumn colors. A broad, sweeping staircase curved up to a landing ringed by an elaborate wrought iron railing featuring lions' heads and fleurs-de-lis.

A young man emerged from a side room, dressed in an impeccable suit with a lavender shirt and a deep purple tie. He looked me up and down. *"Qui est-ce?"*

"Je vous présente Astrid Llewelyn," said Brandt. *"Elle est un chasseur de licorne."*

"Bien sûr." His gaze turned appreciative. *"Bienvenue, Mademoiselle. Je m'appelle Jean-Jacques. . . ."* He went on in French. Apparently, he was some sort of secretary.

"Bonjour," I said.

"Come on," said Brandt. "Let's go meet the boss lady."

He led me into a sitting room lined with ice blue wallpaper and furnished in cream silk and dark wood. Feathery golden flowers exploded from the tops of vases half as tall as me, and a petite, dark-haired woman sat at a spacious antique desk and looked up as we entered.

She stood, and as she did, I saw two massive white shapes move from underneath the desk and come to stand on either side of her. For a moment, I thought they were unicorns, then realized they were dogs—enormous white-coated dogs whose heads were practically at chest height. She moved around the side of the desk and the dogs came with her like snowy sentinels.

"Astrid Llewelyn," said Brandt, "I'd like to introduce you to Isabeau Jaeger, the current head of Gordian Pharmaceuticals."

The woman extended her manicured and bejeweled hand to me. "Astrid," she said pleasantly, her French-accented voice lilting over the syllables and making my name sound like *Astreedt.* "I believe you knew my husband."

The thing about a unicorn is, when they come at you, you can just shoot them. I'm far less capable of dealing when it's a human bearing down on me with a very sharp weapon. And a mention of Marten Jaeger was one of the sharpest I could imagine.

I stared at Mrs. Jaeger and wondered how quickly I could run without a unicorn chasing me.

"Yes," I stammered. I knew him. I hated him. I watched him die.

Her hand, slim and fine and cool as spring, slipped into mine. Her eyes were silver blue, just like the walls of the room and the moonstone necklace she wore, and shiny black hair fell in waves to just above her shoulders. "I'm sorry, *ma chère*, does this trouble you? I know the way he died was most horrible."

"I'm so sorry for your loss." The words shook from my lips, and I prayed they did not sound quite as hollow to her.

"*Merci beaucoup*," said Isabeau Jaeger. "We were quite shocked to hear of it. You see, it had been many, many months since I'd last spoken to him." She turned her back to me and moved toward the desk, her giant dogs trailing in her wake, their noses practically reaching her shoulders, when she stopped. "We were estranged, Astrid. I could not support his policies. Not the ones about our company, not the ones about the kirin, and most certainly not his thoughts regarding the young ladies in your monastery."

I stood dumbfounded. No one had ever mentioned Marten's wife. Was their "estrangement" why?

Isabeau gestured to the armchairs near her desk. "Please have a seat. I am very glad to have the opportunity to speak to you. I am ashamed to admit I've felt far too uncomfortable to approach the Order of the Lioness these past few months. I should have contacted you at once, but I had no idea what reception to expect. You'd be justified in slamming the door in my face."

I sat down on the chair—plopped, really.

"Can I get you something to drink? Perrier, perhaps? Or chamomile tea?"

I shook my head, and watched as she scratched one of her dogs behind an ear. Its lips parted and I saw a flash of white fangs even longer than Bonegrinder's.

"Do you like dogs, Astrid?" Isabeau asked. "These are Great Pyrénées. They are sheepherding dogs from our French Alps. As beautiful as einhorns, no?"

"I wouldn't know," I said. "I've never seen an einhorn."

She beamed. "We must do our best to correct that. They are the loveliest of all unicorns." Her smile faded as she continued to caress the dog's neck. "At one time, I had hoped a sheepherding dog could do the same for unicorns. I was mistaken."

How many dogs had they lost before that became clear? I folded my idle hands in my lap. "What are their names?"

"The male is Gog," she said, pointing. "And the female Magog. It was a joke of my husband's. Some Alexander story about giants who guard the gates of hell." She pursed her lips. "He had it wrong, of course. The giants were the monsters trapped *beyond* the gates."

Brandt slumped into a seat beside me and started scarfing brightly colored candies from a nearby crystal dish.

I sat forward in my seat. "Madame, I have to tell you, I tried so hard to stop the unicorn that killed your husband. I couldn't—"

"I believe you, Astrid," Isabeau said, and sat behind her desk again. She kept her face down for a moment and when she did speak, there was a catch in her voice. "Marten reaped what he sowed. He was very hard and very greedy, and I could not bear

107

to live with him like that. We went our separate ways, but I did not supervise him. And so, I feel like I must apologize to you. I did not know how twisted his ideas had become. Had I any notion of his behavior to the women in your Order, or the way he would withdraw and give support at a whim, or his evil dealings with the kirin unicorns or those boys, I would have stopped him. It was shameful. It was criminal. Had he not died, I would be working now to see him justly punished for his actions."

Her expression was somber, but not devastated. Certainly not as wrecked as I'd be if I found out my husband was a scumbag like Marten, though I supposed she'd had several months to adjust to the idea, and several more to come to terms with the fact that he'd been killed by a unicorn.

I cleared my throat. "That's actually why I'm here. I've been looking for Seth Gavriel—"

"You and the authorities, no?"

I looked at Brandt, who was still involved in his candies. "Brandt said you might know where he is?"

Isabeau gazed at me sadly. "If I did, I would certainly inform the police, just as they have asked. All I know is that Seth was under the protection of my husband. Marten gave him money, set him on the run. If he should use his company credit card, we'd be able to trace him. He's either too clever to use it or so stupid he's lost it. But trust me, Astrid, should we ever have an inkling of what has happened to that young man, we shall contact the authorities."

And yet, all this time, the Bartolis' investigator had been chasing the wrong card! "If you know what credit card Seth has, why didn't you tell us at the Cloisters?"

Isabeau looked confused. "The Cloisters? I have given the

information to the police," she said. "Who are most likely to track such things. I didn't think it would be useful to you, and we are tracking it as well, but I can give it to you if you wish. I will do whatever I can to help. It's such a terrible thing."

My shoulders relaxed like the limbs of a bow at rest as Isabeau spoke.

"We all want to find the secret to the Remedy," she went on. "It could be the most important medical breakthrough of this century. Yet it will not be had at the price Marten sought to pay."

The phone on the desk rang twice, then Jean-Jacques poked his head into the room and aimed a stream of rapid French at Isabeau.

"Forgive me, Astrid," she said. "I must accept this call. We can talk more in a few minutes, yes? And in the meantime, maybe Brandt can show you our herd. I understand you were friends in the States."

Their herd? I looked at Brandt, who rolled to his feet, then pulled me to mine.

He kept his hand on mine all the way out of the room and down the hall, and I was pretty much grateful for it, as my mind was busy spinning the information it had just received.

All this time I'd been terrified by the idea of resumed contact between Gordian and the Cloisters. Would they be furious over what we'd done to the kirin? Over what we'd let happen to Marten? I'd never expected a reception like the one I'd just received. I'd never thought that Gordian was anything other than utterly under Marten Jaeger's thumb. I never thought that anyone there would consider what we'd done to be justified.

Especially since I hadn't reached a conclusion on that myself.

Brandt seemed oblivious to my inner turmoil, chatting about our hometown as we walked through the corridor.

"Hold on," he said as we reached the back of the house. He ducked into a side room and emerged with a small paper sack. "You okay, Astrid? You look like you did that time you got a B on your chemistry test."

I swallowed. "It was a C. A C-minus." I'd completely screwed up my orbital calculations and spent the next week on makeup extra credit.

"How traumatizing," he joked.

I turned my face toward my feet, trying to remember a time when a C-minus on a test was the most traumatizing event in my life.

"You still want to be a doctor?" he asked as we exited the house.

"Yeah. But it's hard lately. I haven't been in school, even."

"The hunter people didn't put you in school in Rome?"

"They tried," I said with a shrug. "But we'd missed the application cutoff. It was disappointing."

"For you, I'm sure!"

The back of the château featured a large stone patio that ran the entire length of the building and spilled down toward the lawn in a series of shallow terraces. Beyond that, the dome of the greenhouse rose above our heads, glinting in the intermittent sunlight breaking through the persistent clouds.

"What have you been doing for school?" I asked him.

"A better question is what haven't I been doing?" Brandt spread his arms wide. "I'm living in *France*! Our dinky little high school can eat its heart out."

How was France supposed to help him on his SATs?

110

Brandt led me down the terraces, and the moment my feet hit the grass I felt them, the way the taste of salt in the air signals you've reached the sea. *Unicorns.* The sense of them bubbled within me, crowding out my thoughts of home and chemistry and even Marten Jaeger's death gasps. The world warped as we moved forward, and the alicorn knife in my purse seemed to hum against my hip.

Brandt was studying me, not even bothering to conceal his wry grin.

"You've got a lot of them in the woods," I said, surprised by how breathless I sounded.

"Can you count them?"

"No. There are too many." Their thoughts overwhelmed me. Hunger, fear, rage, weariness, despondency, despair. "These are einhorns?"

"*These.*" Brandt laughed. "Amazing."

Not as amazing as what I'd started to touch back when I'd been doing yoga at the Cloisters.

We neared the greenhouse. "What's in there?" I said, trying to subdue my instincts to sprint toward the forest. It was still possible to have a civilized conversation, unicorn magic and all.

Brandt shrugged. "More of Isabeau's experiments. Medicinal herbs and stuff. She's all about finding cures in the natural world."

As we rounded the back of the glass dome, I saw that the forest itself was ringed with high chain-link fences topped by massive loops of barbed wire. More barbed wire was woven through the links.

"Is this supposed to keep the unicorns in?" I asked skeptically. Steel barbs probably wouldn't even slow them down.

"No, it keeps the crazy people out." Brandt pressed a code into the lockbox on a double-row security gate, and a buzzer sounded as we went through to a slim open area beyond the actual start of the trees. Inside the woods, I felt the unicorns stir and come forward. The air was dappled with sunlight as the clouds moved in the sky. Beneath the fire and flood that marked the presence of the animals, I caught the odor of a coming rain. It was the perfect weather for a unicorn attack.

I stepped between Brandt and the approaching monsters. "Um, this is a little unsafe. I'm getting some scary flashbacks to the last time we were in the woods."

"Really?" Brandt raised his eyebrows suggestively. "Remember what we were doing then?"

Making out on a blanket. I blushed as he stepped around me.

"Here they come!" He pointed. A half dozen einhorns stepped out of the grove.

Just as Isabeau had promised, they were magnificent. Tall and elegant as deer, with slender white limbs and long, curving necks. Their large eyes were black and shiny as obsidian, surrounded by eyelashes as snowy as their fine coats. A graceful spiral horn the length of my arm stood at attention in the center of each of their foreheads. Long white tails like lions' tails flicked with curiosity behind them.

Around each of their necks lay thick collars supporting chunky black boxes that blinked with green and red lights. My steps faltered.

"Electric collars, see?" Brandt pointed out a line in the dirt in front of us marked with little red flags. "They can't cross this point." He moved up almost to the line while I watched the silent unicorns, transfixed.

"How did you do this?" I asked, astounded. Unicorns could not be kept in captivity. At least, that's what I'd always been told.

"How do you think?" said Brandt. "A hunter caught them for us."

A hunter? Who? "Where is she now?"

Brandt lifted his shoulders and reached into his paper sack. "Uh, she . . . got out of the business."

The unicorns watched him warily, though a few cast their eyes toward me and back to Brandt. Their thoughts seemed alien to me, like a favorite dish cooked by a different chef. It wasn't the pure, untempered rush of emotion like Bonegrinder's, nor the flickers of concrete images like the kirin's. It certainly wasn't the karkadann's complicated imagery that could, after a fashion, pass for speech in my head. I struggled to separate the sense of each unicorn into their individual thoughts, a process made all the more difficult as they suddenly united under a single desire.

Food.

Brandt was holding out a giant steak. He waved it at the unicorns, clucking his tongue.

"Brandt!" I said in surprise.

"Relax." He chuckled. "They know they can't go past the line."

He must be right, for though I could feel their hunger, shimmering like the mottled sunlight through my head, none of the unicorns stepped forward, despite Brandt's persistent teasing.

"What?" he cooed to them. "No one wants a nice raw steak? Yummy."

And then, from behind the others, I saw a unicorn move

forward. A juvenile male. Mangy, with raw patches and scabs showing through his white coat, and so skinny I could count his ribs. I'd never seen a unicorn with wounds like that. Had he been gnawing on his own skin, then? Or were his regenerative powers failing? The unicorn's black eyes trained on the steak as he hobbled forward.

For a moment, his thoughts bubbled up above the others. *Starving. Hadn't eaten in days. Smaller than the others. They got to food first. They stole it from him.*

"Brandt," I warned.

"Yummy bloody meat," said Brandt, and drew his arm back as if to toss it to the unicorn.

The unicorn lunged at the barrier and Brandt jumped backward.

I heard a pop and a sizzle, and the unicorn stumbled.

"Crap!" Brandt cried, turning my way. "Did you see him go? He almost got me!"

Behind the barrier, the unicorn was shaking his head, dazed, and getting back to his feet. He began to growl, lips pulling back to reveal sharp white fangs.

I reached for my purse as the unicorn started forward again. This time it broke right past the barrier and galloped toward the steak still in Brandt's hand.

My ex-boyfriend turned around just as the unicorn reached him. It lunged at the steak, spearing right into Brandt's hand. Brandt cried out.

The unicorn collapsed, the vibrating hilt of my alicorn knife buried deep in its throat. Blood pooled around the steak still clenched between its jaws. The other unicorns scattered, terrified. I rushed forward, watching Brandt's expression dissolve into pain as he struggled to pull the horn out of his hand.

Too late, too late! And this time, there'd be no ancient vial of the Remedy to save him. What an idiot, to wave a piece of meat at a starving unicorn! If only I'd pulled out my knife the second I saw them come out of the woods. If only I hadn't wanted to see the einhorns up close.

"Man, that stings," said Brandt. He shook his hand free and looked up at my stricken face. Then he smiled. "You okay, Astrid? Aww, that wasn't your first time, was it?"

I froze as he calmly held out his punctured hand. The wound knit together before my eyes, leaving behind nothing but a small, helix-shaped scar.

8

WHEREIN ASTRID GETS AN INVITATION

"Y ou're—" I stammered. "You're immune."

"Yeah," Brandt said. "You gave me the Remedy."

"I mean . . . you're immune like a unicorn hunter. You heal instantly from alicorn wounds."

"Yeah," Brandt repeated like I'd lost my mind. "*You gave me the Remedy.*" He pulled the alicorn knife out of the dead unicorn's neck and examined it. "This is really nice. I've never seen anything quite like it."

And I'd never seen a boy heal like a hunter. What was some alicorn carving compared to that?

He handed me the knife. The surviving unicorns cowered deeper in the woods. The acrid smell of fresh blood mixed with the scent of fire and flood. "You've got killer aim, Astrid. For a second I thought that knife was going to go right through my arm."

"But you'd have healed from that, too?" I asked. "It's alicorn."

"Yeah. All alicorn, just like you." Brandt nudged the corpse of

116

the unicorn with his toe. The steak slid from between the creature's death-slacked jaws. "We're going to have to get someone to come by and clean this up. What a mess. Poor guy." He looked up at me. "Hey, you all right? How many *have* you killed?"

"Dozens." I turned away from the corpse on the ground.

"Well, don't worry about it," said Brandt. "We've got plenty here, and that one was attacking me. You were well within bounds to put it down."

I studied the blood staining the knife in my hands. Not dark like kirin blood, but a bright crimson. Lighter than human blood, thicker than zhi's. "I knew the Remedy healed the poison. I didn't know it made you immune. I didn't know it made you like me."

"Just in terms of alicorn wounds," Brandt said, walking toward the exit. I caught up to him by the doors, still holding the knife awkwardly in my hands. "Which we basically discovered by accident. This isn't the first—or rather the second—time I've been gored." He held the chain-link gate open for me. "Remember how scared I was the first time? I totally flipped out."

"What else has it given you?" I asked as we passed back onto the château's lawns. "I mean, I know the whole idea of the Remedy is that it can cure poisons or diseases or wounds other than the kind made by unicorns—but so far, that's all I've seen."

"Well, I haven't been sick once since your mom doused me," Brandt said. "But that doesn't necessarily mean anything. Gotten a couple cuts and scrapes falling off my bike, though, and those heal normally. The truth is we don't know. Isabeau doesn't believe it's a panacea, by the way. Not like her husband did. She doesn't think it can cure everything there ever was. But if it can neutralize poisons—any poisons, which is what the legends say—it would revolutionize a lot of medical treatments. The way they talk . . . it sounds pretty cool, actually. Like a cancer therapy where you could flood the patient's entire body with really powerful chemo then shoot them up with the Remedy before the drugs could attack healthy cells."

And that was only the beginning. "So that's why you have these einhorns? For testing?"

"Yep. Historically, they were the best source of the Remedy. Gordian's still trying to figure out why. Or how."

"And you?" I asked him as we went up the terraces to the patio. "They're still testing you?"

"I'm still on the payroll." Brandt opened the door to the house. "Look, I don't know a lot of this science stuff. I didn't even get a C on that chemistry test you whined about back home. And I bet Isabeau's off the phone by now. You can probably talk to her as much as you want."

Yeah, right. *Hi, Isabeau. You know how you didn't seem to mind that I let your husband die? Well, how do you feel about the fact that I just went out into your backyard and stabbed one of your pet unicorns in the throat?*

Brandt paused in the tiny entrance foyer and I almost ran into him. He braced his hand against the door to the main hall and smiled down at me. "It's really good to see you again, Astrid. And just now, to get a taste of what you're able to do— it's amazing."

There was no place for me to back away, nowhere to put my hands except to clutch even tighter the hilt of the bloody alicorn knife. "Thank you."

"I'm so sorry I never appreciated you when we were together."

My mind raced alongside my heart, but I couldn't blame it on unicorn magic. "It's fine," I said, head bowed. "I don't even think about it anymore."

"Don't you?"

Suddenly, his nose brushed mine, and I stumbled back, gulping. "What are you doing!"

Brandt held up his hands in defense and stepped back. "Sorry. I thought—"

"I have a boyfriend." And even if I didn't . . .

His mouth fell open. "A *boyfriend*?"

"Yes, Brandt," I snapped. "Is that so difficult to believe for a freak like me?"

Hurt bloomed in his blue eyes. "Hey, I apologized for that. I was wrong, and it was a jerk thing to say." He sighed. "The way I broke up with you was a huge mistake. Breaking up with you in general was an even bigger one."

Today was the day to listen to people tell me things I'd never expected to hear. "Thank you," I said softly. "Your apology is accepted. But, um, I still have a boyfriend."

"I'm surprised to hear that," he said. "Not because of *you*, Astrid. But I thought the Order of the Lioness—"

"It's kind of on the down low," I explained. "I'm not supposed to be with Giovanni, but no one's ever told me explicitly to stop." At least, not recently. Not since he'd devoted his school's van and his enrollment at said school to help us defeat the kirin.

"Giovanni?" Brandt cocked his head at me. "An Italian?"

"American," I said. "But his mom's Italian, and he was there studying last summer. He's at college in New York City now."

A knowing look came into Brandt's blue eyes. "Ah, a college boy. Nicely done."

I rolled my eyes, bracing for his assumptions. *And he doesn't mind that you don't put out?* Gah, what was I doing here, talking to Brandt Ellison? I had a criminal to track down. I had Cory to protect. I had answers to get out of Isabeau Jaeger before I left this château and Gordian behind forever.

"I don't have a girlfriend, since you're not bothering to ask," Brandt said.

"I didn't think you did." I was tired of clutching the bloody knife, but I could hardly put it back in my purse. "Since you tried to kiss me."

"I apologize for that, too. I read your cues wrong." He stuck his hands in his pockets. "Wishful thinking, maybe."

I snorted.

"Or maybe I just found it really sexy, the way you saved my life with a flick of your wrist."

"I didn't save your life," I said, ignoring the "sexy." Sexy! In bloodstained cargo pants? Right. "You're immune."

"A horn through the heart still kills, Astrid."

I said nothing and ignored the way he was looking at me.

After a moment, Brandt sighed and opened the door to a small powder room nestled under the stairs. "If you want to wash the blood off your hands."

Did I ever.

As soon as the door shut behind me, I breathed a sigh of relief. Even in this tiny, windowless room, I felt the shuddering fear of the unicorns. Now that I was alerted to their presence—and they'd been alerted to mine—I felt them out there, wandering, nervous, fearful of my unexpected and unexpectedly violent presence.

I scrubbed the blood off the knife as well as I could, but chose to dry it off on the leg of my cargos rather than risk staining one of Isabeau Jaeger's fluffy white hand towels. I washed my hands, letting the water run as hot as it could until my skin turned pink. Steam billowed up from the faucet to fill the space and fog the mirror.

I covered my eyes with my warm hands and took several deep breaths, smelling herbal soap and no trace of unicorn blood. After a moment, I felt better. Maybe the unicorns were calming down, or maybe I was. I lowered my hands and went to wipe the steam off the mirror.

Sexy. Ha! And trying to kiss me! Either Brandt was feeling pretty desperate these days or he truly was affected by the way I'd saved his life by killing that einhorn. And I found that a difficult belief to swallow, as the time I'd *actually* saved his life, back in Washington, he'd repaid me by loudly dumping and humiliating me in front of half our high school.

Look at me. My hair was mussed, frizzing up out of its braid, not helped at all by the dry recycled air of the plane from Italy or the motorcycle helmet Brandt had made me wear in Limoges. My T-shirt dye had faded from its multiple washings, since I had so few clothes in Rome, and my cargo pants were an unflattering mess. And then, of course, there were the scars. One alicorn scar laced down my left forearm like a twisted bracelet of shiny red flesh. I'd received that one in Cerveteri, as well as a matching mark in the hollow of my left shoulder. I had another on the back of my right wrist and still another on the inside of my right elbow. And these were just the scars he could see. I had alicorn scarring at the base of my ribs, in my left leg, and near my right hip. Bigger than them all was the enormous star-shaped puncture wound on my back.

I'd never thought of myself as beautiful like Phil, but before

I'd started hunting, I'd always considered myself reasonably attractive. Cute enough to get the interest of someone as popular as Brandt back in high school. Cute enough not to repulse Giovanni when we started dating.

And yet, ever since he'd left Italy, I'd stopped caring entirely about my looks. I couldn't even remember the last time I'd worn my hair down instead of back in this utilitarian braid. I'd spent most of my days swathed in a camouflage-colored split skirt habit, and even when I wasn't wearing nun clothes, I was dressed in bloodstained hunting gear. Scarred and grungy, yes. Sexy? Certainly not.

What was Brandt playing at?

I reached back into my purse, but this time, I pulled out my cell and saw a text message from Cory.

How's it going? Did you find him?

How was it going? Well, zero Seths, but my unicorn score for the day was already at one. I'm sure Cory would *love* to hear all about that. Not to mention that rather than following our plan, I'd been touring the Gordian Pharmaceuticals facility with my evil ex-boyfriend.

There was a knock on the door. "Astrid?" Isabeau. "You are all right?"

I shoved the cell phone back in the purse. "Yes. I'll be out in a moment."

I opened the door to see her standing there, her expression one of concern. "I understand we had an incident."

"I'm so sorry," I said to her. "I thought it was going to kill Brandt."

"*C'est pas grave,*" she said, waving her hand. "It might well have. Foolish boy, to tease it thus. I am glad you were there to protect him. I shall have a word with him. No doubt he was showing off for you, as young men will." She clucked her tongue. "Shall we go for a walk in my greenhouse? There will be no unicorns—or young men—there to distract us."

I was astonished. Isabeau Jaeger appeared to be the kind of woman to take everything in stride.

She led me back through the patio and toward the greenhouse, chatting about the history of the château—"it was once thought the spring near this property possessed healing waters purified by the horn of a unicorn"—and of her "abhorrence" of her estranged husband's more "radical" ideas. I trailed behind her, soaking it all in.

We went into the greenhouse, and I blinked in surprise at the sudden silence in my head. From within, I could not sense the unicorns anymore, and the air smelled green and wet.

"Wow," I blurted.

She smiled at me. "Yes, it is very beautiful, is it not? I love to walk here." She reached for a nearby pot and broke off a twig of a leggy plant covered in tiny yellow and white daisies. "Here."

I smelled the flowers. "Chamomile?"

"*Oui,* yes, very good. Do you have much interest in plants?"

"Um, not especially?"

"Pity." Isabeau frowned. "I had heard you liked medicine."

"I do," I said, taken aback. "How did you know that?"

"*Ma chère,* you received an award for your service at the hospital in Washington. These things are online. Also, your science fair prizes." She tapped her lips with her finger. "I could find much more given some time."

123

"Right." So she'd read up on me while Brandt was showing me around. I'm sure she'd gotten a full report from Brandt when I'd been washing up, as well.

"And of course, I have seen your mother on television."

I forced a smile.

Isabeau turned and walked on. "My mother—she was a nurse. Very interested in natural medicine. She taught me so much. I studied biochemistry because of her. And yet, I believe many of the answers to our most pressing medical needs are hidden in plain sight. Not in chemicals, but in the bodies of the living things of this Earth." She waved a hand back at me. "Take your chamomile. It grows as a weed, in ditches, on roadsides. And yet it is a miracle. It calms the nerves, helps you sleep, soothes your stomach"—she paused and looked over her shoulder at me— "or brightens blond hair."

I grabbed for my braid. My hair was already way too light. Practically colorless. In the summer, if I swam in pools too often, it turned neon green.

"A weed that can do all that! Is that not a miracle?"

"Yes," I agreed.

"So then imagine the potential of something much more rare. Something much more precious."

"Like unicorns?"

"*Bien sûr.*"

"And that's why you have the herd of einhorns back there."

"It is a touch more complicated," said Isabeau, examining the wilting leaves of another plant. She picked up a small spray bottle, spritzed the plant, and moved on. "Do you know how antivenin is made?"

"From horses, right?"

"Yes. The venom of captive snakes is milked then injected into captive horses. Over time, the horses build up immunity to the venom. The antibodies in their blood are then drained and processed to create antivenin."

"Does that work for unicorns?" I asked.

"No," said Isabeau. "Right now, the Remedy is the only known antivenin for alicorn poison. And we do not know how to make the Remedy. There is something still missing."

But Marten had told me he'd discovered the secret. Had he just been lying to me in an attempt to save his life, or had he been telling the truth—a horrible thought—but never had the chance to pass it along?

"And yet, we keep the einhorns for the day when we can process vast quantities of Remedy. They are our horses and our snakes in one."

"And you keep Brandt for the same reason?" I asked.

Isabeau gave a short, musical laugh. "He would not appreciate being thought of as a lab rat, I think, Astrid. You have heard, perhaps, of the creation of the first vaccine for smallpox? It was made from the antibodies of a young milkmaid who had survived a much less dangerous disease—cowpox. Cowpox made her immune to deadly smallpox, and thus, the vaccine formed of her antibodies was named for 'vacca'—for cows."

"So you're saying that Brandt is a milkmaid."

"In the end," said Isabeau, "that is precisely what he will be."

I bet he wouldn't be happy about that, either.

"The making of medicine is not a perfect process. Look at the antivenin example. We must have captive animals, and the horses do suffer. The snakes as well. None of it is pleasant. But for that, how many lives—*human* lives—are saved?"

I nodded in agreement. Animal testing: horrible, but capable of producing life-saving results. We'd reached the back of the greenhouse by now, and Isabeau drew her hand over the condensation gathered on one of the triangular glass panels.

"Do you see that?"

I peered through the glass. About a hundred yards away, a tiny tent village blossomed among the weeds beyond the edge of the manicured lawn. I saw people moving around the tents, hanging laundry, cooking meals. "Who are they?"

"People whose passions run as strong as mine," said Isabeau. "That is public land, and as near as they can get to our unicorns. They protest the use of animals in medical testing. I think it bothers them most that the animals are as beautiful as einhorns." She straightened. "I also think they would not like what you did in the forest."

"I bet." I stood up, too. "And the fact that unicorns are endangered probably makes them more vehemently against you." Against both of us. They should probably be talking to Phil.

"*Oui.*" She plucked the chamomile from my hands. "Pity they are not so sensitive about the poor flowers. I understand their desires. Like I said, it's not a perfect system. But more than that, I understand the desire of the mother who loses her child to tumors. Or," she added, "of the daughter who loses her mother to a loose unicorn. Like your friend Cornelia."

"You know Cory?"

"*Bien sûr*, Astrid. The Bartolis came to Gordian for help when they first tried to open the Cloisters of Ctesias. It was there that my husband and I first disagreed. It was there that we went our separate ways."

"Oh." I frowned.

"I still do not believe in my husband's ideas. However, he was right about one thing. We did need hunters. We do need them. Perhaps Brandt told you how we first came to capture our herd?"

"He said it was a hunter. Who was she?"

"A young woman who wished to live a private life. She has left her hunting behind her now, and we have promised to keep her identity confidential."

"Does she have any sisters?"

Isabeau laughed again. "I don't think so. But what I do know is that while she was here, it was easier to keep the unicorns quiet and at ease. A hunter can soothe their thoughts, even as they excite hers."

I shook my head. "I don't know what you're talking about."

"Of course you do. You have a pet zhi at your Cloisters, do you not?"

"Yes."

"And you can give her orders?"

Not ones she'd necessarily listen to. "Yes, but zhi are different. They're domesticated."

"Einhorns are different as well. You shall see."

Um, not so much, unless there were a lot of einhorns in England.

Isabeau circled around me in the aisle between the plants and leaned against one of the trays. Giant exotic flowers created a golden halo about her head. "Astrid, these protesters are a problem. Their presence incites the unicorns, and an incident would jeopardize our entire operation. What has happened today has made me realize how dangerous our position is, even with our current precautions. We need a fail-safe." She placed her hands on the tray on either side of her. "I have a proposal for you. I would like you to stay here and guard the einhorns."

I merely blinked in response.

"I understand that the Order has had some money problems since your falling out with Marten. If you would agree to stay here, we could pay them for the trouble of lending us one of their best hunters," Isabeau continued. "If we cannot get you, I would be more than happy to hire another one from Rome. But I would prefer it be a trained hunter from the Cloisters, rather than a girl with hunter powers who does not know how to use them. We have had problems with that in the past."

"Oh, you mean like when your husband drugged up Valerija and kept her around like unicorn catnip?"

Isabeau pursed her lips. "How horrible. I didn't know about that. And it isn't what I'm speaking of. You have seen Brandt here. He is very happy. I would have you work for me, Astrid, not be my captive."

"Well, that's a relief," I said. I should probably be heading back to the airport now.

"I believe your coming here was an act of providence. I would like to mend fences with the Order of the Lioness. We need your expertise and abilities, and you need our financial support."

"Not really. The Church has been helping us out."

"And you find the strings they attach more tolerable than those of Gordian?"

"Less dangerous to our health and happiness, that's for sure," I replied.

"I am not my husband, Astrid," Isabeau said. "I do not know how to convince you of this but to repeat the ways in which this is so."

I looked away. This was true, and perhaps it was uncharitable of me to snap at her like that.

"As I said, I would be willing to hire any experienced hunter to guard our unicorns, but I would prefer it be you."

"Why? Did Brandt say something to you?"

She sniffed. "Brandt is a silly boy who thinks silly boy thoughts. You must endeavor to ignore him. And as for you, *ma chère*, I saw your records. I know you love medicine as I do. I cannot imagine the frustration you must feel in your nunnery. You are given only a bow, when what you long for is a beaker. Here, when you are not on duty, I would be able to provide tutors for you. There is a university in Limoges—and at the university, a whole building named for my mother. I can arrange for you to take introductory classes, just as I have for Brandt."

Was that what Brandt had been doing in Limoges? Taking classes?

"You can study your chemistry. I would show you the work we do."

I swallowed. I'd heard these sorts of promises before, from my mother, from Marten. And I'd still ended up without any education, trapped in an ancient monastery, polishing weapons all day long.

Isabeau took in my skepticism. "We could draw up a contract if you like. I would guarantee the things I am promising you. Support of Gordian, tutors, tuition for laboratory classes at the university, your working hours . . ."

All of this sounded *way* too good to be true. A fair bet, it probably was. I shook my head. "I'm on assignment already. I'm supposed to escort Cory back to England. We're going to watch over each other and I'm going to be with her tutors, so

129

that solves the whole issue of my education you seem so concerned about."

"How excellent," Isabeau said, her tone one of false cheer. "The Bartolis must have quite a chemistry lab in Neil's bachelor apartment in London."

I'd give Isabeau Jaeger this: her aim was as true as any hunter's.

"Would you not rather have this than your bodyguard job in England? Cannot another hunter protect the Bartoli girl?"

"Can't another hunter protect your little lab rats?" I asked. How many times had I begged for any info from Marten, only to be promised answers and lied to? There was no way Isabeau could be telling me the truth.

"Yes," she said. "But I want a Llewelyn."

I rolled my eyes. *This* again! First her husband tries to render Phil and me ineligible because we're Llewelyns, and now Isabeau was aiming at a new way to get a Llewelyn hunter out of the hunting game. As if it really made any kind of difference. Judging from Grace's skills, they should be concentrating their efforts on *her* family: Bo.

"Forget it," I said, and turned to leave. "You're barking up the wrong tree, lady. All this obsession with Llewelyns is useless. I'm not some kind of great hunter, I'm not anything special, and I don't care to play these kind of games."

Isabeau said nothing as I walked back down the long aisle, thoughts churning. Part of me longed to stay here, where there was science being done, where I was free to wear what I liked, to learn where I wished. All I had to do was watch over a few einhorns already in a vast cage.

And yet—it was Gordian Pharmaceuticals. I couldn't forget

that. Their lies were as common as the pervasive ones about how special I was supposed to be because of my last name. The whole thing was a lie—lie upon lie upon lie.

"Take the chamomile with you, Astrid," Isabeau called from across the greenhouse. "It will keep you calm when you leave here. It will drown out the cry of the unicorn magic."

I spun to face her. "Yeah?" I shouted back. "Is that what the last hunter here told you?"

"No," she said. "I learned it from my mother. She was a Llewelyn."

9

WHEREIN ASTRID MAKES A CALL

Cory picked up on the first ring. "Did you find him? What did he say? Oh, I wish I could have seen the look on his face when they nabbed him!"

"Chill," I said into the phone. "It wasn't Seth."

"Pardon?"

"It wasn't Seth. Your PI has been following the wrong blond American teenager."

"But the Gordian credit card—"

"Belongs to Brandt Ellison."

"Your ex-boyfriend?" Cory asked, incredulous.

"It gets worse." I filled her in on Brandt's current situation, Isabeau Jaeger, and the offer she'd just made me.

Silence reigned on the other end of the phone. I tapped my fingers against the windowsill. I was alone in a small study on the ground floor of the Gordian château, as far as I could get from the einhorn enclosure in the back. A small cup of chamomile tea sat cooling on the sideboard, its scent wafting throughout the room, curtailing all trace of unicorn.

I wondered if the trick would work in the Cloisters, or was the place too woven through with bones and magic for even the strongest tea to make a dent?

"Cory?" I said at last.

"I don't know what to say."

"Do you trust her?"

"Yes," said Cory. "But don't mind me. I trusted her husband as well, remember? In fact, I recall not liking her very much, since she seemed so disinterested in hunters in general."

"Seems she's changed her mind about that."

"Just as I've changed my mind about Gordian."

Me, too, but what *was* Gordian? If it was the policies of the person in charge—if that person was Isabeau—maybe things would be different this time. And if Isabeau was as disinterested in hunters as Cory said, that boded well that she really wanted nothing more from the Order than to hire one hunter to guard her precious lab rat einhorns.

Maybe everything was what she claimed. She didn't want to sponsor or control us the way Marten had—she just wanted a simple cash arrangement, to pay me for services rendered.

"What should I do?" I asked Cory.

"Get on a plane to London," she replied. "As planned. I could be getting attacked by unicorns as we speak."

"But she wanted me especially," I said.

"Well, so do I."

"Really?"

There was a pause. "Come on, Astrid, you're my best friend."

This time, I didn't say it out loud. *Really?*

"I know that you and Phil . . . have this special bond and all.

I'm not hurt. But yes. You are."

I'd had one other best friend in my life: Kaitlyn, back home. She'd dumped me as quickly as Brandt after the return of the unicorns had branded me a freak. I hadn't even spoken to her since I'd come to Rome. And it stung, sure, but I also had Phil, who I'd always loved far more than any of my regular friends.

I wondered if what Kaitlyn did to me hurt as much as knowing the person you considered your best friend didn't like you as much as you liked her. I wondered if knowing that felt anything like it did when I realized that no matter what Phil and I had shared in the past, I was outside the loop when it came to her feelings for Neil.

"Thank you," I said. "That's really sweet."

"Sweet?" Cory snorted. "That's what you say to blokes you're blowing off."

"Well, it *is* sweet," I said.

"And you *are* blowing me off." Cory sounded impatient. "Are you coming to protect me or not? Remember, I've been through the lab rat scenario with Gordian and so has Valerija. It always ends badly."

"You're right," I said. "Still, I should call Neil and Phil and tell them about this offer."

"Have you figured out a way to explain to Phil that you're in France, or shall you leave Neil to face that music alone? Oh, and please leave me out of the story, if at all possible."

Good point. How was I going to relate the news to the Cloisters without revealing the truth? Phil would know there was something the three of us were keeping from her.

"Maybe it would be better if I were the one to stay," I said slowly. "After all, besides you, I'm the hunter who most under-stands the danger Gordian poses."

"Valerija," Cory pointed out.

"Phil and Neil would never trust Valerija on her own," I said.

"She's not like that anymore," Cory said. "She's actually changed a lot. You just don't notice because we all play with knives now."

"Good point."

Cory sighed. "What does this job at Gordian have that England doesn't?"

Funny. Isabeau had just asked me the same question, in reverse.

"Is it Brandt?"

I almost laughed. "Brandt? Please. I'll tell you what I told him: I have a boyfriend."

"Ooh, why did you have to tell him anything? Did he make a pass at you?"

"It's stupid. He just thinks he's a player. And, um, he was kind of turned on when I killed a unicorn for him."

"He's a sick bastard if that does it for him."

"Tell me about it."

"So if it's not Brandt," Cory wheedled, "why would you even consider this? Just come to England."

I knew why, but I hesitated to admit it.

It was this strange herd of unicorns, whose thoughts were like nothing I knew. It was the potential of the Remedy that lay in Brandt's blood, that was hidden in the lab on this property. It was Isabeau herself, who'd awakened in me all the hope I'd once held for Marten.

And even more hope than that.

My mother. She was a Llewelyn.

There was a beep on the line. "Oh no," said Cory. "That'll be Neil. What should I tell him?"

"Tell him to call me so we can work out a plan."

"So he can kill the messenger? Think not. You're on your own, there. Must go." She hung up.

I plopped into a sleek, silk-upholstered armchair, feeling even more confused than before. On one hand, I had made a commitment to Cory that I'd stay with her in England. On the other, I could be in London for two or three weeks—just long enough for Gordian to hire a different hunter—then Cory might recover and we'd both return to the Cloisters for good. Then what?

Of course, this could all be a moot internal argument anyway. There was a good chance that the moment Neil and Phil discovered where I was, they'd swoop in and scoop me up. They'd been more hurt by Marten Jaeger's betrayal than anyone else.

There was a soft knock on the door and Isabeau Jaeger entered. "Pardon my interruption, Astrid, but it's getting rather late. I was wondering if you've arranged for accommodations in the village or back in Limoges."

My eyes widened. Right. A hotel room. The kind of thing you never thought of when the only places you've ever lived were your mother's apartment and the nunnery where she'd dumped you. Even on a hunting assignment, I'd always had a tree stand of my very own. "I'll be all right."

She raised her eyebrows. "Yes?"

"I'm fine." I still had some cash. If Limoges was a university town, there'd be a student hostel somewhere around where I could crash.

"Because you are welcome to stay the night here if you wish," Isabeau said.

"Here?" I said.

"I live here," Isabeau replied. "As does Brandt, and a few of the scientists."

Then why was Brandt checked into a hotel in Limoges?

Isabeau went on. "It would give me a chance to speak to you more about my plans for our hunter—whoever she might be—as well as talk a bit more about our family connection."

"That's really not necessary—"

"Nonsense. We are, after all, related. How could I turn away a member of my own family?"

I checked out the window, surprised to see the sky darkening. How had the afternoon slipped away from me?

"All my clothes are at the airport," I said.

"I'm sure I can find something for you to sleep in," Isabeau replied.

I clutched the cell phone in my hands like a lifeline. "Why . . ."

"Yes, *chère*?"

"Why are you being so nice to me?" I whispered.

Again with the musical laugh. "You are perhaps more used to potential employers abusing you? That strikes me as counterproductive."

I squeezed my eyes shut. "No, I mean . . . after what happened to Marten. I was there, you know. I was there when— I couldn't stop it, I swear. If only I could have . . ."

Could have what? If I could have run my sword through Bucephalus, who'd saved my life several times over? If I could have killed that unicorn before he'd murdered Marten, would

I have? I wished I could give an unqualified yes, but the truth was I didn't know.

Isabeau's cool hand brushed my cheek. "Don't cry, Astrid. It is very terrible to see a man's death. Any man. Even you, who live with life and death every day, cannot watch it impassively. Even a doctor, who makes a life's work on the subject, is helpless in the face of death. There are some deaths we cannot prevent, though we would give our own lives to try and though we will curse our impotence for the rest of our days."

Tears spilled over my eyelids, and I bowed my head even farther into my chest. "Thank you," I said, though what I wanted was to press into her hand. I wanted Isabeau to hug me, the way Phil or my mother would hug me. She was smaller than me, but somehow I knew I'd feel safe in her arms.

"Come. Stay the night here, and have dinner with me."

"And Brandt?"

"Brandt will not be dining with us." Isabeau pursed her lips. "His earlier behavior was unacceptable."

"Oh, I didn't mind," I said. "He didn't know I had a boyfriend."

"*Pardon?*"

"When he . . ." I tried to back away from the topic, but Isabeau's gaze had me nailed. "Tried to kiss me, earlier."

"He did." Her expression was unreadable. "That was not what I referred to. Rather, I meant his behavior toward the einhorn. One does not tease a pitiful animal." She tilted her head as she regarded me. "Or a dutiful unicorn hunter."

"Please don't say anything to him!" This was so embarrassing.

Isabeau shook her head in exasperation. "Of course not, Astrid. I am not one of your nuns here. So will you stay?"

"For the night," I hedged.

"A start," said Isabeau. She clapped her hands. I heard a scuffle in the hall, then Gog and Magog's large white forms filled the doorway, gazing adoringly up at their mistress. For a moment, they reminded me of Bonegrinder, until I realized I couldn't sense their thoughts.

Dinner was pleasant; we ate chicken and vegetables and salads with goat cheese. Isabeau sat at the head of the table, and her dogs curled around the back of her chair, not begging, but not leaving her side, either. She chatted about local festivals and the neighborhood cuisine, which seemed to feature more than its fair share of chestnuts. Autumn was a beautiful season in the area, and being so far inland meant a respite from a lot of the tourists who flooded the coast.

"Of course, you're familiar with tourists, living right around the corner from the Colosseum," Isabeau said.

"Grateful to them," I said. "My Italian is still pretty poor, but lots of tourists mean lots of people who know some English and work in the area."

"I think it's important to take advantage of your travels, Astrid. When you decide to stay here, I will engage tutors for your French studies, as I have for Brandt. He's improved immensely, you know."

It was like that all through the meal. *When.* Not *if.* "Yes, I've noticed."

"I speak five languages," Isabeau continued. "And my husband put me to shame with seven."

"Marten knew seven languages?" I asked.

"And English was his worst." Isabeau chuckled, then stared

139

into her wineglass. "Dessert, I think."

Dessert was pastries and tea. "My mother was English," Isabeau explained, "and I'm afraid I picked up the habit from her."

"English and a Llewelyn," I said.

"Not by name, but yes, that was her family." Isabeau placed a pastry on her dish. "I believe it was an offshoot of your own mother's. Mine knew her heritage, of course, but had far more important issues to deal with than old family legends. She came to France a teenager and a nurse and worked for the Red Cross—and the Resistance—during the occupation. My father was a physician, and after the war, they married and settled here."

"Since unicorns were not around during your mother's lifetime, how did she know anything about herbal therapy for hunters?"

"She was very interested in studying alternative medicine, which was only starting to come back into fashion. Her family history included many records from medically minded unicorn hunters. There was information about the Remedy, but also on wound treatment, mental health, menstrual relief."

"Medically minded Llewelyns?" I asked. Cory wouldn't believe that. To her, all the hunters in our family were killing machines.

"*Oui!*" Isabeau smiled. "You are part of a very long tradition. My mother loved the idea of 'old family recipes' and wrote many books on herbal remedies based on her family's store of knowledge. Would you like to see them? We have some in the library."

I nodded, though French medical tomes were probably way beyond my understanding. I put down my untouched cup of chamomile tea and followed Isabeau from the dining room. The library turned out to be a small sitting room beyond Isabeau's office decorated in the same ice blue and cream. The walls were covered in shelves crammed with books of all shapes and sizes. Some were new paperbacks with brightly colored spines; others were old, with cracked leather or canvas bindings embossed with faded gold lettering. There seemed to be some method to the shelving, however, because Isabeau beelined right for several large volumes on a lower shelf. They were aged hardcovers, probably from the 1970s to judge from the dark green and gold color scheme as well as the picture on the cover, which featured a pretty woman standing in an herb garden. She wore bell-bottoms and had backcombed blond hair, but her face was identical to Isabeau's. Her name was listed as Claudia L. Landry.

"The L is for Llewelyn," Isabeau said. "Which was most certainly not my mother's middle name nor her maiden one." She shook her head and ran her hand lovingly over the portrait before handing the book to me. "A silly affectation, perhaps, but she was very proud of her heritage."

"I know what that can be like," I replied. I flipped idly through the book, which seemed to be some sort of encyclopedia of herbal lore, shot through with illustrations of various plants and flowers. "Did your mother wish she'd been a unicorn hunter?"

"My mother never even imagined it," she said. "Unicorns were long gone in her time. She did like the idea of a chain of educated, powerful women, however. She loved that her ancestors were working in medicine in a time when many women weren't even literate." She lifted her head. "We are both from a long line of very powerful daughters, Astrid."

I wasn't. My mother's side was descended from Clothilde's brother, and a long line of males—hence the fact we were actually named Llewelyn. And from my father's side, well, there was my father at the very least. Still, I knew the drill. "Believe me, I hear that often enough. The way the people at the Cloisters talk, we're practically superheroes."

"All women are superheroes." Isabeau took the book back. "Unicorn hunters or not."

I looked at her curiously. "So you don't regret missing out on being a unicorn hunter?" My mother did. Even Marten had seemed jealous that the abilities belonged only to the females of the family. "You don't wish they were around when you were . . ." Don't say eligible. Don't say eligible. " . . . younger?"

"Not a bit!" She shuddered. "I have no interest in hunting—unicorn or otherwise. I've always liked chemistry and medicine. And if I wanted a hobby, there was gardening. I like flower arranging, too, come to think of it."

I could hardly compare unicorn hunting to flower arranging, and my face must have shown it.

"I do not mean to belittle your skills, Astrid," she added. "And I do think of it that way. You have a marvelous skill, and one that is very useful to my work. Which is why I wish to hire you. The same way I would hire a skillful architect to build my house or a skillful chef to prepare my food. I can admire your abilities without being envious of them."

"My life isn't something to envy," I said softly.

Isabeau regarded me. "No. I don't think it is."

The bedroom she led me to was spacious and placed near the front of the château, at the farthest possible corner from the einhorn enclosure. The walls were papered in a subtle gold and cream stripe, and the bed linens matched in shades of gold, beige, and ivory. Lamps burned in every corner, and a tall vase of white flowers stood near the door.

"I'll get you something to wear and be right back," Isabeau said. "The bathroom is right through that door."

The bathroom was almost as big as the cell Cory and I shared at the Cloisters, and featured a claw-footed tub with a high back, a marble vanity, and gold fixtures.

I was almost afraid to touch it.

Isabeau returned with a pair of white satin pajamas. "This probably isn't your style," she said, "but it'll do for the night."

"Thank you." The material felt almost cold to the touch, and slipped over even my bowstring-calloused fingers as if made of water. "You've been way too kind."

"I've been nothing more than civil, Astrid. I'm sorry if your experiences have led you to expect anything less." She came closer and tucked a strand of loose hair behind my ear. "I don't believe you are being properly looked after, *ma chère*."

I swallowed heavily and looked away.

Isabeau still seemed to be looking at me. "Were you my daughter and charged with such a difficult duty, I would wish for someone to take very, very good care of you." Her voice broke on her final words. "Have a good night."

I looked up, but she'd already turned away.

Once alone, I decided to run a bath. I couldn't even remember the last time I'd taken one—they didn't have bathtubs at the Cloisters—and this tub was especially lovely. There was even a selection of bath oils placed nearby, all in pretty glass vials stopped with tiny corks and smelling strongly of fresh herbs. I picked the one that reminded me most of chamomile and sprinkled it liberally into the bathwater, then sank in up to my neck and closed my eyes, breathing in the scented steam and letting the heat seep into my bones.

I soaked until I was pruney and ready for sleep, then wrapped myself in a big towel and combed out my hair in front of the beautiful mirror. I put on the silky pajamas and padded back into the bedroom, breathing a sigh of relief. For the first time in ages, I'd sleep under a ceiling not studded with the bones of murdered unicorns. I couldn't feel their buzz in my head. I couldn't even sense the ones in the yard anymore. The satin I wore didn't irritate my scars like most of my shirts. Instead, it almost seemed to caress the raised bumps on my skin. The bed sheets smelled like lavender, and the scent of herbs misted their way through my unicorn-wracked senses.

I laid my damp head against the cool, fragrant pillow, and breathed a deep sigh of relief.

Were you my daughter . . . I would wish for someone to take very, very good care of you.

But I wasn't her daughter. At best, I was her extremely distant cousin. She was a Jaeger. The head of Gordian Pharmaceuticals.

I sat up, startled into wakefulness by my sudden comprehension. Isabeau was all of these things. And I really, really wanted to work for her.

I wanted to see what was going on here. I wanted to take part in the search for the Remedy. I wanted to fulfill my duty as a unicorn hunter, but I hated life at the Cloisters. I hated being stuck there, polishing weapons and wearing habits and traveling around killing wild animals. Here, I could protect people from the threat of killer unicorns without necessarily having to kill them. It was win-win.

Besides, if I stayed here, I could keep an eye on Gordian, make sure they weren't doing anything sketchy. I would be right here if, by chance, they did hear anything from Seth. I could go back to school—I could take college-level science classes.

And I could learn more about some Llewelyns that I actually respected. Medically minded Llewelyns like Isabeau was talking about. Like Isabeau herself.

When Clothilde Llewelyn had wanted to leave the Cloisters, she hadn't taken the coward's way out, availing herself of the services of an actaeon who'd strip her of her powers and leave her in the lurch. She knew that her duty was not necessarily to the Cloisters but to the human race. She was charged with protecting people from unicorns, whether that meant killing them or sending them away from the human population for good.

Or even watching over a herd to make sure they didn't escape their dedicated enclosure.

I could fulfill my duty as a hunter right here, and I was far more suited to the job than anyone else at the Cloisters. Couldn't say that about the position as Cory's bodyguard. Any of the other girls could do that, maybe even more skillfully.

I'd take the job. I just had to convince my friends it was the right choice.

10

Wherein Astrid Breaks the News

"Well, it's no secret you've been miserable here," Phil said when I called her. "Which is why I agreed to let you go with Cory in the first place."

"So, in your mind, there's no difference between me living in London and me working for Gordian Pharmaceuticals?" I asked.

She sighed. "Whatever, Astrid. You didn't seem to think I needed to know what you were up to when you left here. Why do you want my approval now?"

Maybe because she was my most trusted confidante. Or had been until recently. Neil's revelation had been accepted, begrudgingly, but now Phil was mad at us for keeping secrets. Or as she'd put it, "conspiring against her to undermine her authority as donna."

Perhaps it was good I wasn't at the Cloisters this morning.

"It's not your approval I want," I said. "Just your understanding. I'm doing this partially for you, you know." I'd come to France for her to begin with. "The extra money will come in handy at the Cloisters. It'll relieve some of the pressure you've been under, some of your dependence on the Church. You can concentrate on your conservation efforts."

"Don't you think there's a particular irony to helping support my conservation efforts through precisely the kind of exploitation my efforts are trying to eradicate?"

I didn't know how to respond to that.

My mother was even less approving. "I don't like this, Astrid," she stated from across the ocean. "You'll be wasting your talents. Doing what? Playing security guard for some corporation? That's no way to distinguish yourself as a hunter."

"I'm not interested in distinguishing myself as a hunter." Not half so interested as I was in, say, finishing high school. "And the money they're paying me will be supporting the Cloisters."

"I told you, once the book deal comes through, I'll have plenty of money for the Cloisters." My mother sighed. "Unicorns are so hot right now. And you could be at the forefront of that, too, if you'd just— This is such a waste, Astrid. Can't one of the lesser hunters do this instead?"

"For the last time, Mom, I *am* one of the lesser hunters." Plus, Gordian could offer me school and science and safety, which I needed far more than any of the dubious glories of unicorn hunting in Italy.

"That's ridiculous," Lilith said. "You, whose first kill was to single-handedly take down a re'em—"

"Hardly single-handedly," I said. Dorcas and Phil had helped, and the unicorn in question had been very distracted at the time, intent on killing Ursula and Zelda.

"Who survived an attack from an entire pack of kirin—"

No thanks to Lilith. She'd been the one to send us up against

147

that pack. "*Barely* survived," I corrected. Even then, my survival had been thanks to the timely intervention of Bucephalus.

"And the only living human to face down a karkadann—"

Is *that* what she'd been telling the people on the networks? No wonder they thought I was some sort of unicorn-hunting wunderkind.

"You've got such a compelling story, Astrid. And now, to give it all up and live in obscurity—"

"You've got that right," I countered. "I want to *live* in obscurity, Mom. Not die a unicorn-hunting celebrity. These battles are not fodder for the nightly news. These girls are taking their lives in their hands every time they go after a unicorn, and—"

"And you've left them to do it alone, without your significant skill set and experience." Lilith clucked her tongue at me. "Not very responsible of you, Astrid. And to think you once wanted to be a doctor, to save people's lives."

I always found it very difficult to speak to my mother. Now that our conversations pertained to actual life and death situations, it had become nearly impossible. I *had* saved people's lives. What had she ever done but put them in danger and profit from it?

Finally, I called Giovanni. We hadn't spoken since before I'd left the Cloisters.

"After everything that happened with Gordian?" he asked, suspicious. He, too, had been taken in by Marten Jaeger last summer. "How can you trust them?"

"This is different." I explained Isabeau's position and summarized her offer. "There are so many benefits to my being here. School, and a more regular schedule, and less danger. And I can keep an eye out for Seth."

"I say let the police handle that," said Giovanni. "And as for less danger, it's you alone with a whole herd of unicorns. How is that less dangerous?"

Giovanni had an especially difficult time imagining unicorns as anything other than the bloodthirsty kirin. I decided to change the subject.

"Also, I can ditch the habits."

"But you promised to send me a picture of you wearing one!"

"Over my dead body."

"Darn." Giovanni laughed. "You know, I've got a reputation for being straightlaced around here, what with the whole dating-a-nun meme that's made its way around campus."

Quite a change from the hard-partying reputation that had gotten him kicked out of his last school. "Yeah, I heard something about that when I called the other day. About me really being a nun. Though you'd think that would make you sound like even more of a bad boy."

"You mean because I'm stealing you away from your religious vows?"

"Something like that." Though it turned out I didn't need Giovanni to play actaeon. There *were* alternatives to life in the Order.

"I'm still worried about this," he said. "How do you know they're going to keep their word this time?"

"Well, it seems to be working out well for Brandt."

"Brandt?"

Oh, right. I explained, as briefly as possible.

"Wait, you're living in France with your ex-boyfriend?"

"That sounds a lot worse than it is," I admitted.

"Very un-nunlike behavior," Giovanni agreed. "Should I be worried?"

"Of course not." I rolled over. "He's just another person in the house."

"A boy person."

"Yes."

"That you used to date."

"The very same."

"Who is not three thousand miles away."

I smiled. "You jealous, Giovanni?"

He was quiet for a moment, taking the question far more seriously than I'd meant it. "No," he said at last. "I mean, not like I don't trust you. But of him, yes, I'm jealous. I want what he has. I want to be near you."

I smiled, though I knew he couldn't see it. I wanted that, too, but for now, I'd take this. A job, a chance, Giovanni on the phone saying he missed me. For now, it would be enough.

Under these inauspicious circumstances, my tenure as an employee of Gordian Pharmaceuticals began. Isabeau sent into the city for my belongings, and when they arrived, her mouth dropped open.

"Rags," was her verdict, wrinkling her nose at my pile of faded T-shirts and cargo pants. "And summer clothes. I can't have you traipsing about the grounds in these."

I looked over my meager wardrobe. "Things get ruined when I hunt in them," I said. "I don't want anything too nice."

"You're not a nun here, Astrid," Isabeau argued. "And if you do your job right—protecting the people around here from unicorns and vice versa—there'll be very little to worry about in terms of bloodstains, either. Besides, you'll need winter coats, school clothes. I absolutely refuse to let an employee of mine look like a hobo. We can go to Limoges this afternoon and visit the shops."

She took in my stricken expression.

"Unless you'd prefer to travel to Paris for your clothes."

I choked. "I can't afford—"

She waved me off. "Naturally, Gordian will finance your wardrobe, Astrid. Just like your room and board. Don't even think of it."

"Thank you, but I really can't let you—"

"You let the Catholic Church give you these horrid green things, *oui*?" She gingerly poked at the corner of my hunting habit.

"Well, yes, but—"

"I refuse to be upstaged by the Pope, *chère*." Isabeau laughed. "Particularly when it comes to fashion."

I drew the line at Paris, though Zelda would probably have struck me dead if she knew.

Isabeau dragged me to half the shops in Limoges. We bought wool pants and belted raincoats, cashmere sweater sets and silk tops, and a new pair of hiking boots to hunt in. We bought skirts "for school" and knee-high boots in both black and tan with leather satchels to match—"only get the kind with pockets large enough for your hunting knife, *chère*"—and fingerless leather gloves in case I had to shoot something after it got cold. Isabeau wanted us to consider party clothes, but I took one look at a rack of low-cut, sleeveless dresses and backed away slowly.

Even in the highly unlikely scenario that I'd attend some sort of formal event, I'd never wear an outfit that so clearly revealed my hunting scars.

"How silly," Isabeau had said. She'd laid hands on my shoulders in the latest shop's open-plan dressing room and faced my bare back toward the mirror. "Your scars are a part of you, Astrid. They mark you as a survivor."

Her hand hovered, fingers splayed wide, over the scar that spread out like a starburst from the center of my back.

"You do not deny that these things happened to you, do you? You fought with a unicorn; you emerged victorious. Did this not happen?"

"Yes." I looked away from my reflection. "But it's so ugly."

"No." She lowered her hand and turned back to me. "What happened to you was ugly. It was painful, horrible, terrifying. And that's what you see when you look at these scars. You see being attacked. But what you should see is the strength of your own spirit. You survived—something almost no one else would." She put a hand on the scar near my elbow. "And you saved a life." She pointed at the scar beneath my ribs. "You were brave and strong, and you persevered where many people would not." Her eyes met mine. "Your scars are beautiful, Astrid, because they reveal the beauty of the woman who lives inside your skin. *Tu te sens bien dans ta peau.*"

And then she made me buy some new camisoles, lingerie, a silk robe, and a bathing suit.

After shopping, we stopped for coffee and snacks at a café, and Isabeau mapped out my work schedule. Keeping the unicorns pacified would be paramount, and she explained how they'd discovered with their last resident hunter—whose name and family origin she still refused to divulge—that the einhorns' wildest behavior tended to coincide with the hunter's periods of absence from the château.

This took a period of discovery? It seemed blindingly obvious to me.

"And yet," Isabeau said, "it is not practical or advisable for you to be constantly on call—or even on site. How can we go shopping if that is the case?" She smiled at me. "How can we enroll you in classes at the university? No, it will never do. So we've learned a few tricks that can, for a short time, delude the creatures that you are still nearby."

I leaned in, interested. "A unicorn-hunting decoy?"

"Exactly," she said. "Or more correctly, a scarecrow. Clothes you've worn work well, as does varying your schedule so that they never know when it's you and when it is simply your essence, left behind as a reminder."

"But unicorns don't use scent or time to sense my presence," I replied. "They do it just as I do—through magic."

Isabeau cocked her head at me. "Is that so? I have always understood that hunters interact with the unicorns using every sense. A hunter can see and smell things we cannot."

"Yes, but those are the—" I paused, searching for the right words. The ones that would make me sound at least *marginally* sane. There was a definite distinction between believing in the magic, as Isabeau did, and listening impassively to a hunter describe how she doesn't really *look* at the unicorns she shoots anymore, just pinpoints their location on the massive, magical radar in her mind.

"Those are the native powers—the ones all hunters are born with, regardless of training. If we work at it, we've got so much more. It's almost as if they're part of our own bodies. I know where unicorns are and how they move just like I know where my own hand is."

"Hmm. So now, you never bother to use your other senses? Those 'native' ones?"

I supposed not. In the Cloisters, the buzz of the trophies and the ever-present odor of unicorns had grown so commonplace—too ubiquitous to, say, pinpoint Bonegrinder's location without tapping in to her thoughts. "My unicorn senses are more general—are they there or aren't they?—and not nearly as perceptive for the purpose of hunting as the magic I started using once I was attuned."

"There are machines," said Isabeau, "that can calibrate a change in temperature down to the tiniest fraction of a degree." She took a sip from her cup and grimaced. "But I do not need them to tell me when my coffee has gone cold."

And as she gestured to the server, I marveled that Isabeau was the only person I'd spoken to in months who wasn't the slightest bit impressed by descriptions of my magic.

"The unicorns in the enclosure," I said. "Are they . . . healthy?"

Isabeau nodded, her expression somber. "You have noticed their rashes, perhaps?"

Rashes? "Yes, and they seem . . . hungry."

"We feed them plenty," she replied. "But they are natural predators. It is not the same. We do the best we can for them, but it is impossible to re-create their environment as if they are still in the wild." She shrugged. "You are familiar with the legend that a unicorn cannot be captured?"

"Of course." Bonegrinder was a refutation of that.

"The real trick, Astrid, is keeping one alive in captivity."

Next, we visited the university, where Isabeau showed me the botany building that had been named for her mother and introduced me to the head of the chemistry department, a Middle Eastern man who was so clearly charmed by Isabeau that, for a moment, I thought he was going to offer to tutor me himself.

Later, as we drove back to the château, I felt my head spinning. This was all happening so fast. Twenty-four hours earlier, I'd been a de facto nun and a high school dropout living in a ruined church made of unicorn bones. Now I had bags and bags of fashionable French clothes, had enrolled in a remedial yet college-level chemistry seminar, and was relaxing on the buttery leather seats of a BMW on my way back to my gorgeous suite at a beautiful château in the French countryside.

I stared out the window at said countryside and stretched my senses out as far as I could, searching for any sign of unicorn. A taste of the monsters now would help me focus. But I felt nothing as we zoomed along.

One of the things that had so frustrated me—and Phil—at the Cloisters was the way the Bartolis were willing to accept the old ways at face value, even despite our limited knowledge of what exactly those old ways were. Cory truly believed in the idea of family castes: that different unicorn-hunting families were inherently better equipped to handle certain unicorn-hunting tasks. As a Llewelyn, I was supposed to be one of the best hunters there, despite facts to the contrary. And yes, maybe we knew what an actaeon was or who every don of the Cloisters had been back to the Order's founding, but we had a terrible time understanding even the basics of unicorn behavior, or the smallest part of our training. As it had been a mystery passed down from hunter to hunter, that kind of thing had never been written down in the records. We'd never known that the unicorn-encrusted walls of our nunnery had been built to help attune us, that there was magic in our ancient weapons that outstripped any of the advances and conveniences afforded by modern bows and arrows.

We didn't even know about the purifying effects of chamomile. How many nights had I gone to sleep with headaches from the buzz of the trophy wall that no amount of painkillers seemed to dull? I wanted to know what other knowledge about hunters Isabeau and her mother had. The more records we could find from hunters, the more we might understand what the lifestyle we were trying to rebuild and—more—what the magic were really all about.

The previous hunter at Gordian—the one who'd helped to capture the einhorns—she'd not been trained at the Cloisters. Her abilities were likely only what came naturally to us, unless she'd figured out a way to teach herself.

Or unless she had some sort of ancient records that taught her. Maybe taught her something even we didn't know!

"The guard you had before," I said. "Did she ever have to kill one of the unicorns?" Prior to attuning our magic, hunting had been a far more difficult and dangerous prospect.

"We were very fortunate," Isabeau said. "She had no interest in hunting, which is why she eventually chose to rid herself of her powers. The hunter's main occupation while here was drawing the unicorns in so she could fit them with electric shock collars."

"But that's so dangerous!" I said. "What if they'd attacked her?"

Isabeau shrugged, eyes on the road before us. "It is the way it has been done in this country for centuries." She gave me a quick glance. "Surely you have seen the tapestries."

I shook my head.

"Not even a picture?" She clucked her tongue. "Perhaps we shall have to go to Paris after all. The Musée Cluny has some. But it is the tapestries in New York City that are most instructive.

They tell a story of the hunt for the unicorn. They say that the virgin sits in a grove and waits for the einhorn to come. It is attracted to her, in the way that all unicorns are, and comes to her, and lays its head in her lap. And then, she slips a collar over its head and leads it into captivity. To her, the unicorn is gentle and calm."

"The einhorns didn't look calm yesterday."

"And why do you think that is?" Isabeau smiled at me as we pulled into the drive leading to the château. "You say you were listening in on their thoughts."

"As well as I could," I replied. "I'm not used to that . . . kind of unicorn, and there were so many at once. They took me by surprise. Their thoughts were . . . strange to me."

"Were you frightened?"

I ducked my head. "A little."

She parked the car in front of the château and stepped out. Gog and Magog came bounding toward her from around the side of the house. I was surprised that Isabeau let them wander around loose, with the unicorns so nearby. Wasn't a big haunch of Great Pyrénées dog every bit as appetizing as a steak? I watched her greet each dog, ruffling the fur on the necks and scratching them under their chins. For just a moment, I expected Bonegrinder to do the same thing— come running up to me, soliciting a cuddle. But the zhi was back in the Cloisters, avoiding Phil and trying to get the other hunters to spend time with her. I hoped Rosamund would comb her hair. I hoped Ilesha would let her sleep on her bed.

"So, Astrid," Isabeau said, handing me several shopping bags, "why do you think that the events in the einhorn enclosure yesterday unfolded as they did?"

"Because when there are unicorns around, I never miss?"

She laughed. "I'm not talking about your considerable skills with a dagger. I'm talking about the animals' behavior."

Oh. She wasn't asking me as a hunter. She was asking me as a scientist. She was asking me to analyze my observations and compare them to the previous observable facts. According to all her evidence about einhorns, which was much more than mine, the presence of a hunter calmed the animals. I wondered if einhorns were like zhi in that respect. After all, I could keep Bonegrinder under control.

And I could easily compare Bonegrinder's demeanor to the attitude of the zhi that Cory and I had hunted the day she'd been injured. Those unicorns had been terrified, but they also knew we meant to kill them. Bonegrinder had no such fears.

"We riled them up, Brandt and I," I said. "Brandt because he's not a hunter and he was teasing them, and me because"—I weighed my words—"because they'd never seen a hunter who was actually a *hunter* before." They'd been attracted to me like they were to all women with my birthright, but when they tasted my thoughts—if they did—they saw I was ready to kill them, primed for it. That I'd killed many creatures like them before and thought nothing of it at all.

"Precisely," said Isabeau. "If you were sitting quietly, if you weren't thinking about slitting their throats, they would be as easygoing as one of my dogs. This is the way of the einhorns. It's one of the reasons we chose them for our captives." She swung the rest of the bags from the car trunk and shut the door.

"But I *am* prepared to kill them," I said. "To keep the people around here safe. I don't know if I can turn that off." I followed her up the drive toward the front door.

"You'll have to try," Isabeau said. "It's important that you stop thinking like a predator, and start thinking like a prison guard."

11

Wherein Astrid Walks a New Path

For a prison guard, I soon found that my duties were extraordinarily light. Every dawn, I made my rounds of the enclosure, checking to see that the fences and the electronic restraints were intact, doing a quick head count of the unicorns. After the unfortunate incident on my first day, there were eighteen left, and I tried to track all of them before heading into breakfast.

Though back in Italy my experiences had seemed to indicate that most unicorns were active at dawn and dusk, einhorns—or at least the captive ones at Gordian, belied that evidence. I would occasionally find some prowling the edges of their enclosure, but most remained hidden well inside the woods, and when I ventured into the enclosure to check on them, their thoughts tended toward the dreamlike.

After the early-morning rounds, I had a few tutoring sessions. Isabeau had hired a recent college grad from Connecticut to cover English literature and history classes for Brandt, and told me I was welcome to take advantage of Brandt's French tutor as well, though he was obviously more advanced than me. To my surprise, I discovered that because of the difference in our curriculum, Brandt and I would only rarely have our classes at the same time. Isabeau presented this as a positive, saying I'd learn much faster in a single-sex, one-on-one environment.

"Studies have shown that all-female education helps build confidence and promotes learning in young women."

I'd crossed my arms, feeling the muscles bulging beneath my new sweater. Given that I could outrun, outshoot, and out-throttle any unicorn, plus had a grade point average well above his, I doubted that my ex-boyfriend posed much of a threat to my confidence.

Then again, there had been a time I almost slept with him to enhance my social standing. I hardly remembered that girl.

"You'll see Brandt plenty, I'm sure," Isabeau had argued. "Schooltime is for you to learn."

I liked my tutor, Lauren. She had super curly hair, spoke German *and* French, and was taking a year off to earn money before graduate school. She was also fascinated to meet a unicorn hunter.

"I've read about you guys in the news, of course, but—I guess I was expecting something a little more . . ."

"Innocent?" I asked. I got that a lot. People expected me to walk around in a white dress and a veil. After all, our position as hunters proclaimed our sexual status more obviously and dramatically than a purity ring.

"I was going to say 'comic book superhero.'"

"Sorry to disappoint," I said. "The Church didn't approve our vinyl jumpsuits and capes."

"Is it true you usually wear habits?"

"Recently." I shrugged. "It's for image, really. All summer long I wore cargo shorts and T-shirts."

"Wild." Lauren shook her head. "Okay, let's get to work. I thought since we're in France, we'd start with the Napoleonic Age. . . ."

Before my arrival, the Gordian staff had a habit of feeding the unicorns at noon, so when my morning classes were done, I headed back out to the enclosure to watch the proceedings. Basically, a few staffers carted in some giant sacks of meat and tossed them over the boundary, then ran back behind the fences. I stayed within the enclosure, on the other side of the electric barrier, and waited for the unicorns to approach.

"Usually they come by now," one of the staffers said to me. "I think they are still afraid of you."

Yet I could feel them yearning for the bags of meat, their longing radiating out from their hiding place within the trees. I watched carefully, but no unicorn emerged from the protection of the woods that first day until I'd left the enclosure and returned to the château.

In the afternoons, I did homework—an odd concept, considering that my studies took place in the same library where my morning classes had been. I'd never known any homeschooled students back in the states—I wondered if they called it homework.

If I saw Brandt then, it was a quick glimpse of him playing video games in his room, or bounding down to the kitchen for snacks, or running out the door to his motorcycle, helmet swinging by the strap from his fingers. He'd wave or grin at me, but I never got another invitation to join him, and my kirin-striped helmet lay unused on a cupboard near the side door. He continued to spend the odd night in hotels in Limoges. Either he had a very late night class at the university, or—something else. Every time I asked Isabeau, though, her answers were vague.

"Boys shall be boys."

I wondered sometimes if he was embarrassed about trying to kiss me, or if Isabeau had warned him to keep his distance. Not that it mattered.

My favorite was the evening rounds. Though I relished long days spent beyond the reach of the unicorns, a cup of chamomile tea on my desk wafting its cleansing scent through the rooms of the château, there was still something to be said for the magic. As the sun set, I'd wander past the greenhouse, slip inside the einhorn enclosure, and stretch my senses out toward the unicorns. One by one I'd feel them alert to my presence, and the concerns of the day would slip away. Historical facts, scientific figures, new French words—even the old, familiar English ones—all faded before the bright focus of hunter magic.

I'd glide down the wooded paths, my arms free of weapons, though I kept the alicorn knife in a bag at my side, and take stock of the unicorns. It didn't take me long to differentiate their thought patterns, and even more, to expect them—whether or not the einhorns saw fit to show their faces.

Always lurking nearby were three males, young, constantly hungry, split between curiosity and fear. The einhorn I'd killed had been part of their bachelor band. The three that remained trailed me on my walks and, day by day, dared to come closer.

They were different than the other unicorns I'd known. As silent and graceful as kirin, they floated through the forest, drifting in and out of the patches of fading sunlight like ghosts, pale and ethereal. Blink and you'd miss them—even if you *were* a hunter.

Their hair was short, showcasing their bony knees and the ribs beneath their skin. Most had sparse manes running down their heads and necks, starting around the spot where the horn sprouted from their skulls. The manes lay matted at the base of their necks where the electric collars rubbed against their skin. Their wide-set eyes were dark and fathomless, with no irises or pupils that I could see.

The first to approach me was the tallest, with legs a few inches longer than the others—a few inches longer than even he seemed to know what to do with. Once, when I stood still for a few moments, he came close enough to nose at my bag. As soon as I breathed, he bounded away, but the next evening I brought a package of sausage and waited to see if he'd do it again.

The sausage produced very quick results. Not only did Stretch return, but he brought along his two friends. One seemed to be suffering from the same skin condition as the einhorn I'd killed, for his fur was spotted with bare, red patches. I examined them closely, for I'd never seen a unicorn's ultra-regenerative hide be anything but utterly pristine.

At least until I filled it with arrows.

This must be the rash Isabeau had mentioned. Did their regenerative ability weaken in captivity? If so, would they even be useful as a resource for the Remedy?

Blotchy was accompanied by the third unicorn, a skittish young male for whom even the promise of fresh meat didn't seem enough to get him to come near me. I tossed a sausage into the brush and he leaped after it, bouncing into the bushes with such enthusiasm and glee that he reminded me of a large, sleek

Bonegrinder, and I laughed out loud.

The einhorns scattered, and though I sat still on the forest floor for another half an hour, none approached me. I wondered how long it took for the hunter before me to capture all of them, or if they were especially cautious around me because I'd first introduced myself by killing one of their own.

Or maybe they knew I could read their minds and were horrified.

The following day, instead of Stretch, Blotchy, and Jumps, a new einhorn began trailing me down the unicorn-trampled paths in the wooded enclosure. This one, from the taste of her thoughts, was a female, and she was ravenous. Nothing would have brought her out of hiding except for the scent of the meat I carried. I dropped a bit of sausage behind me and walked on, casting quick, magic-enhanced glances back to see if the einhorn followed.

She did. She was another young one, barely an adult, who trotted behind me on legs that seemed far too slender for her bloated body. I wondered if she, too, was ill—certain types of malnutrition caused bloat, especially if she was gulping whatever food she could find before another unicorn grabbed it away from her. Alternately, maybe she'd swallowed something she shouldn't have—a plastic bag, perhaps. Or it could even be a tumor. It was impossible that so many other unicorns in this enclosure looked starved and she was this fat.

A few pieces of sausages later, and Fats was practically in my lap. At the edge of my consciousness, I could feel the three males poking around, keeping their distance but drawn in by the food. Beyond that, I could feel the other unicorns lying in wait, curious and cautious. On the edges of their minds, I tasted regret and anger. Though their thoughts were not firm and human-shaped like a karkadann's, I could still snatch images from their minds. Memories and fears that passed, to my consciousness, for fully formed thoughts.

Not only did they remember what I'd done to that other ein-horn, but they also remembered what the other hunter had done to them. She'd drawn them in, clasped those collars around their necks, and captured them. Now, they were trapped, and once the wildlife of these woods had been consumed—all the rabbits, voles, and foxes—they were utterly dependent on the largesse of their captors.

I laid a sausage in my open palm and held it out to Fats. She tottered closer, her nose twitching as it shifted into high gear. Her thoughts fell into grateful, Bonegrinder-like patterns, and I bit my lip, not realizing until now how much I missed the little zhi. I felt her lips on my skin, the soft grazing of her fangs as she snuffled up the treat, and I laid my other hand lightly on her head, just behind her spiral horn.

Fats froze as I ran my fingers through her mane, scratching the red, shiny scars that marked the places where the electric collar bit into her skin. In spots, her regenerative hide even grew over the edge of the collar, the way I'd seen Bonegrinder's flesh heal over a bullet. We remained like that for a few moments, Fats with her neck awkwardly stretched over my lap while I scratched her head, until something startled her and she sprinted off.

Not like Bonegrinder at all. I must keep that in mind.

Their behavior fascinated me. They weren't tame like zhi, yet their attraction to hunters seemed even stronger. The second I came to the enclosure, I felt their attention turn my way—even if they were frightened, even if they were wary—they knew where I was and their thoughts held a certain fascination with my every move. They weren't devious like kirin, either; their thoughts remained open and easy, with a certain malleability to their minds—almost as if they invited me to peek inside or share my own feelings.

It was strange, this magic. I was used to the altered state I slipped into while hunting, and even the low, idling hum of readiness I experienced in the Cloisters, but this felt odd. Every time I was in the enclosure, the magic washed over me at full tilt, and yet, there was no outlet for my energy. I didn't have to chase these unicorns; I didn't have to hunt them. My body didn't know what to do with itself; I buzzed for hours after every encounter.

The next morning, Stretch was there to meet me at the boundary, his associates lingering in the brush and watching me with wide black eyes. His thoughts showed he resented having given up his food to the female yesterday, and he planned to be the first unicorn I met on my rounds.

"Hello," I said to the einhorn, and it did not deter him. I turned my back on the animal and marched into the forest. He followed, and when I didn't immediately reward him with a sausage, he started nosing at my bag.

"Watch it," I said, and when I turned around again, he shied back. Blotchy and Jumps were a few more yards back on the trail, Fats hid in the brush even farther away, and then there was a new unicorn sniffing around the perimeter of the group. Another male, not as sure of himself as the three I'd come to know. I divided my sausages into five bits, threw Fats her share, and held Stretch's out to him. He paused for a split second that seemed far longer in my unicorn-awareness, then snatched it from my hand, retreating again before he chewed.

Blotchy and Jumps were still too close together to throw them separate bits. I knew they'd fight, which didn't seem conducive to my "keep the unicorns pacified" prime directive. I clucked my tongue at them, holding out more sausage, but they held their heads back, even as Stretch lunged for more.

Then, from out of the bushes came the new unicorn, the fifth unicorn. His mouth was parted, his tongue dangling out from between his fangs. Stretch looked up and growled at his approach, and he growled back, then licked his chops. His tongue flopped down again, as if too swollen to withdraw into his mouth.

Was every unicorn in the enclosure suffering from an ailment of its own?

I tossed Tongue his sausage, then walked toward Blotchy and Jumps, my hands outstretched and filled with their portions of meat. They backed up as I came closer, Stretch hot on my heels.

"Come on," I coaxed. "It's okay, you can have it."

The unicorns clustered around me, jostling one another to get closer to the food I offered them. Velvety snouts pushed against my hands, my arms, my neck, and I ducked to avoid their swinging horns.

"Watch out, you vicious monsters," I said, chuckling, reminded more than ever of our house zhi. They pressed closer, nosing in my bag for more meat. By now, Blotchy and Fats were in a tug-of-war contest over the wax paper wrappings on the sausages, while Jumps and Tongue waited to see what was left. Stretch stood guard over us all, face at the level of my shoulder, head tilted back and horn well out of the way, as if in response to my warning.

I glanced up at him. "Can you understand me, fella?"

Stretch stared straight ahead, eyes unblinking.

Guess not.

The others seemed only to understand the language of food. I wished I knew more about the differences between the species. The kirin and re'em I'd fought never seemed to want more than to skewer me, but Bonegrinder, a zhi, was subservient to me, and was known to occasionally obey the commands of a hunter. I never considered that she could read my mind, nor the other unicorns, and yet, the karkadann had considered our telepathic link to be as much a part of our powers as speed and aim.

And if the karkadann thought nothing of reading my mind, did it mean that the other unicorns could do so as well? Were they always reading my mind, as I was reading theirs, and understanding it in whatever way they could? Was the reason Bonegrinder had stopped loving Phil a result of her lost magic but not in the way we all thought? Was it just that, for the first time, Bonegrinder couldn't sense, telepathically, how much Phil adored her?

As Isabeau had said, was our reliance on the magic blinding us to what our natural senses might easily be able to convey?

The sausages gone, the unicorns began nuzzling me for more. The odor of fire and flood filled the air around me, emanating off the unicorns in waves. Beneath it, I could smell dampness and animal, their musty coats, their waste and festering wounds. Their thoughts crowded in on me, too: hunger, pain, desperation, and fear that burned almost as brightly as the magic that bound us. My hands were in their fur, my cheek against their manes, my blond hair tangled with their white as their tails flicked rhythmically in the fading light. I could hear their noises, soft snuffles and lowing that sounded somehow like the cross of a cow and a cat and the hum of the bones on the Wall of First Kills back in the Cloisters.

I caught my breath and reveled in their nearness, suddenly hungry for the feel of them, the scent, the strange comfort their nearness brought me. I wanted this.

I hadn't known.

This must be what Alexander felt in the company of his karkadann. Here, alone, communing with the unicorns, the magic between us flowing like the tides of an ocean, I could understand why he'd loved Bucephalus, why Bucephalus had stayed so long with him. This strength, this power, these thoughts that blinked through my brain at the speed of enchantment—I could do anything! I could take over the world if I wanted, could lead armies into battle, could change the entire course of history.

In the distance, there was a sound— a car backfiring or the crack of thunder—and the unicorns scattered. In seconds, I was alone in the woods, as the magic dissolved into the dying sunlight. My hands dropped to my sides, and the rest of the world came back into focus. Yes, it must have been thunder. Now, without the pull of unicorns, I could feel the drop in air pressure, the scent of rain on the breeze, and the blackening sky.

I hiked out of the woods, feeling drained by my encounter, yet strangely alive. Neck-deep in the combined magic of these beautiful creatures, I found it easy to forget about reality for a few moments . . . but I had to remember that an even better world waited beyond. Since coming to France, I'd been sleeping better, studying better, *dressing* better. I had my own room, I—mostly—set my own hours, and as long as no humans were injured by an escaped einhorn, I answered to no one. Working for Gordian was a way to parlay my hunting onto a path with a non-unicorn-hunting future. It was like Giovanni had said: it was okay to be a unicorn hunter, but I needed to think about who I was when I was just Astrid as well.

At the Cloisters I was simply another member of the Order, no matter what noises my mother made about supposed "glory." I was just another hunter who followed the rules of the Church and the missions of the don. Another hunter who waited in the nunnery, surviving days of interminable boredom punctuated by moments of abject terror on the hunt.

But here I could concentrate on my own life—one without magic. I could drink chamomile tea and do my schoolwork and spend most of my time without being reminded that just beyond the walls, right behind the greenhouse, there was a herd of monsters—breathtaking, magnetic monsters—that only I had the ability to subdue.

That only I had the ability to speak to.

Before I knew it, a month had passed at the château. The weather turned cooler, and the geodesic glass panels of the greenhouse misted over with condensation in the mornings and evenings. Brandt traded in his T-shirts for sweaters, peacoats, and preppy-looking scarves in a blue stripe that brought out the color of his eyes. The leaves in the wood grew golden and began to gather on the forest floor. I rustled through them on my rounds, a steady pack of unicorns trailing behind me, their numbers increasing every day as they slowly learned I meant them no harm. Or maybe they'd simply do anything for increased food rations. They certainly appreciated the addition of sausage to their diet, and they looked less scrawny by the day.

Phil sent me regular reports of progress, or lack thereof, back at the Cloisters. She was making baby steps toward saving the unicorns. Neil hadn't managed to find any new hunters. The girls had killed three kirin and two zhis, and a new report had just come in about a pack of einhorns in Poland. They were sending out a team next week. Did I have any einhorn tips?

Cory's reports were similarly status quo. They'd sent Valerija to guard her, as the runaway was free to go where she pleased. Additionally, Valerija would probably most benefit from the English lessons she'd get while living in the United Kingdom. Things had been relatively quiet for them. Valerija had sensed the presence of unicorns on the Bartoli's country property, but they'd kept their distance. She'd killed a few on assignment in the neighborhood, and folks seemed happy to have unicorn hunters in residence, which made Neil optimistic that his future schemes would receive a good reception.

Cory related that, during all this, she sensed nothing of the unicorns' presence. And all of her doctors' tests came back inconclusive. One said it could be MS, another hypothesized lupus, a third suggested chronic fatigue syndrome. Since her most notable symptom was her inability to access unicorn magic, there wasn't a lot of information on the subject.

Five weeks after I arrived in France, I was headed out on my morning rounds of the einhorn enclosure when I saw Isabeau standing in the hall, surrounded by her staff. One of the Gordian scientists was with her, wearing a long white coat and sharing notes on a clipboard.

"Astrid," Isabeau called, beckoning me over. "I am happy to have caught you."

The scientist handed her a large syringe.

"You were a hospital volunteer in your hometown, yes?"

"Yes."

"Are you familiar with giving injections?"

"Sort of." We hadn't been allowed to do it at the hospital, but I'd observed it many times. In an emergency, I could probably handle the situation.

"On your rounds today," Isabeau said, "would you please take this and inject it into one of the unicorns. We'd like it to be a . . ." She looked at the scientist as if for clarification.

"*Un jeune masculin*," he said.

"A young male, if at all possible. Thank you, *chère*." She handed me the syringe and turned back to her notes.

The scientist spoke to Isabeau again in rapid, rushed French.

"Oh, *oui*, yes. Astrid, make sure that you do not inject the animal until you have come very close to the boundary. I would not have you be forced to drag it out like dead weight, and obviously, we cannot bring our carts within the enclosure."

I eyed the needle. "It's a sedative?"

Isabeau gave a quick jerk of her head. "No, it is an anesthetic. A euthanasic. How do you say it? To put the unicorn down."

12

Wherein Astrid Makes a Kill

Isabeau found me in the greenhouse, still gasping for breath, face buried in a chamomile plant, though I doubted anything would drown out the images of the unicorns fighting over the sausages as I laughed in the woods.

"Astrid! Whatever is the matter?" She came striding down the aisle, her steps long and sure despite her short stature and the tottering height of her heels. Gog and Magog trotted behind her, their ears perked, their eyes as dark and piercing as any einhorn's. "Why did you run away from me?"

"I—I was just taken aback, that's all."

"By what?"

"I didn't realize I was being asked to kill one of them."

She stopped then, and her expression was one of confusion. "*Je ne comprends pas.* You are regularly asked to kill unicorns. You killed one in your first hour here. Why should this request cause you to flee?"

"I—" She had a point. "I was just surprised. I didn't realize . . . that this would be part of my duties."

Her confusion gave way to amused bafflement. "But you're a unicorn hunter. You're the only one who can kill them."

"Right, but—" There was no point explaining. Yes, I killed unicorns. All the time, with rarely any thought. I, who could see right into their hearts, who could taste their terror as my arrows pierced their chests—I'd still killed dozens.

Though perhaps my favorite part of this job was that until now, I hadn't had to kill anything.

"Why do you need it?" I asked.

"For our experiments. We use the parts of the unicorn in our attempts to re-create the Remedy. This is the reason we keep the animals here to begin with."

"Yes." I nodded miserably. I knew that, too. They were not just captives there for my amusement. They were lab rats. I needed to snap out of this shock.

"This way, the anesthetic, it is quick. Humane. And painless. So much better than one of your weapons." Isabeau handed me the syringe I'd dropped in the hall. "This is part of your job, just as killing one that escaped would be."

I swallowed. My job was to be a unicorn hunter, not a unicorn executioner. I'd never killed one that wasn't either actively or about to attack something. And yet I couldn't argue with Isabeau's point. I couldn't get squeamish over a gentle euthanasia when I seemed to have no problem with the prolonged, painful death of a mis-shot arrow.

Though it had been quite some time since I'd hit a unicorn anywhere that didn't bring a quick death.

"I need sausages or some other meat. To tempt him over to me."

Isabeau's eyes narrowed. "I thought they found your

hunter wiles temptation enough."

"Please," I croaked, then hated myself for it. "I can give him a last meal."

Her face softened. "Yes, *chère*. That is only fair."

I headed into the enclosure armed with my knife, a packet of meat, the deadly syringe, and a jaw filled with firmly gritted teeth. This was my job, my duty. And how was giving one unicorn a peaceful, painless death any worse than stabbing one in the neck from ten feet away?

Perhaps it had been a bad idea to name the unicorns that followed me through the forest every day.

I let myself through the gate, then marched across the no-man's-land and past the electric barrier, chin held high, telling myself to just stick the first young male unicorn who wandered by. I was not going to play favorites with the lab rats.

Please don't let Stretch come first. Please don't let Stretch come first.

The forest was still and quiet that morning, the thoughts of the einhorns as dim and insubstantial as the mist coating the ground at the base of the trees. They must be asleep, dreaming of food or freedom or whatever lay in the hearts of captive monsters. Fine, I would wait. I was good at waiting. How many sleepless nights had I spent up on the cramped and vertigo-inducing quarters of a tree stand? At least here I could be on the ground.

I sat down a few yards into the wood, my back against the trunk of a tree, and removed the meat from my bag. The combination of hunter and fresh food should provide an irresistible combination to any nearby unicorns.

It didn't take long. Within minutes, one approached. I could taste its thoughts. Driven by a hunger that seemed to consume the creature from the inside out, the unicorn moved toward me. I tensed. This was not any of the einhorns I'd known. He was wary, angry, and did not trust me. Fury burned in his belly in the place of food, and for the first time since coming to France, an einhorn reminded me less of a zhi than of a kirin and its endless rage. He'd kill me if it meant more food.

I reached into my bag for the syringe, and the unicorn took off. I leaped to my feet, scattering food, and had already rushed in the direction of the fleeing unicorn before I remembered that I wasn't hunting. I didn't need to chase after this one unicorn. Another would come.

Even if this was the only one I'd met whose life I felt comfortable ending.

I plopped back onto the ground and dug the heels of my hands into my forehead. No. I wasn't going to play favorites. Any of these unicorns would do—the ones I knew, the angry one who'd almost attacked me—it didn't matter. Their lives were all forfeit for the good of whatever people Gordian would be helping once they were able to formulate the Remedy. I'd killed dozens of unicorns to save the lives of people and livestock. Surely it was no different to kill a few more, even if the people I was saving didn't even know it yet.

Slowly, the presence of more unicorns invaded my senses. I looked up. Blotchy and Jumps stood a few trees away, watching.

Okay, boys, which of you is it going to be?

But they couldn't understand me, and if they could, I doubt they'd be waiting there, drooling over meat I intended to use to lure one of them to his death.

I rose to my feet and began walking back toward the electric boundary, dropping lumps of meat as I went. My plan was to bring the unlucky unicorn as close as possible to the edge of the enclosure before inserting the needle into its vein. I knew how to give injections, but I would need to distract the unicorn long enough to perform the procedure. Even with my magic-enhanced speed, it might be tricky to keep the animal still once I stuck a needle through its thick hide. Unicorns were pretty quick, too.

I cast a glance behind me. Both unicorns followed, snarling at each other as they rushed from one bread crumb of meat to the next. I felt other unicorns emerging around us, drawn in by the scent of food. I grimaced. Great, an audience.

Jumps realized that if he let Blotchy claim the rearmost sausage and ran straight to the next one, by dint of his longer legs, he could jump the line and get most of the food I dropped. He started gaining on me.

Whoever wins loses.

Jumps drew closer and closer. I waited for him near the boundary and when he reached me, I palmed the syringe in one hand and held out a huge lump of meat in the other.

"Here boy," I whispered, tamping down my fear and projecting nothing but comfort on the slim chance that he could feel some of the turmoil in my mind. He leaned in to take the meat from my hand and I closed my fingers around it—hoping he wouldn't choose to overcome that barrier by just biting them off—and slipped my other hand around his neck. He tensed up for a moment, but remained intent on the meat.

As Jumps pulled the last bit of sausage from between my clenched fingers, I slid my pinky through his mane, searching for a vein in his neck. I had to do this quickly. Even now,

Blotchy was catching up to us, nose still buried in the leaves, looking for any forgotten meat.

There. The needle slid in and I tightened my grip on the unicorn as I depressed the plunger.

The einhorn jolted once, and I held on, using the force of his jerks to draw us closer to the line. The unicorn gasped.

Respiratory failure followed by cardiac arrest.

I knew what was happening now. Jumps stumbled to his knees and I followed, holding on with both hands.

"Shhh . . ." I whispered as he twitched then went still. His terror faded like an echo inside my head.

I took a deep breath and straightened. There. Done.

At the edge of the woods, a line of unicorns gathered and watched me, their fathomless eyes filled with reproach.

"I had to," I said to them, and began to drag the body across the line. As I pulled Jumps over the boundary, a shock jolted through us both and I dropped his hooves and fell back onto the ground.

"Ow!"

The other unicorns didn't move, just watched me with interest.

Okay, next time, I'd need to think this through. Rubber gloves, maybe, or simply release the collar before I pull the corpse over the—

Jumps's chest began to rise and fall.

No. That was my imagination. Or maybe some sort of left-over muscle spasm.

He lifted his head, then struggled to push himself to his feet.

"Oh my God," I whispered, still splayed out on the ground.

Jumps took a few staggering steps, horrific choking noises coming from his mouth. His eyes were wide now, rolling in his head so I could see the red sinews that held his eyeballs in place.

But his mind—oh, his mind! Inside his head was nothing at all. No fear, no pain, no thoughts, just a vast black chasm.

"No!" I cried, reeling in horror.

He fixed me with his bloody stare and, gasping, collapsed once more.

As one, the unicorns at the edge of the woods turned from their fallen friend to me.

What had just happened? The unicorn was dead; I could have sworn to it. I saw it die; I felt our link break. Had it been the electric shock, somehow reanimating its heart and nerves?

And yet, the way it had glared at me. . . .

Breathing hard, I crawled toward the body and placed my hands on his neck, searching for a pulse. Nothing. My fingers in front of his nostrils found no breath. And, most of all, the chasm had closed.

My shoulders shuddered and I bowed my head.

Jumps's hoof shot out and kicked me in the stomach. I flew backward and my head slammed hard against the earth. I wheezed and covered my belly with my hands, squeezing my eyes shut in pain.

Just a nerve response. That's all.

And then I heard the worst sound of all, a unicorn scream. It seared through my ears, shrill and desolate, then straight into my brain, where it echoed from a place beyond memory, into instinct no cell in my body could ignore. *Make it stop.*

I rolled to my feet, clutching my aching stomach with one hand and reaching for my knife with the other.

I staggered toward the body of Jumps, which was flailing and grunting, trying to push itself to its feet. It was dying. Again.

"I'm sorry," I said, and slit the unicorn's throat. Blood poured from the wound to soak the leaves around our feet, and the unicorn fixed me once more with its gaze, as black and deep as the void fading from both our minds.

Jumps went limp and I kneeled near his head, burying my face in my bloody hands.

Sometime later, I heard a motor and looked up to see some of the Gordian staffers pulling up outside the fences with a small truck. They stared through the links in horror, speaking to one another in French.

I rose, letting my hair hang in front of my face so they couldn't see the streaks of blood, so I didn't have to look at them. My eyes burned like alicorn venom, but no tears fell. The men came through the outer ring of fences, and the surviving unicorns sprinted back into the woods.

I waited, head bowed over the corpse, until I realized the angry string of French emanating from the one in the white coat was aimed at *me*.

"*Salope Américaine!*" He grabbed my arm, and the unicorns were close enough so that when I shook him off, I knocked him from his feet.

His jaw was slack with shock as he looked up from his spot in the dirt, but I didn't change my expression, just stared at him grimly from beneath my fall of hair, like the blood-spattered girl at the end of a horror film.

He grunted, stood, and started speaking to his companion.

"*Mademoiselle, pardon.*"

I turned my baleful glare to the assistant.

"He says the specimen is ruined. The blood, it was important to keep inside. That is why you were instructed to use the syringe."

"I used the syringe," I snapped. "It didn't work."

As the assistant translated, the scientist snorted and flicked a blood-soaked leaf off his leg.

"It didn't!" I exclaimed in French, turning on him. "He went down, but he kept coming back to life."

The scientist rolled his eyes.

"They have amazing healing powers. You know this," I argued straight at the head scientist. I knew enough French to manage that. "And also, the famous purification ability. Don't you see? I gave him the poison." My French failed here. "He was neutralizing it."

The scientist laughed. This time he didn't go through his assistant but spoke to me in English. "I do not listen to an ignorant child. You know nothing of medicine. Just magic."

The blow hit harder than the unicorn's hoof. I gulped, seeking some sort of response, as the scientist continued his conversation with his assistant.

The younger man translated, "We will need a new specimen."

I shook my head. "Not without shooting or stabbing. I can't get one otherwise."

"We will provide you with another syringe."

I switched back to French. "No. It doesn't work!"

The scientist practically growled at me. "You will do as you are told."

Oh, I would, would I? Not in these woods. I gave a nearly imperceptible shake of my head as unicorns coursed through my veins, wild and free even in this pitiful, dying little forest. I

181

said nothing. I didn't need to.

The scientist and I stared each other down while the assistant wrung his hands. Finally, the scientist cursed and walked off, and the assistant began to lug the corpse toward the gate.

"Hang on," I said. "I'll help you." I leaned over, grabbed my alicorn knife from the puddle of einhorn blood, and wiped it off on the dying grass.

I was so fired.

After depositing the dead einhorn on the flatbed of the cart, I watched the assistant drive away, then limped back up to the château. The scientist had already gone inside, no doubt to tattle to Isabeau about what an intractable bitch I was. *Salope.*

Whatever. At least back at the Cloisters we only killed unicorns that were an immediate threat to ourselves or others.

With difficulty, I made it up the stairs to my room, my abdominal muscles screaming in pain with every step. Now that I was out of range of the einhorns, my superstrength had fled, and I could feel the full power of that kick. I'd be lucky if there was no internal bleeding.

It was the middle of the night back in New York, but I needed to talk to Giovanni right now. I felt hollow and faint, reeling with rage and pain and other feelings I was too scared to attempt to identify. I might wake him up, but he'd done it to me before, too, calling during his evenings, way after bedtime here in the quiet French countryside.

But Giovanni wasn't in bed. Instead of his sleepy voice at the other end of the line, I heard pounding techno music. "Astrid!" Giovanni attempted to yell into the phone.

"Are you at a club?" I asked him. That was unlike him. Last

summer, Giovanni had preferred museums to nightclubs and gelato to alcohol of any kind. Had he fallen off the wagon?

I did the math. It had to be after three A.M. where he was.

"Astrid!" he shouted over the beat. "Now's not the best time!"

"I'm hurt," I sobbed into the phone. "I got kicked by a unicorn today." And that wasn't even the worst part.

"I can't hear you!" he cried. "Can I call you back in the morning?"

I flicked the phone closed and squeezed my eyes shut. Who knew where I'd be by then?

In my posh golden bathroom, I stripped and assessed the damage. A dark bruise was already spreading across my entire torso. Maybe I was hemorrhaging. Maybe when Isabeau came in to fire me, I could ask her to call the hospital. In the meantime, I could enjoy this place while I still had it.

I washed off the blood and put on a loose-fitting dress that wouldn't rub against my waistline, then called Lauren and canceled our lessons for the day. Obviously, if I lost my job I'd no longer enjoy the educational patronage that Gordian was providing. And anyway, I needed to lie down for a while.

I eased myself onto my bed, tugging gently at the hem of the bluish gray silk so my dress wouldn't bunch up beneath me. I rested a hand on my stomach and my head on the lavender-scented feather pillow, and I let my eyes drift close.

I don't know how long it was before there was a soft tap on the door.

"Come in," I rasped without moving. Here it comes. I heard Isabeau's voice, tried to sit up, then cried out as my bruised abdominal muscles activated.

"You're hurt." She rushed over to the bed. "What happened?"

"Got kicked by the einhorn . . ."

"Let me see." I moved my hand and she pulled up the front of my dress. I winced as she softly palpated my stomach. "You need a cold compress for this. And some painkillers. And I will have a doctor come to look at it."

"The same doctor I saw this morning?" I asked, suspicious.

Isabeau straightened. "That man is no longer in my employ."

"What?" I shoved myself up on my elbows. "Why?"

She looked into my eyes. "Astrid, I am going to tell you something and you must listen very carefully. You are *never* to let a man lay a hand on you in anger. Do you understand?"

I bit my lip.

"Yes, I made sure I got a full report."

I talked past the lump in my throat. "But it was my fault. I messed up; I ruined the unicorn—"

"Even if you had," Isabeau said, her face hard as stone, "it would still not be a reason for him to touch you. Nothing would warrant that. But you did not mess up. You tried to follow our directions. There were complications that none of us could have foreseen, and you were faced with a loose unicorn, outside the boundary. It could have endangered everyone in the château, and you protected us. You did your *job*, Astrid."

I gulped, but it was like there was a balloon in my chest, growing bigger and bigger with each of her words. "But what about your research?"

She shrugged. "We face a setback. Obviously we can't risk losing more of the unicorns until we have perfected the euthanasia technique. So that experiment will be put on hold."

"It worked," I said. "At first. But then it's like it came back to life. I was wondering if it had something to do with their rejuvenation ability. Like maybe the blood was neutralizing the poison, even after his heart and lungs had stopped, and . . . I don't know, allowed it to start again. . . ." I trailed off, remembering what the scientist had said about my ignorance.

"It's possible," Isabeau agreed. "In fact, it is very likely that you are correct. We'll have to keep working on the problem. But you must not blame yourself for what happened this morning. We gave you faulty equipment. It was our mistake, and it will not happen again." She smoothed the edge of my dress. "We cannot risk the danger. You're too valuable to us."

I burst into tears, rolling onto my side as carefully as possible and curling my body into a tiny spiral.

"Astrid." The bed dipped, and I felt Isabeau's hand on my arm, the soft fall of her hair on my brow. *"Ne pleure pas, ma petite. Ma petite chère."*

I turned over and wrapped my arms around her waist, laying my head in her lap.

"Shhhhh," she said, stroking my hair. "Don't cry."

But I wanted to cry. I wanted to cry and cry for poor Jumps, and for all the pain in my stomach, and for the fact that Isabeau believed me, that she stood by me, and that she thought I was more important than research that could turn her into a billionaire or even save the world.

After a few moments, the tears passed, but I didn't move, and Isabeau didn't stop caressing my hair.

"I suppose you shouldn't go to your lessons today," she said.

"I've already canceled them." I sniffled.

"Is that so? Well. I will go get you a cold compress, tea, and perhaps some soup? Would you like me to bring you some books? Or maybe a magazine? I have some English ones. I think you should try to rest until we see the extent of the bruising."

I agreed and Isabeau left, returning in short order with an ice pack, some herbal ointment, and a tea made of ginger and stinging nettles. I'd changed into loose pjs and climbed under the covers.

"You'll like this," she said, handing me the mug. I'd quickly learned that when she said that, it usually meant I would most emphatically hate it. Stinging nettles tasted about like you'd imagine—like dirt and leaves brewed in hot water—with the added kick of spice from the ginger.

"Honey?" I choked.

Isabeau laughed. "Drink quickly. It'll help with the bruises. How is the compress?"

I patted it. "Cold. Feels nice."

"You just rest. Here, I brought you something special." She laid a large book on my lap.

"*Hildegard of Bingen: Selected Writings,*" I read. "What happened to British *Vogue*?"

"You'll like this better, Astrid. It's about a medieval nun—"

"A hunter?" I scowled.

"No, a scientist. And a composer and a writer. Hildegard of Bingen was one of the smartest women that ever lived, as a matter of fact. She wrote several books on diagnostics and medicine, including one that talks about unicorns. She ran her own monastery and served as an adviser to popes and kings."

"She had skull-cracking visions and spoke in tongues," I read from the back of the book.

Isabeau smiled. "Well, we don't have a problem with magic

around here. Especially magical nuns."

"I'm not a nun," I said.

There was another knock at the door and Brandt stuck his head in. His arms were filled with a video game console and controllers. "I heard we have an invalid?"

I tossed *Hildegard* aside as he entered, dragging a little cart with a TV perched on top.

"I've only got about ten games." He handed me a controller and a stack of disks. "But I want to see if the unicorns have helped you get any better with first-person shooter."

"The good news is," I said, "I couldn't get much worse." Back home, Brandt used to tease me that I could play only the nonviolent games—the ones where I had to stack blocks or roll things into balls or race cars. But of course, that was before I'd killed anything. Times had changed.

Brandt plugged in the television, hooked up the console, then slipped in a disk. He hopped up beside me, jostling both the tea and the cold compress on my tummy. He fluffed a spare pillow behind his back and handed me a controller. "Okay, hunter. Care to wager?"

I pulled myself into a more upright position and arranged my pillows and compress. "Sure. Five euros?"

"That's all you've got? Isabeau, are you ripping off this poor girl? She's the one taking her life in her hands."

Isabeau folded her arms. "No, you're certainly not a nun, Astrid."

"Fine," I said. "Ten."

As Isabeau made her way to the door, Brandt clicked through to the start menu. "I say we take on some zombies first."

That worked for me, too. After all, I'd already killed one today.

13

WHEREIN ASTRID CONTEMPLATES
THE MEANING OF LOVE

That evening, Giovanni called back.

"Sorry about last night," he said. "It was crazy around here."

"Sounded like it." Brandt was gone by now, and I was still resting in bed, having downed several more cups of Isabeau's herbal remedies as well as a dish of beef stew. "What was going on?"

"It was awesome! Some of my friends organized this giant scavenger hunt. It took us all over the city. We were out all night."

"Is that so?" I asked, skeptical.

He chuckled. "It wasn't like that. The strongest thing I had to drink was espresso."

"Good to hear."

"Jeez, you sound like my mother. So what's up?"

I hesitated, not eager to ruin his good time with tales of euthanasia and bruised ribs. "Nothing. I just miss you. I'm glad you had a good time."

"It was the best. Or," he corrected, "would have been if you'd been here."

I rolled my eyes at that.

"Oh, there was even a unicorn clue. My team was giving me hell over that one. We could have gotten five hundred points for a unicorn bone."

"Oh, that's awful! I could have gotten you one so easily!"

"Yeah, they were furious I didn't bring home any souvenirs from Rome. *Dead* unicorns are rare enough around here that they make the news anytime there is one." He cleared his throat. "We, uh, really need some hunters over here."

"I'm sure Phil and Neil are working on it."

"And your mother. She was on TV again the other day. It's so weird every time the topic comes up at school. We're lucky in the city. To most everyone at school, the unicorns are something that is happening somewhere else, to someone else, but I can't forget that day in the van. I don't know anyone else who has even seen one."

"You know a lot of us," I said.

"Well, you know what I mean. Regular people."

I swallowed. Regular people. Right.

"Are you okay, Astrid? Why did you call me in the middle of the night? Did something happen?"

"Sort of. I killed a unicorn today, and it was—awful. I've just gotten so used to *not* having to do that."

"And I've gotten used to not worrying that I was going to get a call in the middle of the night saying you'd been gored."

"I wasn't gored," I said. "Just kicked. Hard."

"Oh no. Astrid . . ." He whispered a curse into the phone. "And you let me go on about a stupid scavenger hunt?"

189

I toyed with the lace edging my pillow. "It's okay. Isabeau came and took care of me." *And Brandt*, I almost added.

"I'm so sorry," he said. "That sucks, because you really seemed to like this job."

"I still do," I replied. "I've just been spoiled. Today was a bad day—but a bad day here is like every hunting day at the Cloisters." My voice broke.

"Astrid . . ." Giovanni said softly. "Shhh, it's okay. I wish I could hold you."

Him and me both.

"It's just that—" I began. How could I say this to him? Giovanni, who called me Astrid the Warrior and said I was the bravest person he'd ever known. What else could this confession be but cowardice? "It's just that I don't think I'm cut out for killing things."

"I know," came Giovanni's voice, kind and strong and true. "I wouldn't love you if you were."

I turned my face into the pillow and squealed. No wonky Italian this time; the actual L-word. Except, he hadn't said it in a way that would make it easy to respond. I wouldn't love him if . . . if what? I couldn't imagine the scenario.

So maybe I should just say it. For the first time. On the phone.

No. Not on the phone.

"Astrid?" came his voice. Did he even know what he'd just said? "Still there?"

"Yes." My voice sounded breathless. "I—"

"I have to go."

"Oh." My mind raced. "I'll, um, send you an alicorn. You know, if you ever need it for a scavenger hunt again."

He laughed. "Unicorn hunters give the best gifts. Take care, Astrid the Warrior. *Ti voglio bene.*"

And then he was gone.

After several days of Isabeau's doctor-mandated TLC and Brandt's video games (I am happy to relate that I now positively rocked at first-person shooter), the bruise had mostly stopped hurting, and the mark on my belly had faded to a sickly greenish purple. I celebrated my first day back on the job with an extra long walk through the einhorn enclosure, and though I sensed the unicorns enough to do a head count—seventeen and counting—I didn't see a single one.

On my way out of the forest, I swung around the far side of the enclosure—the end that bordered the edge of the Jaeger property and the beginning of the public land. The protesters remained, their tents looking all the more bright and cheery beside the dying greenery. Clotheslines, bikes, folding chairs and tables, and other camping accoutrements lay scattered about the grounds, and the scent of burned meat hung in the misty air. If I could smell it from here, I marveled that the unicorns didn't risk life and limb to burst through both electrified boundary and barbed wire. And I could see, sticking out of the back of one of the protesters' trucks, the piles of signs they wielded every day at the entrance to the château. Though the words were in French, the images were not: gory color photos of the horrible things that happen to animals in laboratories. At one time, they might have made me wince. But I'd seen enough blood and pain by this point that they didn't really bother me, and I doubted they bothered the scientists who committed these acts, either. So who were the signs supposed to affect?

Perhaps they served as some sort of perverse encouragement to the protesters who wielded them. They were certainly devout, leaving family and friends and job to come here and camp day in and day out for the sake of their beliefs.

As I turned to go, I spotted movement from one of the tents. A tall black man slid out and straightened, stretching in the gray dawn light before he spotted me.

I steeled myself for an assault of words I probably wouldn't understand, but instead he raised his hand and waved, cocking his head to the side as if curious.

I waved back.

As he seemed to have no interest in coming closer or shouting to me across the campground, after a moment, I turned away and walked back into the woods.

After my lessons were over that morning, I called the Cloisters.

"Astrid?" Phil answered on the first ring.

"I'm fine." This had become our standard greeting ever since I'd left the Cloisters. No amount of argument about the relative gentleness of the einhorns would sway Phil into believing it was safe for me to be here alone.

"I thought you were our lawyer calling back." Phil's tone brightened. "Yesterday was the most amazing day. One of my letters has actually gotten some attention!"

"We can afford a lawyer?"

"The unicorns can!" Phil said. "She works for the Center for Biological Diversity. It's an environmental foundation devoted to protecting endangered species. They're funded by grants or something. Anyway, she's interested in taking on unicorns."

"Oh," I said. "Great."

"It *is* great," Phil said. "This woman, she's worked with polar bears, she's worked with tigers; she's one of the preeminent lobbyists for wild predators. And that's the great thing about our petition to have unicorns recognized as an endangered species!" You could practically hear Phil beaming all the way from Rome. "Apparently, it's pretty much impossible to get an animal listed as endangered without years and years of scientific research to show they are—especially if they're some random thing like a rock lichen or a clam. It's way easier if it's a big, beautiful animal like a bear or a tiger . . . or a unicorn."

"Even if they'll eat you?" I asked.

"As long as they can put its picture on T-shirts or turn its likeness into stuffed animals, you can get the public on your side. That's what the lawyer said, anyway. And we're in luck, because unicorns have always been so popular. Maybe even more popular than bears!"

"That's . . . great. Really."

"So anyway, she's going to draft a petition to send to the Department of the Interior to add unicorns to the list of endangered species in the United States. Things are really bad over there, especially out west. There was this whole story in the news a few weeks back about some state government getting so worried about a herd of kirin in some canyon somewhere that they dropped napalm on them. Can you believe it?"

Yes. But I wasn't about to say that to Phil.

"And it gets even better. She's also going to put me in touch with people who can do the same with petitioning CITES—"

"Who?"

Phil sighed. "Sorry, you haven't been around. You've missed so much. The Convention on International Trade in Endangered

Species. It's basically the committee that decides on worldwide endangered status for wild animals and plants. I want to make the capture, trade, and cruel treatment of unicorns illegal all over the world."

"Lofty goal," I said.

Phil paused for breath. "And how are you?"

"Oh, you know," I said. "Killing unicorns for pharmaceutical testing."

She laughed. "Well, not much longer if I have my way. Meanwhile, everyone around here is engaged in the same activity, so don't feel too bad."

Far easier said than done. Only, where was I supposed to draw the line? How could it be okay to kill an entire pack of kirin, but not the single zhi we had living in the Cloisters? And maybe I saw the point the protesters were trying to make. Why was it okay to imprison and half starve this herd of einhorns until we were ready to kill them in the name of scientific testing? If Phil got her way, did that mean we wouldn't be allowed to kill any unicorns, even the ones who were about to eat people? Who *had* eaten people?

For all that Isabeau and I liked to imagine that the nobler side of being a unicorn hunter involved the production of the Remedy, I couldn't seem to move past the inscription on Clothilde's sword. TO VANQUISH THE SAVAGE UNICORN. If Phil didn't get things changed soon, we'd vanquish them right back into oblivion.

I needed to stop thinking about this, so I asked, "How's Neil?"

A pause. "Fine. He didn't get that hunter, you know. The American one? And then a week ago, he tried to contact a few more in Sweden and was totally given the brush-off. He's a little down about recruitment at the moment."

Of course, that wasn't what I was asking and Phil knew it.

"And how are you and Neil?" I spelled out.

"We're friends and colleagues," Phil said. "As we've always been."

"And that's all?"

"It's actually quite a lot."

"But is it enough?"

"Drop it, Astroturf." After a moment, her tone returned to normal. "So how are your classes? Are you learning lots?"

We talked about school for a while. Phil remained undecided about whether she planned to return to college the following semester or risk losing her scholarship and take the entire year off for her Save the Unicorn crusade. She'd also decided to switch her major from Media Studies to Biology and Public Policy. "If I do manage to pull off any movement on the unicorn front, I'll probably be able to score an academic scholarship or grant, so Dad won't kill me for getting kicked off the team."

"But Phil," I said, "don't you want to play volleyball anymore?"

"Of course I do," she said. "But that doesn't mean there aren't more important things for me to be doing right now. Come on, Asterisk, you know that better than anyone."

I said nothing.

"So how are things there other than classes? Isn't it lonely?"

"Well, I don't have to share a bathroom with ten other girls, if that's what you mean."

"There are seven hunters left here, Astrid. And that's when no one's out with an injury, too. Not exactly a full lineup."

Was she asking me to come back?

"Who do you hang out with over there?" she asked. "Brandt Ellison?"

"Sometimes," I said. Actually, pretty regularly the last few days.

"Is he any less of a cretin than he was back home?"

"Well, I never thought he was a cretin, remember?" I replied. "I was dating him."

"If I recall correctly, you were simultaneously dating him *and* thinking he was a cretin. The two aren't mutually exclusive."

"Well, he's decidedly less cretinous when your relationship is utterly platonic," I said. "Like the other day, I was hurt and he was really sweet, bringing me some video games and—"

"Wait. Asteroid, you were hurt? What happened? Why didn't you call me?"

I explained what had happened when I'd tried to euthanize the einhorn.

"I don't like this. Not at all. I'm really sketched out by the idea that you don't have any backup out there. I would never send a hunter out alone."

"Honestly, aside from this one instance, it's the most boring job in the world."

"One instance could have meant your life. What if, instead of kicking you, that unicorn had bitten off your hand? Or your head?"

"Einhorns aren't big enough to bite off my head."

"Not the point, Astroturf." Phil was quiet for a moment. "I'm going to talk to Neil. We might have to call this Jaeger woman and see if we can send another hunter out there to assist you."

"You were just complaining how few you have left at the

Cloisters!" I cried. "And you want to reduce the numbers even further?"

"I want to keep you safe, yes," was Phil's only response. "However that comes about."

"I *am* safe," I argued. "The other day was an anomaly, and Isabeau has assured me that nothing like that will happen again. Phil, you have no idea how easy it is here. I don't need backup. These unicorns—they're utterly trapped. Between the electric collars and the fences, they're practically domesticated. They're actually pathetic in a lot of ways—skin and bones. They don't look healthy enough to escape even if there weren't barriers."

"Really?" Phil asked. "That's terrible. Do you think you could take some pictures? I know the lawyer would love to see exactly what kind of cruelty the unicorns are facing."

I was pretty sure that would be a breach of my contract with Gordian. "They aren't being cruel! There's plenty of food, and the enclosure's very nice. Unicorns just don't take well to captivity, that's all."

"Bonegrinder's doing fine," Phil said.

I grimaced. That was my argument. "Einhorn are different."

"What does the vet say?"

"Vets are a tricky prospect with unicorns, given the danger and their inherent resistance to sedatives. Still, I think I can help a vet with getting them diagnosed and if he has to give them shots."

"You haven't yet?" Phil exclaimed. "Where is my wannabe doctor cousin! Asteroid, I'm shocked."

And perhaps she was right to be. Most of the unicorns I knew were wild, and if any suffered from health issues, it hadn't mattered. After all, the point was for me to kill them. Bonegrinder seemed healthy enough—she'd never been to a vet or received any kind of vaccination, but then again, there weren't any laws regarding the licensing of a pet unicorn, either.

But there must be laws regarding the welfare of animals used in scientific testing. The captors needed to be held accountable that none of the creatures under their care suffered needlessly. I would bring that up with Isabeau the next time I saw her.

Except her secretary, Jean-Jacques, informed me that Isabeau was away on business until the following morning. In the afternoon, I did my homework, checked on the unicorns again, and in a fit of entirely unexpected homesickness for Rome, made spaghetti for dinner.

No, I didn't miss the Cloisters. But I missed Lucia's cooking, and I missed Cory, and I really, really missed Phil.

Without Isabeau around, and with Brandt on his usual nightly excursions to who knew where, the château turned into a ghost town, haunted by the two pale wraiths of Gog and Magog, who wandered, graceful as einhorns, from room to room in search of their mistress. I watched them skulk around while I ate my dinner. A few times, they gave me a perfunctory sniff, as if making sure that I wasn't hiding Isabeau under my shirt along with her herbal, bruise-reducing ointments. Though the dogs had never been particularly unfriendly to me, they cared about no one and nothing except for Isabeau. Not exactly hornless Bonegrinders, despite their shaggy white fur and long legs.

I missed Bonegrinder, too. It would likely take a while for the einhorns to trust me after the euthanasia disaster. If they ever deigned to come near me again, that was.

After dinner, I headed back into my room and tried to

decide how best to entertain myself for the evening. There was that Hildegard book, which I'd cracked, read the part where she recommends that you travel faster with shoes made from unicorn hide, and tossed it aside. Brandt had left me with his video games, which might help pass the time. Or I could call Giovanni. Again.

I hadn't heard from him since he'd accidentally blurted out the L word. Was he regretting saying it? Was he avoiding me? He'd gotten off the phone quickly enough afterward, as if terrified I'd call him on it. I'd left him two messages in the past two days that he hadn't yet returned, and I loathed the idea of becoming that needy girlfriend who left strings of messages on his phone.

I dialed his number. After a few rings, it went to voice mail. "Hey, Giovanni. It's me. It's just really quiet and boring around here tonight, and I miss you. Give me a call if you get a chance."

There. That was light and easy. I didn't sound desperate or pathetic or clingy.

Except, maybe a little too disinterested? Like I only called him when I was bored? I didn't want him to think that. I was sure that over in New York, there were dozens of cute coeds who found him absolutely fascinating, who wanted Giovanni to whisper sweet Italian nothings in their ears, who would never for a second weigh the pleasures of a video game or the writings of a medieval German nun against even the most casual chat.

Girls who he didn't have to say he loved over the phone from three thousand miles away.

Did he even mean it? It had kind of slipped out. Not, "Astrid, I love you," but part of something else. Granted, it had been

199

part of the most beautiful thing that anyone had ever said to me. What did it matter if he'd said the words or not when he so obviously meant them?

Meant them, and then didn't call me back for days.

Maybe I should call back, make it clear that I really did want to talk to him. Though, that's what I'd done in my last voice mail.

And where was he, anyway? If you counted back the hours it was—okay, it was about three P.M. He was probably in class with the ringer turned off. I plopped on the bed. Long-distance relationships really sucked. I wondered if he ever sat around like this, counting up the possible and terrifying reasons that I hadn't returned his messages, or if that kind of worry was of strictly female provenance.

Naturally, because I *returned* his calls! I lived for them. I hated coming back from a visit with the unicorns to find that I'd missed a chance to speak to Giovanni. He never had to spend a minute worrying that I wouldn't call him back, that I was entertaining some other boy, that I was out doing something really fun without him, and didn't care. He knew my life. Unicorns, school, bed. How fortunate for him that his girlfriend wasn't halfway across the world in a city famous for never sleeping. That she was shut up in a sleepy French village, in a remote and lonely château that, except for the clothing options, might as well be an Italian nunnery.

I picked up a controller and cued up the video game where I got to shoot zombies. This would do for passing the time. Besides, there was so much pleasure in killing things that exploded into tiny red pixels instead of actual blood. It made for a nice change.

Sometime later, there was a knock on the door and Brandt poked his head in. He checked out my indecently high score on the screen then whistled. "I'm afraid I've created a monster."

I paused the action. "Hey, what's up?"

"Nothing. I was going swimming downstairs and wondered if you wanted to come along."

Swimming. Now there was a novel thought. Isabeau had shown me the indoor pool beneath the ground floor on my first day here, as well as insisting that I purchase a bathing suit on our shopping trip, but I had yet to take advantage of them. "Sure," I said. "I'll grab my suit."

Brandt smiled. "See you down there."

After he was gone, I changed into the suit I'd bought. It was a plain navy tank suit with a white trim along the neckline, slim straps, and a scooped back that I didn't realize framed my enormous back scar until I was standing before my bathroom mirror and picking out a towel.

The scar shone, as dark red and shiny as if I'd never taken care of it. Not true. All the hunters worked on their scars, lavishing them with cocoa butter and vitamin E and every other treatment designed to reduce the appearance of scar tissue. Nothing worked. My other scars were small, though. The one on my back was a traffic-stopper.

I loosed the elastic on my hair and shook out my braid, allowing my hair to drop over my back like a curtain. There, that would help.

I wrapped myself in a short white robe, tied the belt around my waist, grabbed a towel, and slipped my feet into an unlaced pair of sneakers. Perhaps I should buy flip-flops next time I was out, that is if Brandt and I were going to

201

make a pool date a regular thing.

No, not a date. A pool rendezvous. No, that was even worse! A pool . . . *outing*. Or inning, since it was right here in the château.

I started toward the door, but stopped when I heard a buzz from my phone. I unearthed it from my bedcovers and checked the display. A missed call from Giovanni. He must have called back while I'd been changing and I hadn't heard the phone in the bathroom.

I hesitated, standing there in my suit and wrap, with my towel slung over my arm. If I called him back now, we'd get in a long conversation, and I'd miss the swim. However, I could call him back after the swim. It was much earlier in the States. There'd be plenty of time, and I'd still manage to have some fun tonight.

I dropped the phone to the bed. Let Giovanni be the one to wait and wonder for once.

14

Wherein Astrid Crosses the Line

†

The pool room at the château was tiled and misty with chlorine-scented air. Brandt had left the overhead lights off, so the entire room was lit with a pale blue glow from the pool lights shining up from beneath the water. Some sort of dance music pulsed through the space, competing with the sound of water lapping against the steps. Brandt was swimming laps, his strong arms churning through the water with swift, powerful strokes. Back home, when we'd been dating, I'd actually attended a few of his swim meets. I'd sat in bleachers for hours to watch him swim for five minutes and fifty-four point ninety-one seconds, during which I'd see the occasional arm or leg and a whole lot of splashing. According to the newspapers and our high school's sports program, Brandt was very good. Hadn't made it any more fun to watch.

He surfaced near the edge and grinned at me. "Hey there!"

I dropped my towel on a bench and started to untie the belt of my wrap. He pulled himself out of the pool and went to turn down the volume on the stereo. Droplets of water ran in streams over his shoulders and down his bare back. I glanced at his leg, where his alicorn scar stood out against his skin.

He caught me staring. "Yeah. My claim to fame." He pointed at my arm. "I see you've got a few as well."

I put my hands behind my back and fanned out the base of my hair to make sure my largest scar remained covered. "Professional hazard."

He smirked. "One of many?"

I blushed, then waited until he dove in the pool to follow him.

"So," he said, settling into a lazy backstroke, "tell me for real. How are you enjoying working for Isabeau?"

I swam after him. "What do you mean? I love it."

He looked skeptical.

"I do!" I swept up alongside him. "You have no idea what it was like for me before I came here. Not knowing if I was going to survive from day to day, not knowing if I'd ever even finish high school! I feel like I was in a war and I've been pulled out of the hot zone and given a cushy desk job. I love it."

We'd reached the other side of the pool now, and Brandt grabbed hold of the ledge, then pushed his feet against it, ready to push off. "I guess I never thought of it like that," he said, and shoved away.

I finished my lap and rushed after him.

"I suppose this is relaxing, comparatively."

"And luxurious," I added. "My own room, my own bathroom, my own tutors!"

Brandt laughed as he reached the far end many strokes ahead of me. "You're the only girl I know, Astrid, who considers more attention from your teachers to be a luxury." He tugged my hair softly as he went by. "Goody two-shoes."

I didn't finish the lap or chase after him, but set my feet down on the bottom of the pool and waved my hands through the water, watching him pull himself effortlessly through lap after lap.

"I like school," I said with a shrug. "Much better than killing things. Science was always my thing, remember? You had swimming, Phil had volleyball. I had school."

"Not anymore." He stopped a few feet away and mimed aiming a bow at me. "You're ten times more athletic than I am now, Astrid."

I looked away. "That's different. It's magic."

"And you don't practice anyway?" He reached forward and squeezed one of my biceps. "These muscles are magic?"

I twisted away, crossing my arms over my chest and spinning in the water until I no longer faced him. "These muscles are gross."

"Well, I'm jealous of them. I'd need a personal trainer—oh my God."

The ends of my hair floated in front of me on the surface of the water. My back was completely exposed. Oops.

"Astrid," he whispered, and then I felt his palm press flat against the scar.

A sensation akin to electric shock shot through the twisted marks everywhere his skin touched mine, and yet, I did not pull away. There was something else there—something familiar.

"What happened to you?"

"What do you think?" I mumbled.

"I've never seen an alicorn scar like this."

I turned my head to cast him a glance over my shoulder. "Yes, well, this is what happens when you get run through. When a kirin decides to skewer you like a human kebab and carry you off like a trophy. This is what happens when you should be dead, immunity to alicorn poisoning or no." I pushed off from the bottom and swam away from Brandt, away from his touch, away from the look of pity in his eyes.

"Astrid, wait up!" And because he was so very much faster than me, I had barely reached the wall when his arms caged me in on either side. "I didn't know what happened to you. I'm sorry if I was being flippant about the whole hunter thing. You're right. Once you've been through that, I imagine life here feels really peaceful. And about the scar—I didn't mean to make you self-conscious about it."

He held my gaze, his eyes as brightly blue as the pool water glowing all around us.

"It's all right." I reached for the wall to steady myself, expecting him to push off for another lap. But he didn't move.

"It's hard," he whispered, so softly I almost didn't hear him over the tiny waves lapping at the ledge. "To be so close, to have this glimpse of what it is to be a hunter, but never to truly understand. . . ."

I swallowed. "What do you mean?"

"The things you see, the way you feel them. I can almost touch it. I feel a twinge sometimes, in my leg, when they're near."

"Really?" Our legs bumped against each other under the water, but he still didn't move back.

"Sort of. Like déjà vu, almost. Like a memory you can't quite reach. A sound you can't quite hear."

It was hard for me to hear any sounds at the moment, with the way my blood seemed to be pounding in my ears. Brandt *knew*? He knew what I felt out there in the woods sometimes?

His eyes never left my face, blue and burning. "I've never told them that before," he said. "I couldn't imagine them understanding. Not like you."

"Oh," I replied, for it was the only thing that seemed to fit.

"Because we've been through so much together," he said. "Back at home, with the attack, and how you saved my life. How you *changed* my life. And now, here in France."

I said nothing, because on that night in the woods back home, both of our lives changed. His for the better; mine for the worse.

"Things are so weird now. We're so far from home. And the other day, sitting around playing video games with you—it felt like old times. It felt like *home*."

I gave him a weak smile. "Yeah, it did."

"Even though we're both caught up in this search for the Remedy. In this quest to change the world."

When he put it like that, my doubts about the captive einhorns melted away. We were working for the greater good. Had the einhorns been free they'd be nothing more than a target for my arrows. Here at the château, their suffering might lead to a major medical breakthrough. To saving thousands of people's lives.

"And I wonder," he went on. "With your boyfriend . . ."

I steeled myself for whatever he was about to say. "What about him?" I asked.

"Nothing." He looked down, his eyelashes shading his gorgeous eyes.

"Liar." It came out like a challenge.

A challenge Brandt was more than willing to take. His elbows bent and he leaned in, pressing me between his body and the pool ledge. "I wonder"—he breathed in my ear—"if he can possibly understand you the way I do."

I caught my breath, pinned there with him, with the sensation of his flesh against mine like the touch of a brand.

"Does he know—what it's like?" he whispered.

Yes. I tell him. At least, I try. I nodded, weakly.

"He can't. How can he know what it feels like, to have that poison in your veins? To taste death in your mouth, to come so close, and then the Remedy—the magic—comes burning through, and everything"—he lifted his head and met my eyes—"everything becomes completely clear."

I shivered.

"Astrid," he murmured, closing his hands at the ledge behind my head. "Please." His cheek rested against mine, his breath hot on my throat.

Except "please" was what I wanted to say, too. *Please, move away. Please, this is very confusing. Please, touch me some more.*

Sensations flooded through me: the sound of water all around us, the currents tangling our legs together beneath the surface, Brandt's jaw sliding against my face, the rush of the blood in my ears, and the beat of his heart against my sternum, and over it all, the strong scent of chlorine, stronger than any chamomile, a cloud so thick no unicorn could penetrate it.

But a siren could. Alarms rang out from every corner of the room, echoing off the tiles and shuddering over the surface of the water.

"What's that?" I said.

"It's a breach." Brandt's face turned hard. "The electronic barrier around the einhorns is down."

I ducked under his arm and pulled myself onto the ledge. Water poured off me in rivulets as I sprinted for my shoes. My short white cover-up clung to my wet form as I wrapped it around my body and headed out the door.

Brandt hurried behind me, but he wasn't as good at running in his flip-flops. I dashed up the stairs and out the back door, pausing only for a moment to grab my alicorn knife from its holster near the door.

"Be careful!" He puffed.

"Stay back!" I cried, and slammed the door in his face. Immunity or not, I didn't need him out here if there were loose unicorns about.

The alarms were even louder out here, an air raid siren set to full blast. As I raced around the edge of the greenhouse, my damp feet sliding in my unlaced sneakers, I could feel the einhorns. The sirens had scared them, and they were flitting around inside the woods, still contained by the fences, but for how long?

The full moon shone brightly on the misty grass, which was slick and silver with an early dew. At the edge of the lawn lay the fence, and as my unicorn senses expanded, I could make out every link in the chain, its shadowed diamonds fragmenting the forest beyond. I skidded to a stop by the gate and gasped. Someone had smashed the lockbox and yanked out the wires. The electric boundary was down, all right, and so was the lock on the gate.

Brandt came running up now, and behind him, panting and lugging a toolbox, was Isabeau's secretary, Jean-Jacques.

I whirled to face them, and the unicorn magic made them seem sluggish. I saw their mouths drop open in slow motion as they noticed my speed. Brandt was still wearing his wet bathing suit, but he'd pulled on both a shirt and his leather jacket to protect him from the cold night air. I couldn't even feel the temperature beneath the rush of fire in my veins.

"I said stay inside!"

Jean-Jacques set the box on the ground and flipped open the lid. He pulled out a giant flashlight and spoke to Brandt.

"He's here to fix the electronic boundary," Brandt translated.

"He's taking his life in his hands," I said. "As are you. Now, help me get over the fence."

"The fence?" Brandt raised his eyebrows. "The one with all the barbed wire on top?" He glanced down at my wrap, which ended mid-thigh. "You sure?"

"Yes." I tugged on his sleeve. "Take this off. I'll throw it over the wire."

He glanced at the top of the fence, almost fifteen feet above our heads. "What if you miss?"

I fixed him with a glare.

"Right. Superpowers." He slid off his jacket and handed it to me. "Try not to get too many holes in it."

"At the moment," I said, tossing the jacket over the fence, where it landed perfectly, "I'm trying not to get too many holes in you. Boost me up."

"Boost you all the way up there?" Brandt shook his head. "Impossible."

"Boost me," I repeated. "Then get out of here."

He shrugged. "Fine." He interlaced his fingers and knelt,

holding his hands out to me.

I stepped in his palms, and as he stood, pushing me up, I leaped.

As it turned out, we didn't need the jacket after all. The bottom of my sneakers touched lightly on the leather as I vaulted the fence then landed softly on the grass on the other side.

The sense of unicorns roaring through my veins, I glanced back at the men. Jean-Jacques had paused in his work to gape at me in awe. Brandt wore a similar expression.

"It *is* different with a trained hunter," I heard him whisper as I ran off.

The unicorns sensed my presence and began zigzagging through the forest, jumping and racing over roots and branches, only half aware that their world had just gotten ever so slightly bigger. If they dared to test the boundaries, I was done for. If I could jump over the fence, it would never hold a unicorn.

I raced around the side of the woods, sticking close to the tiny plastic flags marking the electric boundary and watching for any signs that a unicorn had broken past. Inside the woods, they were moving too swiftly to get a head count. Here and there I felt the familiar thoughts of the ones I knew—Fats and Stretch, Tongue and Blotchy—each running, awoken by the sirens and unsure of their meaning. My presence was doing nothing to calm them down.

My wrap flapped against the top of my thighs as I sprinted through the edge of the forest, leaping over fallen branches and ducking under tree limbs. My damp hair whipped against my face and I wondered if this was what it felt like to be a real huntress of Diana, running wild beneath the moonlight in a little white toga, weapon in hand, prey loose in the woods.

Though it was doubtful that ancient, mythological hunting parties wore sneakers.

On the other side of the fence, the protesters' camp came into view. With my unicorn-hunting senses at full tilt, the people running from tent to tent with their flashlights looked like sleepwalkers—ridiculously slow and clumsy.

It must have been one of them who'd sneaked onto the property and destroyed the electronics.

"You morons!" I shouted, though I doubted any of them spoke English. "You're going to get yourselves killed!"

One of the men turned, and I recognized him from that morning. He stared at me, and unlike all the others, he did not seem awed by my speed, by the magic coursing through my body. He regarded me steadily, without curiosity, without surprise. Was this the idiot who'd smashed the power box?

"Did you hear me?" I screamed.

"Behind you," he replied calmly.

I whirled to see a unicorn charging out of the woods and straight at me, its movements masked by the jumble of the others' terrified emotions. Its feet flew in slow motion—one step, two—galloping toward the boundary with no fear and no hesitation. It knew there'd be no resistance, no shock. And then it would leap over the fence and freedom, sweet freedom. . . .

I drew my knife. *Stop*, I commanded the unicorn in my head.

It rushed forward.

I pulled back my arm to throw. *Stop!*

It lowered its head, horn aimed at me, still running.

The knife flew from my hands.

The unicorn reared back on two legs, screaming, the knife

stuck hard in her foreleg.

"Shhh," I said, running to meet the wounded unicorn. It wasn't a fatal blow, but an incision with an alicorn knife wouldn't heal the way a regular wound would. *Shhh*, I repeated into her mind.

Miracle of miracles, the unicorn quieted and stopped rearing. She limped a few feet toward me, grunting softly, and I put my hand on her neck, patting softly to distract her as I pulled the knife from her flesh.

Her pain rocketed through both of us and we staggered together. I put my hand over the wound to try to stem the flow of blood. Had it been a mistake to remove the knife? Would she die of blood loss? I'd purposely tried to miss any vital parts.

There was a soft thump behind me and I spun around. The protester stood on the other side of the fence, pointing to a spot in the grass. I looked down.

A small plastic case with a red cross on the cover. A first aid kit. I raised my eyes to the protester, who touched his fingers to his brow, then turned and walked away.

I snatched up the case and returned to the einhorn, who was limping around on her bad leg.

"Hold still," I said, and yanked out some absorbent pads and an elastic bandage. Now I was patching up a unicorn!

The unicorn stopped stumbling and remained calm.

"Ah, so now you listen like a zhi, huh? Is that all I have to do, threaten you with death?"

The unicorn looked at me with terror-filled eyes, but didn't flinch when I touched her leg. Her thoughts radiated fear and pain and a sort of bafflement that, despite the fact I'd just stabbed her, I meant her no real harm.

"This is what happens when you try to make a break for it," I explained to my little man-eating friend.

Breaker nudged me with her nose.

I put pressure on the wound until the blood flow slowed, then got some gauze pads and packed them against the incision, wrapping tightly around the unicorn's leg with the bandage. Short of stitches, this would be the best I could do. I fastened the bandage with metal clips, then put my hands lightly on the unicorn's leg, bending and moving it to make sure that she couldn't dislodge the bandage while running.

It was then that I felt them. Awe, rising like a giant bubble, growing to push out every other emotion: all the pain and the fear, and the curiosity, and the excitement engendered by the alarms. I raised my head and saw we were surrounded by a circle of unicorns. There were Stretch and Blotchy and Tongue and Fats, there was the angry one I'd seen the day I killed Jumps, and some other unicorns I had caught only glimpses of—old, young, healthy, starving, standing around me like pale ghosts in the moonlight, staring at me with their fathomless black eyes, their white bodies sleek and solid but for the dark, dead collars at each of their throats. Breaker's blood felt sticky between my fingers and I balled my hands into fists at my side. The unicorns didn't move, just stared at me as a group, as one. I felt tiny points of pressure at the edge of my mind, as if they were leaning into it, separated from actually hearing me, from actually communicating with me, by the thinnest membrane of misunderstanding and mistrust.

I took a deep breath and thought of everything soothing. Full bellies and quiet glades, grass cooled by evening dew and large shadowy dens beneath the roots of great trees. A moon that lit up the sky and meat still warm with the blood of a beating heart.

The unicorns came closer. They *listened*.

A mother's fur, the scent of fire and flood, a caress from the hand of a hunter, her softly shadowed thoughts pushing all the fear from your brain . . .

As one, the unicorns bowed before me, touching their horns to the earth, and I released my hands. I was a goddess. I was Diana, the Huntress, the Mistress of the Animals.

One by one, the lights on their collars blinked back to life.

15

WHEREIN ASTRID TESTS THE LIMITS

†

I spent the night in the enclosure, just to make sure there were no unexpected occurrences. Brandt brought me dry clothes and blankets and I huddled inside them, knees drawn up to my chest, staring across the electric boundary at the château and wondering what in the world had happened that night.

Who was I? Was I a unicorn hunter? Was I some kind of magical unicorn homing signal? Was I a horrible, faithless girl who was about to make out with my ex-boyfriend while my current boyfriend left messages on my voice mail? And if I was this last one, how was I planning to crawl my way back? Was I supposed to tell Giovanni what had happened—though nothing had, actually, happened? Was I supposed to just push it all out of my head? Was I supposed to never get near Brandt again? These were the types of things I'd probably know if I had any real experience with boys; if I hadn't been living in a convent; if my only two relationships hadn't been with boys whose lives I'd saved from the vicious killer unicorns *I* was responsible for drawing in to begin with.

Last night, Brandt had almost made sense to me. Being with him in my room, in the pool, it almost felt like the old days. Neither of us could ever go back, but he knew me well, an Astrid who'd never been a warrior, and he'd liked that girl enough to date her back home. And now that he knew me this way, he still seemed to like me. And he was up to his neck in my new world as well, graced with the same scars, working toward the same goal, in whatever weird way Gordian managed to find a use for him. Whenever I was lucky enough to get Giovanni on the phone, I listened to him talk about his life in New York: his classes and his friends and his all-night scavenger hunts. It seemed so alien from my world. And how could I bring up unicorns in that context?

How could I make him understand what it felt like to live here, among them? How could I tell him that I'd come to long for the scent of fire and flood, to reach out to the unicorns, to pry into their minds just to get a taste of the wildness that nothing, not even electric boundaries and razor-topped fences, could touch?

I could stand in the moonlight and make an entire pack of venomous monsters bow before me. How was I going to explain that to Giovanni? At best, he'd respond with a vague "cool," or say he was proud of me, but not really understand what I meant. At worst . . .

I knew what the at-worst would be, because I felt it, too. At worst, he'd ask what kind of sad, sick individual I'd become to manipulate a bunch of weak, captive unicorns in that way. I was pretty much one step up from a lion tamer with a chair and a whip. These weren't my pets, these weren't zhi; they were wild. Even in captivity, they were the wildest animals I'd ever known, and yet I was making them perform for me like dogs on leashes.

Because I could.

I curled myself into an even tighter ball.

In the dream, Bucephalus called to me in the voice of Giovanni. Somehow, with the sort of logic that only made sense in a dream, I knew it was Bucephalus who spoke, though it sounded like my boyfriend. He was angry, furious that I'd broken our end of the deal.

I wasn't quite sure what deal he was talking about.

His anger pulsated through my mind, drawing me in like the flickering signal from a lighthouse. I was searching for him, stumbling through a tangled wood, my feet catching on roots and vines determined to stand in my way. Here and there I saw a flash of einhorn disappearing into the woods. Even they ran from the wrath of a karkadann. And yet, I drew closer.

Where are you! I called to him. *Where have you been!*

But he was too angry to respond.

The wood in the dream suddenly gave way to a clearing bathed in moonlight, and I stopped short in recognition. It was the garden outside the Borghese museum, the spot where I'd first kissed Giovanni. The place where I'd first met the karkadann.

Bucephalus was there, as massive and deadly as always. In the voice of Giovanni, he spoke.

This is what you wanted.

No, it wasn't. I tried to tell him, but he didn't understand justice in human terms. He didn't know how we did things today. Giant, three-thousand-year-old monsters could do as they pleased.

The karkadann stepped aside, and there, on the ground near his hooves, lay the body of a young man, his face bathed in blood.

It was Brandt.

The next thing I remember was the feeling of dew on my face and Isabeau's voice in my ear.

"Astrid? Wake up. It's morning and all the unicorns are safe."

I blinked my eyes open and pushed myself off the ground on my elbow. There was a crick in my neck, and I could feel the grit of dirt on my cheek. Isabeau looked crisp and fresh in a starched suit, with pearls at her throat and her hair falling in a sleek black wave.

"Rise and shine, my unicorn hunter!" Isabeau laughed. "You are a dedicated employee, *chère*, but there is no reason to sleep in the dirt like a dog."

I shoved myself to my feet, wincing at the stiffness in my body. "There was sabotage—"

Isabeau clucked her tongue. "I have heard all there was, and I shall be dealing with it. And I thank you for your service above and beyond the call of duty. Now, you should go inside and clean yourself up. You have class in the city today, no?"

I did, but man I was sore. All I wanted was a long soak and then maybe to nap in my real bed. I stretched.

She watched me trying to roll out my shoulders and shook her head, as if reading my thoughts. "Astrid, you *do* have class in the city today. I will have to insist upon it. Your injury has already put you behind on your studies. This job is important, but so is your education."

This job was the only reason I was getting an education. If the unicorns had escaped last night, if they'd killed someone, then my being here would be proved utterly useless, and I'd have to leave it all. Leave my tutor and my gorgeous suite, leave the chemistry lab in Limoges and the herd of einhorns I was coming to know well. Leave Isabeau. Leave Brandt.

That last bit might not be a bad idea.

"Thank you," I said. "You've been really outrageously good to me."

"The only thing outrageous," she replied, "is that you think such things are anything other than common human decency. I want to find the Remedy, but not at the expense of your safety or your future. You will have a life after your unicorn-hunting days are over, Astrid. I insist upon that, as well."

I looked down, not sure of how to respond.

"Come, let's get you cleaned up and dressed. A coffee, a pastry—you'll feel much better."

She put her arm around me and led me out of the enclosure and up toward the house. We parted at the stairs, but I still said nothing, and as I returned to my room and got in my gorgeous marble bath, I couldn't shake the feeling that I'd just been reprimanded by a parent.

Still, she was right. I'd missed a few classes after the unicorn had kicked me. It was time to get serious again.

Isabeau's driver took me to Limoges, waited while I attended my lab sessions, then took me home and dropped me off in front of the château when I finished.

I began to head upstairs to change, when Jean-Jacques stopped me. "*Mademoiselle*, Madame Jaeger would like to see you in the garden."

"Is something wrong with the fence again?" Had the power gone down while I'd been away? I about-faced and started rushing back down the stairs.

"No, no. She would like to show you something. And also, last night. I want to say, eh, *merci, Mademoiselle. Je n'ai pas peur quand vous êtes ici.*" *I do not fear the unicorns when you are here.*

I smiled. "*Merci*, Jean-Jacques."

Behind the house, on the green lawn that stretched between the greenhouse and the unicorn enclosure, Isabeau stood, a bow in her hands. "Astrid!" she called gaily, waving me over. There was a large target set up near the edge of the lawn and a sheaf of arrows in a brand-new quiver. "Surprise!"

I took the steps off the patio into the grass, the heels of my boots sinking into the turf.

"I know it is not the ancient bows you are used to," she said, "but look!" She handed me the quiver. I pulled out one of the carbon arrow shafts, but instead of being tipped with a practice point or even a barbed alloy hunting point, I saw the telltale gray of a bone chip. Grace would drool over these. They were so much nicer than her homemade attempts.

"I had them made from the alicorn of one of the dead einhorns," Isabeau exclaimed. "A weapons maker in Orleans. Aren't they lovely?"

"Exquisite," I said, tapping my finger lightly against the tip. Sharp. "You want me to use them? You want me to kill the whole herd?"

"No!" Isabeau looked shocked. "I want you to have practice. You haven't used a bow since you've been here. I thought you might miss it. There are practice tips as well, see?" She pointed to a box holding extra points, fletching, and nocks. "And then, if you need to use the bow for real sometime, we have it here. You will not be restricted to your knife, as you were last night."

"Thank you," I said.

Isabeau frowned. "You don't like them."

"I do," I said. "And you're right, I have missed my archery."

Isabeau stepped back. "Try it! I would love to see you shoot."

I shrugged and screwed off the alicorn tips of several arrows, replacing them with practice points. Then I shouldered the bow and picked my way across the lawn until I'd reached the far edge. I took aim and fired. One, two, three arrows, directly into the center of the target. I shot four more into the cardinal points within the pencil-drawn lines of the outermost circle. Then I returned to Isabeau.

"Perhaps," she said wryly, "you don't need the practice after all."

"The unicorns are right there," I said. "I can shoot whatever you'd like."

"I'm certain any university would like to have you on their archery team."

"Yes, as long as they don't mind keeping a zhi around as a team mascot." Actually, that wasn't entirely true. With all my experience, I was a pretty good shot even without the magic. "But thank you for the gift. They're beautiful." I fingered the box of alicorn points. "Actually, you know where these would really come in handy?"

"*Bien sûr*, Astrid. I have already sent a set to the Cloisters."

I smiled.

"Holy crap, Astrid!" Brandt came dashing across the patio. "I saw you from my room. That was outrageous! Do it again!"

Isabeau's mouth formed a thin line. "She's not a circus

performer here to do tricks for you, Brandt."

He ignored her. "Come on, Astrid." He yanked the arrows out of the target. "Do a star pattern. Or a B. Can you write my name in arrows?" His blue eyes bright with anticipation, he held out the shafts.

"Enough, Brandt!" At the sound of Isabeau's rebuke, Brandt's hand dropped, his smile faded.

"Busted," he whispered, then winked. He turned to face Isabeau. "You're a real killjoy, you know that?"

"And you are a disobedient employee and a willful child."

"A child, huh? Is that how you think of me, boss lady? Interesting. Never would have guessed that."

"Enough," she said coldly.

"Or is it really just that you think of *her* as a child?" Brandt cocked his thumb at me. "*Your* child."

I clutched the gorgeous quiver, torn between running to Isabeau's defense and wondering if Brandt had a point.

"I said *enough*." Isabeau's voice had turned dangerous, as icy as the time she'd told me never to let a man hit me.

"Brandt," I said, "come on. Isabeau takes good care of both of us. You know she does. And of course we're still children. She's aware of that. That's why she's making sure we go to school and—" I reached out and touched his shoulder and he whirled to face me, his grin back, his eyes almost wild.

For a second I thought he was going to grab me, but he didn't. He just stared at me in a way that sent a flush all the way into the toes of my new boots. "Hey, Astrid," he said in a tone of false casualness. "You want to go swimming again later?"

I flushed deeper, and then, without waiting for an answer, he strode off.

A few moments of silence passed, stretched longer by the nearness of the einhorns in their enclosure. I could feel the way the wind twisted every leaf on the trees, could hear the elevated rate of Isabeau's heartbeat. She was afraid.

I swallowed. "I'm not sure what just happened here."

She shook her head and plastered on a smile. "It is nothing. An old argument between us. He does not like the restrictions I put in place as a condition of his continued employment. When we argue about them, we both become rather ill-tempered."

"What restrictions?" I laughed. "He said that, too, but to me, living here's been a breeze."

"That is because you are a good student, Astrid. You like to work; you feel a strong sense of responsibility to your job and your studies. You're not here to waste anyone's time."

"And Brandt is?" I said. His French had improved by leaps and bounds. Every time I saw him with the tutors, he seemed as engrossed in his work as I was.

"Brandt . . ." She hesitated. "I shouldn't talk about him like this. Suffice it to say that he doesn't always make things easy on me. He knows his position is unique enough that he can take advantage of it."

And mine wasn't. Sure, unicorn hunters were rare, but if I didn't measure up, she could always send to the Cloisters for another one. There was no more Remedy, and if they were using Brandt to help synthesize it, they needed to keep him willing to play their games.

I wondered how much he was getting paid to sit around the château and donate little vials of blood. Actually, in all the time I'd been here, I didn't think I'd ever seen him with a Band-Aid on his arm. Then again, with the weather getting colder, he'd mostly been wearing long sleeves.

Except in the pool last night. I blushed again, and Isabeau raised her eyebrows.

A few days later, I exited my chemistry lab to find Brandt sitting on the steps of the Landry building.

"Fancy meeting you here," I said, tapping the toe of my boot against the stone.

"Not too surprising," he replied. "I've been waiting for you."

I raised my eyebrows.

"I thought it would be fun if we stayed in the city this evening. A little escape."

How different we were. Gordian *was* my escape. "I don't know. I've got some work—"

"Come on, Astrid!" he said. "I'm bored. I can't spend another night out in the country."

"Then go on another of your mysterious trips," I said. "Where was it last time? Iceland? Ibiza?" According to Isabeau, Brandt liked to blow off steam on the Gordian dime, hopping from European party capital to European party capital.

"Alone? That's no fun, either."

"Get a girlfriend."

"Good idea." His blue eyes said a lot more.

"I'm unavailable."

"Oh, believe me, I know." He stood, slowly, as if examining every inch of skin showing between the top of my boots and the bottom of my skirt. "And since that's the case, what's the big deal if you hang out with me tonight? Just friends."

The big deal was the pool, and he knew it. "Why?"

"I told you," he said. "I'm lonely. I'm . . . homesick." He looked away. "I'm sorry, but you remind me of home. And sometimes I just want . . ."

"Things to be like they used to be?" I asked softly.

He nodded, not meeting my eyes.

I caught my breath. Well, that I could understand. "Okay," I said. "Let's have some dinner. Something American."

He grinned.

We went to a fast-food restaurant and ate burgers and fries. We stopped at a clothing shop and charged new pairs of blue jeans to Gordian. We skipped coffee in favor of Cokes, lamented missing Halloween, and discussed putting together a Thanksgiving dinner.

"They have turkeys in France, right?" Brandt asked as we walked down the street together. I laughed.

Rome had been a wonderful city, and I'd enjoyed exploring it with Giovanni. I'd loved the pasta, the gelato, the endless parade of famous works of art. But we'd never gone out for burgers. And sometimes, every once in a while, as wonderful as the food was in Italy, as spectacular as it was in France, I just wanted to have a greasy fast-food burger. I wanted to eat regular pizza. I wanted peanut butter sandwiches and milk chocolate and the sight of the Pacific Ocean and a little piece of home.

Just like Brandt.

We passed a bar with young people and dance music pouring in equal numbers into the street.

"Let's check it out," Brandt suggested.

I hung back.

"Come on," he said. He tilted his head to listen to the music. "That's Madonna. She's American."

"Barely," I argued as he pulled me inside.

But it turned out to be a lot of fun. The crowd was composed mostly of students from the school, and I got to practice my ever-improving French. It had been ages since I'd gone dancing, and these kids were really into it. Brandt would disappear and reappear throughout the night, never hovering, but always making sure I was still having a good time.

So I was shocked when I felt my phone buzzing in my bag and noticed on the readout that it was well after midnight. Followed instantly by dismay when I recognized the number.

Giovanni.

I hurried out of the building, but the music followed as I answered.

"Astrid? Where are you?"

"Out."

"At a club?" he asked. "That's . . . odd."

I pursed my lips. What? Was he so used to finding me tucked safely in bed by the time he called? "*I've* never had a problem with partying, *G*."

He chose not to respond to my jibe. "You're not alone, are you?"

I hesitated.

"Astrid? You shouldn't go to a nightclub without a friend."

"Don't condescend to me!" I snapped. "You're two years older than me, not twenty. I know what I'm doing."

"You *are* alone? Astrid, come on, that's not safe."

"I'm not alone," I replied. "I'm with Brandt." Even as I spoke, I regretted it, remembering where I'd been the last time he'd called. In the pool, with Brandt. And now I was at a club with Brandt.

Silence. Then, "You told me you hardly ever see him."

"Did I?" I said lightly. "Well, I guess this is one of the times."

He didn't say anything, and my eyes began to burn.

And then, horribly: "Well, don't let me interrupt you."

"Giovanni, wait!" I cried. "There's nothing— I just wanted a night off. I'm in Limoges, and Brandt's here, too, but there's nothing going on. We're just hanging out with some of the college kids. It's totally innocent."

I could hear him sigh. "I . . . trust you, Astrid."

He shouldn't, I thought.

"And, yeah, you should totally be able to go out and have fun. It's just a lot harder for me to picture you having a social life when I know you're not with Phil or the girls at the Cloisters but instead hanging out with some guy you used to date. Especially when he's not three thousand miles away and I am."

"Proximity is not how I choose my men," I said. It wasn't, it *wasn't*.

But that wasn't Brandt's only argument. He didn't think that Giovanni and I had anything in common. He would be more than happy to point out how Giovanni would avoid this nightclub like the plague, and I wanted to dance all night. How Giovanni didn't understand thing one about unicorns or the Remedy, and it had become Brandt's whole life—and mine.

"Look," I said. "I can't talk now. I'll call you later, okay?"

"Fine," he said, and in the word, I sensed the same frustration I felt whenever he blew me off.

I stuck the phone back in my purse and turned back to the nightclub. I hated to think that Brandt was right.

We didn't arrive back at the château until nearly dawn. Brandt had wanted to stay in Limoges—maybe get rooms at a hotel, as he had so many nights in the past—but I demurred. Despite his use of the plural when suggesting rooms, I didn't think spending the night in a hotel with Brandt would endear me to my boyfriend. Or Isabeau.

However, all the lights were on at the château when we pulled up outside, and I began to think that, hotel or no, Isabeau was already unhappy.

She met us in the entrance hall, her face a thundercloud. "In the future," she said, "I wish to be given advance notice of any all-night excursions."

"Chill out, Madame Jaeger," Brandt said.

"I will not," she replied. "Astrid, what if we were to have had an emergency here last night?"

"Same as if you were to have one while I'm taking my classes in town," I replied. "You call on my cell."

Her expression didn't soften.

"You said varying my schedule would be fine." I stood my ground. "I should be allowed to go out."

"All night?" she asked. "I doubt your mother would let you do something like that."

"Not unless it involved putting me in a life-threatening situation," I snapped.

"What are you mad about?" Brandt asked, a smile playing about his lips. "Make up your mind. That she left you here alone with the big bad unicorns or that she went out without begging you for permission first?"

Isabeau turned to him. "I am not angry," she said. "I am simply informing you both that should my wishes be disobeyed one more time, there will be consequences. Do you understand, *Monsieur*?"

Brandt's smile vanished. "Whatever," he said, and stalked off.

She looked back at me and shook her head. "It is unfortunate that you chose last night to exercise your freedom, Astrid. I had a surprise for you."

"What?"

She eyed my outfit, which still reeked of cigarette smoke and club sweat. "Go wash up," she said. "Perhaps when you come back, you'll see them."

I headed back into my room, took a quick shower, then changed. By the time I got back downstairs, the sun had already crested the horizon, and Isabeau was exiting her office, her face set in stern lines.

"Astrid, it goes without saying that I'm disappointed in you. In Brandt, I have come to learn to accept such behavior. But I expect more from you."

"More than what?" I asked.

"You have a strong sense of what your duty is," she said, "and yet you continually feel the need to test yourself. Staying out all night with a boy?"

"Nothing happened!" I snapped. "You know that being out with a guy doesn't necessarily mean sleeping with one, don't you?"

"I know that Brandt would take every opportunity he can to make it mean exactly that." She shook her head. "You dated him, so you know that, too."

Suddenly, even through the haze of herbs in the hall, I felt the unicorns jolt awake to a new presence. I stiffened. "There's something . . . happening. In the enclosure."

"Ah, yes," said Isabeau. "It's your surprise."

16

Wherein Astrid Sees Something New

†

I found them standing by the gate that led beyond the fences and into the einhorn enclosure. They were dressed in long coats and hats to keep out the morning chill, but I still recognized them instantly.

"Cory!" I cried. "Valerija!"

Cory squealed and came running at me. "There you are!" She threw her arms around me. "Hi! Hi hi hi! Sorry, we couldn't wait any longer. Well, Val couldn't, anyway. She's been dying to see these einhorns."

Val? I shook my head. "What are you two doing here?"

"Visiting you, of course. Checking out the operation."

"Do you know the code?" Valerija asked, still at the gate. The unicorns within lurked at the edge of the forest, curious about the newcomers.

"You could have given me some warning, you know," I said.

"And ruin the whole point of a surprise inspection?" Cory asked. "Of course, when we came, we thought we'd be surprising evil Gordian Pharmaceutical scientists, not you on an all-night

231

date with some bloke who is not your boyfriend." Cory crossed her arms. "Should we be reporting back to Giovanni?"

"He knows," I mumbled. And didn't like it one bit. And what, no lecture from her about the evils of unicorn hunters dating? Not that Brandt and I were *dating*.

"There's something more," Cory said. "The Cloisters received a report about a unicorn sighting near Bordeaux a few days back."

"A *sighting*?" I asked. That was about a three-hour drive from here. "Not an attack?"

"There was no interaction," Cory said. "No casualties."

That was unusual. "Why haven't I heard anything about this?"

"To be honest, we thought there was a chance you already knew."

And hadn't told them? Cory took in my bafflement.

"Astrid, from the description—it sounded like a karka-dann."

A karkadann! Could Bucephalus be near? I remembered the dream I'd had the night the electric boundary went down. I hadn't had that dream in months. It couldn't be a coincidence.

"Phil seemed to think that if it was—well, maybe it was coming to see you."

"And if not," Valerija added, "that you should not go to it alone."

"There are several concerns," said Cory. "There's no record of any hunter killing a karkadann except for Clothilde. And that story isn't true. So if it's not Bucephalus, it's extremely danger-ous."

"If it is Bucephalus, he's still extremely dangerous," I said, annoyed. "I watched him murder a man in cold blood, remember?"

"All the more reason to think even two hunters aren't enough," Cory said.

"So we just let it ravage the countryside, then?" I asked.

Val turned away from the woods. "But it isn't," she said. "There is no news of an attack on a human. Not even on an animal. Just the one person saying they saw it."

"Maybe it was a hoax," I suggested. "Like someone saying they saw the Loch Ness Monster."

"Perhaps," Cory said, still skeptical. I had to agree. This wasn't a public news item, or I'd have heard about it already. This was a private report to the Order of the Lioness. And the fact that this alleged karkadann hadn't attacked anyone made it seem even more likely to be Bucephalus. He'd know that the quickest way to bring the wrath of unicorn hunters down upon him was to hurt a human. I'd heard nothing from him since this summer. It made me think he was staying deep in the wild.

But why would he surface only a few hours away from me? Did he need my help again? Or, like last summer, was he looking to help *me*? That was silly. The only thing I needed help with now was making sure I didn't ruin my relationship with Giovanni.

Again, I recalled my dream and the image of Brandt dead in a pool of his own blood.

That kind of help I could do without.

I shuddered. "So what do you want to do? Day-trip over to Bordeaux and check it out?"

Cory hesitated. "I'd been hoping you would say you and the

unicorn had a nice little visit and that would be the end of it. I guess we'll have to call in more hunters."

"Or," I said, "here's a novel idea. Why don't we just leave it alone?"

Cory said nothing. Valerija looked confused.

"It's like Valerija said. It didn't do anything. It's not bothering anyone. What right do we have to kill it?"

"It's dangerous," Cory said. "It could kill dozens of people—"

"But it hasn't!"

Her brow furrowed. "You want to wait until it does?"

I looked down, took a deep breath. "No," I said. "But I don't want to murder something, either." I was through with all that.

Cory didn't respond, and Valerija cleared her throat.

"Come on, let us in," she said, rubbing her hands together. "Enough talk. I want to see the einhorns."

"I don't think that's a good idea," I said. "What about Cory's . . . disability?"

"Oh, it's fine," Cory replied. "Val will take care of them if they get rowdy. She's my knight in shining armor."

"And they won't get—what this word is?—rowdy," Valerija added. "We have done some tests of our own. Unicorns still sense her like a hunter. It just doesn't work the other way 'round."

Wow, her English *had* gotten good.

I let us all into the enclosure, and as soon as we were past the electronic boundary, the einhorns came for us. The usual crowd surrounded me, snuffling for food, and when their search proved fruitless, they started sniffing at Valerija and Cory.

"Wonderful!" Valerija exclaimed. "They are extraordinary."

"They're beautiful," Cory agreed. "If a bit thin."

"Can you feel them?" I asked her.

She touched one on the flank. "Yes, very soft."

"You know what I mean."

Her expression dimmed. "No, not at all." She and Valerija exchanged long glances. "It's gotten worse and worse. And the doctors can't find any medical reason for it."

"I can't believe I'm saying this, but what about a nonmedical reason?" I examined my friend. She looked paler than usual, but it wasn't summertime in Italy anymore. Also, she looked thinner. A lack of pasta or something more sinister? "Is there anything else that could be causing this? I mean, you don't have a boyfriend, right?"

Another quick, inscrutable glance between Valerija and Cory.

"No," Cory said. "No boyfriends. The doctors are wondering if it's something connected with hunting. An allergic reaction, maybe, or a disease of some kind that vectors between hunters and unicorns."

"But what unicorn have you been in contact with that none of the rest of us have?" I asked. "Bonegrinder would have brought with her any disease those unicorns in England had."

"Or," she continued, "maybe it was something Gordian did to me back when we were still trying to figure all this stuff out. Back when we were testing Bonegrinder and me, before the Cloisters opened."

"We want to ask Isabeau," said Valerija, coming close. She grabbed Cory's hand and squeezed it. "Because they could have also done it to me. It may be any time now that I lose my powers, too."

Cory gave Valerija a very serious look, and placed her free hand on top of their joined ones. "You won't. I promise."

I stared at them, more confused than ever.

"You know what?" Valerija said at once. "I think I'm going to go for a quick walk around the woods. Bye!" She scurried off, and the einhorns trailed after her.

"Cory . . ." I began.

"She's doing so well, don't you think?" Cory said.

"She's not the only one," I drawled. What was with all the hand-holding and mysterious glances?

"Astrid, you have no idea what her life was like before she came to us. She lost her mum, too. You know. Just like me."

"Oh." I looked after Valerija, into the woods. I'd never spent much time getting to know the runaway when she'd first come to live with us. Frankly, she'd scared me, and with good reason, as she'd turned out to be a Gordian spy. Though Phil had even been her roommate for a while, I never got the sense that they chatted much. Only Cory had been friendly from the start. No wonder Valerija had volunteered for the job of watching her.

"Not exactly like me, though," Cory went on. "Her mother was . . . troubled. Alcoholic, other drugs. And when she died, Valerija was left living with her mum's old boyfriend. He, um, tried to hurt her, and that's when she ran away."

"That's terrible. She never told us."

"It's hard for her. Not just the language barrier, but everything. You know how hard it was for her to tell us about Gordian and all last summer. But we've grown quite close, so . . ."

"How close?" I asked.

She pursed her lips. "We have a lot in common."

Oh yeah. Valerija the druggie runaway and Cory the rich, pampered princess. But maybe who we used to be before we were hunters didn't matter so much after all.

"We do!" she insisted. "And she's so much better now. I can't wait until they see her back at the Cloisters."

"No more pills?" I asked.

"Hasn't in months," Cory stated, her eyes shining with pride. "Says the unicorn magic's the only high she needs."

"That's . . . nice, I guess." Was that what being high felt like? Magic? Was that why I craved being near the unicorns?

"I know, odd, isn't it?" Cory shrugged, and I gave a little chuckle to cover up my own confusion. "But that's what she says. Which makes me even more scared for her—if she catches whatever this thing I have is." She leaned in. "Because to tell you the truth, I don't know if I much mind the other drawbacks. I find I don't miss hunting."

"I'm right there with you," I said.

"And I'm certain I'll be safe in the Cloisters. We're going back, both of us. I don't need to take one of their few hunters away for bodyguard purposes."

"How magnanimous of you," I joked.

"It was Val's idea." Cory checked for the other girl in the woods, but she was too far within the trees. From the echoed thoughts of the unicorns surrounding her, Valerija seemed to be in seventh heaven. If I closed my eyes, no doubt I could feel her myself, the pinprick node vibrating to me through a string of unicorn consciousnesses.

If I wasn't careful, Valerija might steal my job.

And then where would Cory be?

"She gets so few interactions with unicorns in London, she's worried she might lose her powers and not even know it."

"I think she'd know it," I said softly to Cory. If I closed my eyes, I'd feel Cory, too. I'd notice everyone, because the unicorns did. They knew each of us here in the woods. They knew the protesters beyond the fence, cooking their stews and washing their clothes and painting their signs. "Right now, though, I'm more worried about you."

She looked straight into my eyes, and most of what I saw there was concern for me. Me, alone here without the support of other hunters. Alone here with Brandt. Left alone to ponder the ethics of killing unicorns who had never hurt anyone at all.

But she didn't say any of that. Instead, she said, "Believe it or not, I've never been happier."

I took a deep breath. "Because of Valerija."

She nodded. "Because of Val, yes."

Well, then.

"Astrid?" Cory looked apprehensive. She clasped her hands together. "What are you thinking?"

The edge of my mouth quirked up. "That I'm not the only one with a penchant for dating ex-Gordian spies."

Cory blushed red to the roots of her hair then hugged me. "Thank you."

"For what?" I asked facetiously.

"You're the only one who knows. Neil would throw a fit."

"That's very close-minded of him."

"No, silly!" She laughed. She was doing that a lot now. "Because we're hunters. You know how he feels about people in the Cloisters being together."

I rolled my eyes. Did I ever.

"And because Val is . . . well, he can't stop thinking of her the way she was when she first came to us."

Well, the drugs were gone, the knives had ended up being an asset, and she'd definitely come out of her shell. "Pretty sure he'll see that's no longer the case," I said. I was pretty sure he'd see everything else, too. Oh, to be a fly on the wall of the Cloisters when they showed up there!

"You're okay with it, aren't you, Astrid?" Cory asked. "I know I haven't been fair to you with Giovanni, but now I realize I was . . . kind of jealous." She looked like she might cry.

"Of me?" I asked, stricken.

She wrung her hands. "Um . . . of Giovanni."

Valerija appeared again, just in time. "Okay, enough of the unicorns. Let's have some breakfast."

I spent the rest of the day in a sort of fog while Isabeau gave Valerija and Cory the grand tour. I trailed behind them on their visits to the château and the labs, and gave short answers to the questions that the three of them aimed at me.

This was too much to process after an all-nighter. Bucephalus, here? Cory and Valerija, here? Cory and Valerija . . . together? How had I never picked up on the fact that Cory's disapproval of my boyfriend was tinged with other feelings? We'd shared a room in Italy and I hadn't picked up on it. It was official: I may be able to read the mind of a unicorn, but when it came to my loved ones, I was completely clueless.

If Cory and Valerija were an item, what did that mean for their magic? Could they be together, for real, or were they trapped under the same restrictions I was? I doubted this was a loophole the Catholic nuns had considered. I wondered if the goddess had.

And if they could be together, how unfair was that? Stupid magic.

The one person we failed to see all day was Brandt, and when the other girls asked about him, Isabeau simply waved her hand and said that Brandt had gone on a trip.

"Already?" I asked. "But he was up all night."

"You seem to have plenty of energy, Astrid," was all Isabeau deigned to reply.

"Well, we're not particularly interested in him," Cory said. "But if you have any information about another ex-boyfriend of one of our Llewelyns . . ."

"You speak, I suppose, of Seth Gavriel," said Isabeau.

"Anything at all," Cory said brightly. "Last known location, if you bought him any clothes or vehicles before he left . . ."

"If you know of any fatal allergies . . ." Valerija added, and I became acquainted with her smile.

"Alicorn poison," Isabeau replied, returning Valerija's smile. "And should the legal avenues for some odd reason fail, I might recommend its application. Believe me, I should like to see that young man brought to justice as much as you. I do not know your friend Philippa, but I know Astrid loves her very much, and so I love her as well. First and foremost, I believe in the law. But I admit that I can also understand your desire for real revenge. Don't forget I, too, am a Llewelyn."

Cory leaned over and whispered in my ear, "I take back my earlier impression. I really like this woman."

The rest of the day passed with the kind of discussions I usually loved. Isabeau turned over all the files she had on Cory and Valerija, and helped them cross-reference the tests they'd undergone at Marten's lab, trying to discover if anything Cory had experienced might have triggered her condition.

"You were exposed to alicorn venom here," Isabeau explained, holding up a sheet of paper, "but it was not the first or last time. I can't imagine how the effect would change."

"And this one is just a standard blood drawing," I said, pointing to another sheet.

The tests on Valerija had been similarly mundane, and since Marten had used her as a guinea pig after he was done with Cory, none of the tests had overlapped.

"I'll make up copies of these files to take with you," Isabeau said to Cory. "And if there's any other information I can get—or tests I can assist you with—let me know. You're correct; your condition is quite curious."

Valerija stared at her wide-eyed, as unbelieving as I'd been when I first came here. I beamed. All Jaegers weren't cut from the same cloth. Then again, Isabeau was really a Llewelyn.

They also talked endlessly about their research—Cory into the history of hunters, Isabeau into the history of their medicine. They shared information and promised to send each other sources that the other might find helpful. I was actually surprised by the extent of familiarity Isabeau had when it came to the topic of hunter genealogy. Perhaps *she* could help me find my father's family.

And apparently, Isabeau found a kindred spirit in Cory. "I've been reading the work of Hildegard von Bingen," Cory said over tea. "Are you familiar with her?"

"Am I!" Isabeau exclaimed. "I've been trying to get Astrid to read her for weeks."

"What?" I looked up from the file containing Cory's medical information. "Oh, right, the German nun. Wasn't really my thing."

"Really?" said Cory. "Despite all the ancient medicine?"

"A lot of it was just ridiculous. Unscientific."

"Quite scientific for the time," Isabeau argued. "And yes, some of it is nonsense, but a lot of it was based on real observations of herbal remedies. Things that are still used today. You should try her again, Astrid. She believed in the marriage of science and mysticism. There is no truer example of that than you and me."

I smiled indulgently. "Okay, I'll try." If Phil wasn't in the job already, I'd wager that Isabeau would make an excellent Cloisters donna.

"I was fascinated with the whole idea of *viriditas*," Cory said. She turned to me. "Hildegard was obsessed with it. It means God's power of creation, but also freshness, vitality, life-springing-forth, and all that."

"All that," I repeated with a laugh.

"Well, I really liked what she said about how creation can be any kind of life. It can be an herb garden, it can be a baby, it can be a work of art, or a medical discovery—"

"Or an organization of women built from nothing, Cory?" Valerija interjected.

Cory blushed. "But she was speaking to her fellow nuns, who maybe thought that since they were spending their lives in convents, rather than getting married and having children, that they had nothing to contribute to the world."

"She was an early feminist," Isabeau agreed.

"But also," Cory said, really on a roll, "it was like we nuns, we virgins—whatever—we had extra *viriditas*. We had more *viriditas* than anyone else in the world."

Isabeau straightened. "What an interesting way to view it." She pulled out another book. "Cornelia, did I show you these? It's a family tree of the Saint Marie branch living in Alsace-Lorraine."

I didn't have much of a chance to talk to Cory privately, though I did exchange a few words with Valerija.

"She has told you, yes?" Valerija asked when I took her to show her the alicorn arrowheads. I'd promised her half my stash.

"Yes," I said. The target was still set up across the lawn. I handed her my bow. "Try them out."

"I am—" She hesitated. "I am happy, Astrid. And I think, I hope, she is happy, too." She picked up my practice bow, aimed, and shot. Bull's-eye. "When I started hunting unicorns, I felt very useful. I felt useful for the first time ever. And I didn't want to take anything."

"Because of the magic?" I asked.

"I thought it was," she admitted, setting down the bow. She didn't look up. "But then I was sent to be with Cory, and I was useful there, too. And there was no magic."

She looked up and smiled. "Okay, there was some magic."

I rolled my eyes and laughed. "But what does it mean? You know, for the rules."

"I do not know," said Valerija. "And I do not want to risk anything. It is too dangerous for all of us right now, to not be hunters. Besides," she said, and touched the arrowheads reverently, "it is still what makes me useful."

Cory and Valerija stayed into the late afternoon, then headed out, having booked a late flight to Rome. I wished they could stay at least overnight, but Cory was keen to see Neil and cross-reference the family trees Isabeau had shared with the records at the Cloisters. She hoped they could scare up a few more hunters.

I made another plea to Cory to delay assembling a hunting team in response to this alleged karkadann report, and she reluctantly agreed, though she dropped several dark hints that if anyone was killed by the unicorn, it would be on my head.

I resisted reminding her that even if we did send every hunter in the Cloisters after a karkadann, we'd almost certainly have casualties.

"We'll give Phil and Neil our report," Cory said. "I think they'll be pleased with your work here."

"Give them my love, too," I said. "And if at all possible, don't tell Phil about the whole Brandt-nightclub thing."

"Right." Cory grinned. "I think there's enough to talk about without getting into that."

After they left, I did my rounds at the einhorn enclosure, then went back to my room to study, without much success. There were too many thoughts whirling through my head. The karkadann, Cory and Valerija, the meaning of our magic, Cory's mysterious illness, my fight with Giovanni . . . At long last, I gave up and wandered downstairs to find Isabeau in her library, reading.

She looked up from her book as I entered. "I was hoping I'd see you again tonight. I am afraid I may have given you the wrong impression this morning. I think you are very responsible, Astrid. I hope you know that."

"Thank you," I said stiffly.

"And I know that things that seem inappropriate are not always so, just as you said. You are not a stupid girl. And I do not expect you to make stupid choices."

"Brandt is a stupid choice?" Not that I was *choosing* Brandt.

She gave me an incredulous look. "I know that Brandt is very handsome." When I said nothing, she went on. "But what of this boyfriend of yours in America?"

"Giovanni," I said. "He's great. There's nothing going on with Brandt and me, you know. He's my ex. We're just friends."

Isabeau closed her book and looked up at me. "Your Giovanni. Does he respect your duties as a unicorn hunter?"

"Of course!" I said. "I wouldn't be seeing him if that weren't the case."

"Hmm." Isabeau tilted her head to one side. "He sounds like a very nice young man. I'm sure it is not easy for him."

I looked away. "Easier if he lives on the other side of the ocean."

"Indeed. But he is devoted to you?"

"I don't know. I guess he is. He said he would be."

"It is difficult to have a long-distance boyfriend. Especially when you are both so young. And the fact that he respects your role . . . He sounds very special, Astrid."

Way to make me feel even more guilty. "Thank you."

"Brandt would not," she stated, and returned to her book.

My mouth dropped open. "I—"

She didn't look up from her pages as she spoke. "I tell you this not as a warning, Astrid, but as a reminder. If at any time you wish to leave your life as a hunter behind . . ."

"I don't." I said. "I . . . made a commitment."

"You are too young to make a commitment that will last you the rest of your life."

"Isn't that what I'm doing, though?" I asked, my voice unable to conceal the bitterness. "If I die, if I'm maimed—won't that last the rest of my life, too?"

She nodded. "This is true. And you *can* leave. Many have. But if you do make this decision, do not go to Brandt. Be with your boyfriend, for he must love you. And you, *ma petite chère*, deserve to be loved."

I wasn't sure how to respond to that, so after a reasonable amount of awkward silence, I asked her what she was reading.

"A funny old book of medical cures," she said. "Not unlike the book of Hildegard's. As I said earlier, I find it quite amusing that these old medics were wrong as often as they were right."

"Have things changed much?" I asked. "It seems that we're still discovering that things we thought were good for you were bad or vice versa." Like margarine and butter.

"True, Astrid." She smiled. "I was just reading the most horrible passage, though. Ironic, given our discussion. I was reading about an old wives' tale that said a man could cure himself of venereal disease by sleeping with a virgin girl." She shuddered. "Can you imagine?"

Unfortunately, I could. People could be real sickos. Phil could attest to that.

"The virgin's purity was thought to be so overwhelming that it would cleanse her lover of his sickness." Isabeau clucked her tongue. "And yet all it would really do was confer upon her the same suffering."

I made a face. "That's so gross. I'm glad people don't think like that anymore."

Isabeau looked down at the page. "Indeed. *Si près et pourtant si loin.*"

So close and yet so far.

I awoke to screams of anguish, and it was several moments after I sat up in bed that I realized the sounds were entirely inside my head. My body flushed with magic—a unicorn in the enclosure was crying out in pain. I hurried to dress and ran out the door.

The moon was obscured beneath a bank of clouds tonight, leaving the woods bathed in darkness. Were it not for the magic, I probably wouldn't be able to see my knife hand in front of my face. The mind-scream continued as I rushed toward the enclosure and keyed the new combination into the gate locks. After the sabotage, police had come to question the protesters about their involvement, but I didn't know if they'd made any arrests. And yet, were they to try breaking in again, surely it wouldn't be a unicorn that ended up in pain? They were trying to save the animals, not hurt them. I remembered the man who'd thrown me his first aid kit after I'd hurt Breaker.

Once I'd crossed the electronic barrier, I could sense the einhorns more clearly. Many were awake, their thoughts focused on the suffering one: Fats.

Had she fallen? Had she been attacked by one of the others? Had her illness suddenly turned acute?

Another scream rent the night air, one that existed in the physical world. It was followed by bellows and grunts, and I banked right and ran into the center of the woods, toward the origin of the noises.

By the time I arrived, it was all over. Fats lay huddled and panting beneath the wilting leaves of a scraggly bush, and nestled between her twining hooves was a tiny, hornless ein-horn, its downy, paper-soft hide still slick and shiny.

I stopped dead, and the knife fell from my hands.

The baby's eyes were shut, tissue-thin lids closed over impos-sibly large black orbs that jutted from either side of its face. It mewled, snuffling at its mother's belly until it found her teats. Fats licked the baby all over, nosing it softly until it was pushed fully against the warmth of her body.

I dropped to my knees in the leaves, tears springing to my eyes.

Fats lifted her head and faced me, blinking slowly and hold-ing my gaze as I struggled to speak. Some magic greater than unicorns choked my senses, burned everything but the vision of this infant, drowned all but the swell of protectiveness emanat-ing from Fats and flowing straight into me.

I crawled toward mother and baby on shaking limbs, feel-ing as faint as the first time I was poisoned by a karkadann. There was nothing else in the world beyond these woods and these einhorns. The moment in the pool dissolved; my awk-ward, aggravating conversation with Giovanni melted away; the thwack of the arrows into the heart of the target faded; Cory's bombshells vanished into the air. I had never existed before this moment; there was nothing more important than this uni-corn.

It was only in some dim, distant, human part of my brain that I realized these thoughts were not my own. They belonged to Fats. She was *making* me feel them. Her child, her love, her fundamental instinct to protect this infant at all costs.

I drew in a breath and reached out my hand to touch the baby.

Yes. It was as soft as I'd thought, and as warm, and as sacred. Fats curved her neck over the child, the blinking lights on her collar a crude barrier when she nuzzled against its skin. She turned to face me again, only a few inches away this time.

"Yes," I said aloud, though this was nothing like talking to the karkadann. There were no words in my brain to translate, just a vital need. "I'll help you. I'll protect her."

Fats sighed and lowered her head, exhausted by her ordeal. And I stood guard over mother and child all night, watching the baby twitch and nuzzle against its mother, watching until the first rays of dawn broke through the trees and made the baby's bare white skin glow as if lit from within. It was then that I named it.

Angel.

17

WHEREIN ASTRID GOES NATIVE

Of course, Angel was a terrible name for a man-eating monster, but somehow that didn't matter as the days passed and I kept up with my secret vigils. I saw the baby through Fats's eyes—it was tiny, not terrible; sweet, not savage. The short days and long nights of winter made it easy for me to keep an eye on mother and baby, and I took to regularly spending my evenings in the enclosure. With Brandt still out of town and Isabeau increasingly wrapped up in her research, there was no one to talk to after my classes were over and no one keeping a close eye on whether or not I slept in my own bed.

The dangers to Angel and Fats were twofold. With the constant food shortage among the einhorns, it was difficult for any individual unicorn to get enough to nourish itself, let alone enough to sustain a nursing mother. Though Isabeau had increased the unicorns' food allotment twice on my request, it seemed that no amount would keep these animals satisfied. They'd already consumed all the creatures—rabbits, badgers, stoats—that had once lived in the forest. They needed a larger territory to hunt and survive.

This difficulty was a product of their species—traditionally, it was known that unicorns could not be captured, only killed. Bucephalus had even told me of his suffering when he rode with Alexander. The truth was, they would wither in captivity, even if they were given all the fresh meat in the world.

And what of Angel, born into a cage?

Above all, it was vital that no one in the château discover there was a new unicorn in the enclosure. I didn't know if I could bear to place an electronic collar around the baby's neck, but I was positive I would never be able to inject Angel with any of the new serums I knew the Gordian scientists would soon be ready to try again. Angel may live on their lands, but I balked at the idea that the tiny unicorn was their property.

Then there was the danger it faced from the other einhorns. More than once I'd noticed some of the other unicorns skulking nearby as I stood guard over mother and child. Some seemed only curious—like Breaker, Stretch, and Tongue—but there were others, like that angry one, whose thoughts tended toward the violent. I worried what might happen if the angry one came upon them when I wasn't there. Fats was weak all the time, losing weight rapidly and constantly exhausted from feeding her baby; and Angel was utterly defenseless with no horn. Defenseless, fat, and probably very tender.

I asked Isabeau to give the animals even more food.

"With the colder weather now, they need to bulk up and protect themselves from the elements," I argued. "Also, I'd be happy to take it to them myself." Perhaps a peace offering of massive amounts of meat would keep the more threatening einhorns at bay.

Isabeau agreed, and the strategy seemed to work—for a while at least. The einhorns ignored Angel in favor of the chunks of meat I threw at them, and I was able to give Fats a larger portion of food that was strictly her own and didn't require scrambling to snatch out of the jaws of the other unicorns. She began to lose that famished look that had turned her name into such an irony, and I rested better during the few hours of sleep I caught each morning between the dawn and my first classes with Lauren.

Angel grew like a weed, with silky white hair and spindly legs so long I began to entertain myself with notions of the unicorn's paternity. *Stretch, you rascal.* After a few weeks of nursing, the baby began eating regurgitated meat from its mother's mouth, which was a lot more difficult to witness, but still fascinating from a scientific standpoint.

I suppose after you've seen unicorn guts, unicorn vomit isn't so disturbing.

And meanwhile, there were those stretches of dreamtime, alone in the woods with nothing but Fats's soft thoughts and the near-silent flicker of the baby's impressions in my brain. I immersed myself in both, marveling at the way they swirled together, their connections to each other far stronger than my magic-induced link. My gift had nothing on Fats's natural ability. The tiniest twitch of Angel's consciousness registered to Fats, even if they weren't together, even if she was out foraging for food she'd never find, leaving Angel alone in the brush with nothing but a besotted unicorn hunter for protection.

Though I recognized the influence Fats's own maternal instincts had on my emotions, I allowed it to continue. After all, this was my job. I was supposed to be attuned to the state of the unicorns. When they were scared or anxious, I remained alert.

When they were calm and passive, I could relax and devote my mind to other things. I was employed as a unicorn keeper, and in protecting the baby, I was keeping the unicorns as best I could.

The fact that I was keeping this one a secret from my employer? Well, let's leave that aside for now.

"You seem tired," Isabeau said to me one morning in mid-December as she found me staring bleary-eyed into the coffee press.

I yawned. "It's just winter. Gray weather will make anyone tired. Trust me, I grew up in Washington."

"How are your classes?" she asked.

"Fine." I gulped down a cup of too-strong, too-bitter coffee and made for the door. She stepped in front of me.

"I'm sure the unicorns are fine. Talk to me for a moment."

I slumped. It had been four hours since I'd seen Angel, and the scent of chamomile and coffee lingered thick in the air, masking my magic. Was the baby okay? Did it need me?

"You've been so withdrawn lately. Ever since your friends visited. I am worried you are homesick for them?"

"No, I—" I tried to sidle around her, but for such a petite woman, Isabeau could certainly fill a space. Okay, then. "Well, maybe a little, with the holidays coming up." Perhaps now she'd let me be.

Apparently not. "And you spend so much time with the unicorns. All night, every night? Astrid, I told you there was no reason to sleep out there."

"How do you know—"

She looked amused. "The lockbox on the gate, Astrid. It keeps a log of every time the code is pressed. How else could we

253

handle the enclosure's security?"

I pursed my lips. "And what other movements of mine are you monitoring?"

Isabeau took a little half step back, looking surprised. "None at all. Why? Should I be spying on you, *ma chère*? Is there anything you are doing of which I would not approve?" When I didn't answer, she went on, "Of course we keep an eye on the lockbox, Astrid. After the sabotage . . . Isn't that why you've been going out there at night? Same as you did the night the boundary was shut down?"

"Yes," I lied. "I don't trust the protesters." But I didn't fear them or *for* them, either. Things had grown scattered and sparse at their camp ever since the night of the break-in, partially given the police interrogation that had followed the situation and partially because the weather had become too unpleasant for any but the most die-hard animal lovers to stay outside all night.

I suppose I now fell into that group myself.

"There are other ways to deal with them than risking your health," Isabeau said. "I appreciate your dedication, but not at such a great personal risk."

"Everything I do is at a great personal risk," I grumbled as I walked by her. Even if I wasn't taking my life in my hands every time I tried to hold off a hungry unicorn, I was risking my future by concealing Angel's presence from Isabeau and Gordian. If I got fired and sent back to the Cloisters, what would happen to my education?

And she thought I was afraid of catching cold?

I zipped through my rounds that morning, taking quick stock of the perimeter while reaching my mental feelers into the woods to sense Fats and Angel, together and asleep. As I neared the side of the enclosure closest to the protesters' camp, I paused. Standing by the fence was the same tall black man, and as usual, he was watching me.

I kept moving.

"Hello," he said, and put his hands on the link. "Hello there. You are American?"

"*Oui.*" I kept going.

"I know what you are," he said. "*Vous êtes un chasseur de licornes.*" *You are a unicorn hunter.*

Give the man a prize.

"You walk among them. You command them."

And this guy stood there and watched.

"So I ask you," he called, raising his voice as my circuit began to take me away from him, "why it is that you can bear to see them like this? They are wild creatures! You must know this is torture for them. A torture much greater than they can suffer, even within the terrible laboratories! Please! Listen to me!"

I stopped now and turned back to face him, but I said nothing. How could I? Yes, the einhorns were suffering here in the enclosure; I knew that better than anyone, just as he'd surmised. And yet, if we could find the secret to the Remedy through their pain and captivity, well, then, wouldn't it be worth it? We weren't making cosmetics here. We were trying to save the world.

Besides, what was the alternative? Let them out? Hardly.

"What is your name?" he asked softly.

"Astrid," I said. "*Comment vous appellez-vous?*"

"René. It is very nice to know you, Astrid."

"You don't know me," I said.

"But I do. I watched you for many days and nights. I watched you heal the unicorn you cut—in the leg, no less.

You are a very poor hunter, I think."

I narrowed my eyes. "Oh, is that what you think? Should I start listing my more impressive kills?"

"No, I also watched your skill with a bow. I know how talented you are. You are a very poor hunter," he repeated, "because your heart is not in the kill."

"Shooting fish in a barrel," I snapped, approaching him. Who was he to observe something like that? That was my own private business. "I wasn't put here to kill any of these animals. Believe me, when I should kill, I kill." I crossed the electric boundary and came near the fence.

"And what if what you should do is something else?" Up close, he was younger than I'd thought, maybe only a few years older than Neil. Figured. It's not like anyone old enough to have real responsibilities could take off months from work to go camp out in a pasture and watch a bunch of captive unicorns. Of that I was sure.

René was very handsome, with strong, chiseled features, dark skin, darker eyes, and a clean-shaven head. He was dressed in a pair of black slacks, hiking boots, and a forest green sweater under a black slicker. He didn't look like the militant environmentalist type, the ones who didn't wash or bathe, who tied themselves to trees or disabled lockboxes or committed acts of ecoterrorism. More like a graduate student on holiday.

"I'd get away from the fence, if I were you," I said. "The monsters can smell your blood from all the way in the forest."

His eyes widened, but his hands dropped from the links and he stepped back.

"Your presence here puts them in a constant state of agitation, do you know that?" I said.

"But you are here to soothe them."

"They belong to Gordian."

"They belong to themselves and to the Earth," he replied. "You know that, else you would not sleep out here as they do."

Did everyone in the world know where I was spending my nights? I gritted my teeth. "Can't you see how important this work is? Do you know how many people we can cure if we continue to experiment on these animals?"

"Yes," he said. "But even if it were a million, or ten million, is it worth the destruction of this species? Are there even a million unicorns? Are there a thousand? Do you know?"

"No," I said without thinking.

René stared at me. "Do you know how many you've killed?"

I whispered, "No."

He nodded slowly and shrugged. "Perhaps you should."

"Perhaps I should have counted how many lives I've saved with the unicorns I've killed," I said. I could start with every hunter in the Cloisters. "Perhaps I should count the lives of every person in your camp."

"René!" He turned to look at a man in the camp. The second man scowled. He was white, older, larger, and wore a scuffed leather jacket. Some animal-rights activist. "What are you doing talking to her?" the man shouted in French. "She's one of them."

I rolled my eyes.

René turned back to me, a smile playing about his lips. "You are not one of them," he said to me in French. "Are you? I think, Astrid, that you are one of us."

The bellow of a unicorn broke the morning stillness. Instantly, every other animal in the enclosure was awake and on alert. I spun on my heel and sprinted into the woods, my conversation with René utterly forgotten. Disorder reigned in the minds of the monsters, with a ribbon of violence spreading through like a sickness. I quickened my pace, beelining for the epicenter of the excitement.

By the time I arrived, it was to find Stretch and the angry unicorn facing off against each other, legs spread, heads lowered, horns glancing blows as each einhorn tested its limits against the other. Nearby lay the body of a third unicorn—dead.

Neither einhorn noticed me as I came closer, struggling to project calming thoughts. They clashed, then withdrew, but any time either attempted to approach the corpse, the other attacked again. I wished I'd thought to bring my bow—there was no way I could hold off two unicorns with only my little alicorn knife.

The angry one charged at Stretch, causing him to gallop off into the brush. Then, before I could stop him, he rushed back to the corpse and fastened his fangs around a spindly leg, dragging the body away. Upon closer inspection, I could see that the dead unicorn was Tongue. I ran forward, knife drawn.

"Drop it!" I cried. The unicorn looked at me and growled, teeth still firmly clamped around the corpse.

I could feel Stretch returning, and suddenly, he was upon us, and had grabbed up another of Tongue's limp legs. A tug-of-war ensued in which the minds of both unicorns were so firmly fixed on their prize that all the calming thoughts in the world were having no effect at all. I felt like a child stamping my foot in frustration. And yet, I kept my knife at my side. They weren't threatening people, nor Angel, merely each other. They were acting like animals in the wild, fighting over food. Horrible, macabre food, yes, but food nonetheless. There were many

258

animals that turned to cannibalism in starvation situations. I'd read stories of polar bears attacking cubs.

I detected no injuries on the dead Tongue, which both soothed and worried me. It was good to know that the unicorns weren't killing one another, but if Tongue had died of some sort of illness, I probably shouldn't let them eat the body, lest they fall ill as well. I'd always wondered if Tongue might be sick, but hadn't given it much thought after Fats gave birth. After all, I thought she'd been sick as well, and I'd been utterly wrong about that one.

The growling grew in both volume and intensity.

"Drop it!" I cried. "Drop it, drop it, drop it!"

They paid me no mind. And what could I do? Kill them both? I wouldn't be able to get Tongue's corpse out of the woods on my own anyway, even if I wasn't forced to hold off hungry unicorns—hungry unicorns used to me feeding them meat— while doing so. And with the einhorns in such an agitated state, I couldn't risk bringing a nonhunter into the enclosure to retrieve the body.

A better argument for backup I'd be unlikely to find.

But instead I just stood there and watched them tear Tongue to pieces.

Later, I collected what little of the corpse I could find, drew blood from both unicorns, and the lab tested it all for known diseases, but found nothing. Still, there might be illnesses, pests, and parasites somehow specific to unicorns. Who knew how many other species the creatures had brought with them in their Reemergence? From what Phil had told me of her research, every animal had the potential of being its own mini-ecosystem.

Saving a flagship species, be it the polar bear or the Brazilian tree monkey or the killer unicorn, introduced the possibility of saving a dozen far less adorable but no less worthy species that depended on the other for survival.

Including parasites. The potential was mind-boggling, since whatever had ailed Tongue was *resistant* to the unicorns' natural self-healing properties. That had to be one hell of a disease. Perhaps it even had something to do with Cory's illness, as her doctors had suggested. Maybe the reason they couldn't identify it was because it was a virus that started with unicorns. I wondered if Phil would take that into account in her proposals to various conservation groups. If it turned out that the unicorns had brought superbugs back with them from wherever they'd disappeared to, it was doubtful society would want anything more than to eradicate them and their possible pandemics from the planet for good this time.

More disturbingly, the possibility of a unicorn-specific disease led to all kinds of speculations on who, exactly, was susceptible. Perhaps Cory was right and it was a disease that vectored only to hunters.

Isabeau confirmed these fears. "Remember cowpox and the milkmaid, which led to a vaccine for smallpox?" she asked me. "It first required the maid to grow sick with cowpox. She got it from the cow." We asked Cory to send more tissue samples to the Gordian labs to test against Tongue's.

I also convinced Isabeau to dose the einhorns' feed with antibiotics, lest whatever had killed Tongue spread to the rest of the unicorn population. Officially, sixteen unicorns remained in the enclosure. Sixteen . . . and Angel.

Whether it was a simmering malaise, a side effect of the

antibiotics, or the coming winter, the unicorns seemed to settle down. More often than not, I found them sleeping in dens
they'd carved out at the roots of the trees. I wished again that
one of the ancient hunters had done some sort of behavioral
study on the animals. Did einhorns hibernate like bears? How
long would it take for Angel to mature into an adult? When
would Phil and her environmentalist allies be able to get a study
like this off the ground?

Though it never got quite cold enough to snow, the nights
neared freezing, and I finally gave up my vigil over the baby
unicorn. More and more of the protesters vanished from their
campsite, probably similarly disillusioned by the gloomy winter
weather. Even René seemed to have given up—at least, I never
spoke to him again.

And Brandt remained nowhere to be seen. I'd never bothered
getting his cell phone number, and after Isabeau's warnings, I
couldn't bring myself to ask her for it. But I hadn't spoken to
him since the night we'd spent in Limoges, and as his absence
stretched longer and Isabeau continued to leave him out of all
conversations, I began to worry that she'd sent him away for
good.

In contrast to the silent woods, the château itself bustled with
activity. Isabeau explained that, for all her life, her mother had
thrown a massive soirée on the solstice, and it was a tradition
that Isabeau had retained over the years, rolling the Gordian
holiday party into the event and turning the night into one of
the finest galas in the region.

I'd never been to anything that could be construed as a gala.
Birthday parties, yes. I'd even attended Uncle John's office
Christmas party one year, for which he rented out the entire

261

back room of a nice Italian restaurant back home. But watching the preparation for Isabeau's solstice party was witnessing event planning on an entirely new level. The château crawled with maids, florists, lighting designers, caterers, sommeliers, decorators, and all manner of staff.

I'd retreated from the hubbub and was studying in my room when Isabeau knocked on the door. She entered carrying a large, glossy black box tied with a white silk ribbon.

"It's utter madness out there. You're wise to avoid all this, Astrid." She placed the box on my bed. "How are you doing today? You're looking so much better this past week or so."

Amazing what a few full nights of sleep in my own bed could do. "I'm fine. What's the box for?"

Isabeau smiled broadly. "An early Christmas present from me to you. It's a dress for the gala."

I laid down my pencil. "I thought it was just for grown-ups."

She laughed. "'Grown-ups'? That makes me feel old! Astrid, you are not a child, and I don't think of you that way. Don't take Brandt's silly words to heart. Besides, it is a party for all my employees, and you are one of those as well." She patted the lid of the box. "Don't you want to try on your new party dress?"

I shot out of my seat. The box lid was emblazoned with an unfamiliar French name, but I knew no one but the most famous designers, anyway. I untied the ribbon and lifted the lid. Within, swathed in layers of silver tissue paper, lay a pile of shimmering silk the color of mist in the moonlight. I lifted the dress from the wrappings. The material flowed like cool water over my hands. Sleeveless, with a wide boat neck, the dress fell in slim, draping lines to the floor. The bodice was simple and plain, with a dropped waist accented by clusters of crystals that looked like dewdrops. More crystals were scattered near the neckline, and shimmering organza scarves in the same blue-gray flowed from each shoulder.

It was, quite easily, the most beautiful item of clothing I'd ever held in my hands.

"Not exactly a camouflage habit, eh, Astrid?" Isabeau asked.

Dropping the dress to the bed, I threw my arms around her. "Thank you! It's stunning!"

Isabeau hugged me back, laying her dark head on my shoulder. "I'm happy you like it. Now, let's see if it fits."

I realized the problem as soon as I got into the bathroom. Though the front of the dress possessed a neckline that would reveal only my collarbones, the back fell in a low, thickly-draped swoop three-quarters of the way to the waistline. It was gorgeous—on some other girl.

I cracked the door. "It's backless."

"*Très chic*, no?" Isabeau's expression faltered. "Oh. Your scar."

My scar. I stared down in disappointment at the dress in my hands. There was no way around it. The draping, not to mention the shoulder scarves, would prevent me from wearing any sort of shawl or cardigan over the dress.

"*Chère*," came Isabeau's voice from the other side of the door, "will you not even try it on for me?"

But I didn't want to. I didn't want to put this magnificent gown on, knowing that I'd never be able to wear it. I didn't want a taste of what it would have felt like to be some other, very pretty girl.

"Please, Astrid? For me?"

I stared at my reflection in the mirror and bit my lip. Even just holding the dress up, I knew the color was perfect for me. It made my light hair look luminous and pearlescent and high-lighted my eyes. I draped the dress over the edge of the bath, then reached for my braid and undid the elastic holding the end in place. I shook my hair loose, fluffed it up until it fell in braided kinks to my waist, and pulled my shirt off.

A storm broke on the evening of the party. The wind whipped around the walls of the château, whining like some sort of injured wild thing. The moon was completely obscured by the dark clouds—that is, if there was any moon. The weather did not deter any of the guests, however. The château was packed with people, music, noise, and scents: of food and wine, of flowers and burning candle wax, of people's perfume and the human odors the perfumes attempted to mask.

I could not sense fire and flood. I could not feel the unicorns. I stood by a long window near the landing outside the ballroom, looking out over the backyard and the einhorn enclosure. The last time I'd seen Angel had been early this morning, before Isabeau had taken me to the salon to get ready for the party. I'd had a pedicure and manicure—the manicurist despaired over my short, ragged nails—then a massage followed by a facial that left my skin feeling tingly and tight. They'd tinted my eye-lashes and styled my hair, grumbling again when I insisted that I didn't want an elaborate updo. To pull off Isabeau's beautiful dress, my hair had to remain long and loose. Period.

It was far too late to check on the baby. I was dressed in my gown and a pair of silver, high-heeled sandals, and a freezing rain was battering the grounds. I hoped everything was all right in the enclosure. Try as I might, I couldn't sense the einhorns.

At least here, on the stairway landing, things were dim and quiet, with the bulk of the brightness, crush, and noise of the party in the next room. Isabeau had introduced me to many people this evening, but their names and faces had blurred together, and I'd quickly tired of their exclamations of delight and surprise at meeting a real, live "*chasseur de licornes.*" I hated the way their eyes lingered on the scars on my arms and hands, on the calluses that even the most intense manicure could not completely erase. I folded my arms behind my back, draping my scars beneath the fall of the organza scarves.

I was alone again now, away from conversations that moved too fast in French and the whispers and glances that I knew were about me, about magic, about all the rumors they'd heard regarding hunters. My mother would probably be completely in her element. I just wanted to escape to my room . . . or to the woods.

"You look like a goddess," said a familiar voice at my back. I turned and there was Brandt, wearing a tuxedo like he was born in it and holding out a glass of champagne. "But I suppose that was the point."

I lifted my chin and felt the ends of my hair brush against the base of my spine, the edges of the scar. I hadn't expected to see him tonight, hadn't even considered what Brandt would think of me in this dress.

Hadn't considered Giovanni, either. This dress was for me. I *was* a goddess.

"When did you get back?" I took the flute, and he clinked his glass against mine.

He smiled. "This afternoon, while you were out getting pretty. Surprise!" He leaned in. "Miss me?"

And regretted every moment I did. But no way I'd admit it. "You've been gone for like a month. What have you been up to?"

Brandt sipped his champagne. "That, *mon petit chou*, is a secret."

I clucked my tongue. "My French is getting better, you know. I'm not a cabbage."

"No, you're a goddess, like I said. Like Diana. I take it Isabeau picked that out for you?"

I smoothed my hand over the silk at my hip, painfully aware that Brandt noticed every single curve in the material. "Yes."

He nodded. "Figures. Have to dress up our pets in the appropriate costumes, don't we? After all, not too many folks can boast a unicorn hunter in their entourage."

I sipped my champagne instead of replying. It wasn't a costume. It was me—the one I never got to be, all wrapped up in habits or hunting clothes. Isabeau had seen it, and here I stood. More beautiful than I'd ever been in my life.

At least Brandt recognized that. I wasn't that girl he'd made out with on an old tartan blanket back home. I wasn't the girl he'd felt free to dump after she'd saved his life. I was something more. Something incredible.

"I really wish you'd stop talking that way about Isabeau," I said. "She's been nothing but wonderful to both of us. Who is it that paid for your month-long vacation to wherever it was?"

"The good people at Gordian Pharmaceuticals." He raised his glass to them. "And believe me, if Isabeau could get me off that payroll, she would."

"I don't see why you're still on it, to be honest," I said. "I mean, a few vials of your blood, what more can they possibly need you for?"

"Why would you want to get rid of me?" He put on an adorable frown.

"What's the difference?" I said, as lightly as possible. "You're never here."

"A-ha! So you *did* miss me."

"I—" I looked away, gripping the stem of my champagne flute. I took another drink, a long one, to make up for my silence.

"It's okay," he said. "I missed you, too. I always miss you, Astrid."

I turned around and caught my breath at the longing in his bright blue eyes. He was standing so close to me. But there was nowhere to go with the windowsill right at my back.

His voice lost some of its intensity. "And look at us now, all dressed up. This is like that prom we never did go to."

"Did you go to prom?" I asked, my mouth dry. "After I left?"

"Yes," he said. "But I don't even remember who it was with."

"Liar." He remembered. And he probably slept with her, too. I had to keep that in mind. That was Brandt.

Except, that was *also* the old Brandt. The one who hadn't seen his life flash before his eyes after being gored by a unicorn. The one who hadn't run away to France to be part of a science experiment that might change the world. The one who hadn't gotten a dose of the Remedy, who hadn't the slightest idea what it felt like to have magic coursing through his veins.

I'd changed so much this year. Was it so difficult to believe that Brandt had changed as well?

He shook his head a single time. "I swear. I can't remember any other girl but you."

I rolled my eyes and turned away again to look out into the night. "Now I know you're lying."

There was a soft clink behind me and then I felt his hand on the nape of my neck, drawing my hair off my back. "I swear to you I'm not."

A second later, his fingers, cooled by the champagne glass, began tracing the whorls of the scar on my back.

I flinched, but didn't move away as the lines of the scar ignited beneath his touch. His fingertips buzzed against my skin. I shouldn't let him do this. "Brandt—"

"I'm in love with you, Astrid," he whispered in my ear. "Don't you get that?"

I turned to face him, which was probably a mistake, because he didn't back up a single inch, and I was left leaning against the freezing window, pressed between the winter storm and Brandt, who was burning hotter every moment. "No. You can't be."

"I am," he insisted, his words trapping me more firmly than his touch could. "I went away, thinking I could stop it, but it didn't work. I went away, thinking that maybe it was the idea of you—your strength, your magic, the fact that you saved my life. The fact that you, Astrid, are the girl that got away because I was too much of an idiot to realize what I had. But it wasn't. It wasn't. I love you, Astrid."

"Stop saying that," I managed to choke out. "I have a boy-friend."

"A boyfriend on the other side of the ocean. I couldn't bear to put an ocean between us. I came back because I couldn't even bear to put a few measly city-states between us. I need you, Astrid."

The winter glass sizzled against my scar, and Brandt drew impossibly closer, until the silk of my dress rasped against his body.

"Please," I begged. "Stop talking like that. It's confusing."

"It's the truth," he argued. "How can that confuse you? Would you rather I lied to you, said things I didn't feel? *That* would be confusing." He rested his head on my bare shoulder for a moment, breathing as hard as I was, then leaned over to my ear, his words coming in a rush of warm breath. "If you didn't want me, too, you wouldn't be standing here."

That was my cue to move. But I didn't. A storm raged within me, hot and cold swirling together, stealing my breath and all my more rational thoughts. Brandt melted against me, his weight pushing me hard against the glass, his left thigh sliding between my silk-encased legs. I gasped.

"Now who's confusing?" Brandt said, and kissed me.

My lips didn't part, my hands remained clenched at my sides, but I didn't push him away. I didn't move my head to the side. I let him kiss me. I let him moan into my mouth, to punctuate each press of his lips with a murmured promise, with a whispered oath.

"You are so beautiful . . ." He drew the champagne glass from my fingers and set it on the window ledge. "So powerful . . ." His hands trailed up my sides and wove themselves in my hair. "So amazing . . ."

And then, somehow, he was standing between my legs, trapping me in a tangle of silken skirt. Somehow my hands had made it around his shoulders, clinging as if I was drowning in my dress and the tidal wave of Brandt. Somehow, my lips were parted, and his tongue was in my mouth, and I didn't mind at all. I knew this, I remembered this, and this time, I wasn't thinking about what it all meant. Brandt smelled like home, he tasted like my old life, and his kisses set my nerves ringing

with a chord I knew well. It was unicorn magic and somehow—
somehow—he was able to connect to it.

"Oh, wow," he murmured. "Can you feel it?"

"Yes," I whispered.

"Can't I please, please, *please* just touch you? Can't I be with
you? Oh God, Astrid, please, don't turn me away. . . ." He kissed
me again, and I felt it in every cell of my body. "I'd do anything . . . I'd do anything to be with you . . . to feel for even a
moment what you feel all the time—"

And then he was ripped away from me. I slid against the window, breathless, and stared. Brandt's eyes were wild; his arms
reached for me in vain. But Isabeau Jaeger, a vision in black vel-
vet, her face darker than the storm outside, held on to him by
the collar of his jacket.

"Enough," she said.

18

Wherein Astrid Takes a Stand

I was sent to my room. I don't know what happened to Brandt.
After twenty minutes, Isabeau came to my door.

"It goes without saying," she said, staring at a spot above
my bed, "that I am disappointed with your behavior. This is
not some nightclub where one overlooks or ignores such crude
activities in dark corners."

I hung my head.

"I expect better from my guests, and better from my employees." Now she looked me in the eye. "And on top of that, Astrid,
what did you think you were doing? Have I not told you about
Brandt?"

I opened my mouth to speak.

"And what about your Giovanni? Don't you care about
him?"

My words broke on a sob. *Giovanni.* This was so much
worse than that time in the pool. I'd actually cheated on him.
I'd made out with my ex-boyfriend. I'd let Brandt ply me with
champagne, and tell me he loved me, and weave such a gorgeous

spell that I'd forgotten everything that Giovanni and I had been through together. I was horrible.

Isabeau's face softened. "Oh, *ma petite*. Do not cry. You aren't the first woman in the world to be taken in, to be told pretty lies by a man."

"He wasn't lying," I muttered.

"Did he tell you he loved you?" She crossed her arms. "Trust me, he lies. Brandt is like an addict. He has a taste of power, and constantly lusts for more. I am just thankful I found you two before any damage was done."

"*Damage?*" I snapped. "Damage like me giving my virginity to him, you mean? Certainly couldn't have that! Is that what really bothers you about my being with him? It's okay for me to have a boyfriend, but only if he's safely overseas? Maybe Brandt's right and I am your pet. Can't have him *damaging* your precious unicorn hunter!"

Isabeau held my gaze for a moment longer, then walked to my desk. She picked up one of my course books and studied the spine. "I hate that term," she said. "The language is all wrong."

"What?"

"A man *taking* a woman's virginity. A woman *giving* it to him. It's inaccurate. The truth is there's nothing to actually possess, whether it's gift or theft. The act destroys the item."

"Virginity doesn't mean anything," I said. "Not unless someone makes it mean something. Not unless some stupid goddess decided it did thousands of years ago—or whatever it is that makes us work like we do." I sniffled, then cleared my throat, willing the sobs back into my chest. "Not unless you're a hunter, and then, yes, it destroys the magic."

"And you want that, Astrid?"

272

I thought of Angel huddled against Fats for protection from the storm. "No," I said. "Not at the moment."

"Good answer." She set down the book. "You hunters, you have a word for those men, do you not?"

I nodded. "An actaeon."

"Yes. The man who watched the goddess in her bath. The men who risk their lives to steal the hunters' most valuable possession."

I swallowed. "They weren't stealing it," I said. "Those hunters, the ones that utilized an actaeon—they wanted out of the business. Like that hunter who worked for you before me. She found one, didn't she? I mean, they don't call them that anymore, but that's what she did. She gave some guy her virginity. She got out."

"No, we don't call them that anymore," Isabeau agreed. "But that is not the point. And there is no giving. An actaeon can seek to possess the power of a hunter, but he never will. All he can do is erase it."

I snorted. "A minute ago you called it stealing. So what is it, Isabeau? What are they stealing, and who are they stealing from? You?"

She looked me in the eye, a slight smile playing about her lips. "No, Astrid. No one ever steals from me."

The following day, I was instructed to bring Angel to the Gordian laboratories. Instead, I tendered my resignation.

"How did you know?" I asked her as I packed. Isabeau sat at my desk, Gog and Magog lounging on either side of her, and ruffled the fur around their ears. I supposed that now I was no longer an employee, I couldn't begrudge her right to have her dogs in my bedroom.

"What, *chère*? Oh, someone saw the baby unicorn. Such a sweet thing. I wish you'd mentioned it to me earlier." She shook her head sadly. "Won't you reconsider? I've already called the Cloisters for another hunter, but they say they'd like to debrief you first. Something about you leaving under 'mysterious circumstances.' I tried to tell them it was nonsense, but—"

Nonsense! Phil had been on my side from the word *go*. Guarding the lab rats was one thing, turning over a baby unicorn to who knows what kind of experiments—that was another.

The thing that was most infuriating was how Isabeau was so calm. I was seething, and she was acting like this whole thing— my life upended, my future uncertain—was nothing more than a minor inconvenience.

"And we won't be able to move the colt until we have a new hunter in place. Who knows what might happen to it all alone out there?"

I looked up from my suitcase, jaw set. Isabeau was playing dirty pool. "That's kind of the reason I'm quitting, isn't it? So you *can't* move it?"

Isabeau looked baffled. "But that's such an empty gesture. The colt—Angel, as you call it—is ours to do with as we'd like, just like all the other animals in the enclosure. I thought you had accepted this."

"Well, I've un-accepted it."

"That won't matter," she said, her voice mild. "It is ours whether or not you are with us. There is no other option for it, anyway. You know it can't be released into the wild, and it would never survive without its mother. All you are doing with this stance of yours is delaying our eventual possession of this creature, and possibly putting it in extreme danger by abandoning it to the others without a hunter guardian. It's very foolish." She watched me picking through my wardrobe. "Do take the silk scarf, Astrid. It looks so lovely with your winter coat."

I sighed. I wouldn't need half these clothes back at the Cloisters, but I hated to leave them. "This would be so much easier if you *acted* angry with me."

"But I'm not angry with you, *ma chère!*" Isabeau exclaimed. Her dogs stared at me, echoing her amusement. "We have a difference of opinion; that is all. I don't want to see you leaving over it, but I am respecting your decision. And hoping," she added, "that in time you'll change your mind. I hate to see you give up your studies."

"There are tutors at the Cloisters now," I said.

"Not *private* tutors," she argued. "Not laboratory sessions at the university."

I clenched my teeth and kept on packing.

"Truly, you won't find a better position than this one!"

"If it's so great," I said, folding up the last of my sweaters and stuffing it into my overfull suitcase, "then I'm sure you'll have dozens of hunters lined up to take my place." I bet Grace or Melissende would come in an instant. They'd have no compunction whatsoever about turning Angel over to be vivisected or whatever other gruesome thing the scientists had planned.

And I wasn't convinced that this whole thing wasn't a punishment for making out with Brandt. Had Isabeau known about Angel all along, and had she been indulging me until I'd disobeyed her? I was sure Brandt would agree with that hypothesis—crazy as it sounded—and yet, I hadn't seen Brandt since he'd been yanked out of my arms, and I didn't know his phone number or how to contact him, either.

Speaking of people I hadn't contacted: Giovanni. Once I did, I'd have to tell him about my infidelity, and I could bear only one major upset in my life at a time, thank you very much.

I struggled to zip up my suitcase, sitting on it to squeeze the edges together.

Isabeau sighed and went over to my closet, where the blue gown still hung from a hanger on the back of my door. "You aren't taking this?" she asked, running her hand along the gorgeous, shimmery fabric.

"No room," I mumbled. "It'd get crushed if I tried to shove it in my suitcase, and what do I need a party dress for at a nunnery?"

She cast me a glance over her shoulder. "Please change your mind. You aren't doing anything but making us wait a few days. You aren't helping the unicorn."

"I know." I swallowed until I could breathe again. "But I'll sleep better at night knowing it wasn't me who handed him over."

Another sigh, and she returned to the bed. Gog and Magog tracked her every move with their big white heads. "Consider this, then. Here you have it easy, months and months where you are never asked to kill a unicorn. That is not the case at the Cloisters. Remain here, Astrid. You seem to have lost your taste for unicorn hunting."

I bristled, because she was right. Just like René. They were all right. Still, at least at the Cloisters, I'd never been asked to kill a defenseless unicorn. The ones I'd put down were the source of imminent danger. "Then maybe I'll get out of the business entirely."

"No, you won't," Isabeau said, quite confident.

No, I wouldn't. Dammit. For a moment, I might have even mistaken her smug tone for my mother's. "Well, I guess I'm done. I suppose you won't let me into the enclosure to say good-bye to them?"

Her voice was as brisk and businesslike as ever. "You know perfectly well why I cannot do that. But I'd be happy to drive you into Limoges." She laid a hand on my shoulder. "Last time, *ma chère*. Do not do this. Yes, I can have another hunter, and yes, the delay is a small annoyance, but it is nothing to the thought of losing you. We have been so happy here. And it feels so right, to employ you over all other hunters. We are Llewelyns, remember?"

I *had* been happy here. I looked around my lovely little room with all its luxuries. My wide desk, my school notes. My golden marble bathroom, my beautiful wardrobe. The bouquet of chamomile on my bedside table, the books that Isabeau had lent me. I thought of how well I'd come to know the einhorns; of my simple, self-set schedule; of the evenings I'd spent talking to Isabeau about science and medicine and the history we shared.

And then I thought about Angel, of the miracle I'd witnessed the night of the unicorn's birth. I thought of what I'd done to Jumps, of the horror I'd felt when he just wouldn't die. I thought of the way the einhorns had stood in a circle and bowed to me, of how hungry they always were, a yearning that no amount of butchered meat could hope to satisfy.

I thought of Clothilde, and how she couldn't live with the destiny that had been chosen for her, and what she was willing to sacrifice to follow her convictions and escape.

"Yes," I said, lifting my chin, "we are Llewelyns. And so you know perfectly well why I cannot allow myself to do this any longer."

Fire and flood assaulted my brain the second I walked through the front door of the Cloisters, lugging my suitcase behind me. Everything looked exactly the same: the cracked cobblestones in the outer court, the weathered bronze doors with their bas-relief carvings of hunters and unicorns, the dimly lit rotunda with its dusty statues and its enormous tableau of Clothilde and Bucephalus—and me dragging a suitcase. It might as well have been eight months ago and my first visit to the place.

Except there stood Phil, looking staid and somber in a con-servative navy skirt and a high-necked white blouse, her hair pulled into a bun at the nape of her neck, and a large golden ring with a ruby red stone dangling from a chain around her throat. Bonegrinder stood obediently by her side, then swept into a bow as I approached.

"Asteroid!" Phil cried, and ran forward. "It's so good to have you home!"

Home. I supposed this was the closest I could come. I no longer had a home in Washington, my mother having months ago abandoned the rooms over Uncle John's garage for a more upscale loft in LA—the better to be convenient to her booking agent. And my room at the château was no longer mine, either. All I had left was this nunnery.

But here, in the circle of Phil's arms, that didn't seem so bad.

She didn't lead me up to the dorm rooms as I'd expected, but into the don's quarters, Bonegrinder trotting along behind us and snapping at the wheels of my suitcase. "There's been some musical chairs going on with the room assignments," she said. "Obviously, no one wanted to keep sharing once you, Cory, and Valerija left two empty rooms, so they spread out a little. Your choice right now is to stay with me or move in with Melissende."

"You, please," I said.

"Thought so." She grinned. "Of course, this could just be a temporary arrangement. Zelda is leaving, you know, and then you can have her—"

"Zelda is leaving?" I repeated. "How? Is she sick, too?"

Phil blinked at me. "No, she's just . . . quitting. You know."

"Did she get an actaeon?"

Phil giggled. "She got a boyfriend. Some guy she's known for years apparently realized how much he really felt for her when it became clear she was risking her life with this gig. She's going back to France—"

"Back to modeling?"

"No," said Phil. "University. I'm thrilled for her, actually, even if it does mean we're down another hunter." She started counting off on her fingers. "Ilesha can't hunt until her stitches close up, and Ursula's out until the cast comes off. Cory's still hunting blind, which makes her more of a liability than anything else, but that doesn't matter because she and Valerija and Grace got it in their clearly genius heads the other day to have an offal eat-off—"

"A what?"

"Brains. Tripe. Gross stuff that, really, no one should ever have to smell, let alone put in their mouths. Anyway, they are still in bed with food poisoning. Which is all we need right now! You certainly returned at the right time."

279

I did the math. That left us with . . . four hunters? Including me? Yikes. "How is recruitment going?"

Phil's expression turned dark. "Sore subject. Don't bring it up to Neil when you see him, okay? We've been having some terrible luck recently."

"Why, what's going on?" I sat down on the edge of her bed. Bonegrinder leaped up beside me and nuzzled until I scratched her at the base of her horn. "I know he didn't get that girl from America a few months ago—"

"Her family wasn't interested," Phil said. "Some nutty theory that unicorns are demons or something. Anyway, that's par for the course. Lately it's been even weirder. We get a tip about a possible hunter, or we track down a family line, but by the time we contact them, they've decided to relinquish their eligibility."

"What?" I exclaimed.

"Exactly." Phil shrugged. "I mean, who can blame them? Especially with all the stories your mother has been pushing to the press about how dangerous our lifestyle is, how we're taking our lives in our hands every day. Yes, it's all very glorious—just like she wants it to be—but the whole 'band of brothers' thing doesn't necessarily market well to the average fifteen-year-old girl."

That was for sure. Only a few months ago I was trying to submarine my eligibility as well.

"There was one in Ireland last week, one in Greece two months ago . . . It's been really demoralizing for him," Phil said. "Especially with Cory not doing any better."

"And you getting ready to go back to school and leave us," I added.

She looked away.

I grabbed her by the shoulders. "Phil. You *are* going back to school, aren't you?"

She said nothing.

"You promised!" I cried. "Your scholarship!" At least someone in this family had to continue on to college.

She pulled away. "Volleyball doesn't seem that important to me anymore," she said. "Not like moving forward with unicorn protection. I've been putting all my effort into that lately. Even if I did go back, I'm not in any kind of training shape. I'd be a pathetic addition to the team. So instead of doing that and wasting everyone's time, I'm going to do this. My contribution toward making the world a better place. I'm going to save the unicorns, Astrid. It's really going to happen. And then we won't need hunters, and all this recruitment stuff won't matter, and everyone will be safe."

This fantasy again. Oh, Neil and Phil were perfect for each other, to be sure. They both saw a prescribed end to this life. They both thought if they put their futures on hold for a few months, a few years, they could achieve a permanent solution for us all. But it was a pipe dream. I knew that now.

"How?" I asked, throwing up my hands. "How will preventing us from hunting the dangerous ones make us all safe? Believe me, Phil, I'm not hanging around here for the glory. I'm doing it because if I don't, people will die. People *have* died. People are dying in unicorn attacks all over the world. So you save the unicorns. How are you going to save the humans?"

"Same way Clothilde did," Phil said with confidence. "We'll create a sanctuary for the unicorns, a place where they'll be safe. A preserve . . ."

"Captivity," I said. Bonegrinder looked curiously from me to Phil. "I've seen unicorns in captivity. It's not a pretty sight."

"You've seen unicorns in a tiny enclosure with no resources, like being in a zoo. I'm talking about a vast tract or tracts of land, separate from humanity, where they can live in the wild and—"

"We tried that," I said. "Clothilde and Bucephalus did. It didn't work."

"It did," Phil said. "For a hundred and sixty years."

"Bucephalus told me last summer that their hiding place is gone. They reemerged because their last preserve was destroyed." Gordian had been my preserve, but I'd lost that, too. Nothing lasted.

"Because there was no protection for it. But we can do it again. We can find another place. We can convince them—"

"Them the unicorns or them the lawmakers?" I asked. "You honestly think you can walk into one of these big government meetings you have planned and tell them that we have the magical ability to talk to unicorns and convince them to go hide out in a giant nature preserve?"

"No," said Phil. "*We* don't have that magical ability. But you do."

The image of the einhorns ringed around me popped into my head, but I pushed it away. "Bucephalus has been keeping his distance for months, Phil. He's the only one who could pull off something like that. And I don't know if it would work again. From what I understand, the kirin are still bitter about their exile. I doubt they'd retreat willingly from mankind."

She stood firm. "It's the only option, Asteroid. Either we find them a wild space, or we hunt them to extinction. Don't you see that's the only possible end to this?"

I laughed, bitterly. "You see an end to this. That's sweet. The only end I see is getting out, like Zelda, like all those missing recruits. Like you."

Phil shook her head, looking near tears. "I'm not *out*, Astrid. I still have a duty to this place, magic or no magic. And I hate seeing you like this. I know this past year hasn't been easy, and I know that a lesser person than you *would* have run away, *would* have gotten out. We *have* to believe there's a solution; don't you get it?"

No. No, I didn't. My solution had been to run away from hunting and become a prison guard, but somehow, that was even worse. Angel was probably even now trapped in some sterile cage in the bowels of the Gordian labs, awaiting some horrible, scientific fate. I couldn't save that unicorn. I couldn't protect any of them. I couldn't do it at the château, and I couldn't do it here. And Phil, no matter what she wanted to believe, wouldn't be able to do it, either.

Maybe Cory was right, and the only solution was to kill them all. Except, the hunters themselves were dropping like flies. Four unicorn hunters. René needn't worry about the fate of the unicorns. It was mankind that was toast.

Bonegrinder whined and licked my hand.

19

WHEREIN ASTRID REACHES THE PEAK

Two days after my arrival, the remaining members of the Order of the Lioness gathered in the rotunda to bid Zelda Deschamps adieu. She stood with her luggage all around her, one hand resting casually on the waist of her boyfriend, David. They were flying to Fiji for a vacation and . . . whatever.

"Should be a good break from the weather," Phil said bravely. I'd caught her crying this morning. She and Zelda had become close friends ever since I'd left for France. It made sense. At eighteen, Zelda was the nearest in age to Phil, and they probably had more in common than anyone else. I remembered when she'd first come, how Phil, Cory, and I had marveled that the gorgeous, black Parisian model had even been eligible to be a unicorn hunter.

"Should be a good break from a lot of things," Zelda joked.

Rosamund had been inconsolable since dinner last night. This morning, her eyes were as red as her hair as she embraced her old roommate and wailed. "Must you go?" she asked. "It's not too late."

Zelda looked lovingly at David, affection and desire shining out of the depths of her dark eyes. "It's way too late." He smiled back at her, every bit as besotted.

I swallowed thickly, thinking of the way Giovanni used to look at me. I still hadn't called him, not even to tell him I was in Rome. I'd picked up the phone five separate times. A few times, I'd even dialed the number, but I couldn't bring myself to press the send button. As soon as I heard his voice, I'd have to tell him what I did.

And then I'd never hear his voice again.

Cory, Valerija, and Grace stood, bleary-eyed and obviously longing to return to bed. The worst of the food poisoning had passed, but they all looked as if they'd need a few days to get their energy back.

I'd brought Cory some soup and lemon soda my first night back, and confessed to her what I'd done with Brandt.

"Don't worry," she'd responded. "We all do stupid stuff. Like that time I ate headcheese. Oh, wait. That was yesterday." She groaned and clutched her stomach. Food poisoning or not, I didn't like the look of her. She'd grown thinner and paler than ever, and spoke of occasional fevers or aches in her joints.

"Giovanni doesn't have to forgive you for that."

Cory eyed me carefully. "I hate to say this, Astrid, but you must be prepared for the fact that Giovanni might not forgive you."

We'd been interrupted then by Grace, returning from one of her many trips to the toilet. She grunted at the bowl of soup and bottle of soda I'd brought her, then collapsed on the bed and covered her face with a pillow. From what Cory had told me, she was bitter about getting Cory as a roommate, but after Neil and

Phil had learned about Cory's relationship with Valerija, they'd decided this arrangement worked far better.

Grace Bo as chaperone. I'm sure she loved it.

David had come into town last night, and we'd all heard their story, which was romantic enough to wow half a dozen teenagers trapped in a convent. Seems he and Zelda had been friends for years. Like her, he'd been a teen model, but he'd grown tired of the industry and quit in favor of École Polytechnique, which, as far as I could tell was the French equivalent of MIT, and which David always called "X" for some reason utterly unknown to me. Smart dude. During a fall holiday from classes, he'd gone to a party with some old modeling friends and ran into Zelda, who was on similar leave from her hunting duties.

"We talked all night," Zelda had cooed.

They'd talked about their world post-modeling and how the lifestyle had never really suited either of them.

"Which was why we were hiding out from the party, if I recall," David had said.

He told her about how much he was enjoying X, and she talked about how she regularly feared for her safety on unicorn hunts. She showed him her scars.

"He thought they were beautiful."

I'd grimaced at that, remembering Brandt.

By morning, they were an item, and they remained so even when Zelda returned to her bow and her habit and her life at the Cloisters. They e-mailed and texted constantly.

"It's kind of weird to fall in love on the Internet," Zelda had said.

"We were in love already," David replied. "We just found out about it on the Internet."

It was a short jump from there to Zelda deciding that she could no longer stay with the Order of the Lioness. Not just because of David, she was quick to point out. But because David had reminded her that there was a whole world out there she was giving up.

"I want to go to school," she said. "I want to study classics."

"Why bother?" Melissende had asked. "We're already living the lives of vestal virgins."

And now Zelda was leaving. A romantic, tropical getaway with her handsome boyfriend and a new life as a student in the *classes préparatoires*, which were like special study courses French kids had to take before they could even hope to apply for their own entrance exams into one of the *grandes écoles*.

I was so jealous I could spit. Apparently, to get the life you've always dreamed of, all you had to do was bide your time and be lucky enough to meet a fantastic, supportive boyfriend who wanted you to go to college just like him—and then be smart enough not to cheat on him.

Oh, and also be willing to walk away from the unicorn magic, from your birthright, from the massive guilt you felt not just for the people you would have been able to save with your special abilities, but also for the unicorns you failed to help in their time of need.

Zelda approached Phil next and hugged her tight. "I will miss you, *amie*."

"Me, too," I heard Phil murmur into Zelda's shoulder.

"It is time for you to leave as well. The Order has no place in the modern world."

"You're right," she said. "But *I* have a place with the unicorns."

I liked to talk about giving up my powers, but I'd never been able to go through with it. And now, knowing what I did about the einhorns suffering at Gordian, about the plight of the Cloisters and their ever-smaller circle of hunters? Now that I knew exactly what Phil was sacrificing, even without magic? For sure I'd never abandon her. Just as, last summer, before she'd found a cause to sustain her, Phil had promised not to abandon me.

"You mean you have a place with Neil." Zelda drew back and looked my cousin in the eye.

Phil said nothing, and I bit my lip, throat burning with even more jealousy. What had Phil told Zelda that she wouldn't tell me?

And then I felt Phil fumbling for my hand, and I unclenched my fist and allowed her to take it. She squeezed, hard, and somehow, that was enough. I relaxed. Neil might be real, or he might never be, but Phil and I were forever.

Zelda knelt near Bonegrinder, who looked up at her with blue eyes filled with more adoration even than David's.

"*Adieu, malodorant monstre*," she said with a laugh. "I didn't think I liked animals, but you are okay."

Bonegrinder thwapped her tail against the mosaic floor.

"I suppose we shall never meet again," she said. "But if we do, please do me the honor of not killing me."

Bonegrinder licked her face, and Zelda crinkled up her nose. I wasn't sure if that was the zhi's version of a promise, or merely a taste test.

That afternoon, Phil received a report of a re'em attack in the Monti Simbruini Park outside of Rome and gathered the troops together. During my absence, she and Neil had procured their own van to help transport us to and from hunting sites, and the four active hunters—Dorcas, Melissende, Rosamund, and me—loaded up our weapons.

"This is going to suck," said Melissende, climbing into the van. "All the really good hunters are out sick."

Phil ignored her, I said nothing, and Rosamund clutched her rosary and stared straight ahead. Phil had told me that the Austrian pianist had rarely attended hunts lately. I'm sure if she were less religious, Rosamund would also be seeking a way out of the biz, and if she were less forthright, she'd probably be faking her own injuries to make sure she stayed on the bench.

"I hate re'em," she said softly once we were on the road. "I haven't seen one since the night we were attacked outside the Cloisters, remember?"

I shivered. Of course I did; that re'em had been my first kill.

"Don't worry," said Dorcas. "Astrid and Melissende have both taken them before. If it's only one, we shouldn't have a problem."

Rosamund stared out the window and said nothing.

The city gave way to suburbs and then countryside, and then even more rugged terrain as we traveled up into the Apennine Mountains. The ground was spotted with gray slush, and gusts of winds buffeted the van as Phil concentrated to stay on the winding mountain roads. Deep ravines and sharp peaks met every turn, punctuated by pockets of dense woods. Though only about forty miles from Rome, this land made a perfect hiding spot for a re'em, or even a whole herd of them, for the park boasted pockets of wild deer and boar, brown bears, and even a few wolves.

The sky was dim and gray, even though it was just past

midday as Phil stopped the van at the entrance to a hiking trail.

"This is where the witnesses found the bodies," she said. She distributed walkie-talkies as we got our gear together. Our arrows, I noted, were all fitted with the alicorn points that Isabeau had had made.

"How did they know it was a re'em?" Rosamund asked, sniffing the air. There was no scent of fire and flood up here, just the freshness of evergreen and snow and rock.

"They caught a glimpse through binoculars," Phil said. "It was up near the top of this trail, by the peak."

"At least it was keeping its distance from the towns," I said. "Like the bears and the wolves that live here."

"I know." Phil frowned. "You're preaching to the choir here, Astrid. I'd say live and let live, too, but it's killing hikers now. There are some big ski resorts around here, and we just can't risk any more attacks. Especially when we're so close to getting protection."

So kill a unicorn to save a bunch of other unicorns? I wondered what the policy would be had it been a bear that had attacked those hikers. How far out into the wilderness would you have to go before the rights of people gave way to the rights of wild animals? Was there ever a time when the animals took precedence?

Phil's point of view sounded oddly like Isabeau's. She was willing to kill unicorns to develop the Remedy, which might save human lives, and she didn't see much of a distinction between what we did and what she was doing, though hunters killed only unicorns who were actively threatening people. The end result was the same: you could kill unicorns to save people.

That was the rule, right?

"Let's separate into two teams of two," Melissende said. "We can take either side of the trail and contact one another if we sense anything." She waved her walkie-talkie—one of the other bonuses from the Gordian largesse.

"Sounds good."

"I'll go with Dorcas," she added, casting a distasteful glance at Rosamund, whose hands were shaking so hard she'd just spilled the entire contents of her quiver into the slush.

Dorcas and Melissende took the left-hand loop, and I waited for Rosamund to gather her bone-tipped arrows together.

"You take care, Asterisk," Phil said.

"You, too," I said. "Remember to stay down in that van."

She saluted me. "Don't worry. I don't want to get anywhere near a re'em."

Rosamund and I started up the trail, sliding a bit on the slippery, lichen-covered rocks pockmarking the terrain, and keeping our senses alert for any trace of unicorn. I decided I had been spoiled by my months wandering in the tiny, flat woods behind the château, carrying nothing more than my alicorn knife and the occasional steak to feed the einhorns. Scaling a mountainside with a bow, a full quiver, my claymore, the alicorn knife, and a full first aid kit was an entirely different prospect. Our progress was slow and arduous and accompanied by a lot of puffing.

"See anything?" Melissende's voice came crackling over the radio.

I caught my breath long enough to shoot back a no. She didn't sound winded in the slightest. Maybe they got the flat side of the trail. So unfair.

There was very little sound up here except for the whistle

of the wind and the creaking in the branches of the occasional grove of trees. We hiked steadily uphill for another forty-five minutes, not talking much, listening to the crunch of gravel beneath our hiking boots and the soft clinks of our equipment shifting around as we walked.

It was hard to believe I was less than fifty miles from one of the oldest cities in the world. Beyond the edge of the trail, there seemed to be nothing out here that bore the touch of man. I found myself wondering if my einhorns would like this place, if Angel would have enjoyed frolicking in the snow or chasing hedgehogs and martens around the rocks.

Of course they would. They would like any life outside the confines of their pitiful little grove, trapped, unable to hunt or chase or be safe. I'd known them too long and too well. I'd seen into their dreams and fathomed their desires. This was all they wanted. I'd abandoned them because I realized how much I wished they could have it. Out here, like this, it seemed easier to imagine Phil's dreaming coming true. Easier to believe that there could be someplace in the wild where unicorns could live free and happy.

And then I remembered that we were out here to kill a unicorn for trying to do exactly that.

"They said they found corpses." My words spilled out.

"What?" Rosamund said, understandably.

"Corpses," I repeated. "The unicorn that attacked those people—it didn't eat them after it killed them."

"So?"

"That's kind of weird, don't you think?"

Rosamund shrugged. "I don't know. Perhaps it had plenty of food stored for the winter. Perhaps it was scared away by something—a bear, maybe."

"Unicorns aren't afraid of bears."

"A lion, then."

"There are no wild lions here. A wildcat, maybe. But a re'em wouldn't be afraid of that, either. Besides," I added, "other animals can't eat carrion tainted with alicorn venom. It's poisonous to them as well."

"Well, then, I don't know," Rosamund said. She hugged her arms around her shoulders. "I'm just cold and wet and tired. Do you feel anything yet?"

I shook my head. "You?"

"No." We kept walking, and Rosamund began to hum softly, a slow melody I recalled she used to play on the piano down in the chapter house.

"So tell me," I said as we puffed along. "Does music have charms to soothe the savage beast?"

"What?"

"It's, um, a saying."

"Oh. I could not say. Bonegrinder seems to like it when I sing, but she likes everything we do. I don't know if it would work on another kind of unicorn. Wouldn't that be nice?"

"Yeah."

We were silent for a few more yards, then Rosamund spoke again. "Astrid?"

"Hmm?"

"Do you love Giovanni?"

I stopped walking. My instinct was to say yes, but if I loved Giovanni, would I have kissed Brandt? Would I have let my ex-boyfriend put his hands all over me? Wouldn't I have contacted Giovanni as soon as it happened to confess the truth? If I loved

Giovanni, wouldn't I have spoken to him in the last few days?

"Why?" was all I said.

"Because I was thinking of Zelda. She loves David, and she left for him. But you are with Giovanni, and you don't leave."

"It's not as simple as love," I said. "I thought you believed that as well. You said you didn't want to have sex until your wedding night."

"I don't," said Rosamund. "But I would also like to have a wedding night."

Touché.

"I've never been in love," Rosamund said. "I had one boyfriend, but it was only for a week, at a music camp. We went to a dance, and he kissed me under the stars."

"Sounds nice," I said. Still no trace of the re'em.

"I probably would have had more boyfriends if I weren't so busy with my music."

I turned to look at Rosamund, at her long, wavy red hair and her elfin face. "Definitely."

The walkie-talkie crackled again. "We see her. It's a re'em. Big one, too."

"Are you within range?" I asked back.

"No, we—" I heard a shouted curse, then the radio went silent. I stared left over the ravine that separated us from the lower part of the trail, wondering what the quickest route was to the other team. Rosamund scanned the landscape, searching for movement.

"Do you see them?" I cried.

"No." She closed her eyes and raised her face into the wind, sending out feelers of magic. I breathed in, hoping to trace the telltale scent of fire and flood, but felt nothing.

"I hear them!" she shouted. "The chords. Over here!" She took off, sprinting up the path, which wound around a large boulder and headed to the right.

"Wait!" I cried. "Rosamund, that's the wrong way!"

But she kept running, and I followed. After all, who was to say that Melissende and Dorcas hadn't already passed the ravine? Their path appeared to be flatter. Maybe they were able to make better time than we were.

Sure enough, on the other side of the boulder the path turned into a series of long switchbacks that Rosamund was blithely ignoring in favor of cutting straight up the mountainside. I panted behind her for a few yards until suddenly I could feel a tingle of unicorn magic. It bloomed inside me and I breathed clear again, my strides lengthening as the world seemed to slow and shrink around me. There were unicorns on this mountain. Several of them.

Melissende's voice came over the radio. "It's coming toward you! Get ready!"

"I know!" I said. "I can feel it. You guys okay?"

"Yes." Now Melissende did sound out of breath. "Oh, it got Dorcas in the arm, but she'll live. She's hanging back while her wound closes. I hit it in the flank with an arrow, but that doesn't seem to have slowed it down any."

"Good to know."

"I'll meet you. Are you still on the path?"

"Sort of. We're cutting through some switchbacks, still heading up the mountain. I can feel it now." Threaded through the scent of fire and flood was great terror, a hunger, and something that felt like . . . loneliness? No, abandonment.

The switchbacks ended abruptly in a copse of thickly threaded evergreens. I plunged through it in seconds and out the other side, where a boulder field seemed to have provided some shelter from the mountaintop elements for the trees to take root. A maze of rocks and tiny peaks jutted up all around me, making it impossible to make out the entire trail. Rosamund was nowhere to be seen, but it felt as if the unicorn was everywhere at once.

I ran faster. "Rosamund!" I called. "Arrow on the string!"

The words whipped away from me on the wind, and then I tripped on a rock and fell, sprawling, the momentum of the magic carrying me several more yards before I stopped.

That's when I heard it. An enormous bellow. And then, over the crest of a ravine to the left of the trail came the re'em, growling and snorting, its galloping hooves pounding the earth, kicking up massive clods of dirt and gravel and snow. This unicorn was even larger than the one I'd killed in Rome. It had to weigh at least fifteen hundred pounds. It tossed its wide, oxlike head wildly about, swinging its great ridged horn from one side to the other as it ran. The green shaft of Melissende's arrow still jutted from its side, and dark red blood ran from the wound in a fanning stream down its dun-colored flank.

I scrambled to my feet, pulling my bow from my shoulder and an arrow from my quiver. With the stopped-time speed of my hunting magic, I scanned the trail ahead for any sign of Rosamund or Melissende, but could find neither. "Rosamund!" I hissed. She must have ducked out of sight when I tripped.

I climbed a boulder, the better to catch sight of my quarry. The re'em galloped toward the rock field, bellowing long and loud. I paused, my bow at full draw. I felt more than one unicorn. Several, in fact. Thanks to my practice at doing a head count back at Gordian, I could detect at least three unicorns in the immediate area. Was this unicorn I was about to shoot responsible for the deaths of those hikers, or was it a different one? A more remote, wild area could not possibly be found. Was it possible that Melissende had injured a unicorn who was just trying to escape mankind?

It didn't eat the corpses. . . .

In the middle of winter, yet. Food must be scarce up here, and yet the man-eating unicorn had left its kill behind. Why?

Why else does an animal kill? For food, in defense, to protect its territory . . . and how could anyone deny that this rugged mountaintop, a home to wolves and bears, was not the perfect territory for a monster?

I heard the thwang of an arrow, and the re'em stumbled, a second green shaft sticking in its hind leg. Melissende climbed out of the ravine, limping slightly as she ran, and reached for a third arrow. By this time, the re'em was closer to the rock field, quartering toward me. I could hit it right in the heart. If I wanted to.

You seem to have lost your taste for unicorn hunting. . . .

I reached out to the unicorn with the tendrils of my mind, remembering how I'd bent the einhorns to my will. *Calm down. Stop your stampede.* Maybe there was still some way. Still some other solution. Like that time with Breaker when the fence went down. Maybe I could make it listen.

The re'em was staggering now, trying its best to run with blood still streaming from both arrow wounds. I didn't know if it was listening or just dying. I skidded down the side of the boulder, back to the earth, and reached into its mind.

Fear, despair, sacrifice. There was no chink in this armor of terror, no way to get inside and speak to it.

Melissende tripped and fell, her bow bouncing out of her hands before she could fire off another shot. This was my last chance. I shut my eyes and took a deep breath. I was an arrow, straight and true. I was an arrow, sent to penetrate the mind of the savage unicorn.

The chord began to ring in my head, the one Rosamund always heard while hunting unicorns. I felt her now, crouched behind a boulder a few yards over. I felt the pinprick of Melissende, halfway across the field. And the unicorn, buzzing, glowing, dying. I felt it crying out, felt it flailing around for the tiny, flickering, oh-so-familiar swirls of the other unicorns. They were gathered nearby. So very, very near . . . so small . . . so helpless . . . so alone . . .

Oh my God.

My eyes shot open as Rosamund jumped out of her hiding place, arrow on the string. She fired into the unicorn, her shot hitting it in the shoulder. I rushed toward them both as the unicorn lowered its head to charge.

"No!" I screamed, passing by boulder after boulder. "No, wait! She's a mother! She's just protecting the babies."

The steps of the charging unicorn faltered as I spoke her secret aloud. She raised her head and stared at me with fiery, furious eyes.

It's the last thing I remember.

20

Wherein Astrid Loses Her Mind

Bonegrinder hopped up on my bed. I felt the depression of the mattress beneath each of her little hooves, felt her sniff my face, then shift and settle down on her haunches alongside my right thigh. The ridges of her screw-shaped alicorn pressed against my calf.

"Morning!" Phil said. There was light on the backs of my eyelids and I squinted.

"Bright."

"Indeed. Comes along with the mornings. How are you feeling today?"

"Not bad," I said, opening my eyes and shoving myself up in bed. "Kinda sleepy, though."

Phil stopped, her brow furrowing slightly. She carried a tray in her hands. "Wow. Okay. Feel like some eggs this morning?"

"Sure," I said.

"Sure," she repeated, as if she'd never heard the word before. She set the tray down on my lap. I looked at the dish as Bonegrinder lifted her head to sniff, then snort at the obvious lack of meat products. There were some scrambled eggs, a lump of what looked like polenta or some other grain mash, and applesauce. But no silverware.

I looked up. Phil was sitting next to me with a spoon in her hand.

"Can I have that?"

Phil blinked, glanced at the spoon, then at me. "Um, sure."

Well, at least now she knew the word. I took the spoon from her and ate my eggs—which, by the way, are not particularly easy to wrangle with a spoon—and then the applesauce. I tried the grain, but it felt bland and sandy in my mouth, so I put the spoon down.

There was a sound in the hall. Bonegrinder hopped off the bed and went to investigate. I felt my eyelids flutter closed.

Fire and flood in my nostrils. Bonegrinder was back.

"Astrid?"

Man, I was sleepy. I rolled onto my side.

"Astrid? Can you hear me?" Phil's voice.

"I wish I couldn't," I said. "It's the middle of the night."

"Oh my God," she said.

"What?" I said. "Did your watch break, or did you lose all sense of circadian rhythms?"

"Circadian," Phil repeated in a monotone.

I sat up and peered at her through the dark. "Yes, circadian rhythm. It's like our bodies' natural alarm clock."

"I know what it is," she said. "I just—" Her voice caught on a sob, and then she was hugging me so tight I couldn't breathe. Bonegrinder growled until Phil released me.

She turned to the unicorn. "You stay, you hear? You

stay." She ran from the room.

Weird. Bonegrinder curled up next to me, and I fell asleep, my hands buried in her fragrant fur.

I dreamed.

"Watch this," I heard through a fog.

Sometime later, there was Bonegrinder, nuzzling against the hand I'd left draped over the edge of my bed. I scratched behind her ears until she bleated. "Hey there, Sweets."

"I don't believe it." Neil's voice.

I sat up. "Um, privacy, Neil? This is my *bedroom*."

"See what I mean?" Phil said. "We have to leave her here."

"Yes, that would be ideal," I said, and covered my chest with my hands. "Or, you know, at least knock first."

I heard Neil blow on his whistle. "Bonegrinder, come." The zhi trotted away.

When I woke up the next time, Bonegrinder was sitting on my feet, and Phil was perched near my left hip. "Good morning." She gave me a nervous smile.

"Good morning," I said, sitting up in bed. That's when I saw the other people in the room. Father Guillermo. A man in a suit. Neil. And Ilesha, holding Bonegrinder's attention by dangling a piece of bacon in the air.

"How do you feel this morning?"

I shrugged. "Fine, why do you ask?"

"I was just curious."

"Okay. So here's something I'm curious about. Why are all these people in my bedroom?"

Father Guillermo and the man in the suit gasped.

Ilesha's eyes widened, but she was concentrating on Bone-grinder. I could feel her subduing the animal, keeping the zhi in place and calm.

"That's a good question, Astrid. Maybe you can figure it out. Do you know this man?" Phil pointed at the guy in the suit.

I shook my head. "Should I?"

"This is Dr. Sachetti."

"Pleasure to meet you."

"Signorina." He nodded.

"He's a neurologist," Phil said.

A neurologist? My hands clenched the sheets. "Why is he here?" I asked, suddenly very afraid. "Does Cory have a brain tumor?"

"Astrid," Father Guillermo asked. "What's the last thing you remember?"

"Neil and Phil barging into my bedroom earlier," I said, giving Neil the stink eye.

"Before that," Phil said.

"You waking me up in the middle of the—"

"*Before* that," she pressed. "Before this bedroom."

I stared in turn at all of them. What was going on here? Were they saying I had amnesia or something? How ridiculous. I *wished* I could have amnesia, and forget all the crap I'd been through. Forget messing up with Giovanni. Forget missing Angel. Forget killing Jumps.

"The hunt yesterday," I said, shrugging. "The re'em on the mountainside."

Phil burst into tears. Neil came to her and put his hands on both her shoulders.

"Phil, what's wrong?" I asked. I leaned forward to cover my hand with hers.

"That was more than a month ago," she said, or rather cried.

I dropped back against my pillow. "Was I injured?" I asked. "In the attack?"

Phil nodded miserably.

"Why—why didn't I heal?"

"The unicorn didn't gore you, Astrid," Neil said, when it became clear that Phil had lost the power of speech. "It slammed you into a boulder. It cracked your head open."

My hand shot to my scalp, where beneath my fingers I could feel the prickles of shorn hair, and the long, jagged ridge of a scar. My jaw went slack.

"You were in a coma—" he said.

"Let me see."

Ilesha's face twisted uncomfortably, which only made me more determined. I threw off the sheets, dislodging Bonegrinder, and put my feet on the floor. I was wearing long underwear, but I didn't care.

"Astrid, wait—"

I stood up, though my legs felt weak, and my head felt light.

Light-headed. There was a funny joke. I wonder how much of my brain got left on the mountainside.

"A coma," Neil repeated. "For a week. We didn't think you'd wake up. But the swelling went down—"

On the far wall, over the dresser, there was a mirror. And there, standing in the reflection, wearing a set of pink long underwear and a horrified expression, stood Clothilde Llewelyn.

Not the Clothilde in the tableau in the rotunda, with her porcelain face and long blond hair. No, the real Clothilde. The hunter, the one with the buzz cut and the body ravaged by a lifetime of fighting unicorns. A fresh scar ran from her temple all the way back to the nape of her neck. Dark, bruiselike marks rested above her cheekbones, which stood out like knives against her wan, skeletal face. But that wasn't all.

There was something wrong with her eyes. I didn't know these eyes, these strange alien eyes. They were dark, almost black, with a crescent ring of icy blue shining out from each iris. I blinked, and she did. I reached out to the mirror and our fingers touched. Behind her, Phil stood, tears dripping down her face, and put her hand on Clothilde's shoulder.

"Astrid." I felt her touch and turned.

"You said a month ago." To Phil. And then, to Neil: "And you said I was in a coma only for a week."

"You've been sick," Neil said carefully.

"Like, with the flu?" I asked, though it sounded inane even to me.

Ilesha was biting her lip so hard, I expected to see blood at any moment, though whether she was about to laugh or cry I couldn't be sure. Bonegrinder sat at the foot of my bed, staring, her tail swishing on the covers. The smell of fire and flood raged through the room.

"*Signorina*," said Dr. Sachetti. "Please to sit down."

I whirled on him. "Apparently I've been sitting down for a month! Now tell me."

He shied away. "It is a very curious thing, a human brain. You do not know at all times what will come back."

"After a week," Phil said through her tears, "you woke up. But, Asteroid, you weren't *you*."

I covered my mouth with my hands, hoping it would somehow keep my breakfast down.

"You weren't you until the other day, with the eggs."

I didn't have amnesia.

I had brain damage.

"Hey Astrid," came Phil's voice. I was staring at myself in the mirror. I was wearing an oversized sweatshirt and a pair of yoga pants I didn't remember putting on. That happened a lot, I was told.

"What's wrong with my eyes?" I asked, sensing the unicorn behind me. It wasn't Bonegrinder.

"It's called heterochromia," Phil said as I turned. There was a certain weariness in her voice, the kind I'd learned meant that she'd already explained this to me. "It might go away, but either way, it won't hurt you. It's actually not so uncommon after traumatic . . . head . . . injuries . . . or, you know, with some breeds of dogs."

I whirled around and she flinched as she got a good look at me. "Breeds of *dogs*?" I repeated. A strange unicorn hunter stood there, a zhi at her side. This zhi was slightly smaller than Bonegrinder had been when I first met her, with a coat more silver than white. The hunter looked nervous. I couldn't blame her.

"Or people!" Phil said. "People have it, too. Alexander the Great."

Great, one more thing we had in common. I turned my gaze to the girl. Young, with a short cap of sleek black hair and wary eyes. She wore jeans, a cap-sleeved blouse, and a golden cross around her neck.

"Who is she?" I grumbled. My eyes were ruined. My brain was ruined. *I* was ruined.

"We're going to try an experiment."

I didn't want to try an experiment. I wanted to go back to bed. I wanted the unicorn to leave so I could bury myself in fog again and forget what had happened to me. The zhi flopped its tail, and I tried to push the magic from my mind.

"Astrid, this is Wen."

Wen waved. Which was kind of funny.

"Wen is new here, and you haven't met her yet. She's from America. Do you remember we tried to get her to join us last fall, right when you left for France?"

I shrugged. There were lots of hunters we tried to get.

Phil moved on. "And this is her pet zhi, Flayer."

I looked at the zhi. The zhi loved Wen. The zhi loved Wen more than Bonegrinder loved any hunter in the Cloisters. It was beautiful. I hated to see it. I hated that the magic was the only thing that worked in my head. Right now, all I could see was their love. I thought of Angel and wanted to cry. Angel was probably dead by now, and I hadn't been able to stop it.

"Astrid." Phil's face filled with concern. "What's the matter?"

"I'm just thinking about the einhorn baby I left at Gordian," I said. "I should never have left him. I feel awful."

Wen's eyes widened. Apparently, I was scary now that my brain was broken.

"And the re'em's babies. Do we know what happened to them?" I asked. "Did Rosamund and Melissende find them?"

"Who is Rosamund?" Wen asked.

Phil frowned. Something started to ache inside me, but it was tough keeping it all together at once. Angel hurt, Phil sad, Flayer loving, Astrid angry . . . There was something else, but how could I ever remember it all? What were they even talking about?

"What do you mean?" I asked Wen.

My cousin stepped between us. Her don's ring swung from the cord around her neck. "You know what, maybe we can talk about this later," she said. "I'll bring Bonegrinder by and we can have a nice little chat."

My eyes became scary little slits in my scary, scary face. "Where's Rosamund?" I asked. The ache grew stronger. "Rosamund should meet Wen, too. I'm sure they have a lot in common." I reached around Phil and poked Wen on her cross.

Wen stepped back, grabbing at her throat. The silver zhi growled.

That's right, little unicorn. Fear me. See how scary I am, with my freaky hair and my freaky eyes and my ugly, ugly scars?

Phil's mouth had become a thin line. "Now you're doing this on purpose, Astrid," she said, her tone angry. "Stop and think for a second."

I stopped. I thought. The ache reached down into my heart and squeezed hard, its claws raking every inch along the way— my eyes, my throat, my lungs. I couldn't breathe, couldn't speak, and tears welled up to drown the pale crescents floating in my skull. Now I remembered.

Rosamund was dead.

She'd died trying to save me. The re'em had gotten her right through the heart. She'd never have a wedding night.

I sat down on the floor and covered my face with my hands.

"I'm sorry." I sobbed through my fingers. "I'm sorry. I'm sorry."

Even through my moans, I could hear Phil sigh. I was disappointing her. I looked up at Wen, who hadn't deserved this. "I apologize. I forget things sometimes. I'm brain damaged, you know."

"Not now, you're not," said the girl Wen.

"What?" I said, taken aback.

"Not now," she repeated. "That's what they told me, anyway. If you're around a unicorn, everything works just fine."

I blinked at her. They'd told me that, too. Sheesh, were they telling everyone?

"And she's getting better all by herself, too," Phil said. "She just sometimes likes to pretend otherwise."

"Why would I do that?" I asked from the floor.

Phil sighed. "I don't know, Asteroid, because you're a brat?"

I frowned. "I'm sorry. I'm so sorry about Rosamund. I'm so sorry. . . ." I started crying again. Phil knelt beside me. Wen knelt on the other side. They both held me.

"Is it always like this?" Wen asked Phil.

"This is the third time she's remembered on her own," Phil replied. "It gets better every time."

"Well, that's good news," I said, hiccupping. I wiped my eyes. "I like your zhi, Wen. He's kind of big for his age, huh?"

"How do you know that?" she asked.

I shrugged and held out my hand for Flayer to lick. I knew a lot of things when the unicorns were around.

It was the only time I did.

Cory looked better than I did, though that wasn't saying much. Though she still insisted that her illness was related only to her ability to access her hunting magic, everyone else knew that she was growing weaker by the day. She suffered from stomach pains no one could diagnose. Allergies whose source no one could pinpoint.

"Ironic," I said one day as I was brushing out Bonegrinder.

"All I have left right now is my unicorn magic."

"Together," Cory rasped, "we'd be the perfect person."

Valerija excused herself from the room. Later, I discovered she'd scrubbed down half the statues in the rotunda before she burned off her frustrated rage.

Wen forgave me our inauspicious meeting. I started giving her archery lessons. As long as Bonegrinder was around, I was still great at archery. She also let me watch Flayer while she was in classes. Phil didn't think I was ready for classes again, and she wanted me to spend as much time with the unicorns as possible.

Dr. Sachetti said that though there was no scientific basis, the changes in my cognitive functions were probably due to the enhanced focus that we claimed our unicorn hunting magic gave us. When our magic was active, our focus increased. He hypothesized that this increase, which he wasn't able to explain, triggered my neural pathways and repaired the broken ones.

Simply put, being around unicorns was healing my brain.

Not that we could test it. No one would let us bring Bonegrinder into a room with a CAT scan.

Phil said she didn't care how it worked as long as it did, which Dr. Sachetti and I both agreed was a very limited way of thinking. I don't mind saying that Dr. Sachetti was actually quite impressed with my opinion on the subject. Because, if we didn't know how it worked, how could we make sure it kept on working? I wanted to get fully back to normal.

As soon as I knew what that was.

Even in the presence of the zhi, I was still missing stuff. For instance, I saw Zelda three times before it occurred to me that she shouldn't be there. "What about David?" I asked Phil in a whisper that, it turned out, was far too loud.

"Zelda heard about you and Rosamund when she landed in Fiji," Phil explained. "Grace called—the rest of us were too much of a mess to try. We just wanted to tell her, you know? They'd been roommates. But she came back anyway."

"She broke up with David?" I asked. Zelda, polishing a sword at the other end of the Cloisters courtyard, shot me a glare.

Phil sighed and told me we could talk about it later. Except we didn't—or if we did, I don't remember.

Rosamund's death had hit all the hunters pretty hard. Dorcas, they said, rarely left her room anymore. Ursula had apparently been barred from going on any hunts.

"Her parents?" I'd asked Cory.

"No," she replied. "Her sister."

A few days later, I surprised Melissende in the middle of target practice. I hadn't seen her since the accident. At least, I didn't think I had.

"Hi," I said from the courtyard gate. She cast me a quick, furtive glance, then hurried over to the target to retrieve her bolts.

"Are you done?" I picked up her crossbow.

In two long strides she was upon me and snatched it out of my grip. "Don't touch that!"

I held up my hands. "Sorry!"

"You'll—" She grunted and turned away.

"I'll what?" I asked. "Break it with my clumsy hands? Shoot you accidentally?"

She froze, back to me. Her black hair was pulled up in a messy ponytail, hanging in tangles against the shoulders of her black sweater. "Shoot me on purpose," she said without turning around. "What difference does it make?"

My brow furrowed. "The difference is you'd be dead?"

Her shoulders hunched and I heard her take a sharp, shuddering breath. And then she ran off.

I think I didn't see her again for a few days, but it was tough to tell time now, what with my odd sleeping schedule and the way events sometimes got confused in my head. I know that one day Phil came to take me for a walk outside the magical safety net of the Cloisters. We were supposed to get gelato.

I don't remember much of the gelato. But I do remember coming back to myself beneath the statue of Clothilde and Bucephalus in the rotunda. Phil was dabbing at my face with a napkin, and my fingers were sticky with melted goo.

Melissende stood in the door to the chapter house, her face a mask of disgust. "Don't you think this is a waste of time?" she asked Phil. "Lock her up; throw away the key."

"Hey, I'm right here," I snapped.

"No, you're not," she said in a monotone. "You're still up on that mountain. I left you there smeared across a cliff face."

Phil stiffened, and the napkin paused in its trip across my cheek.

"I killed that re'em, and I saw that you—at least"—her voice shook, but she pressed on—"still had a heartbeat. I had to pick, though I knew there were other unicorns around. And I knew they might—"

"Stop it," Phil whispered.

But Melissende had no intention of stopping. "*Eat her*," she blurted out. "But what could I do? You were dying. I carried you down the trail . . . but it didn't matter."

"I said, stop it!" Phil whirled on her.

"You're kidding yourself, Phil. *Your* Astrid is gone. Rosamund's

311

dead, Astrid's brain dead, Cory's as good as dead—we're all going to end up like that if this keeps up. That's why I won't let Ursula go on a hunt."

Phil turned back to me, returned her attention to my fingers. "Then leave. If you feel like that, then just leave. Get rid of your eligibility."

"No way." Melissende gave a bitter laugh. "Leave so one day some unicorn can sneak up on Ursula and actually succeed in killing her this time? I'm okay with dying, as long as I can make sure that never happens."

Phil had moved herself between Melissende and me. I pushed her aside, ignoring the stickiness of the gelato still clinging to my fingers. "Thank you for saving my life, Melissende. I appreciate it immensely, and someday, I promise I'll be well enough to return the favor."

She snorted. "You? Hunt again? Don't count on it, genius." She walked away.

I looked at Phil. "Don't worry about her. She's wrong. Soon I'll be well enough to help again."

Phil didn't respond.

But things were improving. Time was I couldn't remember anything that happened when I wasn't around a unicorn. Time was, Phil told me, that I couldn't even string a sentence together unless Bonegrinder was sitting on top of me. But I could even read again now. First in the Cloisters, with the background buzz of the artifact net, and then, during my therapy sessions in the hospital, with nothing remotely related to unicorns anywhere around.

I was getting better. One of these days, I'd be back in classes. One of these days, I'd be a doctor.

But maybe only if they let me bring Bonegrinder to my medical school.

Weeks passed, and I threw myself into training. It was easy. In fact, unicorn hunting was the only thing that was easy anymore. I'd tried picking up my calculus textbook the other day, but the numbers just blurred together. The same thing happened when Phil gave me her latest environmental presentation to read. I'd tried to concentrate on it for forty-five minutes, then threw the papers to the floor, went outside, and hit fifty-seven bull's-eyes in a row.

The scar on my head had shrunk down somewhat, and the doctor told me that once my hair grew out, no one would notice it anymore. I asked to visit Rosamund's grave, but Phil told me her parents had taken her body back to Vienna.

"Then let's go to Vienna," I said.

But Phil just shook her head and ignored me.

That night, I shot sixty-three bull's-eyes in a row.

That's the part I really hated about all this. Because I sometimes got confused or said outrageous things, everyone simply wrote off completely rational suggestions as utterly preposterous. Why shouldn't I go to Vienna? Hadn't I traveled across the ocean a year ago all by myself? Hadn't I gone to France all by myself? Now I couldn't go to Vienna with a companion? It was ridiculous. I wasn't even planning to leave the EU. I couldn't visit the grave of the girl who'd died trying to save my life?

Rosamund would have thought that was ridiculous as well. I knew she would.

I missed her music in the chapter house. Sometimes I went down there and placed my hand on the trophy wall and closed my eyes and breathed until I could hear the chord. It wasn't the same as Rosamund at her piano, but it was still nice.

Phil and Neil wouldn't let me hunt, either, as if afraid I'd get "disoriented" in the middle of the action and, I don't know, shoot Grace by mistake. Again, ridiculous. How could they be arguing on one hand that I was constantly getting better and on the other hand that I couldn't tell the difference between Grace Bo and a unicorn?

"To start with," I muttered as I shot my seventy-fifth bull's-eye, "Grace is a bitch. And she walks on two legs."

After my eighty-second bull's-eye, I dropped the bow to the ground. What was the point of all this training if I wasn't allowed to hunt? What was the point of teaching my mind to do math again if I wasn't going to be able to be a doctor? What was the point of growing my hair out to cover my scars if no one was ever going to let me beyond the doors of the Cloisters?

I kicked at the alicorn-shaped columns. Flayer and Bonegrinder paused in their game of tug-of-war over an old hambone to look at me curiously.

I screamed at the sky.

"*Señorita?*"

Oops. Father Guillermo stood at the entrance to the rotunda, his hands folded before him. Great. Now I looked crazy in front of the priest.

"Are you all right?"

"Of course not," I said. "I'm brain damaged, haven't you heard?"

"Hmm . . ." Father Guillermo began a lazy circuit around the edge of the courtyard, keeping a wide berth between himself and the two zhi. I had to admit, Wen had pulled off something miraculous with Flayer. He seemed to understand that humans were not for eating, and ever since he'd been around, Bonegrinder, as if in solidarity, had been relaxing around nonhunters as well.

"I imagine this must be very frustrating for you," Father Guillermo said.

"That's putting it lightly."

"*Cogito, ergo sum*," he said. "Do you know what that means?"

"No."

"It's more Latin. Descartes, actually. A philosopher. It means, 'I think, therefore I am.' It means that our minds are the only things we can trust. Everything else in the world could be a lie, except for the fact that we can think. We think, therefore we are."

"And if I can't trust my own mind . . ." I began.

Father Guillermo nodded. "Then you can't know who you are."

I laughed. It was much easier for me to laugh these days. Everything seemed so funny. Either funny or truly tragic.

Or both.

"I didn't even know who I was *before* this happened to me, *Padre*. I wanted to be a doctor, but I was really a high school dropout. I was supposed to be a unicorn hunter, but I didn't want to kill them anymore. I thought I was in love with my boyfriend, but I kissed another guy. And I thought all the time. I was the thinkiest person I knew."

He studied me for a moment. "Then perhaps you are looking for a different piece of philosophy, Astrid. *Cognosce te ipsum*."

"And what does that mean?" I asked as he finished his circuit of the courtyard and drew close to me.

He laid his hand upon my brow as if blessing me. "'Know thyself.'"

For some strange reason, my bruised cerebrum found it much easier to learn Latin than to wrestle with derivatives, tangents, and secants, so when I finally was allowed to resume my course work, I dropped calculus in favor of ancient languages. I rationalized the change with the argument that if I ever got better enough to start thinking in terms of premed again, the Latin would come in handy in anatomy classes.

And then I laughed at the idea of me *rationalizing* anything. I must be getting better if I'd made it that far.

Armed with a grammar primer and a dictionary, I roamed about the Cloisters, finding inscriptions and graffiti that I happily translated, to the amusement of Phil and the delight of Father Guillermo, who'd taken me on as a pupil. The inscription at the base of the fountain in the courtyard said, "To Honor the Sacrifice of a Sister of the Order of the Lioness," and dated to the Reign of Terror in France. There was a crude scrawl at the bottom of the chapter house staircase that read, "Death or Flatulence to Dona Maria Therese," which we all found hilarious.

Today I was in the Cloisters courtyard working on a page Father Guillermo had given me to translate. Now that spring was fully upon us, I tried to spend as much time outdoors as possible. The weather was beautiful, cool and sunny, and there were flowers blooming all over the courtyard.

This translation was especially tricky as I was trying it out without the benefit of either of our house zhi. Their absence always made everything seem just a little more misty, but Dr.

Sachetti and Phil believed that it was important for me to wean myself off needing the unicorn magic to concentrate, needing it to think.

"*Et diliges Dominum Deum tuum ex tota corde tuo, et ex tota anima tua, et ex tota mente tua, et ex tota virtute tua,*" I read aloud. I liked reading aloud. It made me feel like I was in a real classroom, instead of all alone inside my broken brain.

Okay, so obviously something from the Bible, what with that *Dominum Deum* stuff. Father Guillermo could be so predictable sometimes.

"And *something* the Lord thy God from the whole of your heart, and from *something something something* . . ." Okay, that made no sense. If *ex tota corde tuo* was "with all of your heart," which I was pretty sure it was, and *ex tota mente tua* was "with all of your mind," and the one with the *virtute* was "with all of your strength" . . .

"*Ex tota anima tua?*" I read again. "'With all of your animals?'"

"Soul," said a voice behind me. "*Anima* means 'soul.' *Animalis* means 'animal.'"

I froze, and it seemed my heart stopped in my chest, which was too bad, since my brain needed all the oxygen it could get.

I slowly turned around, and there he was. Giovanni.

Giovanni.

Giovanni.

21

WHEREIN ASTRID LEARNS HER PLACE

Giovanni stared at me with those steady brown eyes that did all the smiling in his face. Phil tapped him on the shoulder. "I'll be in my office if you need anything."

He nodded, but didn't take those eyes off me.

Giovanni looked different, but who was I to talk? He'd gotten skinnier since last summer, and he'd grown out his hair into dreadlocks several inches long. Some of them were dyed crazy colors. Is this what happened at art school?

"Hi, Astrid," he said.

"Your hair is longer than mine." I ran a hand through my prickly, shorn scalp. Phil said it was elfin. I said it was plague victim.

Giovanni chuckled. "Yeah. Weird, huh?"

"Weird," I repeated. He was still standing halfway across the courtyard. "What are you doing here?" I asked.

"I'm on spring break," he said. "Thought I'd come and see my girl."

I closed my eyes, wishing the fog would come and take me away. *His girl?*

Giovanni's arms wrapped around me. "Astrid," he whispered. "It's okay."

"No, it's not," I said, stiff within his embrace. "I haven't spoken to you in months."

"Yeah, well, you get a pass on phone duties when you're in a coma. It's a rule."

"I wasn't in a coma for months."

"I mean . . . with . . . everything you've had to deal with."

Yes, the everything brain damage. Had Phil warned him what to expect? When Phil had said he could come to her if he needed anything, could one of those things be tips on dealing with his brain-damaged girlfriend?

Was I his girlfriend? Can you have a girlfriend you don't speak to for three months?

Melissende was right. Astrid—his Astrid—the one he'd cared about, the one who'd cheated on him—she'd died up there on the mountainside.

It was amazing that he didn't recognize that already.

"I wanted to fly over when I heard what happened to you," he said, his arms dropping to his sides again. "Phil told me not to."

"You didn't call."

"I did," he said. "I called once. I don't think you remember. It was . . . early on. Phil said maybe wait a bit. So I waited. But I knew I was coming out here for spring break. I was determined to see you."

I didn't say anything, just stared at my hands, tracing the

319

alicorn scar on one with the fingers of the other.

"I . . . came as soon as I could," he offered. "I swear to you I did."

"Of course you did," I said at last. "How's school?"

Giovanni quite obviously did not want to talk about school. He'd come to Rome to see if I was normal or stupid. He'd come to Rome to see if I was pretty or monstrous. He'd come to see what he was going to do about me.

I wasn't sure what he was deciding.

So he told me vague stories about classes and activities and roommates, and I did my best to follow along and not act idiotic or foggy or outrageous, but I kind of wished Bonegrinder were around. It would make this all so much easier. It would make it more obvious to him that the old Astrid was still in my head somewhere and that I was reconstructing more pathways for her to get out on every day.

But then I remembered what the old Astrid had done to him, and how she'd never told him, because she'd cracked her head open on a mountainside before she'd gotten up the courage to confess.

I watched him carefully for signs. I watched his surprise when he looked into my eyes, which never had gone back to being normal. They'd freak you out if you weren't expecting them. They freaked me out every time I looked in the mirror, and I knew they were there.

I watched the way his brows knit in concern whenever he caught a good look at the scar side of my head. I listened to his nervous chuckle every time he made a joke I didn't get, every time I laughed at something that wasn't, it turned out, a joke at all.

"And what have you been up to?" he asked me. "Other than . . . you know."

"Smooth," I said. "Other than rebuilding my brain, you mean?"

He nodded, half relieved that I could joke about it, half worried that I wasn't actually joking. I wondered what the conversation had been like with his roommates. *Hey, you know my girlfriend, the magical nun? Well, turns out she's now a magical retarded nun. A magical, bald, ugly, retarded nun. But hey, you guys go out with the gorgeous, witty models you meet every day on the street in New York City. I only have eyes for my bald, stupid nun. The one who lives across an ocean.*

And they said *I* was the irrational one? What was Giovanni even *doing* here? "Well, you might have heard we have a new hunter," I said, keeping up the appearances that made everyone feel so much more comfortable around me nowadays. "One. Singular. She came with a zhi. Wouldn't come without it, actually. They had to ship them both over in some sort of phenomenally sketchy cargo arrangement. No one has ever tried to transport a unicorn overseas like that before."

Eight hunters left at the Cloisters: Melissende, Grace, Ilesha, Dorcas, Valerija, Zelda, and now Wen. Ursula still counted, I supposed, locked away in her room. Cory and I were on permanent hiatus, though.

Ironic, given that now I probably *could* be the best hunter. It was the only thing I was any good at anymore.

"And Phil's working her hardest to make that illegal!" Giovanni exclaimed, and shook his head. "You know, it's amazing what she's been able to accomplish in such a short time. I know I don't have any right to be, but I'm so proud of her. Every time the whole unicorn issue pops up on the news, I think about how she set this all in motion."

"She's pretty amazing," I agreed. All that work on behalf of unicorns and still had time to spoon-feed me ice cream whenever I got confused.

He hopped up and held out his hands for mine, then pulled me to my feet. "And she's agreed to let me spring you for the evening. So what'll it be, milady? Spanish Steps and people watching? Dinner and fine art? A stroll around the Colosseum and a picture with a super cheesy gladiator?"

Old Astrid would have loved that. Every bit of it. Even if she didn't deserve it from him. I drew back. "None of the above."

Giovanni's brow furrowed. "Come on, Astrid. Phil said you've been dying to get out of here."

"I can't." I crossed my arms, hugging myself tight to keep from capitulating. I didn't know if I'd even like art anymore. After all, I didn't like math so much lately.

"Too much?" he asked. "Okay, we can start small. We'll take a walk down the street and get some gelato. That'll be nice."

"No," I said. "I can't. I don't want to be out there alone." If Giovanni couldn't figure it out, I'd have to tell him. The girl he loved was gone. She was gone even before her brains had been bashed out.

He forced a laugh. "But you won't be alone. You'll be with me." And then he smiled, which Giovanni *never* did, and I, who had spent the last year staring at racks of bones and unicorn innards, thought it was the most macabre thing I'd ever seen.

It had to end. "Well, either you'll leave me to find my way home alone, which is a really scary prospect, or we'll have this incredibly awkward walk back after our fight. I don't want to deal with that, either."

"Our fight?" Giovanni raised his eyebrows. "Why would we fight?"

"Because I cheated on you," I said before I lost my nerve. The patronizing mask Giovanni had been wearing this whole time slipped right off his face. "When I was in France."

He stared at me in open shock.

"Oh, not much," I said. "I mean, I'm still here, aren't I? Still a hunter. But yeah, I did."

I heard him breathe in and out. Saw him tamp down his urge to shout. I saw him get angry, the kind of angry I knew he could get, the kind of angry that had gotten him kicked out of school, but I wasn't scared. This was the right thing to do.

"I kissed Brandt. Almost in the pool. Almost at the club. And definitely the night of the party, when he gave me champagne and told me he loved me." The words came faster now, in a rush so hot they broke right through the mist that always lingered in the corners of my mind when the unicorns weren't around.

Giovanni made a choking sound in his throat.

"I felt terrible," I said. "Right away I felt so terrible. I didn't know what to do. I was afraid to tell you. And then *this* happened, and I never got a chance to."

Then, most horribly of all, I saw him shove his rage away. After all, I was broken now. He couldn't blame *me* for what the other Astrid had done. But he needed to. Her for the cheating, me for not being her.

My eyes burned and my throat closed, and the microscopic part of me that still held out hope for my old life couldn't help but go on, to offer this elegy for something that could never,

ever be. "If I'd called you then," I said, desolate, "I would have begged for your forgiveness. I would have told you that kissing some other guy was the worst mistake I'd ever made, that I have always loved only you, and that I would do anything to make it up to you."

There. I caught my breath. My heart was pounding like I'd just come off a hunt. But my mind was totally clear.

I'd told him I loved him. I'd said it now, when it was worthless. All those months of pouring my shapeless longing into the phone, I'd never said it, saving it up for the moment when I could look him in the eyes.

I couldn't read his eyes.

"But now?" Giovanni asked quietly. Dangerously. For a long moment, we just stared at each other, and I wondered if he saw me. Did he see past the crescents, the bizarre heterochromia that marked me as a descendant of Alexander much more clearly than my invisible magic? Could he see that right now I *was* Astrid? Astrid the Warrior. Astrid the Traitor. Astrid the Broken Doll. And no matter which one I was, I could never, ever have him.

"Now," I said, and cocked my head to examine him, "I think it just means that you don't have to feel guilty when you walk away."

I will give Giovanni credit: after that, he didn't walk away. He practically ran. Without another word, another look, he turned on his heel and marched straight out of the courtyard. I needed no telepathic link to realize he was swimming in fury.

Good. I needed him to drown out the pity.

I hoped he wasn't alone tonight. I didn't want my mistake,

my stupidity, to get him into any trouble. As for me, I sat around and sifted through my brain for every memory I could grasp of him. I recalled our first kiss, at the museum, and the way he'd held me after we decided not to sleep together. I remembered how he'd saved me after the kirin had run me through, how he'd put his hand on my scar and called me a warrior. I savored the memory of him running up to me in the City of the Dead and pulling me into his arms. I thought about the morning he'd met me at dawn and told me that no distance would ever come between us.

Well, he'd been wrong. That was all.

He called a few times, but I wouldn't talk to him or return his messages, and I dared Phil to act disappointed. Luckily, she decided she had bigger fish to fry when it came to the matter of rebuilding my head.

After Giovanni had gone, life at the Cloisters became more unbearable than ever. I always felt on the outside looking in. Looking in on the hunts, on the classes, on Phil's ever-accelerating activities, on her secret conversations with Neil. I was even jealous of the bond between Wen and Flayer, of the one between Flayer and Bonegrinder.

The mist in my mind dissipated more every day, but I was the only one who seemed to notice or believe it. It was as if Phil had encouraged me to a certain level of competence but refused to believe that I could go any further. After sending Giovanni away, I never got another offer of an outing. I'd even asked Father Guillermo if he'd take me for gelato and he'd mumbled something about running it by Phil first. I still wasn't allowed to hunt. Phil no longer gave me her drafts to decipher.

And every time I complained, she just said I was experiencing mood swings and the neurologist had warned her that I'd get frustrated when my recovery hit a plateau.

I was *not* on a plateau, except in terms of my being allowed out of this prison. Besides, if she wanted to see how I handled myself away from unicorn magic, she ought to let me leave the Cloisters altogether. The entire building was a crutch, with its walls of singing bones.

Was it any wonder that Lilith thought it was the perfect location for my television debut?

22

WHEREIN ASTRID MAKES HER DEBUT

L ilith arrived at the Cloisters with a truck full of cameramen, journalists, and wardrobe specialists. "She looks much better than last time," was the first thing my mother said when she saw me.

"*She's* happy to see you, too," I responded.

"Ah." Lilith clapped her hands together. "I see the brain damage hasn't affected your smart mouth. Excellent."

Lilith had come when I'd been in a coma. I knew this because she'd told me on the phone every time I'd spoken to her since the accident. I got proof when she and her agent showed me the footage they'd filmed of her sitting by my bedside and stroking my poor, limp hand.

My mother was right. I looked way better now.

They took over the Cloisters, rearranging the courtyard so it looked prettier and "more classical"—their words. As far as we could tell, it involved removing our targets and dragging several large bits of broken columns into their favorite corner.

"Great," Cory said, watching as they erected the "set." "I've spent the better part of a year trying to make this place not look like a ruin and they're strewing masonry all around the garden."

"There, there," said Valerija, placing a hand on her shoulder. She turned to Phil. "The money is worth it, definitely?"

Phil frowned. "It had better be. No one told me we would lose our practice space."

Then came the fittings. I was shoved back into a hunting habit and fitted with a long blond wig.

"The point of the headscarf is to *cover* the hair," Phil drawled from the door. She gave me a sympathetic shake of her head.

"Eh," said Lilith with a shrug. "This will look better on TV."

"This is a bad idea, Aunt Lilith. I don't think Astrid is in any position to speak on television."

"She doesn't have to talk. This is my visit to my old stomping grounds, my emergency trip to sit with my poor, injured, unicorn-hunting daughter." The staff clucked their tongues. I'd already learned that this was an automatic response, done in unison. My mother's very own Greek chorus.

Phil rolled her eyes. I would have, too, but the makeup person was jabbing at me with eyeliner. Some emergency. It had taken my mother almost three months to come back.

"These eyes are going to look kind of off-putting on video," she said to one of the producers. "Maybe contacts?"

"If the point is that I'm injured," I said, "wouldn't it be better if I was in bed, maybe in my pajamas?"

Lilith considered this. "No, I don't think that sells *hunter*, visually. Besides, we already have bed footage. Trust these people on this, Astrid; they're experts."

Neil joined us at the door to watch the commotion. "This is disgraceful."

Phil looked relieved that he'd come out and said it. Donna or no donna, Lilith was still Phil's aunt.

Lilith turned to him. "Well, we can always leave, if you don't think you want our money. But if we do, I'll also make sure your little campaign isn't mentioned in the piece. I'm sure eight point five million viewers don't need to learn about the plight of endangered unicorns, don't need to see any other side to the story other than the one where they are monsters killing innocent people."

Neil shook his head dismissively. "And presenting the tragic story of an injured hunter is going to somehow convince the world at large to show the animals mercy?"

Lilith shrugged and turned back to me. "That's your problem, not mine. I think she needs more blush. Astrid, you're so pale."

"Sorry, Mom," I muttered, shooting a pointed glance at Phil. "I don't get out much."

Phil stuck her tongue out at me. I giggled.

Downstairs in the courtyard, two cameramen were trying to bait Bonegrinder and Flayer into a fight. Wen and Ilesha stood guard, arms crossed over their chests, vehemently not amused.

"They're just lying there," said one of the cameramen. "Can't you get them to wrestle or something?"

"Yeah," said another. "There's so little footage of killer unicorns close up. This is an amazing opportunity, and these guys look like kittens."

Ilesha gaped at them.

Grace stepped in. "Are you all mad? Do you know the lengths

to which we've gone to make sure these creatures aren't ripping your throats out right now?"

As if to punctuate the statement, something caught Bonegrinder's interest and she began to growl.

"No!" Grace said sharply, and the unicorn settled down. "The day I came here," she said, "this zhi almost killed my mother and my little sister. We've spent months bringing her to a point where she is calm in the presence of people, with great personal risk to every nonhunter who has entered these walls."

The cameramen stepped back, more subdued. Then one said, "Did you get any footage of that attack on your family?"

Luckily, Grace was unarmed. As it was, Ilesha had to tackle Bonegrinder, who'd gotten a bit excited by Grace's sudden rage.

When Phil got word of the incident, she removed the zhi from public viewing. "This isn't some underground betting ring," she explained when the producers complained. Lilith had apparently granted them total Cloisters access. "We're trying to train the pet zhi and make sure they are no danger to the public. But you must remember, they are wild animals."

"I resent that," said Wen. "Flayer is a bottle-fed sweetheart."

"But can you make it growl on command?" the cameraman asked.

The hunters voted to sic a zhi on them. Phil overruled us all.

I was told that the so-called plot of the piece would revolve around Lilith's life on the home front—what it was like to advocate for unicorn hunters while her daughter was overseas risking her neck by slaying unicorns.

"Slaying?" I said blankly. "That makes me sound like some kind of butcher."

Lilith trotted out a phrase I knew quite well by this time. "It plays better. Trust the experts."

"It's just really violent," Phil pointed out. "We're trying to get to a point where our hunts are targeted eliminations of specific problem unicorns—"

"Like what you did in Cerveteri?" Lilith replied. "When you took out an entire pack? Several dozen unicorns in one go? What was that except a massacre?"

Phil and I shut our traps. Cerveteri had been an exception that would doubtless *also* not "play well" on television.

The talent arrived. Her face seemed familiar to me, as well as her perfect coif of honey-colored hair, but the names of American network news anchors had long ago vanished as my brain made room for hunting techniques and methods of sword cleaning.

She swept in on a cloud of pancake makeup and too much perfume, and moved right past Lilith's outstretched hand. "Philippa Llewelyn, right?" she said, closing in on Phil. "The one who writes all those adorable letters to Congress. You're in charge here?"

"Yes," Phil said. "Jointly with—"

"I'm Marianna Matheson, lead on the story. Lilith didn't tell me you were so young," she said.

"She's my aunt," Phil replied flatly.

"So *young*," Marianna Matheson repeated, casting significant glances at the producers. "And so *charming*. How ever did you come to be in charge of this entire operation at your age?"

"Oh, that's easy," Phil began, then saw the look on my mother's face and clamped her mouth shut. "I'm Aunt Lilith's successor," she said instead.

I burst out laughing, startling the three closest staffers. Guess the truth would have pissed Lilith off too much. *After Astrid's mom went nuts, shut down the Cloisters, and locked herself in the weapons hall, blaming herself for Astrid's assumed death, all us teen hunters got together, forced her out, and decided to take charge ourselves.*

Marianna Matheson's smile seemed ready for prime time as she looked at Phil. "Let's get you in makeup. I'd love to have you in on the interview as well."

"But—" Lilith began.

"Oh, it'll be excellent!" Marianna Matheson clapped her hands together. "All three of the Llewelyns!"

Grace and Melissende, standing in the shadows at the edge of the courtyard, rolled their eyes.

We were ushered to the set and placed in armchairs inexplicably scattered on the cobblestones. I was dressed in a full-on camouflage habit, my blond wig artfully arranged under the scarf to make the hair look as full and lustrous as possible. Both Flayer and Bonegrinder, against the protests of Neil and Phil, were chained to the legs of my chair and instructed to lie there like stone statues of unicorns. Wen stood just offscreen with a bag of treats and the unicorns' full attention. Ilesha stood in the parapet with a bow at the ready, just in case.

My mother sat in a nearby chair and gripped my hand as if she actually cared. Phil, who'd managed to squeeze herself into one of Zelda's old hunting habits, sat on Lilith's other side.

Marianna Matheson approached the set, looking over her notes. Flayer lifted his head as she approached, and she froze. "Will they behave? I was told they'd not do anything in the presence of hunters."

"They're chained," was all Phil would say. I snorted. They could yank this chair out from beneath me in a second if they wanted to.

Marianna Matheson looked from me to Phil. "But you're not a hunter, correct?" she asked Phil.

Phil pulled off her don's ring. "Here, put this on if you're concerned. It'll keep them away from you if they attack."

I saw Neil's back stiffen from his place in the shadows of the Cloisters. Even now, given how far we'd come, he hated it when Phil took off that ring.

Marianna Matheson took the ring, and from the grumbling of the staffers clustered closely around us, I wondered if she'd have to fight them for it.

The shooting started.

"Good evening," Marianna Matheson said. "I'm Marianna Matheson, reporting from the Nunnery of Ctesias in Rome, Italy, the world's only training camp for unicorn hunters. As the unicorn menace spreads across the globe, many people have been wondering how to stop these vicious, deadly monsters. Well, tonight we're here to talk to the people whose lives are dedicated to just that. A group of women, all from the same family, who have a powerful birthright, an innate ability to track and control these dangerous creatures."

From the corner of my eye, I could see the camera panning across our little group.

"The Llewelyns are the only people in the world with the ability to be safe in the presence of unicorns. . . ."

Uh-oh. The other hunters would have a field day with that one. Was that Grace snorting in the shadows?

". . . which is why I am wearing this ring." Marianna Matheson flashed the don's ring at the cameras. "The only one of its kind, it is capable of actually repelling a unicorn attack."

Phil pursed her lips, probably already calculating how soon it would be until the Cloisters was burglarized by a mob in search of the ring. There were four people on the screen. Only one of them was an actual hunter.

"Lilith Llewelyn, many of you know. She selflessly gave up her own career to travel to Rome and train her daughter, her niece, and other hunters in their service to humanity."

Lilith's hand tightened on mine. She must have heard my gulp of disbelief. I listened as Lilith presented her usual spiel about the glories of hunting and her dedication to the cause for many years before the Reemergence, dealing with society's ridicule, preparing for the day when she could give back to mankind.

The usual crap.

"Since leaving to help educate the public about the unicorn menace, Lilith Llewelyn's training duties have been taken over by her niece, Philippa." Marianna Matheson smiled at Phil. "But Philippa has a new cause, beyond that of saving people from unicorns." She paused, and nodded at Phil.

Phil smiled sweetly. "Yes. Together with the governments of the world, we are seeking to classify unicorns as an endangered species. With protection, we unicorn hunters can work to remove unicorns to remote and unpopulated locations, places where they won't be a danger to humans but can live out their lives as the beautiful wild creatures they were born to be."

"Splendid," Marianna Matheson said, beaming like a child who'd just gotten a glimpse of a towering gelato sundae. "And we'll be talking more about that later." She returned her attention to the camera. "As you can see, there's a lot more to unicorn hunting than meets the eye. But the life of a hunter is not to be envied. At any moment, they could be killed while on duty protecting humanity from unicorns. And tonight we have a special treat. A mother and daughter reunited. This brave teen has devoted her life and her health to the safety of others. Already a nun at sixteen . . ."

Seventeen. Not a nun. But really, in the scheme of things this lady was getting wrong . . .

". . . Astrid Llewelyn has been permanently disabled by her service."

I heard Phil gasp. Lilith's grip turned suffocating. Was I reacting? I couldn't tell. I couldn't tell anything beyond the haze that suddenly clouded my "normal" contacts, the giant ball of wrath that exploded in my throat.

"Her dreams for the future dashed, her hope of ever finishing school or becoming a doctor—her childhood dream—gone forever. Astrid, how do you feel?"

I closed my eyes for a long moment, and then blinked them open. My fake eyes, as fake as the statue of Clothilde in the rotunda. My hair, fake. My dress, fake. How did I feel?

Fake.

I turned to my mother and gave her a very long, hard look. Permanently disabled? Dreams dashed forever? She had arranged this. Did I need to have those words thrown in my face on national television? They already echoed around inside my empty skull day in and day out.

Flayer's and Bonegrinder's magic flowed into my body, and I yanked my hand from Lilith's grasp.

"I'm putting my life back together," my lips said. "It's hard, of course."

"Of course," parroted Marianna Matheson. Lilith looked concerned, but it was not the expression of parental love she'd so carefully cultivated for this program. Oh, she loved me, all right. Especially when she could get good footage.

Right now, she was very, very concerned about the nature of this footage.

But she hadn't seen anything yet.

"Especially since the accident claimed the life of one of my dearest friends."

Marianne Matheson nodded in sympathy. Beneath the frame of the camera, she was waving furiously at her producer, who looked frantically through her notes for any mention of Rosamund.

She wouldn't find it, of course. Lilith would prefer to be interviewed herself than to give up any spotlight to actual grieving parents, like the Belangers.

"And especially when I wake up every morning to this." I yanked off both wig and habit.

The producer dropped her folder. "Wait, cut. We're not doing a reveal; we're doing a progressive before-and-after—"

"No way," said Marianne Matheson. "Keep rolling. This is better. We'll edit it in." She turned back to me. "Is it difficult for you to see what you've sacrificed and still return to your duty every day?"

"Oh, I'm not hunting now," I said. "It's far too dangerous to put a weapon in my hands, what with the brain damage I've sustained."

Lilith leaned in front of my chair. "Astrid's therapy is progressing at a steady rate," she said. "We're hoping that she'll be in hunting shape very soon. She can't wait to return to her post, slaying unicorns for the good of all humanity."

Enough of this. I stood and walked nearer to the cameras.

"Do you want to see the rest of my scars?" I asked them. "I'd have to take off my top."

"Astrid!" Lilith cried.

Marianna Matheson gestured to the camera to keep rolling.

Phil came over to me and put her arm around my shoulders. "Come on, Astrid."

I looked up at her. "What? Lilith wanted me on TV. You let it happen. Are you surprised I can't stick to the script? Didn't you hear her? My life has been ruined. What have I got to lose?"

Marianne Matheson smiled as the interview descended into chaos. "This is awesome."

Things fell apart after that. Neil and Phil rushed me off set as Lilith got into a screaming fit with the producers and Marianna Matheson. The last thing I heard was her threatening Neil and Phil for sabotaging her big break.

"Asteroid," Phil said as she dropped me off in the chapter house with a firm order to stay put, "that was crazy, but crazy awesome."

"Your mother, however . . ." Neil began.

I put my head in my hands. "Apple doesn't fall far from the tree, huh?"

But as soon as they were gone, I realized that when all this died down, I'd never be able to face them. Not the other hunters, who'd been slapped in the face by Llewelyns, en masse, thanks to my mother's propaganda. Not Phil, since I'd probably forever ruined her chances of getting good publicity for Save the Unicorns. And certainly not my mother.

How could she have done this to me? I'd always known she was crazy, always known she was cruel, but this? This was my life. How could she make me feel so small? So broken?

I thought about France. I thought of how Isabeau had always been giving me books and encouraging me to take more challenging classes at the university. I thought of how there, I'd been free to come and go as I pleased, to lounge in the magic or avoid it. I thought of how there, I hadn't been special because I was a Llewelyn. Maybe there, I wouldn't be un-special because I was broken.

I thought of how Brandt had told me he loved me, which was a thing that Giovanni, after flying all the way to Rome to visit the invalid, had never said. I remembered how obsessed Brandt had been with my scars that mirrored his own. I wondered what he'd think of the one on my head.

I wondered what he'd think of me now.

For someone with brain damage, outsmarting the lot of them was appallingly easy. They didn't shut me in at night. They didn't hide my phone. They hadn't gone through my drawers and taken my passport or the euros I hadn't used since leaving the Gordian château. So that night, while things were still chaotic, I simply called a taxi; stole my alicorn knife and the claymore of Clothilde Llewelyn from the weapons wall in the chapter house; hugged Bonegrinder and breathed deeply of her magic, hoping it would be enough to keep me clear; and walked out the front door.

Magic or adrenaline kept me focused all the way to the airport and past the ticket counter. Waiting for my plane was the worst part, as the sun rose in the sky and I realized that Phil and the others were probably up and looking for me. Even if they did suspect the airport, however, I had a good head start. As long as the plane wasn't delayed, I'd be fine.

As long as the plane wasn't delayed, I'd have enough clarity left to make it all the way there.

By the time I arrived in Limoges, the fog was back. It was all I could do to hand a taxi driver directions to the château. I'd written them down in Rome, just in case. I watched the taxi driver load up my suitcase and the long, thin case that could have been a fishing rod but was actually my sword. I think that was all I'd brought. I hoped I didn't leave any other priceless ancient weapons anywhere along my path.

And then there was the château. The taxi driver took my stuff out and I gave him a big wad of money, which he seemed pretty happy about, and then I walked up to the front door and knocked. It was afternoon now, and late rays of light shone red and violet over the creamy stones in the wall.

After forever, Isabeau answered the door.

"Hi," I said to her. "I've changed my mind."

Isabeau told me that Phil had already called and asked her to be on the lookout for me, but then she promised that she wouldn't rat me out. "You don't have to go back if you don't want to, Astrid."

She'd started crying when she saw me, and then she hugged me close. After that, I'd asked her if we couldn't go out to the enclosure straightaway, because I didn't think I'd be able to talk to her without some unicorns around.

The first touch of their magic was like a cool breeze in the midst of a heat wave. I breathed deep, and relaxed. Okay, I made it. It worked.

"Did you replace me?" I asked.

"We could never replace you, Astrid. And the Cloisters said they couldn't spare another hunter after the accident."

"So what have you been doing?" I looked out over the enclosure. The unicorns were sleeping. Only ten of them left now. I didn't think it would be polite to ask about Angel. The woods looked different in the spring, all budding green leaves and tiny blossoms nestled in the grass. Off to the left, I saw that the protesters' tents had sprouted up again like so many spring mushrooms.

"We've managed." She shrugged. "We found a girl—not trained, of course—and she helped us out when we needed it."

"Oh." I looked down. "Is she still here?"

Isabeau smiled. "No, she got out of the business."

That was certainly a popular option these days. But it would never be an option for me. I couldn't afford to relinquish the magic. It was the only thing tethering me to reality.

"How do you feel?" Isabeau asked me. "Well enough to come inside for dinner, or do you wish to eat out here?"

"I think . . . I think I feel fine." I clenched my hands into fists. I could do this. I needed to learn how.

So we ate dinner, and I told Isabeau about everything I had been through, and how difficult the past few months had been. She listened, nodding and saying comforting things at all the appropriate places. I did my best not to cry, but I can't say I was fully successful.

And then, when we were done, she stood. "Astrid, I want to show you something. Come with me."

I followed her down the corridor, down stairs and through hallways until we reached the passage that led to the laboratory wing. The second we entered, I could feel him.

Angel.

My breath caught in my throat, and Isabeau turned.

"Please do not be upset, Astrid. Your einhorn is fine. He has borne his captivity quite well, and we are learning so much from him."

I prodded gently at his mind, but he was asleep, a sleep so deep that not even the unusual presence of a hunter seemed to disturb it.

"And it is good he is here, too," Isabeau added. "I would like you to feel as comfortable and clear as possible right now."

She crossed to a desk and sat down. It was nothing like the gorgeous antique in her office. This desk was made of simple metal, with plastic trays for stacking papers, a mug with the Gordian logo filled with pencils, and a clunky computer station. Behind Isabeau's chair was a filing cabinet and a shelf piled high with files next to a small refrigerator. I sat down in the folding chair across from her.

"As you know," said Isabeau, "your purpose here was to guard our einhorns. The einhorns' purpose has been to help us discover a way to re-create the Remedy, which is also why we've had Brandt here."

"I remember all that," I said. "I don't have amnesia."

"But what you don't know—what you've never known—is that we *do* know how to make the Remedy. We can make it in tiny, tiny amounts. Doses so small that they are functionally useless. We can't even market them. Our task, since before you and I even met, has been to figure out how to solve this problem, how to synthesize the Remedy on a large scale."

I stared at her. "So Marten was telling the truth," I said. "He did know the secret to the Remedy."

She nodded. "Yes. He discovered it last summer. But it didn't do us any good. We could get a single dose of the compound, perhaps, but we had no way of reproducing it. No attempts to synthesize it were successful. Nothing we tried made a difference."

"But you can do it!" I whispered in awe.

"Yes." She folded her hands in front of her. "We are in possession of over one dozen doses of the Remedy."

"Why didn't you tell me?" All these months, they'd known?

"To know how to make one dose? That is not knowing anything. You as a scientist know that the heart of any experiment is in its reproducibility. We haven't truly made a discovery until that time. So we were waiting to make a real announcement until we had something to celebrate. That never occurred. We had to keep experimenting to try to figure that part out."

That made some sense to me. "So how do you make it?"

She pursed her lips. "It's complicated. And difficult, and very, very touchy. I had hoped that this was something we could produce on a vast scale. I was hoping that the Remedy would be a cure for the masses." She smiled in self-recrimination. "Barring that, I hoped I could make a luxury drug. Even if we had to charge an exorbitant price for every dose, it would be worth it, to save whatever people we could."

"But you can't do that?"

Isabeau shrugged. "No. It is impossible, as rare now as it was throughout history. In this case, the ancients were not hampered by their inferior technology. The Remedy, like the unicorns, like the hunters, is not the product of science. It is the result of magic."

342

"Why?" I asked. "Does it take a large number of unicorns to make one dose?" How many must have died to create the one my mother had given Brandt?

"No," she said. "Nevertheless, its ingredients are incredibly rare. I now understand why it was spoken of with such reverence." Isabeau stopped and looked at me. "I would like to give it to you."

23

WHEREIN ASTRID CONSIDERS THE CURE

The shock wave that followed her statement was enough to wake Angel from his slumber. I heard the rattle of a cage in the next room, the soft bleat of a unicorn.

"You can't be serious," I spluttered.

"I most certainly am."

"You just finished telling me how very rare it is!"

"And therefore why you should feel that I am not making this offer to you lightly. My company has already invested millions of euros in the development of this drug. We have nothing to show for it but a handful of doses. We cannot recoup those fees, even if we were to sell them to the richest people on the planet. So why not instead give one to a person I love?"

Angel began to cry. I followed in short order.

"Please calm down, *ma chère*," said Isabeau. "You are disturbing the unicorn, and we have gone to great lengths to keep him sedated."

"Why?" I sobbed. "Why would you do that?"

"I told you," said Isabeau. "I love you, and I hate to see a young woman with your intelligence, your potential, hampered by this injury. You know that you cannot count on the unicorn magic forever, and there is no telling if you will ever progress past this state."

I cried even harder, no longer caring if it upset the einhorn. Yes, this is what I needed to hear. Not Phil's pandering and protectiveness. The truth. I'd be forever trapped in the Cloisters, forever trapped alone and ignorant. Without the unicorns, without the magic, without being a hunter, I was doomed to eternal fog.

Isabeau handed me a tissue. "I cannot make any promises that the Remedy will cure you of your condition. It may be that it has no effect on a hunter. It may be that it has no effect on a condition that is not a wound or a poisoning. We have not had enough of it to do proper testing. You would be a guinea pig, Astrid, and it may well be that we waste one of our few precious doses of the Remedy on you."

I choked.

"But," she added, "I am willing to try."

I said nothing, just sat there and sobbed until I had no more tears left. Around me I heard the sterile hum of machines, the high-pitched whine of the fluorescent lighting, the scent of disinfectant and medicines and blood. If I closed my eyes, I could sense them through Angel's point of view.

This was his life. This had been his life since I'd left. Every single day of his existence had been spent inside a cage, in a room with latex-gloved hands and needles and bright white lights. He couldn't remember even the large enclosure in which he'd been born. He didn't know the scent of dirt or leaves. He barely remembered the feel of his mother.

And I realized now what a hypocrite I was. Because I didn't care. I wanted the Remedy. I wanted it for my own. Angel's existence was a sacrifice worth making if it meant that I could be cured of the fog that lay around my brain like a chain. I wanted my own freedom far more than I wanted his.

I hated this about myself, but I couldn't deny it.

"Do you remember what Brandt used to say about me, Astrid?" Isabeau asked. "He said that I treated you like a child. Like my child."

I nodded.

"The truth is, I did have a child. I had a daughter, many years ago. She died when she was about your age. She died of cancer, and there was nothing I could do to save her. At her worst, she looked much like you do now: shorn hair, pale face, the despair that gripped her when she saw nothing but pain and suffering for the rest of her short life."

Yes. How did she know? How did she nail every single sensation? How did she do it while dangling before me the apparition of enslaved unicorns?

"If I had this chance with my daughter, I would have used it. But I didn't. Please don't let me miss out this time. Please let me try to help you."

Yes! My brain screamed. Yes, yes, let's do it now! Now now now now now now now.

But—weren't there other people who deserved this more than me? What of Cory, who was growing weaker by the day with some ailment that no doctor had yet been able to diagnose? What of people in the world that were dying—actually dying— that the Remedy might save? Did I have any right to use it in what might be a vain attempt to cure a little brain damage?

Because if I did take the Remedy that Isabeau offered and it didn't make a difference, how would I feel then? How would I feel knowing that it might have been used to *save someone's life*?

I opened my mouth. "Thank you," I said robotically. "It's an honor. But I have to think about it."

Isabeau seemed to understand. She showed me to my old bedroom and left me alone. I didn't unpack; just sat and soaked it in. My books still sat neatly on the shelf above the desk. The clothes I'd left still hung in the closet. The beautiful dress seemed even more beautiful now, its silken folds a remnant from a time when I believed that I retained some trace of the normal girl I'd once been. Once upon a time, I could dress up in pretty gowns, and if I left my hair down, I could almost pretend that I wasn't a unicorn hunter. I stared at my reflection in the mirror. No denying that now. I looked like a monster. I understood now why Clothilde chose to keep her head shaved. She didn't want to hide her scars—she wanted a constant reminder of the person those wounds had created.

I took off my clothes and put on the dress. Without the veil of my hair, every scar I had stood proudly on display—my back, my arms, my hands, my head.

I went to the case and pulled out the claymore. *Domitare unicorne indomitum.* To vanquish the savage unicorn. I held it up and out, copying the pose of the statue in the Cloisters rotunda.

Now I looked just like Clothilde. Now we might as well be the same person.

There was a knock on the door. "Astrid?"

I dropped the sword. *Brandt.* I cast about the room for a robe, for something to throw over my long formal gown. I thought of wrapping my head in a towel. What was he doing here? Isabeau hadn't said a word about him! I'd assumed he'd gone.

"Astrid, open the door. I have to see you. I have to talk to you."

"Um..."

"I know what you look like, and I don't care."

I opened the door, more out of curiosity than anything else. "How do you know?"

He startled at my eyes—they all did—but recovered himself quickly. He took in my attire, his eyebrows quirked. "They told us when you were hurt," he said. "They said they'd had to shave your head in the hospital. But they didn't say anything about your eyes." He examined me. "Your hair's cute. Kind of punk."

"Thank you," I said. "Now go away."

"Why?"

Because there were no unicorns in my bedroom, and Brandt's presence had always been confusing to me, even before I was brain damaged. "Because I'm asking you to, and you've always been gentlemanly enough to do what a girl asks."

"Yeah," he said. "Those are the rules." He was staring intently at me. "But I think I'm kind of over that stage in my life." He came inside and shut the door behind him.

I backed into the room, eyes widening. "Brandt—that was a joke."

"I love you, Astrid. I've told you that so many times." His eyes were wild and he kept advancing, kept coming toward me until the back of my knees hit the bed.

My sword was all the way across the room. I could probably

get to it before he could stop me, but then what? Hold *Brandt* off with a sword? *Brandt Ellison?*

I wondered if this was what Phil had been thinking that night with Seth. That there was no way a guy she knew could possibly threaten her like this. But I was strong, with or without a unicorn. And I had way more to lose.

"Keep away from me, Brandt. I'll—" Scream? Yes, I'd scream, but more important, I'd grab my sword and lop his head off if he tried to touch me.

"I don't like this job, Astrid. I want out. And I think you can help me. I think, with you—it would be different. . . ."

For a second, confusion—*real* confusion—broke through the fear. "Your job?"

"Here, at Gordian."

I stared at him, baffled. "Brandt, there are far easier ways to get out of this job than raping me. Though I assure you if you tried, you'd be more than fired. You'd be dead."

He stopped and blinked at me. "*Raping* you? What are you talking about? I would never, ever do something like that. I love you, Astrid. I know everything you've been through. I know about Phil— God, what kind of monster do you think I am?"

I held up my hands. "You're backing me on to a bed after I asked you to leave. What else was I supposed to think?"

He whirled around and walked away, stabbing both hands into his hair. "Is that what she told you? That I can't control myself? That I'm some kind of wild animal?" He turned to face me. "Well, that's not how it works, you know!" He glared at me, anger staining his face red.

Where was a unicorn when you really, really needed one? I sat down on the bed and closed my eyes, trying to still my mind to make sense of it all. Curse my broken brain. I took several deep breaths, then opened my eyes again. Brandt was still across the room, breathing heavy, his hair standing up all over his head.

"I don't know what you're talking about, Brandt," I said. "How *what* works?"

Now it was Brandt's turn to look confused. "I thought she told you," he said. "I thought she told you all about the Remedy."

"She offered to give it to me," I said. "But I still don't understand—"

He laughed bitterly. "But she didn't tell you about the side effects?"

Side effects?

"Of course not!" he raved. "Because they wouldn't really pertain to you, would they? That's what she thinks, anyway. She thinks it's all about her precious dead daughter. She refuses to even consider it."

"Brandt," I said slowly, in the tone of voice that Phil liked to use on me whenever I got particularly "outrageous." "Please sit down and tell me, slowly and with a lot of detail, what in the world you are talking about. I don't know if it's the brain damage or what, but I can't understand you at all."

His lips formed a thin, angry line and he stared at me for a minute, hands clenched at his sides. Then suddenly he rushed forward and fell to his knees in front of me.

"Please, Astrid, just say you love me. Say you love me and none of the rest of this matters."

"What? No!" I shoved him off my skirt.

"It's Giovanni, isn't it? You think *he's* the one."

"Stop it, Brandt!" I took another deep breath. "And no, for

your information, I don't. But neither are you, so—"

"That's not true!" Brandt said. "I know it can't be. This isn't like with the others. You're different. With you it's love, real love. Oh Astrid—" He lifted his face to mine and kissed me.

I pushed him off and squeezed out around him. "I said stop it." I walked over to the far corner of the room, placing the bed and my suitcase between us, and I picked up my sword. "Now, you stay over there"—I gestured with the claymore—"and I'll stay over here and you'll tell me what the hell you are talking about. What others?"

He knelt there against the bed, his hands out on the sheets as if he was praying, then slumped. "The other hunters," he said, defeated.

The point of my sword lowered to the floor. "Other hunters?"

"That's what I'm doing here, Astrid. I'm not a milkmaid; I'm a scent hound."

"Excuse me?"

"I'm an actaeon."

We don't call them that anymore. How well I remembered Isabeau saying it.

We've been having terrible luck recently, Phil had told me. *We get a tip about a possible hunter . . . but by the time we contact them, they've decided to relinquish their eligibility.*

My hand shot out to grab hold of the desk for balance. "What? How?" I asked.

"It's a side effect of the Remedy," he said. "The way I heal. The way I can almost—almost—touch the magic. I can also sense you. I can sense you like you can sense unicorns."

I shuddered. Yuck. And he'd been sleeping down the hall from me for months?

"And I want you. Oh, Astrid, it's like when I'm near a hunter, she's all I can think about. She's the only thing in the world."

"So you *don't love me*," I hissed. "You have a fetish. You have a fetish and you've been"—the realization struck me with the force of a re'em on a mountaintop—"you've been running around Europe deflowering every girl who might be a unicorn hunter before the Cloisters could get to them! You're disgusting!"

"No," he said. "I'm *helping*. These girls don't want the life you're living, Astrid. They don't want the danger. Can you blame them?"

I couldn't, but that was hardly the point. The reason we were in so much danger was because we had so few hunters. We'd gone up against a re'em with only four of us. I'd almost been killed and Rosamund had lost her life. We were all shouldering that much more of the burden because these other girls chose to get out of their duties. . . . "Then you are a rapist."

"No!" He stood up. "I would never, ever do anything against a girl's will. Never. Marten had it wrong. Marten was too desperate. Seth was a monster. Isabeau and I . . . we're not like that. We approach the girls and tell them about their situation, about the danger they are in, and about what we can do to help them. It's up to them to choose their path after that."

"And you get paid for this?" I asked, appalled. "You're what, a prostitute?"

"They don't always come to me. Some of them have boy-friends—" He sighed pitifully.

I gagged. "Gordian pays you to sleep with unicorn hunters. That's the definition of a whore. It doesn't matter how pretty the packaging is, or what you're *saving* them from."

He hung his head.

Now the truth lay splayed out before me like a rotting feast. "And that rule that bothered you so much about living here, the one you were always complaining about . . . it was me. *I* was the rule. Hands off."

That's why Isabeau was always so scared of him spending time with me. That's why she'd made sure he was kept away when Cory and Valerija had come to visit. Three hunters might have been too much for him to bear.

He nodded without looking up. "But don't you see, Astrid? That's how I know I love you." And now he raised his eyes to mine and started moving forward again. "It's not the Remedy when it comes to you. I liked you before, I like you still, and I like you even knowing I can never have you. Knowing that until you're cured of your brain damage, I can never, ever be with you, because we have to protect you. . . ."

I lifted my sword again. "I am *not* some delicate flower. I do *not* need your protection. *Ever!* Do you hear me?"

He backed away, lifting his hands in surrender. "No, of course not. That's what I love about you! You've always been so brave, so strong. You saved my life. I just mean, the magic . . . your mind . . ." He trailed off. "God, your eyes. They're hypnotic, Astrid. . . ."

"Shut up!" I cried. Everything out of his mouth was a lie. Isabeau had told me the truth. All he wanted was a taste of power. Just not the way I'd thought.

Silence reigned in the bedroom while I worked this all out in my battered brain. Poor Neil. All along he'd been out there looking for hunters, and Brandt had been tracking them down using unicorn magic and seducing them out from underneath us. And as sickening as it was, what could we say? These girls were allowed to make their own choices. We couldn't begrudge them relinquishing their magic, whether they did it with someone they truly loved, like Zelda had planned to, or some actaeon off the street who offered to unburden them of—

Wait. Why? Why was Isabeau trying to sabotage Cloisters recruitment? Marten had struck a deal with a rogue band of kirin: disable the Llewelyn hunters in the Order, and they would assist him in his quest for power. But Isabeau *was* a Llewelyn, and she'd protected me from Brandt's advances. Plus, I knew the einhorns. They were nothing like kirin. It made no sense.

"I don't get it," I said at last. "Why would you do this? What are you gaining from it, except for random one-night stands?"

"I told you," he said, "I'm an actaeon."

"I know what an actaeon is. I just don't see why it's a job."

He smiled then. "Then no, Astrid. You have no idea what an actaeon is."

I leaned on my sword hilt and placed a hand on my hip. "Excuse me? I'm in the Order of the Lioness. We were the ones to come up with the name. We were the ones to kill them with our zhi whenever we caught them in the act."

He sighed. "You think that's all they did? Just deflowered your hunters? You think that they risked life and limb for a little sex? No, Astrid. That's so naive. They were thieves."

I rolled my eyes. "Of virginity?"

"Of the Remedy."

I dropped the sword to the floor.

He went on. "There's nothing magical about virginity. There's nothing special about sleeping with a virgin. *Usually.* But people like you . . . you're different. You know that. The virginity of a unicorn hunter *is* magical. And so is taking it."

I backed against the wall as the room swirled around me. I almost wished the fog would come back, but my mind was as clear as a bell.

Phil, standing in the center of the Cloisters chapter house the night after she was raped, surrounded by bones that would never sing for her again. *But that was enough. For whoever decides these things.*

Seth disappearing on the Gordian dime.

And then, a few short weeks later, Marten Jaeger, cowering before the karkadann in the courtyard, pleading for his life. *I know the secret of the Remedy.*

Last winter, Isabeau in the study, telling me the crazy story of the men who used to sleep with virgins to cure their illnesses.

And then, worst of all, tonight: Isabeau, down in the lab, looking me in the eye and telling me how rare the ingredients for the Remedy were.

Brandt was still watching me.

"You get it from us," I said. "The secret of the Remedy isn't the unicorns."

"No," he said. "It's the unicorn hunters."

24

WHEREIN ASTRID OBSERVES THE EFFECTS

Unicorns were a dime a dozen, Brandt had explained. A thousand doses of the Remedy could be made from the materials gained from a single unicorn. Claudia, Isabeau's mother, had figured out the basic formula by piecing together the medical memoirs of her hunter ancestors. Not that it mattered much to her, as there had been no unicorns around. But no one had been able to interpret the *meaning* of some elements of the formula, particularly the mystical *viriditas.*

And perhaps it meant nothing. After all, many old medieval cures were utter nonsense, and sometimes so-called important steps in medieval alchemy were nothing but a waste of time.

I remembered Cory and Isabeau's conversation about Hildegard von Bingen and her obsession with *viriditas*, which literally meant "greenness." And now—only now—I remembered how quickly Isabeau had changed the subject.

For Hildegard, *viriditas* had meant the power of God, the power of life, freshness, vitality. For a long time after the Reemergence, Brandt explained, Gordian scientists had feared their inability to create the Remedy was a product of the *freshness* of the unicorn materials they used. Maybe the unicorn specimens had to be alive. Or maybe they could be gathered only in a particular season, or maybe they needed some special green herb to stir into the compounds.

Nothing worked.

And then, about nine months ago, Isabeau had a brain wave. One she shared with her husband. Once upon a time, there was a disease called "greensickness," which was actually just a type of anemia that most often affected young women. Another name for this disease was "virgin's sickness," and the cure was believed to be—wait for it—deflowering. Because naturally, the cause of their illness was the burden of their greenness, of their virginity.

Maybe, Isabeau had thought, the *viriditas* of Hildegard wasn't the same thing listed in the formula of the Order of the Lioness. Maybe the creation of the Remedy required a mystical alchemy involving the virgin hunters themselves.

Marten took that idea and ran with it. Enter Seth and Phil. Isabeau was horrified at his methods, but she couldn't argue with the results. They'd discovered the secret to the Remedy.

Even though it would never do them any good.

Magic could not be synthesized. They'd never be able to make more than a few vials of the Remedy. There was only one dose per unicorn hunter.

It was midnight in France, and I stood at the fence of the einhorns enclosure. I'd kicked Brandt out of my room and changed into more appropriate breaking-and-entering clothes. I needed to be with the unicorns tonight. I needed to get my head on straight.

But the code for the lockbox had been changed. I was trapped

357

outside the fence. I began wandering the perimeter, pressing my face up against the links and willing the unicorns to draw closer. They'd never be able to cross the boundary, of course—I'd never be able to touch them—but out here, with the magic, things already seemed clearer.

I would never accept the Remedy.

How could I? Brandt had been right. Actaeons were thieves. They stole the . . . *essence* of the hunter's virginity and they kept the resulting Remedy all to themselves. That was why the hunters, as a group, hated actaeons. If a hunter chose to leave on her own, if she chose to marry and settle down—*her* Remedy was her own to keep, to sell or use as she saw fit. The Remedy we'd used on Brandt had been the one belonging to Clothilde Llewelyn.

These girls, these hunters that Brandt approached—they knew nothing of the Remedy. All they knew was that Brandt was sweet, clean, and discreet. He'd unburden them of their powers and disappear into the night.

Bearing with him something that might one day save their lives.

Isabeau had lied to me. She hadn't kept the secret of the Remedy from me due to a technicality of not being able to reproduce it. She'd kept it from me because she knew I wouldn't approve of her actions.

I could not use it. The Remedy didn't belong to Isabeau to dispense to her friends. It belonged to each person who had helped make it possible to create.

No, the only option was to try it myself. I could ask Isabeau to do it for me. I'd sleep with someone—Brandt maybe—then make the Remedy, then take it and . . . see what happened.

But what if it didn't work? Isabeau had already warned me she had no proof that the Remedy was potent against brain damage. And if I lost my virginity, I'd also lose the magic. If the Remedy didn't work, I'd be stuck in my fog forever.

Was that a chance I was willing to take? Even if it meant the only alternative was stealing someone else's personal cure?

Sacrificing Angel was bad enough. I couldn't sacrifice a sister-at-arms.

"Who's there?" said a voice. I turned, and with the clarity of unicorn magic, I saw René standing about twenty yards down the fence line.

"Astrid," I said, and stopped.

He came forward, a beam from his flashlight cutting through the night. Its glare hit my eyes. "Astrid, *le chasseur des licornes*. You look terrible."

"A wild unicorn," I said. I circled my ravaged face with my finger. "See, this is why you shouldn't be so eager to see these monsters released."

"That does not deter me," he replied. "If you were to go inside and see them, you would know that they do not have much time left. They cannot survive any longer in captivity. You must help us."

"I *must* not do anything."

He came closer and examined me, my shorn head, my long scar. "I have looked you up, Astrid Llewelyn. I have seen your mother on the television."

"Well, that should be your answer right there."

"And I have spoken to your cousin. I am a friend of Philippa."

I narrowed my eyes at him. With the help of the magic, I could see him clearly in the dark. He did not look like he was lying.

"I am a conservationist, just like her. I have helped her with her battle to protect the unicorns. I have read her papers. I have listened to her cry when she thought her cousin—her best friend—would never wake up."

My eyes began to burn, and I couldn't trust myself to speak.

"I know you can make it over this fence with my help. I saw you do it the night the electricity went down. I want you to go inside and see the einhorns. You *will* help us," he said. "I know you will."

The dust puffed up around my feet as I landed hard in the dirt on the other side of the fence.

I turned to René. "How am I supposed to get out of here when I'm done?"

His face fell. "I had not thought of that."

I rolled my eyes. Great. "Never mind. I'll just tell Isabeau that I felt the need to spend the night with the unicorns." She'd understand that. I'll say it kept my head clear while I considered her offer.

An offer that I wished above anything I was the type of person to accept. But I could never live with myself if I wasted a dose of the Remedy when there was someone else out there who really needed it. Someone else it actually belonged to.

I crossed the electronic boundary and headed into the woods. Around me, the unicorns slept, not even stirring as I approached them. This was strange, like the sedation I'd felt in the labs with Angel. Had they somehow figured out a way to manage the unicorns' rejuvenation–happy body chemistry?

As I reached the outermost trees of the grove, I sensed a new smell, one even stronger than unicorn. Rotting meat. A few steps farther in, I practically tripped over a burlap food bag filled with moldy steaks. Another sack lay nearby, torn to shreds, with scraps of meat scattered about the ground and going bad.

I stared at the food with a sense of growing unease. It was impossible that Gordian had taken to feeding them *too* much. So why was this here, going to waste?

A few yards on, the smell grew even stronger, and I came upon the corpse of an einhorn. Several days old from the look of it. Its bowels had been ripped out, and its insides were hollow and mushy. Its fur was patchy and its skin raw in places, but I didn't know if that happened pre- or postmortem. Its face was covered in gore. I couldn't recognize it . . . or I didn't want to.

I sidestepped the mess and kept walking, trying not to gag on the stench. Did no one at Gordian know what was going on here? Food rotting while the unicorns turned on one another? I sensed a conscious presence off to the left and turned. The bushes rustled, and I saw a flash of white. More than that, I tasted familiar thoughts.

Fats. I called to her in my head, but she cowered deeper in the bushes. I wondered what she'd been through in the past few months, if she missed her baby, if she'd fought when they took him from her the way the re'em had fought us when she thought we'd threatened her offspring.

"Fats," I cooed, and held out my arms.

Nothing. Her mind radiated only suspicion. I came closer, and she sprang out, snarling and tossing her head, then raced off. I saw her white hindquarters vanishing into the forest, her long, lionlike tail now replaced with a bobbed stump.

As my exploration of the woods continued, I found two more corpses in various states of decomposition and three more unicorns, each of which vanished as soon as I came close, each of which sported tails gnawed to nothing and open wounds as if they'd been fighting.

At last I reached the center of the enclosure, the roots of the large tree that had once been the den for Fats and Angel. I closed my eyes and stretched out my senses. Ten little pinpricks of light, ten lives of hunger, terror, boredom, and desperation. And beneath all those emotions, something else, something that grated against my senses like the wrongness of rotting meat. Lunacy. These unicorns weren't just withering away in here. They were going mad.

This couldn't continue. The Remedy was a fraud, and so was this experiment in einhorn captivity. Perhaps at some point, it had been worth it to sacrifice these animals for the good of mankind, but not anymore.

But what should I do? I could kill them all, right this moment, put them out of their misery. They were all sick, weak, violent. They might not survive even if I did set them free. They'd certainly be a danger to the people of the surrounding countryside. I could hunt them down, slaughter every last one by morning.

I tipped my face skyward, tasting the spring breeze and the traces of unicorn on the wind.

Cognosce te ipsum. Know thyself.

I *could* kill them all. But I wouldn't.

I returned to the fence line and waved to René. "You were right," I said when he came over. "I'll help you."

We made our plans through the fence. René brought over another man: short, with a scarred leather jacket and an equally pockmarked face. Not that I was one to talk.

I remembered him from before. He was the one who'd warned René not to talk to me. He seemed no less suspicious now. Though he introduced himself as Thierry, his habit of not meeting my eyes made me doubt the claim. They explained their plans to me, passed them through the holes in the fence in little rolled-up bundles of paper. I read each plan with the benefit of unicorn magic and flashlight glow.

And then I laughed.

I rolled the pages up again and shoved them back into the links. "This one," I said, punching it through, "will get you all killed by the unicorns." I punched at the second. "Killed by the unicorns." The third. "And, oh yes, killed by the unicorns."

They stared at the crumpled plans.

"You say you've been watching them." I crossed my arms. "Haven't you seen how vicious they are? You can't just let them roam freely around the countryside. The first thing they'll do is eat everyone in your camp. This fence isn't here for *their* protection."

"What do you recommend?" René asked.

"Me, of course. That's why you came to me, isn't it?"

"We came to you for help breaking into the fence."

They most certainly did not. A tractor could accomplish that. "You'll need a lot more than that if you expect to survive this little endeavor."

"We have people who have dealt with wild animals before." Thierry shook his head. "We've always managed in the past."

I stood in silence for several seconds, and then I said, "I will not assist you until I can be sure that doing so will in no way harm the people in your camp, on this property, or in the surrounding countryside. I'm a unicorn hunter, which means it's my job to protect people from unicorns, in whatever way is necessary."

Thierry narrowed his eyes. René looked increasingly nervous. I stood my ground.

"I believe," René said at last, "that Astrid knows what she is talking about in this matter."

"We're not going to have her release the unicorns only to shoot them dead."

"And I'll shoot them dead in a flash if I have the slightest inkling they'll cause trouble once they're free." My voice was even, my expression mild, but my very presence was scary enough to let Thierry know I was serious. One nice thing about having brain damage, people are inclined to believe you might fly off the handle at any moment. And I came armed.

"We appreciate your concern for us," René began.

"It's not just concern for you," I said. "If you do this, you must promise that no harm will come to anyone in the château, either."

René blinked. Thierry twitched. And in the throes of unicorn magic, I noticed everything.

"The unicorns are freed," I said. "Gordian is untouched. And the second I think a unicorn might become a danger to us, I kill it. Those are the terms."

After a long hesitation, Thierry nodded curtly.

"Now," I said, "the difficult part. What can we do with the einhorns after we free them?"

By morning, when the Gordian technicians came to retrieve me from the enclosure, we'd hammered out a strategy and my partners in crime had returned to their tents. Another nice thing about having brain damage is people don't think much of you. So when I goofily batted at the hand of the technician working the lockbox and pretended not to understand a word of his French, he merely rolled his eyes at me and entered it again, muttering the code to himself.

Step one.

When Isabeau asked me if I'd made a decision, I said I was still torn. And then I told her the truth—or most of the truth. Another nice thing about brain damage is that no one expects you to lie. I told her that Brandt had come to me last night, but I didn't tell her that he'd shared the secret of the Remedy. Instead, I'd focused on his romantic aspirations. I told her that I'd gone out to be with the unicorns, and had been horrified by the state I'd found them in. I asked her why, if they were no longer in need of the einhorns to make the Remedy, they needed to keep the animals, and if the change in their condition had anything to do with a shift in treatment now that they were no longer a priority.

In other words, I gave her one last chance. Isn't that what I owed her, after everything she'd done for me? She'd given me a home, an education, beautiful clothes, a real chance at a future. She'd given me more affection than my own mother, and taught me that there was an actual place for my magic.

And, with that knowledge, I'd realized that my only choice was to save the einhorns. To betray her.

Isabeau reacted about as I'd expected. She blew up at Brandt, then sent him away. (Step two.) Then she pretended to be shocked and appalled that the unicorns were doing so poorly. Then she apologized profusely for both situations, and started explaining to me what kind of new experiments they were using the unicorns for. Just because the Remedy was a bust didn't mean the rejuvenation ability of the unicorns couldn't supply the company with a major scientific breakthrough. Isabeau even took me down to the lab again to show me some of their most recent data.

Step three.

It was actually pretty interesting. Too bad it was over. I couldn't countenance the suffering of the einhorns for anti-aging cream. Saving human lives was one thing, cosmetology another.

Later, when Isabeau was occupied, I packed a change of clothes, my money, and my valuable documents in a backpack, and hid both backpack and sword case out near the enclosure. Yet another nice thing about having brain damage is that when your boss's secretary sees you wandering through your house with your luggage and asks if you're going somewhere, you can just act disoriented and say something nonsensical like, "I'm having a picnic, want to come?" and they write you off.

I *do* want to get better, but at the same time, I don't think I mind people assuming I'm dumb.

After that, there was nothing to do but wait. I'd been a unicorn hunter for a year. I'd spent nights in tree stands, days staking out a field, weeks trapped in a monastery with only my bow, arrow, and target range for company. I'd spent hours upon hours alone in a forest, stretching out my senses for the slightest trace of a monster.

I was really good at waiting.

25

Wherein Astrid Commits a Crime

That night, I waited for a text message from René that everything was in place. Then I entered the einhorn enclosure using the keypad and deactivated the electric boundary. Unfortunately, that was the easy part.

Five minutes of sitting on the ground, meditating and projecting soothing and attractive thoughts toward the unicorns achieved nothing. Not a single one approached me from the woods, and my vision of leading them, Pied Piper–like, in a single-file line toward freedom began to evaporate into the moonless night.

Where were the unicorns that had once circled me in submission? Had I lost their trust when I left them here alone to kill one another? Were they beyond reaching?

I squeezed my eyes shut and tried to identify each animal in the woods, to pinpoint their minds like the blinking lights on their collars had so recently marked out their locations. Ten little unicorns, scared as could be. Ten little unicorns, scared . . . of me.

Once upon a time, I'd been able to make them do as I willed, merely by thinking it. When I met Wen at the Cloisters, I learned that her control of Flayer worked on a similar principle. Their bond was so great that he knew exactly how she wanted him to behave and obeyed.

The re'em could read our thoughts, as the one who'd almost killed me had. These einhorns could read mine if I wanted them to. And if I wanted them to do something badly enough, I could place the compulsion right into their minds. I could make them come to me.

I took a deep breath and called to them. I showed them freedom, and mercy, and endless open ranges. Safety and surcease of pain. Nights without chemical sleep, days without the madness of captivity.

Come to me.

Ah, here they were, drawing near at last. My hand tightened on the hilt of my knife.

Ten little, nine little, eight little unicorns . . .

These were okay. Fats, and Breaker, and a juvenile female I vaguely remembered. They were terrified, but I sensed no violence from them.

Seven little, six little, five little unicorns . . .

Not so with these new ones. Stretch was there, and the thread of his thoughts made the hairs on the back of my neck stand up. What had happened to my playful friend, the one I'd saved from death? He watched me warily, but with eyes that gleamed with bloodlust. I caught my breath. I did not want to kill Stretch, no matter what he'd become. But if he was too dangerous, too far gone . . . I couldn't risk it.

The other two were with Stretch. They waited for him to

make a move. Little thugs, both of them, but if I took Stretch out, then they'd fall in line.

Four little, three little, two little unicorns . . .

More einhorns on the edge of madness. Some of these had killed others, eaten others. Fats and the little girl shied away. I clenched my teeth and concentrated harder. Soothing thoughts, warning ones, containing ones above all. *Just stay here and stay still. . . .*

One little unicorn boy.

There he was, the last of the einhorns. The angry one. The one who had spread his poison of rage through the others. It was Gordian who was to blame for his captive lunacy, but that didn't change the facts. A junkyard dog was mean because of the abuse and neglect it had suffered, but it still needed to be put down.

Stay still, I thought to the unicorns as I hurled my knife through the angry one's eye.

He crumpled to the ground, and the seething pulsation of his thoughts vanished with a pop. The unicorns stood frozen, some crouched in fear, prepared for flight.

Stay.

Run run fly run escape charge run run run dart jump no death run.

Stay. Calm. Done.

And in my mind, I saw Bucephalus killing the head of the rogue kirin. I'd culled the mad unicorn from this pack. I hoped it would be enough.

Another few heartbeats as I retrieved my knife and wiped it off on the grass. The unicorns waited for me.

Okay. Come. Calm.

One by one I led them through the double gates of the fence. They jostled together, snuffling and grunting—one even squealing when another jabbed it in the butt with its horn.

Calm. Slow.

Simple emotions worked best with the einhorns. They didn't have the communication ability of, say, Bucephalus. I led them around the side of the enclosure, skirting close to the fence though there was little point in trying to hide; their white coats stood out like beacons in the night. We went past the remains of the campsite—most of the protesters had quietly packed up and left—and onto the public lands, where Thierry and René were supposed to be waiting with the truck.

But when I arrived, nine little unicorns in thrall and in tow, only Thierry stood there, his face set in grim lines.

"Where is René?" I asked.

"Detained." Curtly. "Keep them back while I open the hatch."

I hesitated. "What happened to him?" Where would René be detained at this late date? He'd been the one to text me only a few minutes ago. Hadn't he?

"It doesn't matter," Thierry grunted. "We just go forward."

The truck was the kind normally used to transport cattle. We'd mapped out a route that didn't require tolls all the way to the French Alps. If the re'em who'd attacked me in Italy could survive in the mountains with her offspring, maybe a small herd of einhorns could as well. As long as wherever we dropped them off was remote enough that they kept away from villages, the move might work.

Thierry went to open the back hatch of the truck. The unicorns' thoughts turned ravenous. Mine turned violent until they settled down. Once Thierry was out of the way, I began to herd them as gently as possible into the truck.

Gently, it turned out, wasn't particularly possible.

Captivity on a few acres of wooded land was hard enough on these creatures. Walking blindly into a dark cage? Not happening. The unicorns bucked and reared, skittered off the ramp and pranced in terrified circles nearby, too afraid of me and my mental threats to run off outright, yet not going anywhere near that dark, cavernous space that smelled strongly of farm animals and slaughterhouses.

Thierry dove underneath the truck chassis. Yes, and they'd been planning to simply let the unicorns run loose. *Morons.* Who was the one with brain damage?

As soon as I coaxed one unicorn inside the truck, another would bound free. Perhaps I should have stolen Gordian's mysterious sedatives, as well.

"We have to go!" Thierry shouted from underneath the truck chassis. "What are you doing? I thought you said you could control them!"

"I'd be happy to see you give it a shot," I grumbled, shoving a unicorn up the ramp.

"We have to go now!" he said. I heard his cell phone go off, and he cursed.

Seconds later, the château exploded.

At the sound of the blast, the unicorns scattered—or at least, the three still outside the truck did. I slammed the hatch down on the others and leaped from the ramp.

"You liar!" I screamed at Thierry. "You promised me!"

"We were supposed to be gone! Get in the truck."

"You liar!" I repeated, and swung at him, my blow

strengthened by hunter magic.

Miraculously, he swerved, then grabbed my arm. "I said get in the truck. We don't have time for this."

I wrenched free of his grip, turned, and ran back toward the château. Isabeau! The dogs! The other employees!

Angel.

I ran faster.

As I neared the building, I saw that the blast had been aimed at the laboratory wing. The house itself seemed untouched, though the fire spreading through the lab had destroyed the dome of the greenhouse and was licking its way toward the roof.

As I stood there, Isabeau came tearing out of the back of the house, Gog and Magog trailing close behind. Her hair streamed out behind her, for once wild and unkempt. Her feet were bare, her eyes brimming with tears that flashed in the firelight.

"Astrid!" she cried. "You're all right. Were you over to see the—" She took in my black clothes and the glisten of unicorn blood, and her eyes widened. "The unicorns."

I felt them a second before they rushed past me, three loose unicorns, each charging full tilt at the fresh meat I'd led them to.

"No!" I shouted, aloud and in my head, to no avail.

Gog was the first to scream as an einhorn speared the dog in the back, near his hips. From the corner of my eye, I saw another chasing down Magog, who'd fled on long white legs so very like a unicorn's, but all my focus was on the third unicorn, the one bearing down on Isabeau.

I'd messed up with Marten—Marten who'd gotten Phil raped, who'd tried to have me killed, who'd plotted behind our backs. But I wouldn't let a unicorn harm Isabeau.

The einhorn lowered his head to charge.

Stretch. I threw my knife, wishing I'd thought to bring my bow.

I wasn't fast enough.

Stretch fell, the knife in his throat, but he brought Isabeau with him. She cried out as she was flung from her feet, an alicorn embedded deep in her side. I rushed forward, dragging the head of the dead unicorn off her. Blood soaked her from shoulder to knee, though how much was hers and how much was Stretch's I couldn't tell.

Isabeau clutched her hands over the wound, shuddering and gasping for breath.

"It's okay, it's okay, it's okay," I babbled, kneeling at her side. "I'll go—I'll go find you some Remedy. I'll fix this. There's time."

Isabeau barked a short, stuttering laugh. "*Et tu, Brute?* What did you think would happen if you let them loose?"

"Not this. I—had a plan. I had . . . help . . ." Blood burbled up out of the wound. Oh God, just like with Brandt.

I heard growling behind me and turned just in time to see Gog leap upon the einhorn who'd attacked him and sink his long jaws into the monster's throat. My jaw dropped.

The einhorn bucked, but Gog's grip remained firm, and he dragged the unicorn down with him and shook until the creature's neck snapped and his terrified mind grew dim.

I glanced at the dog's hindquarters, at the alicorn wound that was even now knitting together.

And then I looked back at Isabeau, who was pushing herself up on her elbows. There was no trace of alicorn poisoning in her face.

"Astrid—" she began.

"You took the Remedy."

"Of course I did," she replied. "With the number of unicorns on my property? It's a fundamental precaution."

"And you gave it . . . to your *dogs*," I spat out.

"They have to live here, too." She coughed, and clutched her wound. "Doesn't heal as quickly as I'd want, eh? Help me up; we have to call emergency services."

Instead I rose to my feet and backed away. *"Your dogs?"*

She sighed. "It was an experiment, to see if it was as effective on other species as it was on humans. The results were fascinating, as a matter of fact. But now is not the time to have this discussion. Even now, our research is burning to the ground! Help me. This will heal, eventually, but meanwhile it hurts like hell."

I turned away from her, toward the lab, where the fire burned ever more furiously. "Everything's destroyed," I said. "The Remedy, all your records."

"I take it *that* wasn't part of your plan, Astrid?" Isabeau clucked her tongue. "You should know better than to try to make decisions on this level. In your state of mind? No wonder you were taken advantage of."

"When?" I cried. "When was I taken advantage of? When I trusted you, though all along you knew the secret of the Remedy? When behind my back you were sending Brandt all around Europe to seduce every unicorn hunter you could find?"

"Behind your back?" she scoffed. The wound was almost completely closed now. "How is what a complete stranger does with her life of her own free will any of your business?"

"If they'd trained to be hunters like they should have," I said, "this never would have happened to me. There would be more hunters. We'd be protected."

"So it could happen to *them*," Isabeau said. "How very selfish of you. Do not take your choice, your sacrifice, and try to thrust it upon some other woman, Astrid. That's hardly fair."

"You lied to me!" But the accusation sounded hollow in my throat. Her lies were nothing compared to everything else she'd given me. A life, a home, her care and affection. A possible cure to this horrible fog.

And Isabeau knew it, too.

"A lie that hurt you not at all," she said calmly. "And in return, you have ruined my life's work, endangered everyone around us, and almost got me killed. Who is winning?"

The windows of the lab burst, shattering shards of glittering glass onto the lawn.

"And your precious little baby unicorn is burning to death," she added. "Unless, of course, you arranged an ill-conceived escape route for him as well?"

I took off.

"Astrid!" she cried as the roar of the fire got louder. "Don't! Astrid!"

A moment later I plunged into the flames.

Fire safety tips came back to me along with the rush of unicorn magic. Angel was here, and still alive. I could feel his terror like it was my own as I dropped to the floor and pulled the neck of my shirt up over my face. Smoke and heat burned my eyes as I slithered toward him. I passed desks, tables, locked office doors, empty lab cages, and some that weren't so empty.

Angel. Just get Angel.

The speed of unicorn magic came in handy here. I flashed

by rooms in nanoseconds, my eyes and brain clear despite the billows of smoke. I came upon Isabeau's office, the place where she'd offered me a dose of the Remedy. Angel was only a few doors away. I could feel him scrabbling desperately at the bars of his cage. And yet, for a heartbeat, I paused.

In her desk were the files about the Remedy. Files that would be destroyed if I didn't do something right right right now.

Like steal them.

I'm coming, Angel.

I grabbed a canvas bag hanging on a hook behind the door and yanked open the drawers, spilling anything that looked remotely interesting inside the bag. File after file, binder after binder, wasting precious seconds.

I had to get out of here. The heat was extraordinary, and I crouched to the ground, where the air remained hazy and cooler.

And then I peeked into the tiny refrigerator. Inside was a tray, and on the tray lay more than a dozen tiny little vials. Each vial was marked with a name—the name of a woman.

The Remedy.

The refrigerator was locked, of course. So I smashed the glass panel on the front, grabbed the tray, wrapped the vials haphazardly in a sweater hanging on the back of Isabeau's chair, and stuffed the bundle in the bag as well. Another five seconds down.

Okay, now, Angel.

The fire sounded closer now, and when I opened the door to the lab where they were keeping Angel a blast of heat hit my face. Though the room itself wasn't burning, there must have been an ocean of flames beyond the far wall.

One second to get to Angel's cage and see him within.

One second to gape in shock. They'd cut off his alicorn. His limbs were twisted and emaciated from disuse inside the cramped cage.

Two seconds to open the cage, another two to rip him from his restraints, heedless of the IV tubes and needles projecting from his skin.

Six seconds. Six seconds too many.

The wall behind us erupted in fire.

I was thrown from my feet, and Angel bounced from my arms and slid across the floor. The little unicorn whimpered, then went still.

I choked, gagging as the heat burned my lungs and throat.

No. I was not going to die here, in a fire. I'd survived count-less unicorns, with the scars to prove it. I'd fought back death from poison, from blood loss, from brain damage. Some nasty little fire wasn't going to get me.

And I wouldn't let it get Angel, either. I'd killed Jumps, and the angry one, and Stretch. I'd killed so many. This einhorn would survive.

No matter what.

I looked through the smoke until I found Angel's glazed, half-closed eyes.

Give me your magic.

Shoving myself to my knees, I swung the handles of the bag back onto my shoulders, heaved the limp unicorn—all fifty pounds of him—into my arms, and hurled us both through the door. Down the hall, past the offices, lungs screaming for air, eyes burning and half blind, nothing but unicorn magic propel-ling us both until I burst through the back door and onto the lawn.

Here, too, the fire had spread, until it engulfed half of the greenhouse. I kept running back toward the park where Thierry and his truck waited for us.

But when I arrived, lungs screaming for relief, eyes streaming, and the pain of what must be burned skin stinging on my back and shoulders, I found that the truck was gone and Thierry with it.

I fell to my knees. I laid an unconscious Angel on the earth. I breathed deeply.

Angel was still alive. I felt his magic, our connection, in every shared breath, in my continued ability to think clearly.

I needed to get out of here. Police would arrive any minute, and I doubted Isabeau's goodwill would extend toward protecting me, even though I'd had nothing to do with the fire. How could Thierry have left me here? And what had happened to René? Had he known they were planning to destroy the lab? Had he discovered that and Thierry kept him somehow from warning me?

I needed to get out of here. I needed to get Angel to safety.

But where? Where in the world would be safe for a baby unicorn with no horn? I stared down at the maimed creature, watching it draw shuddering breath after shuddering breath into its atrophied lungs. I wondered if it could walk on those emaciated legs. I wondered if its horn would ever grow back. I wondered if it would be best of all to simply put this animal out of the misery that had comprised the entirety of his short, wretched life.

Angel opened his eyes and nudged my hand with his snout.

Fair enough. He wanted to live.

I retrieved my sword case and backpack, and stuffed the bag

of files and test tubes inside the pack. Then I strapped my luggage on and hoisted the unicorn into my arms. Angel wasn't light. In fact, he was already far bigger than a zhi, but I had our magic on our side. I set off after the truck tracks, hurrying only when I heard the sound of sirens pulling up to the château.

I came across the truck less than two miles down the road. The engine was running, but the vehicle was at a stop. I approached it, reeling as the unicorns buffeted me with their panic. They were slamming against the slats of the cargo hold. Some had punctured the sides with their horns. It wouldn't hold them for long.

I edged around the side of the truck until I reached the cab.

Thierry lay slumped over the steering wheel, dead. His face showed signs of alicorn venom, and when I peered closer, I saw a puncture wound at his shoulder. There was a ragged hole in the wall of the cab behind him and I could make out a flash of unicorns flitting about inside the cargo hold.

I closed my eyes, projecting stillness.

The unicorns obeyed.

Now what? I was alone. Alone with a truck full of crazed unicorns and a dead man. And the police on their way.

I set Angel on the ground, then opened the door to the cab and pulled Thierry's body out. I *could* just leave him here. The police would find him, no doubt, just as they'd found Marten's body when I'd left it.

Except, this time, I'd been the one to set the unicorns loose. This time I really had been to blame for anyone who died of unicorn poisoning tonight. I was to blame for getting Isabeau and her dogs gored. I was to blame for letting ecoterrorists take advantage of me. I thought they'd just wanted to free the unicorns. I'd believed them when they'd promised me it was so.

One thing about having brain damage is you have a ready excuse for when you act like a moron. But it's not a nice thing.

I was responsible for this man's death. Sure, he'd left without me, but I'd been the one to run off and leave him with a truck full of deadly unicorns. What other choice did he have?

I stared at Thierry's corpse.

Well, besides waiting to see if I'd come back.

I lifted Angel and rested him on the passenger seat, then climbed in behind the wheel.

Okay. Truck. I could do this. With the help of these unicorns, I knew I could.

I drove off.

26

WHEREIN ASTRID TOUCHES THE TRUTH

The Alps were beautiful this time of year. I pulled the truck over at the end of a narrow, lonely road. There was a valley between two mountains off to my left, a vast field of green grass, boulders, and wildflowers open to the sunshine. I hadn't seen signs of a village, resort, or even a farm for miles.

Beside me, Angel blinked open his eyes and lifted his head.

"We're here, little one," I said, and set the emergency brake.

I let the unicorns out of the cargo hold and surveyed the damage. Two were missing chunks of their ears and one was limping around due to a puncture wound in the leg, but they'd all survived the trip. I directed them into the pasture.

Go now. You're free. Stay away from humans.

I didn't know if they'd understand, or care enough to obey even if they did. I hoped the wildlife here would be sufficient to sustain them. There were wild goats, I was sure, and probably plenty of rodents, birds, and other food sources. It was the best I could do for them.

Fats lingered by the guardrail at the side of the road,

381

her eyes on the truck's cab.

I sighed. I couldn't leave Angel with them. I didn't even know if the animal could walk. And, in the wild, without a horn? How would he protect himself? How would he hunt?

Fats whinnied at me, the horsiest sound I'd ever heard a unicorn make.

I looked back at the truck. Angel stood in the window of the cab, battering at the door to be set free.

Fine, then. I opened the door and lifted Angel to the ground. He tottered over to his mother, who butted her snout against him, rubbing her nose all over his fine white coat and the scabs from the needles and tubes. She licked at the spot on his forehead where his horn should have been.

I hung my head.

Curiosity blossomed among the other unicorns, and they drew close to the little one, their minds calming more than I'd felt the entire trip. *Awe, pity, wonderment.*

Angel wiggled under the guardrail and onto the grass.

The other six unicorns circled him, facing outward, ears alert. They stared at me, their eyes as black and bottomless as ever. But I could read their thoughts loud and clear.

Ours. Leave.

In the truck, among Thierry's things, I found a pair of binoculars. Just out of the range of unicorn magic, I watched the einhorns retreat into the mountains, still tightly clustered around Angel. In the distance, against the backdrop of the meadow, they seemed like nothing more than specks of litter, easily blown away and lost to time. Would they survive out here? Had I endangered any people by releasing them?

Was I even a unicorn hunter anymore?

After they were gone, I sat in the dirt at the side of the road, waiting for the fog to descend on the mountain and my mind. I was so tired. Their magic had sustained me all through the long drive. It had overcome my injuries from the fire, the ache in my lungs, and the scrapes and burns on my body. But it was evaporating now, leaving behind only spring sunlight and soft green grass. . . .

In the dream, Bucephalus called to me in the voice of Isabeau Jaeger. Somehow, with the sort of logic that made sense only in a dream, I knew it was Bucephalus who spoke, though it sounded like my old boss. I could hear the anger in her voice, as commanding and firm as always, but underneath it, there was something more.

Understanding.

I was searching for him, desperate to reach him, scrambling over rocks and across fields strewn with gray ice and slick boulders. Here and there I saw re'ems peeking at me from between cracks in the stone, watching me carefully to determine my next move.

I felt their thoughts. They hoped the karkadann would get me, and if he didn't, they were more than ready to kill me themselves.

I called to him. *Help. I need your help!*

It's too late for that, said the karkadann.

The fog was coming now, and I stumbled, slowing, as I saw the field drop away off a cliff. Below me lay a ravine so deep the bottom was wreathed in mist. I reeled back.

"Where are you!" I screamed. And then I turned.

Bucephalus was there, as massive and deadly as always. His

eyes gleamed, not the pits of fire I knew, but with twin crescent moons of pale blue. My eyes. He began to step aside, as he did in every dream, and I knew, I just knew the body he'd show me was mine.

Stop, I begged with every bit of my brain, and because he was a unicorn, he did. Giant, three-thousand-year-old monsters could do as they pleased.

But not when it came to unicorn hunters.

When I woke, my mind was practically clear. I climbed back into the truck and drove down the mountain. In the first town I came to with a train station, I abandoned the truck, bought food, and spent some time looking through the Gordian files I'd stolen. Seemed Brandt had been quite the busy boy this year. Isabeau's notes had been meticulous. She'd charted the details of each hunter they'd "sampled"—her age, her health, her hunter family origins. It seemed, from what I read, that she'd been formulating a theory about which hunter lines produced the strongest kind of Remedy.

I scanned the pages, my thoughts growing foggier the longer I was away from unicorn magic. I had a limited amount of time to make my plans before everything slipped away from me completely.

My mind was already misty when I read the name Llewelyn.

The conductor woke me up as the train pulled into the station. I blinked my eyes open and looked around, disoriented as usual without the benefit of the magic. I stretched my legs, and the hard soles of my boots clinked against the vials nestled inside my backpack.

I rubbed my eyes and peered at the window. A gray, gloomy landscape, like nearly every other train depot I'd passed. A painted metal sign read KIEL. I'd arrived.

I grabbed my backpack and the sword case, shoved the hood of my sweatshirt up on my head, and hopped off the train. It took about twenty minutes for me to get oriented with the map I'd brought along with me, and I seriously considered checking into one of the hostels near the station for a few hours of sleep before continuing on my journey. I hated the idea of arriving at my destination and no longer being coherent enough to complete my task.

Unfortunately, I was running low on funds, so I skipped the taxi in favor of public transport, which took longer, but after all, I didn't want to barge in on these poor people before they were really awake.

The other folks on the bus stared at my scar, my singed clothes, and the long case I carried. I tugged my hood down over my ears and stared straight ahead.

I wondered what made me think I had the ability to pull this off on my own. All alone, without even a unicorn around to give me a jolt of clarity. Either I was truly getting better or I'd gone completely off my nut.

I started to panic as we reached the residential neighborhoods, terrified in equal parts that I'd miss the stop, or that I'd reach my destination unscathed. I began to arrange my speech in my head. Casual, confident, and nonthreatening.

I'm not asking for anything. I'm not asking for anything.

"I'm not asking for anything," I said aloud. The woman next to me on the bus scooted away a little.

I watched the names of the streets and traced our progress on my map. And when we were close enough, I got out.

The address in Isabeau's files proved to be a stately town house on a wide, treelined street. I went up the front steps, the edge of my case banging slightly against the stones, and knocked. The door opened to reveal a young woman, maybe two years my senior.

"*Guten tag,*" I said. "*Ich heiße Astrid—*"

"I speak English," the girl said most charitably. My accent must be wretched. Her short hair was a sort of light auburn and very curly, but her eyebrows and nose were right.

"I'm looking for Marikka Loewe."

"I am she."

"I thought so," I said. "I, um, have something of yours."

Marikka Loewe looked at me skeptically, a skinhead ragamuffin with weird eyes and charred luggage standing on her doorstep. "What is it?"

"It's . . ." I started to slide my backpack off my shoulders. "It's something you gave away. You didn't know you had it. . . ." Maybe I should have just mailed her the vial with a note.

She peered at me suspiciously. Like I said, eyebrows and nose. Or maybe just that I looked like I'd been through a war. "Who are you again?"

"I'm Astrid Llewelyn," I said.

She inhaled sharply. "Llewelyn. You're with the unicorn hunters."

"Yes. I mean, no. I mean, yes. But that's not why I'm here—"

"It is a waste of your time. I am not—"

"I know," I said. "If you'd just let me—" I leaned over to root through my backpack. Contents may have shifted upon travel. The strap of my sword case slid off my arm and bashed hard against the stoop. The clasp came undone, and the claymore clattered out.

Marikka gasped. She scanned the street, as if terrified anyone would see me there with a weapon. "I think you should leave," she said. She backed across her threshold and held the door open at a slit, wielding it like some sort of swinging shield. "Please go away."

"No, wait! Please, this will just take a minute."

She hid behind the door. "I'll call the police."

"I'm your sister!"

She stopped at this.

I squeezed my eyes shut, gathered my focus. "I'm not . . . asking for anything. I'm here to help you."

She stared at me, eyes wide. "Who are you?"

"I told you," I said, shoving the claymore back in its case. "I'm a unicorn hunter. My name is Astrid Llewelyn. And I'm also your sister." I recalled the names I'd read in the files. "Julius Loewe is . . . our father."

Marikka stared into my crazy eyes. "I think you had better come inside."

Marikka showed me into the kitchen and gave me coffee and a biscuit, which helped considerably. I should have thought to eat before I came here.

"My mother died soon after I was born," she told me. "My father was a student. He couldn't take care of me, so he sent me to live with my grandmother. This is her house."

"It's very nice," I said.

"I never see my father," she went on. "Christmas, maybe. But I can give you his information."

I shook my head. "Only if you think he has another daughter."

She snorted. "He might have a dozen, after today. How old are you?"

"Seventeen." I'd celebrated my birthday in a coma.

"I'm nearly twenty." Her face looked pinched. "He didn't waste much time."

I cleared my throat. "He didn't have a . . . relationship with my mother," I said, then realized that might not be exactly comforting. I looked around the kitchen. "What was your grandmother like?"

She smiled. "Strong. All the women in my family are strong. You look like you are related in that way, Astrid."

"Tell me about her."

Marikka told me how her grandmother had hid refugees during World War II. "She worked in the shipyard all day, watching them build U-boats," she said. "And then she'd come home and work all night smuggling slaves." She cocked her head at me. "You look a little like her. Like the pictures from back then."

I retrieved her vial of the Remedy from my backpack. "This belongs to you," I said. "I hope it's still good, but I don't know. They were keeping it frozen, but I have seen it work after hundreds of years sitting on a shelf. So maybe magic lasts."

She examined the vial. "What is it?"

"It's a cure." I took another sip of coffee. "It's a cure for almost anything. And it belongs to you. You can keep it, sell it, save it to use on something really important. . . ."

She examined the label then blushed. "Gordian Pharmaceuticals. What is this, payment?"

"The opposite, actually." So I told her about the Remedy, and

Brandt's part in it. She didn't look me in the eye the entire time I spoke.

"I didn't want to be a unicorn hunter," she said when I was finished. "He told me how dangerous it was. He told me about the wounds he'd seen. . . ." She looked at me and shrugged. "I cannot say that seeing you makes me regret my choice."

I grimaced.

She bit her lip. "I'm sorry. I did not mean to offend you. Your life looks as if it is very difficult."

"No," I said, "I understand. And I envy you. There are reasons I cannot . . ."

Marikka raised her eyebrows. "Oh, really? Me, too," she said. "But you just make the decision and go through with it. It wasn't so bad."

She meant sex with Brandt. Which was a topic so awkward I'd hoped never to bring it up. I wondered if Brandt had known that Marikka was my half sister when he'd bedded her or if Isabeau had just given him a name and an address and he'd gone off on his hunt. Perhaps we weren't so very different, he and I? After all, no one had ever told us hunters about the lives of the unicorns we were sent to kill. No one had stopped to question if the re'em on the mountain was just protecting her young, rather than viciously murdering any hiker who happened to wander by.

"And anyway," Marikka said, "I don't have time for unicorn-hunting training. I'm studying to be a physician."

The revelation hit me harder than Jumps's hoof in my gut. I took a deep breath and centered myself. "How wonderful."

Well, the coffee was done, the Remedy was delivered, and it was well past time for me to leave this poor woman alone and go find some park to cry my eyes out in.

She reached across the table and placed her hand over mine. "Truly, you might consider doing it as well."

I blinked at her. "Doing what?"

"Sleeping with a man. It isn't so bad, and it will release you from your duty. It's very odd. It's been many years since I ever thought of myself as a virgin. The magic has a very old-fashioned philosophy, doesn't it? Very limited."

My mouth formed a little O. So *that's* what she'd thought I meant when I said there was a reason I was still eligible. The lesbian loophole. "I see," I said. Well, who'd have thought that? There was knowledge that might come in handy for two hunters I knew. "No, I'm just a plain old virgin. No boyfriend *and* no girlfriend."

"Oh." Marikka leaned back. "That is very sweet."

"Yeah." We sat in some more awkward silence.

"Are you . . . all right?" Marikka asked me. "I mean, do you have a place to stay?"

"I have a train ticket," I said, gesturing to my backpack. "Lots of Remedy to deliver to lots of distant relations."

"Right." She nodded, then sat up straight in her chair. "I have something to show you. You'll like this. Wait here." She dashed from the room and I heard her feet on the stairs, then an opening door, then more stairs.

Now was my chance. I should leave. I should leave now before I was totally overcome with jealousy for my sweet, pretty, intelligent, studying-to-be-a-doctor lesbian half sister. I should leave before she caught me wailing hysterically at her kitchen table. I pillowed my arms on the table and laid my head on top of them, the material of my hood blocking out the morning light.

The sense of magic prickled across my scalp and down my

spine, radiating outward along the whorls of the scar on my back. With it came serenity, like the feel of cool cotton sheets beneath your body after a long fever. I took a deep breath and raised my head as Marikka came into the room with a linen-wrapped bundle in her hands. Magic sputtered from the package like sparks from a dying fire, and my whole body yearned to snatch it from her hands.

"My grandmother had this hanging over our mantel," she said as she began to undo the bits of twine holding it together. "But I put it away in the attic when I redecorated. I think it belonged to that ancestor of ours. The Llewelyn."

Marikka pulled back the linen coverings. Within lay a small horn bow, gray and shiny with age. Perhaps four feet long unstrung, with a slight recurve and a grip made of creamy wood worn to a shine.

"There were arrows once, too," she said, "but I can't remember where I put those."

I reached out to touch the bow with trembling fingers. "It's beautiful."

"I'll take your word for it," Marikka said. "I don't like weapons very much. But here, look. It's carved." She turned the bow on its side and indeed, I could see a faded engraving curving down the inside of both limbs, the part that would face the hunter whenever she went to shoot.

ANIMAM COGNOSCERE ANIMALIS

"Do you know what it says?" she asked.

I nodded. "Yes. It's a prayer." Or a wish, or maybe just a hope.

The hope I'd had when I stood on the side of the road in the Alps and watched my einhorns disappear forever. The prayer I'd murmured every night above Angel as he slept in the enclosure. The only thing I'd wanted since the moment I'd been forced to kill my first unicorn and known both that I'd had no choice and that I hated nothing more. It was the dream I hadn't wanted to admit I'd held, the power I was just beginning to wield.

This was Clothilde's bow. I had the whole set: knife, sword, bow. And now I knew why she made the choices she had. Now I knew why, despite my training, despite the danger, despite all the hideousness and savagery I'd somehow managed to survive, that I was making the same choices. There were two sides to being a unicorn hunter, two gifts that made up our magic, and neither should take precedence over the other.

DOMITARE UNICORNE INDOMITUM: To Vanquish the Savage Unicorn.

ANIMAM COGNOSCERE ANIMALIS: To Know the Soul of the Beast.